Wildflowers

A streak of moonlight bathed his head and shoulders, outlining the tight muscles beneath his buckskin jacket. His solid, perfect shape reminded her of a Greek statue. Oh, she thought, he's all too real. She shut her eyes as he touched her face once more, caressing the curve of her chin and cheek bones. His mustached mouth moved as he whispered her name against her neck, "Johanna."

She looked at him. "Yes?"

"You didn't answer my question? Will you sing for me?" His pleading tone reminded her of a child begging for a sweet.

He stood apart from her, staring into her eyes as if plumbing the depths of her soul. It made her shiver. "Please, Johanna, sing that tune you hummed earlier."

"No, not now — it's too late."

They reached the wagon, the campfire a glimmer above gray ashes and the lantern glowing by the wagon wheels.

In the quiet of the moment, Ryan reached for her and pulled her to him. "Johanna," he whispered, brushing back the stray strands of hair which fell from her bun; then he unloosened the fasteners in her hair, letting it cascade in a soft flow of red tendrils down her shoulders.

Johanna pulled away, "Ryan, don't!"

"Why not?" He smoothed her hair, "Your hair has the glow of a sunset, and it feels as soft as the morning dew. Johanna," he said meeting her questioning gaze, "you are prettier than any wildflower bloomin' on the prairie in spring."

Her pulse raced, and she pushed her hair back into some kind of neat array, fearful lest someone should spy them together. Ryan remained oblivious of all else, save her, as he captured her hands. He turned them palm-upward, and then gently touched the sores. "To heal your wounds," he murmured, kissing one palm and then the other. The pressure of his lips heated her from her fingertips upward.

Wildflowers

by

Catherine Greenfeder

A Wings ePress, Inc.

Historical Romance Novel

Wings ePress, Inc.

Edited by: Elizabeth Struble
Copy Edited by: Karen Babcock
Senior Editor: Leslie Hodges
Executive Editor: Lorraine Stephens
Cover Artist: Richard Stroud

Wings ePress Books
http://www.wings-press.com

Copyright © 2007 by Catherine Greenfeder
ISBN 978-1-59705-874-2

Published In the United States Of America

June 2007

Wings ePress Inc.
403 Wallace Court
Richmond, KY 40475

Dedication

To Pat Guerrero, my mom

Special thanks to

Rita Rinaldi, Patt Mihailoff, and Mike Powazinik

One

The heavy scent of lilies and damp earth filled Ryan's nostrils; his legs felt weak beneath him. An ache hammered his head as he began to wobble and sway toward the open grave. Some force pulled at him from behind, tugging the bottom of his leather tunic.

"Phew! That was a close one, Uncle Ryan!"

A swift glance at his twelve-year-old nephew brought him back to the painful situation. "Thanks, son." He held the boy's shoulders a moment then studied him. Samuel Majors' dark coloring and shoulder-length hair made him a pint-size version of Ryan's brother Chet.

How could this have happened? Ryan asked himself as he turned to the pine box covered with orange and yellow lilies from the farmer's field and the crumbling, damp earth thrown in symbolic gesture of man's mortality. A deep sob escaped from Ryan, he had fought it long enough. He heard a woman's cry and glanced at the source—Sara Majors, Chet's widow, peered from beneath a black lace veil. A frown creased her brow as her blue eyes bore into his.

Shame heated Ryan's face. The whiskey did its nasty job on him. Rather than obliterating the sorrow, it exacerbated it—making him less able to hold back his emotions. He hiccupped aloud. Reverend Wade shot him a quick glance, cleared his throat then continued with the prayer service.

Ryan shrugged in mild embarrassment, and lowered his gaze onto the faces of Chet's other three children. The dark-haired seven-year-old twins, Maggie and James, stood stiff and somber as the cottonwood trees behind them. Five-year-old Becky, pale and blonde like her mother, clung to the black folds of fabric surrounding Sara's protruding belly. In a few weeks, maybe even days, there'd be another child to care for—a child who would never know the love of its father.

If only I had been at the warehouse, instead of in the saloon, maybe Chet would be alive and they'd have their daddy. That thought weighed like a boulder upon Ryan's chest. As the preacher closed his book, the mourners filed past the family. Sara held both Ryan and Samuel's arms for support. "I must thank the reverend," she whispered to Ryan. "He did a fine service for my Chet,' She leaned close to Ryan then lifted the black veil.

Ryan imagined how she must feel inside. Even with swollen, blood-shot eyes, Sara appeared pretty in a delicate way, like one of the white butterflies that flitted through her garden. "Ryan Majors," she whispered in his ear, "is that whiskey on your breath?"

"A little." He chuckled. "For medicinal purposes."

"In a pig's eye. Don't let the minister find out you've been drinking! He's a strict Methodist and swears alcohol is made by the devil."

"No, but you can act, hic, sure as hell like one!" Ryan said

"Hush up!" Sara yanked on his arm. "Oh! I feel dizzy. Quick, hold my hand." He led her around the graveside then dropped his hold as she stepped up to speak to the minister. "Reverend Wade, thank you kindly for the service." Sara's voice broke on a sob. "Chet would have been quite happy with it. He was always reading to the children from the Bible."

Ryan avoided the preacher's steady gaze. *How could two brothers who grew up in the backwoods among their mother's Pawnee people be so different? Reading the Bible to children,* Ryan thought bitterly, *now there's a right funny twist!* Ryan could barely sign his name. Chet, on the other hand, had learned to read and write so well he ended up heading a warehouse. Not only did he win over the woman they both wanted in their youth, but he became educated as well. "Damn it all!"

"What's that you say, Mr. Majors?'

Ryan felt the minister's gaze boring into him. Who the hell did he think he was with his fancy clothes and words? His being a circuit minister from back east somewhere, Boston or New York, didn't give him the right to act superior!

"You'll have to excuse my brother-in-law, Ryan." Sara jerked on Ryan's elbow. "Chet's death is a shock to him."

"To us all, I'm sure." Reverend Wade gently took hold of Sara's free hand. "If there is anything more I can do, please let me know. My daughter is coming to town next month, so I'll be in Independence for some time. I'd be happy to stop by." A slow smile lit up his face. He playfully patted Beth's head. "Last time I saw my Johanna, she was only a little taller than your Beth here!"

"You'll have a fine reunion," Sara said, "but thanks just the same. You are most kind, Reverend Wade." With that, Sara turned and waddled over to the wagon with her children following their mother like baby ducklings. Ryan helped Sara board the seat. The youngsters clambered inside. Samuel sat beside his mother, grappling with the reins of the mule team.

"Take them home, Samuel. I'll be by soon."

"See ya, Uncle Ryan." Samuel cracked the whip over the mules' heads.

"Mr. Majors," a harsh voice rattled from behind. "It will do no good to your sister-in-law and her children if you take up the evils of alcohol."

3

Ryan grunted as he turned around to face the dour expression of the long-faced minister. "Thanks for the sermon, Reverend Wade. Sara and the children needed it, but I sure as hell don't." He reached into his leather satchel and pulled out a handful of crisp dollar bills. "This is from me, payment for your prayers. I'm sure they'll get my brother into heaven. God knows he don't deserve the wrath of hell."

"I don't imagine so." The minister took the bills from Ryan then tried to hand them back.

"Thank you, but if the widow needs it..."

"She'll do fine. Don't you worry none. I plan to look after my kin."

After a few silent minutes, the preacher pocketed the bills then walked down the dirt-covered trail toward the center of town. Ryan waited a few more minutes before he knelt down to caress the soft earth which blanketed the coffin. "Chet, why did you die? Why? You left Sara and the children! You left me!" Ryan's hand struck a rock, and he winced with pain as he sucked the blood off his knuckles. "Damn you!" Tears stung his eyes. He dabbed them with his dirtied hands.

The cry of a hawk startled him. Ryan watched as the bird circled in the sky above the grave and headed west. A man without faith, Ryan had few superstitions. Yet, having lived among the wild creatures for so long, he took it as a sign. He stood, dusted off his trousers, and shook his fist at the hawk. "Sure as hell, I'll find whoever murdered my brother! Even if I have to go to the ends of the earth!"

~ * ~

May 1848

The first spot of land Johanna Wade noticed as the steamboat chugged up the slow moving Missouri was the riverbank lined with scraggly bushes of wild daisies and primroses. The spindly branches of cottonwoods and weeping willows curtsied under a strong gust as the smoke from the boat clouded the air. For Johanna, the month of her journey from her native Boston had felt more like a year. Staring into the muddy river, she thought back to that fateful wintry day when she decided to come west. It had been so cold that the Charles River froze and the harbor needed to be closed. Despite warnings, daring souls skated on the river.

Johanna had enough trouble making her way through the crowd of dock workers and factory employees who milled about the icy cobblestoned streets. The short distance to Charles Street seemed to stretch on for miles. The urgent message from her aunt's servant made her leave her one-room schoolhouse in the care of her assistant. Was Mabel sick? The thought made her race to the brick-faced home and bang upon the brass knocker until Lottie, Mabel's servant, ushered her inside. Over tea and crumpets, Aunt Mabel produced a letter from Johanna's father. The letter requested that they join him in the Oregon Territory.

At twenty-four, Johanna had entertained the notion of starting anew in a strange land with a man she barely knew, but still loved. The position as a head schoolmistress beckoned her, as had the opportunity to heal from the scars of a broken heart.

The blast of the ship's horn woke her to the present moment. She spied a group of Negroes working on a field across the river. A white overseer cracked a whip in the air, sending a chill through Johanna. *This is the South*, she reminded herself, *slavery is lawful here*. Much as she hated the very word, she knew that more than one of her uncle's voyages to the islands had been to deliver slaves to the South. Now she saw the evidence of that awful business, and her stomach revolted.

That evening, in the confines of their tiny cabin, Johanna sat beside Mabel finishing a light meal of soup and crackers. "Will Father look the same?" she asked Mabel between mouthfuls of food.

"Oh, I have no idea," Mabel said. "Harold was always a strange bird. If it wasn't for you, Johanna, I would not be here. I have no more interest in your father's mission than I do in that temperance society."

"But, Auntie, I thought you supported it."

"When Captain Foster was alive, we had a rather good time and many parties. You remember how the captain earned his money."

"Yes." Johanna sipped her soup then added in a whisper, "Rum running."

"I hated to let Lottie go, I was glad my friend Willimina hired her. At least, I gave her a decent severance pay."

"Don't worry, Auntie." Johanna patted Mabel's hand. "I'm sure Lottie will be fine. Not too many people have your compassion. After all, Lottie would be a slave in many parts of this country. I believe there will be an end to this slavery one day." Johanna put down her spoon. "Just as one day Oregon will be a state."

"Oh, you do?" a male voice asked, suddenly joining in their conversation.

"Yes," Johanna said, frowning at the young man who had entered their cabin. Reverend Stephen Green had a habit of barging in on them. Despite his easy charm and boyish good looks, the blonde-haired Stephen annoyed Johanna with his peskiness. The thought of spending more months with him on the long journey to Oregon filled her with unease. How could the mission board do this to her? Didn't they realize that she and her father could manage the missionary work without any assistance from Green?

Stephen stooped to fit his wiry, six-foot frame beneath the doorway of the cabin. "I see you're enjoying some luxury aboard ship!" His smile softened his sarcasm. The cabin had barely enough space for her and Mabel to turn around in, let alone to sleep and move about. Yet, they managed well enough. Stephen's presence, however, made it too tight for comfort. "Ah, you should come up and get the fresh air, Johanna. Walk about the ship with me." He raked his long, well-manicured fingers through his blonde, curly hair and smiled with such enthusiasm that Johanna almost acquiesced.

"Perhaps later," she answered. "I am a bit tired."

"Oh, well." He turned to Mabel. "And how about the Widow Foster?"

Johanna hated the title he accorded her aunt. She caught Mabel's look of slight annoyance. "No, thank you. Go on, Johanna. Don't stay in this dreary room with me."

Stephen's pouting expression made her feel childish, so Johanna nodded. "Oh, very well. I suppose I could go." As they stood aboard deck, the breeze played with the bonnet on her head, and Johanna had to hold it in place. She eyed Stephen's profile, recalling a time in her youth when she could have fallen for his charm like her friend Anna did. They had been roommates in a boarding school when she introduced Anna to her neighbor Stephen. The son of a county judge, Stephen had inherited a lively wit and a way with words. He quoted from Shakespeare, the Bible, and the law. At sixteen, he held the promise of becoming a fiery orator, or even an actor. But a preacher? "Do you remember Anna McGinty?" Johanna asked as she retied the string of her bonnet. She watched Stephen's expression change from puzzlement to mild amusement.

"Oh, yes I do," he said with a chuckle. "I remember that little wallflower with the freckled nose. She stood about this high?" He pointed to hip level.

"No, she was taller than that and not a wallflower."

"Not really, Johanna. Why?"

Johanna stood dumbstruck. How could Stephen have forgotten the girl whom he had promised to marry if she waited for him to return from school? In another year or two, he told her, he'd be back. Three years went by before Stephen returned from the seminary in upstate New York. By that time, Anna had married another man. The man she'd married had been a cruel one who beat her. "Did you know that she waited for you? She wrote to me from Providence, telling me that you had been her only love. Well..." Johanna sniffled and broke into a sob. "Before I left home, I received word that Anna died. That brute of a man she married had beaten her so, she never recovered."

7

"Oh, Johanna." Stephen took her hands in his. "I am so sorry. I had no idea that she felt that way about me."

Johanna pulled from his grip. "I went to your father's house on Chambers Street, and he informed me that he found a pile of mail—letters from poor Anna that had remained sealed. You never bothered to even open them, let alone answer her."

"I could not lead her on, Johanna." This time a pained expression creased Stephen's face, surprising Johanna. Could those be genuine tears in his eyes? "There is only one woman who I will ever love." He clutched her hands. "You must know it, my dear. Even back then, the only reason I took time with you and your friend Anna was to be with you. Judge Green had other aspirations for me, rest assured, than my becoming a minister."

"And marrying beneath your station wasn't in the plan?"

"Oh, but Johanna, what does that matter now?" Stephen lifted her hand to his mouth and planted a kiss on her palm.

"Leave me, Stephen." She pulled from his grip and rubbed her hand as if to remove dirt. "I've no interest in your plans now, only in my father's mission." Laughter from a crowd over on the far side of the deck made them both turn around. Had she become the spectacle of their laughter? Johanna frowned at the thought. Obviously not, for the four women who were dressed in the most garish lavender and red satin gowns flirted brazenly as they sat atop the laps of lust-filled crew members.

"Pay no heed to those hussies," Stephen whispered. "They've no right to breathe the same air as you, Johanna."

"If you recall the Bible, Stephen," Johanna whispered back, "Jesus befriended a prostitute by the name of Mary." She walked away, anger coiling like a snake in her bosom. Stephen followed her. A cabin boy carrying a tankard of ale bumped into them, spilling some of the contents on Johanna's dress.

"Are you blind?" Stephen shouted in anger after the boy.

The boy turned, bowing to them. "I sorry," he said in a thick

French accent.

"He ought to be whipped!" Stephen began to chase after the boy.

"Leave him be!" Johanna yelled. The ale soaked through the hem of her dress, chilling her skin, and she wrinkled her nose at the smell. When Stephen returned to her side, she said, "It's all right. I'll change my gown, anyway, before we leave ship."

"Johanna, I've been wondering if you have given my proposal further thought?" Stephen pressed her elbow. When she didn't reply, he stood back. "You cannot pine forever. It will not bring your beloved Robert back from the grave."

"I'm aware of that, Stephen," she replied, lowering her gaze, "and my answer is still no. Whatever plans you have do not concern me."

His fingernails scraped the wood of the rail, causing her to look sharply at him. When she did, she felt the hard pressure of his thumbs on her hands as he held them and stared deeply into her eyes. "You are the minister's daughter, Johanna. I'm sure your father would find me a fine and suitable candidate for you." He leaned closer, adding, "Remember, I do have an inheritance which will ensure our comfort in the wilderness."

"Stephen, let go of me!"

"I'm sorry." He dropped his grip and shook his head in pious disapproval. "To think of you alone and vulnerable among the heathen. You need a man's protection. Let me be that man."

"Are you forgetting that my aunt is my escort? Furthermore, I will be in the company of several families. Most importantly, I will be with my father. Can't you get it through your thick skull? I have no desire to marry you or anyone else." The boat rocked and Johanna felt dizzy. She grasped the ship's railing. "I think I'd best lie down, I'm a bit seasick."

"A captain's niece seasick?" Stephen's lips creased in mock disbelief. Johanna walked slowly back to the cabin she shared with Mabel. No sooner had she reached the door than her stomach rebelled and she retched. She then crumpled into a heap inside the cabin.

Mabel cleaned up the mess and administered smelling salts.

"There, there, Johanna." Mabel wiped a damp cloth over her forehead. "We are nearly in port. It must be the terrible food they served us."

Johanna bent over a washbasin, retching again. "Oh, my... what a mess!" She needed to lie down but first she wiped her lips with a handkerchief then took the basin out to empty its contents into the muddy waters. The sharp blast of the steam whistle hurt her ears. Entering the cabin again, she glanced at her reflection in a mirror. The sight of her pale complexion and wind-blown red hair made her feel even worse. She looked ghastly. She didn't want Father to see her like this. She quickly pinched her cheeks and made an effort to put her hair back into a neat bun. On impulse, she fingered the golden locket on her necklace. It opened to reveal the portraiture of her beloved fiancé, now dead for three years. Suddenly the boat lurched to one side with a thunderous bang as the whistle blasted, deafening her momentarily.

"A collision! Oh, goodness!" she screamed, snapping the locket shut and rushing to the door.

Mabel followed her and grasped her arms. "Oh, Johanna!" she shouted as they peered out at the immense stretch of dry land and the semblance of a small town with its waiting dock. "We've arrived!"

"Independence?"

Mabel nodded and gave her a hug.

"Ah," Johanna sighed. Soon she'd be stepping foot on solid ground and meeting the man she'd traveled half a continent to see. Her heart danced with happiness—and more than a little relief.

Two

The Reunion

The horses reared up at the loud piercing blast from the steamship. "Thunder and tarnation!" Ryan shouted above the din. "We know it's here. Why the hell does it have to let out such a confounded noise?" Grabbing the reins on the buggy team, Ryan managed to coax the horses forward through the throng of people lining the dockside.

The minister ignored Ryan's profanity. As soon as they halted, Reverend Wade jumped down and began to run along the cobblestone levee. Ryan imagined the minister meeting a mirror image of himself. He chuckled at the notion of the minister embracing a scrawny, beak-nosed hag in black garb. He longed to get this meeting over with and hightail it back to the saloon and a little rendezvous of his own with the star attraction, Molly McGee. His only reason for being here was a deal he'd worked out with the foreman at the trapping company. He had hired himself on as a trail guide for the minister. It'd only be for a few months, he reasoned, then he'd get the money for his kinfolk and be on his merry way—hunting the varmint that killed Chet.

Overloaded with sacks and barrels of goods, wagons, mules, horses, camp equipment, and travelers, the boat appeared to be sinking into the Missouri. Ryan tied the buggy to a hitching post. He caught up to the minister as the boat moored alongside the landing. The ship's passengers and the waiting crowd exchanged greetings.

Ryan moved forward and missed being shoved into the river by two men carrying lumber.

"Watch your step," one of the men warned.

Ryan found something more important to watch—the face of an angel. Her soft, patrician features were beyond compare. Tendrils of wind-swept red hair slipped from her gray bonnet as she waved a long cloth and shouted, "I'm here!" Her deep blue eyes brimmed with joy as they gazed to a point far from where he stood. Who was she? The crowd pressed in on him as the ship's passengers disembarked. In the confusion and the noise, Ryan lost sight of the beauty. He peered around at the crowd, a motley assortment of young and old, rich and poor.

Local gentries—men in fine suits and ladies carrying parasols—stepped up to greet loved ones and friends. Stocky farmers hawked fruits and vegetables from their wagons. Mexicans wearing bells and slashed pantaloons smoked shuck-rolled cigarettes. A group of blanketed and painted Shawnee bartered beads and buffalo hides for whiskey or rifles; a contingent of soldiers from Fort Leavenworth marched to the strains of the drum and fife.

"Johanna!" Reverend Wade shouted, pointing to someone walking down the gang plank.

"That's my daughter." The minister beamed with pride, nudging Ryan. "Johanna Wade!"

Ryan felt as if a bolt of lightning pierced him and he staggered back in disbelief. For the beauty he had admired turned out to be the minister's daughter. Impossible! Yet, she stepped down with the grace of an angel, dropped her baggage, and rushed to the open arms of the preacher. Her ribbon-frilled bonnet flew from her head, and her hair tumbled across her shoulders.

Struck dumb with amazement, Ryan stood gaping as father and daughter exchanged hugs. When the young woman stood at arm's length from the preacher, Ryan's gaze traveled the length of her, from the high-buttoned, gray bodice jacket, which rounded over her bosom and narrowed at the waist, to the shortened above-ankle-length gray skirt which rested upon her low-heeled shoes. Her demeanor indicated fine breeding. Up close, her features—rounded mouth and dimpled cheeks—gave her a cherubic quality. The tears on her flushed cheeks only made her look lovelier.

"You have grown!" Reverend Wade exclaimed. "Has it truly been twelve years since I held my little Johanna?"

"Yes." She wiped away tears with a crumpled handkerchief. "Twelve long years!"

Her father inspected her from head to toe. "No more little girl with long braids..." He leaned closer and tenderly tweaked her nose. "But you've still got those freckles. Johanna, you're as beautiful as your mother."

She threw her arms about him. "Oh Father, I've missed you so much!"

Ryan paced restlessly, waiting for him to notice her, too. When she failed to do so, he decided to take things into his own hands. He lifted the baggage and strolled over to where father and daughter stood. He lay the baggage down and removed his coonskin cap. "Name is Ryan," he stated, peering at her. She looked up, but another man blocked her view of him.

"Johanna, your bonnet," the man said, handing over the pointed gray bonnet. Clad in black, the man was lean and tall. A black cap crowned his thick blond hair.

"Thank you." She smiled, taking hold of the young man's elbow. She looked at Reverend Wade. "Father, you do remember Stephen Green?"

Reverend Wade looked at the young man a moment then replied, "Yes, of course! You were a youngster when I saw you. And, from Johanna's letters, I learned that you became a minister. So you came to join us?"

"Yes." The man's hazel eyes lit with pride. "When Johanna told me that you sent for her and needed help with the mission, I asked the mission board if I could join you." The two men shook hands.

An older, heavy-set woman in a powder-blue gown rushed up to them. "Hello, Howard!" she bellowed, throwing her arms about Reverend Wade. He pulled away from her powerful grip.

"Mabel Foster, so good to see you." He kissed his sister-in-law's forehead. "How was the trip?"

"A bit rough." Mabel pushed the brim of her bonnet back from her thick auburn hair. "The train crossing was fine. But the steamboat made me ill. Furthermore, we had to stop a number of times to be pulled from the shallows. Alas, we are here." Her blue eyes twinkled with mirth as she smiled at her brother-in-law. "It is good to see you again, Howard, after so many years!"

"It is good to see you both again." Reverend Wade glanced at Johanna then turned to Mabel. "You have done a fine job in raising her. Thank you. We have much to praise the Lord for. Isn't that so, Stephen?"

"Amen," Stephen responded.

Johanna glanced past Stephen, her gaze resting on Ryan. Her expression changed to one of bemusement, as if she had never seen a trapper. She stared at his leather attire, from moccasin footwear up to fringed leather pants and buckskin shirt, she peered at his face, and when their eyes met, she held her breath and lowered her gaze.

Ryan smiled at her. At last she acknowledged him. He stepped forward, and gestured to her baggage. "Carry these for you?"

She didn't respond, but stared at him with such intensity that he wondered if she had heard him. So, he repeated his question.

Finally, her eyelashes fluttered. A crimson hue inched up her neck and face as she gazed at him. She rubbed her face with her hands. "I'm terribly sorry for staring. In Boston, men don't wear animal hide and furry caps with tails."

"No, they wear black linens," Ryan muttered, taking hold of the baggage. He swung one bag too wide and struck Johanna's knee. "Sorry." Why was he acting like a damn fool? And what was that scent she was wearing? Smelled like magnolia blossoms. He definitely needed to get back to the saloon and the likes of Molly McGee. He felt more ornery than usual, and an angel-faced beauty from back east—a minister's daughter, no less—would know little of his heated need. So, why did he find himself ogling the gentle sway of her hips as she walked in the company of the ministers and her aunt? "Women!" he muttered to himself. "I've enough trouble as it is."

Johanna leaned toward her aunt, whispering, "What strange men they have in Missouri."

"Pay no attention to him," Reverend Wade stated. "Ryan is our trail guide."

Mabel mumbled as she opened her parasol to shield her from the sun, "Stodgy old coot, Howard. Boston couldn't keep ya!"

"Now's not the time, Mabel!" Reverend Wade warned.

Mabel shrugged. "I guess some things never change." She took hold of her niece's arm. "Come, Johanna, help me to the buggy."

The two ministers followed behind, armed with Mabel's hatboxes and baggage. They rode in the carriage while Ryan trotted alongside on horseback. His rifle lay before him, resting against the high pommel of his saddle. Every so often, between conversations with her aunt and father, Johanna glanced at him. He sat like a king, his gaze alert to the path before him. And he ignored her. She felt a pang of disappointment.

"Here we are." The minister pointed to a sign for the Noland Hotel. "We'll be here a few days."

The stately white building, reminiscent of a plantation mansion, with its columns and circular verandah, loomed before them. The scent of roses filled the air. Reverend Wade stepped from the carriage and tied it to the post in front of the hotel. Ryan dismounted, secured his horse then walked toward the carriage to offer help. But when Stephen helped the ladies down, he headed toward the luggage. He took down a few pieces and as he reached for a hatbox, he touched Johanna's hand.

The touch of his hand sent a warm tingling through Johanna, and she said demurely, "I'll take it."

"No, I'll take it," he insisted.

Johanna pulled at the box. "Really, I can manage one silly little box."

"Fine. Take it then." He threw it towards her. With a gasp of surprise, she caught the lightweight box. Ryan ignored her wide-eyed stare.

Stephen came over to her and cast a disparaging glance at Ryan. "Are you having a problem, Johanna?"

"No. Please see to your own baggage."

"Very well." Stephen took down two dust-covered suitcases.

Johanna noticed anger blazing in Ryan's eyes as he gazed at the young minister. Ryan turned to her again. "If ya don't mind, I'll take the rest of the stuff inside." Without waiting for her response, he took two armloads of luggage and headed into the hotel.

Johanna stayed at the carriage, waiting for Ryan's return. She needed to talk to him, find out what sort of man her father had selected for their journey. Even more, she felt a need to be near him without all the others around. This sudden interest baffled Johanna.

When Ryan stepped out into the street, she cautiously approached him. His rugged appearance and brash manner were a novelty to her, after her upbringing in proper Bostonian society. Her pulse raced at the sight of his buckskin leggings clinging to his hips and thighs. A soft sigh escaped her lips as she noticed the way the leather shirt stretched across the wide, muscular planes of his chest and shoulders. His raven locks hung past the top of his shirt, giving him an exotic appearance. But it was his eyes—dark brown and almond-shaped that stared boldly at her—that sent a nervous jolt through her being. As she drew closer, his full, sensuous lips curled into an arresting smile. "Oh, my," Johanna sputtered, clasping the ivory cameo brooch at her neckline.

"What's wrong, ma'am?" Ryan grabbed her by the elbow.

She waved her hands in front of her face. "It is warm here, and I am so tired from the long, long journey." She pulled from his grip. "Thank you, but I feel better now." She straightened. "My father told me that you're our trail leader."

"Anything wrong with that?"

Surprised by his sudden insolence, Johanna thought of a new tactic. "Don't be defensive. Let's be friends." She held out her hand for him to shake.

Ignoring it, Ryan turned to his horse. "Man doesn't need a woman friend." He patted the horse's side, took his rifle down and showed it to her. *"This* is my friend. It protects me, helps feed me, and never spurns me."

Undaunted, Johanna came around to face him. "Mr. Majors, we'll be on the trail a long time. Surely we can be friends."

This time he shook her hand. "Don't see why not."

Warmed by the handshake, Johanna cooled herself with a wave of her paper fan. "How long will it take to get to the valley?"

"About four to five months, miss."

"Five months? That's a long time. Do you have experience with leading wagon trains?"

Ryan's gaze narrowed. "Yes," he muttered, "five months is a long time, but we have lots of land to cross. And no, I haven't led wagon trains before."

"What experience have you had?

"I've been from here to the Pacific a thousand times, been hunting round every stream in between, met more Indians than you could ever imagine, and I know a hell of a lot more about it than a bunch of pilgrims from Boston society!"

Johanna crossed her arms in front of her, "Don't be so impudent, Mr. Majors. All I asked was a simple question."

Ryan scowled. "I wasn't being impudent, ma'am, just stating the facts." In a softer voice he added, "We have to leave early before the snow."

Johanna thought of winters back home. "Snow! How marvelous!"

Was she a complete fool? Ryan wondered as he mounted his horse. "Snow in the Rockies is a lot tougher than what you're used to in the city." He glanced at her fine linen dress and soft leather shoes. They would be useless for the trail. The gold locket dangling on her bodice probably cost more than he could earn in a year of trapping. What did she know of hardship and danger? He leaned from the saddle, bringing his face closer to hers. "This will be a hard journey for you and your family, pampered and spoiled as you all are."

"How dare you!" Ryan's horse bristled under her shrill cry.

"You're scaring Daisy! Step away before she stomps you!"

The anger in Johanna's eyes made them sparkle like sapphires. Ryan found them bewitching. To his surprise, she threw back her arm and struck at him, but missed, striking the horse's side, instead. Daisy bucked back then took off. Fortunately, Ryan managed to hang on as the horse took him for a gallop.

He rode around the square then turned back to the hotel. Johanna backed away as he rode up to her. "Now it's your turn!" he shouted. Bringing the horse to a halt, he leaned down and pulled a startled Johanna up onto the saddle.

"Let me down at once!" she screamed, landing sidesaddle in front of him. Ignoring her plea, Ryan clenched her by the waist with one hand while gripping the reins with the other. "Git a move on, Daisy." On cue, the horse trotted away from the hotel, toward the outskirts of town.

Shaken, Johanna grabbed the pommel with one hand and Ryan's waist with the other. "Where are you taking me?" she yelled above the din of the crowd, which whispered and laughed as they watched.

"We're going for a little ride," Ryan replied. "Hold tight now. These people want a show!"

"Take me back!" she cried, pulling on his shirt.

"You little fool, you'll get us killed! Stop pulling on me!" He finally stopped a few yards outside of town.

Johanna opened her mouth to blast his ears, but before she could say a word, he turned her around and crushed her to his chest, kissing her hard on the lips. Stunned, she kicked her feet in frustration. The horse took off, ending the kiss.

"Damn! Hold tight," Ryan warned, turning the runaway horse toward the hotel.

As soon as he stopped the horse, Johanna slid down from the saddle and glared up at him. "Don't you ever, ever do that again!"

Ryan slid down and stood before her. "Seemed to me ya like it."

"About this much," she gritted, slapping him across his face with all her might.

Ryan rubbed his jaw. "Guess I had it comin'." He grinned cockily. "Hell, it was worth the pain."

"Oh, you!" Johanna turned about and rushed into the hotel.

"What the hell got into you?" Ryan wondered aloud as he led his horse to the stable. He had meant to teach the uppity Eastern gal a lesson, not to steal a kiss. And what a kiss—had he been anywhere else, it would have gone further. *Get a grip, man! She's not worth the trouble.* As he rounded the corner, he spied the elder minister, a solemn expression chiseled in his face. His dark eyes narrowed to slits as he glanced at Ryan.

"Mr. Majors," Revered Wade called, heading his way. "Thanks for the help."

"No problem, Reverend."

"I also want to warn you." He gestured toward the hotel. "My daughter looked quite distressed. Word has it that she was taken for a ride by a trapper."

Ryan stood silent.

"Johanna is precious to me," Reverend Wade continued. "I may not have been the best father, but now that she's with me, I intend to do my best to see that no harm comes to her. Let me remind you that you are a hired man, a guide, nothing more!" He motioned with a nod of his head. "And here comes Reverend Green, a fine gentleman, one

I can trust with my Johanna."

Ryan scowled at Stephen Green, who hastened to Wade's side. Fancy clothes didn't make Green a better man. He was still a pup, wet behind the ears.

Stephen sniffed the air, and grimaced. "Mr. Majors, I didn't see your name on the list of guides for hire."

"Didn't put it up there," Ryan replied.

"And how long have you been leading wagons?"

It's none of his damned business, Ryan thought. Deciding to give him as little information as he could, he replied, "I know enough to get you to Oregon."

Stephen glanced at Reverend Wade. "That true?"

The elder minister looked hurt. "Do you doubt my judgment, Stephen? Why, I wouldn't have picked Ryan if he didn't have experience in the mountains."

"I'm wondering why you picked someone who never led wagons before." Green turned to Ryan. "Reverend Wade told me a bit about your past, Mr. Majors. Guess you did spend years in the mountains. It looks to me like you're still carrying the dirt with you."

Ryan clenched and unclenched his fist. *Why I ought to rip him in two, but I need the job.* "At least the mountain air is fresher than the sewage in the cities back East," he replied. "Good day, Reverends." He mounted his horse, pulled on the reins and headed out of town. The sky showed promise of rain, and he wanted to reach the farm before the storm began. Bad enough he stormed inside. There'd be other chances to make the young pup chew his words. At least he could spend a quiet supper with Sara and the children. There, no one looked down their noses at him. Lord, how he hated city folk!

Three

Supplying the Wagons

Johanna opened her eyes as morning light filtered through the ivory lace curtains in her hotel room. She stretched, yawned then wrapped her morning gown about her and went to the window. Through the lace curtains, she peered out at the street below. Shopkeepers rolled out awnings or placed sale signs in their windows. Wagons rolled by carrying emigrants from back East towards the public square where they would camp and prepare for the journey west. Down by the waterfront, dock workers hauled cargo from the ships. Trappers carried pelts towards the trading post.

Their buckskin shirt and leggings reminded her of Ryan Majors. Not since Robert's death had she been so unnerved by a man. He did not have the fair-haired Robert's comeliness and sensitivity, but something about him tugged her in a direction her good sense told her to avoid. The air felt warm. She took off her wrap then walked across to the oak armoire upon which sat a bone-colored porcelain basin and a matching pitcher.

She filled the basin with the water from the pitcher. Lowering her head, she splashed her face then patted it dry with the small towel which hung on a wall. She gazed up at her reflection in the mirror above the armoire. Faint shadows beneath her eyes testified to her interrupted sleep.

Dreams of Ryan Majors had disturbed her slumber. In one, he carried her off on horseback, refusing to return her to the hotel despite her protestations. In another, she saw Ryan struggling with a man, whose face remained hidden until Ryan shot him. The man lay bleeding. Johanna ran to him and screamed. The face belonged to her dead fiancé. The last dream she recalled as she brushed her hair was of her being chased.

A friend in Boston once told her that dreams had meanings beyond the surface. She wondered what hers meant. She missed her girlhood friends. They were shocked when she had told them six months ago that she would be leaving for Oregon. None of them understood why she would leave a secure teaching position with a reputable family for the desolation and uncertainty of Oregon Territory.

Yet, none of them knew the guilt which haunted her. She blamed herself for not doing more to ease Robert's suffering. They could have married before his illness, but they waited and Robert never recovered. Even three years after his death, she had not forgotten how the illness had ravaged his youthful blonde looks and sunk his spirit. The sonnets and love letters he wrote were his final gift to her. She secreted them in her luggage for her journey, as if keeping him with her. Robert's physician, Doctor Watkins, tried to reassure her that nothing she could have done would have saved Robert.

Johanna could not be comforted. A knock on the door startled Johanna from her reverie.

"Who's there?"

"Mabel. We have to meet the ministers."

"I'll be down shortly, Auntie." She crossed the room to her baggage and removed a navy dress. "Might as well wear widow's weeds." She held the dress up against her, staring into the mirror. The simplicity of the garment could not detract from her beauty. She ran a hand through her hair. At least navy was safe, not like the bright frills she once wore. After Robert's death, she'd felt no urge for brightness. Sighing, she tossed the dress on the bed, looked at her wardrobe then held up the emerald green dress. It had been her mother's. Held against her now, it reminded her of happier times. Robert had loved the dress; she had to take it with her even if she wouldn't use it. Even if she wanted to wear it, what need would there be for a frilly dress?

There would be no ballroom dances in Oregon. She returned the dress to the baggage then closed the bag. She put on the navy dress, swept back her hair and twisted it into a bun.

"That's more like it!" she said aloud, pinching her cheeks for color. "A proper schoolmarm in dress and deed!"

"Johanna, are you all right?"

"Yes, Auntie. I'm almost ready."

"The ministers are downstairs waiting."

"Go on. I'll be there shortly." She completed her costume with matching shawl and bonnet. When she descended the stairs, she found Mabel talking with her father in the lobby. He looked cheerfully at her.

"Good day, Johanna."

She smiled. "Good day, Father."

The minister handed her a list. "If you can get these supplies, I'll go about the business of organizing the wagon party."

Johanna took the list, feeling like a dutiful daughter. "Yes, Father."

"This should be enough." He handed her a few dollars. "Stephen is bringing the buggy around for you."

When Stephen arrived with the buggy, both men left. Johanna resented the way Stephen stole the role she had planned for herself, being her father's assistant. Both men treated her as a helpless child. She scowled at them behind their retreating forms. "It's our duty to shop!" She sneered as she helped Mabel up into the buggy.

"Certainly," Mabel replied. She winked at Johanna, adding, "We wouldn't want to disappoint the men, now would we?"

Johanna applied the reins a little harder than needed.

"Don't kill the poor beast!" Mabel warned.

"Which one?" Johanna asked. They laughed, and Johanna drove through town. To Johanna's surprise, Independence proved itself an established western settlement. Its myriad of buildings, from log huts to slat board or brick, catered to the needs of the inhabitants and the transients who used it as a jumping off point before heading west. Signs indicated a fair number of trades: blacksmiths, saddleries, wagon shops, gunsmiths, apothecaries, dentists, lawyers, and banks.

General stores stocked food, hardware, and other supplies. A county courthouse and a sheriff's office signified a penchant for keeping law and order before the road led away from civilization.

A handful of bullwhackers of the Santa Fe Trail rubbed their mud-caked boots on the ground. They swore with such profanities that Johanna felt her face redden from embarrassment. One bullwhacker, a tall, scruffy looking man with a tattered hat, flashed a bowie knife and threatened the saloon owner for not serving him fast enough. A man wearing a silver badge interceded in the dispute and whacked him on the side of the head with the butt of his revolver.

"I think there's going to be a fight." Mabel pointed towards the crowd gathering outside the saloon.

"Let's get away." Johanna struck the horse's flank, urging it to move faster.

She halted outside a shop whose sign advertised the latest in Eastern fashion. A white gown with a bustle trimmed in violet and a matching bonnet beckoned to her, but now was not the time. Supplies needed to be purchased.

"How lovely." Mabel pointed out a row of white, weather-framed buildings. Their peaked roofs, encircling verandas, and neat gardens reflected an earlier French influence. Johanna stepped down from the buggy, tied the horse to the post then helped her aunt down. She enjoyed walking past the shops and the gardens of the residential area. With nostalgia, she plucked a rose that hung across a fence. She inhaled the bud's fragrance. "It reminds me of your garden back home. Here." She looped the rose through the buttonhole of her aunt's jacket.

"Yes, I remember how you ruined my garden."

Johanna laughed. "I was a mere child at the time."

"A mischievous one at that!" Mabel opened her parasol to shield them from the glaring sun. "You were always into trouble, minister's daughter or not. You had your mother's high spirits." She held onto Johanna's elbow.

"I wish that I had known my mother." Sadness and loss gripped Johanna. "Let's go in."

She pointed to a general store. Upon entering, they ducked under the baskets and cooking ware which suspended from the low ceiling. A wooden counter displayed a colorful assortment of yarn, sewing notions, and household tools. Barrels of flour, grain, teas, and coffee lined shelves along the walls. Behind a desk stood a smiling, bald clerk. "Morning, ladies."

"Good day." Johanna replied. She glanced through the colored threads and picked out a few. Mabel held up some calico and floral printed fabrics.

"Can I help ya with anything?" The clerk asked, glancing at their garments. "You look like you're from the East. Ain't that right?"

"Yes." Johanna replied. "We came from Boston."

The clerk followed her around the shop. "Where ya'll heading?"

"Oregon Territory."

"You'll need plenty for that. A hundred sacks of food or more. Got a wagon?"

"No, not yet," Johanna replied.

"Go down the street a bit and you'll get one from Hiram Young's Wagon Shop."

"Thank you." She continued to browse. "We could use these and those." She pointed out the sacks of flour, salt, rice, wheat, sugar, and a display of fabrics.

By the time they finished shopping, they had more than they could carry in the back of the buggy. "How will we ever get these back?" Johanna asked the clerk.

"Tell ya what," the clerk whispered, "I can send my servant Jacob over with it in our wagon later. Where ya staying?"

"The Noland Hotel."

"He'll take your purchases there. That will give ya time to shop."

"That would be kind of you," Johanna said, paying him. She turned around to find Mabel fingering yarns of lace and sewing supplies.

"Add these too," Mabel stated, putting packages of seeds on the counter. "We will need our own garden once we get to the valley."

Johanna told the clerk to add the seeds to their bill. "We'll return after lunch for as much as we can carry back." She tugged Mabel by the elbow. "Let's go, Auntie. I'm famished."

"But this Irish lace, it would make wonderful drapery."

"Not now." Johanna nodded to the clerk, "We'll take it later, thank you."

She pulled Mabel out of the store. "Come on."

As they moved down the steps of the store front, the aroma of baked bread and roasted coffee lured them towards a cafe across the street. Potted red geraniums lined the windows. Diners sat outside at cloth-covered tables.

Over tea and biscuits, Johanna and Mabel discussed their purchase needs. "It will be a long time before we can obtain such goods," Mabel stated. "I already miss my milliner and seamstress."

"We'll have to provide for our own needs from now on." Johanna spread blackberry jam on a warm pastry shell. "I shall miss this fine food."

Mabel held up the white china cup. "I will miss drinking from such fine wares!"

Johanna drained her tea, savoring the delicious blend of leaves with a hint of lemon. She placed her empty teacup down. Mabel picked up the cup and peered into it.

"Captain Weaver had a gypsy friend aboard his ship who taught him to read tea leaves. He showed me what to look for." She turned the cup around a few times. "Hmmm, let's see. This looks interesting."

"Don't tell me you believe such nonsense?" Johanna sighed.

Mabel's face turned serious as she pointed out the patterns of the wet tea leaves. "A bird shape—see that means you are going on a trip."

"You don't need tea leaves to tell me that!"

"And..." Mabel whispered, "you will meet a handsome stranger who will change the course of both your lives."

"Bah!" Johanna laughed. "You can tell that from tea leaves?"

Mabel put the cup down. "Or from knowing my niece."

Johanna felt chilled. Had Mabel sensed her disturbance over Ryan Majors?

"We best be going, Auntie. It's late, and we have to collect our supplies."

Mabel gave her a sympathetic look. "I raised you like my own child. I know your heart had been broken once."

"I'm fine, Auntie. I miss Boston." She smiled. "Yet, I do look forward to a new life in Oregon."

Mabel sat back. "Do you wish you had married Doctor Watkins?"

Johanna stirred the tea leaves with her spoon. "There was never anything more than friendship between us. He married his nurse, Hillary."

"Perhaps there was nothing on your part," Mabel replied. "I never understood why you rejected him. He was a respected gentleman, a fine doctor with a growing practice."

"I need more than that." Johanna glanced away. "Besides I'm too old to wed."

"Johanna!" Mabel clapped her hands in astonishment. "You're only twenty-four. I am twice your age. That doesn't stop me from gaping at every handsome man that crosses my path. I'd take a fine gentleman caller over that Ladies' Temperance Society any day."

"Why Auntie! I don't believe you."

"Dear girl, you have seen little of life and less of men." Mabel continued to lecture.

"Granted, Robert McEntee was articulate and handsome. You were his adoring student who fell for his lofty poems and gallantry. What notion have you of marriage and love?"

"How can you say that? I was betrothed."

"And so naive. Did you think that you were the only female student to receive amorous letters from precious Robert McEntee?"

"Yes."

"Hmpf!" Mabel stood. "I heard enough rumors from the Ladies' Temperance Society to the contrary."

"And you believed those old hags?"

"I hoped they were untrue." Mabel opened her parasol. "What difference does it make now? Robert is dead as are the rumors. Come, child, we are getting late. Your father will think we've run off with one of those ruffians."

Johanna raced ahead, not wanting to hear anymore of her aunt's remarks on Robert. Mabel caught up, breathless and red in the face.

She pulled on Johanna's sleeve.

"Slow down, girl. I am twice your age. And I do know that love doesn't happen with sonnets and sweet music. It is more complicated than that."

When they reached the general store, Mabel leaned on a fence to rest before following Johanna up the steps. She grasped Johanna's arm for support. "The Captain and I had our stormy moments. And many a night I spent on the walk glancing towards the sea and praying the good Lord would deliver my mate home to me. Marriage takes lots of work."

Johanna shook her head. "I'm not afraid of discord. I put off my wedding. Robert never got well." She wiped a tear away. "I could have given him a measure of happiness, but I didn't."

"So you're resigned never to love, foolish young girl! Time is the best test of such things and I'd wager you will change your mind."

"Never." Johanna pushed open the door to the general store. "We're here for our supplies." She told the clerk. "If you don't mind, we will have your servant run up the rest."

"No problem." The clerk looked happy to have rung up the large order.

Johanna struggled with the door and the bundle of fabric as she made her second trip down to the buggy. A trailing end of the cotton material caught on her heel, tripping her. She fell down two steps, landing on the ground with her petticoats spread for all to see.

"Are you injured?" Mabel came down to her aid.

Her pride was hurt, but she was fine. "I can manage." She rose up, pulling her skirts over the undergarments. As she did so, she heard a disturbing whistle.

"Hmmm, nice!" a male voice called.

Embarrassed, Johanna glanced over the crowd of strangers and found the source of the remark to be Ryan Majors. His expression one of pure amusement—at her expense—incited her to sheer anger. *Of all the luck!*

Quite a coincidence, Ryan thought as he reached the bewitching redhead. He had been thinking about her this morning, deciding it had been a mistake to kiss her. He could have jeopardized his job as trail boss. This was his chance to apologize. But how could he with her aunt present? Seeing the mess at her feet, he went to offer his assistance.

"Are you all right?" He stretched out his hand. She glared at him. The contempt evident in her clear blue eyes did not daunt him. He silently gathered up the fabrics and placed them in her hands.

"Thanks!" she snapped.

He noted her wet eye lashes. Had she been crying? Why?

"Mr. Majors, fancy seeing you here." Mabel smiled and elbowed Johanna. "We were discussing how fortunate we are to have such a fine trail leader."

Johanna opened then shut her mouth. She placed the bundle in her wagon and returned to her aunt's side. "We've finished shopping for today."

Ryan looked again at the bundles of fabric and yarn and assorted notions. "Seems to me you'll need more than this to make it to the territory, if all you brought with you were your frocks." He picked out bits of Irish lace. "Fancy rags won't do on dusty trails."

Johanna grabbed the lace from him. "This is not a rag. It's to be made into a tablecloth when we get to the settlement." She placed the material back then tied the bundle. Staring up at him, she replied, "And for your information, we are having the remainder of our purchases delivered to our hotel."

"When I gave the supply list to Reverend Wade, I don't recall fancy frocks and frivolous items. You're gonna need them pots and pans, plates, and blankets. But unless you plan to pick berries for every meal, you better have a hundred or more sacks of food."

"We know that," Mabel interrupted, "The kind clerk in the general store warned us about what to take."

"And we can add to our list before we leave," Johanna stated.

"Oh, I am rather tired from the day." Mabel glanced at Ryan. "My niece here ran me ragged. Would you mind helping me?" She gestured towards the buggy.

"Sure." Ryan helped Mabel ascend the step of the buggy.

"I'll get some more things, Auntie." She rushed back to the store with Ryan dogging her steps. She avoided talking or looking at him as they entered the store, grabbed a package, and returned to the buggy. They put the bundles in the buggy then Ryan studied her for a moment. He had never seen such a serious expression on so young a woman.

"Need a hand?" He nodded towards the step to the buggy.

"No, thank you. I can manage." She lifted the hem of her skirt as she climbed aboard the buggy.

As she sat in the seat, Ryan leaned over and whispered. "We must talk."

She lifted the buggy whip in a threatening manner. He jumped a bit. "Good day, Mr. Majors." Then she prodded the horse forward.

Mabel waved at Ryan as they rolled away. "Thank you for your assistance, Mr. Majors. We will see you soon."

"You sure will." He shouted back. "Very soon."

Four

An Unexpected Dinner Guest

Johanna gritted her teeth at the mere thought of seeing Ryan so soon. In two days the man had managed to infuriate her, embarrass her, and, at the same time, stir up the most wicked of thoughts. Each touch heated her to the quick. And that kiss! It had been a far cry from the platonic pecks her fiancé had given her years ago. This kiss boiled her blood. Like it or not, she had been more than willing to respond.

"What's wrong, Johanna?" Mabel glanced at her with concern. "You have such a queer look on your face—one moment it's one of revulsion, the next a pleasant smile. Has the sun been too strong for you?"

Johanna laughed. "It's nothing, Auntie."

"It's that Ryan Majors isn't it?"

"Not at all." She hoped her aunt would not begin her lecture about men again. The day had been trying enough. When they reached the hotel, Johanna clambered from the buggy and hitched it to the post. She helped her aunt down. "I'll take these in." Johanna motioned to the bundles in the rear.

"Looks like you could use some assistance."

Turning her head at the sound of a man's voice, Johanna came face to face with a smiling Stephen. The smile, however, failed to reach his eyes—those steel blue orbs exuded a haughty arrogance. During their trip to Missouri, Stephen had been the idyllic gentleman. He had indicated he would be of service to her and her father's mission. Since their arrival, however, he had ignored her, focusing on her father and doing his best to ingratiate himself into the elder minister's companionship. With that in mind, she ignored him now.

But Mabel said, "Yes! We could use some help," and held the hotel door for them as they carried the bundles. They climbed two flights of stairs to the landing where Mabel and Johanna were staying. Mabel opened the door to her room and slumped onto a chair; her breathing became ragged as she poured herself a glass of water.

"Rest awhile, Auntie." Johanna pulled over an ottoman and lifted her aunt's feet. "Stephen and I will get the rest.

Mabel looked at Stephen. "You don't mind?"

"Not at all," he replied. When they left the room, he squeezed Johanna's hand. "You must see the horses your father and I bought," he said, looking pleased as punch as he led her downstairs at a more rapid pace than she cared for.

"You're like a child!" she snapped, clutching onto the banister railing. Not in all their years of growing up had she seen Stephen this excited.

He bowed as he held the door for her. "This way, my princess." It was the name he called her when they had been children playing on Boston Commons.

Johanna gave him an exasperated look as she followed him into the cobblestone street. "Thank you."

He let go of her hand and ran to the livery stable. Johanna wondered why Stephen was so gleeful. She entered the dim interior of the stable. A small stream of sunlight filtered through the roof and shimmered upon the floor, which smelled of manure and hay. A shuffling of hooves kicked up dust. As they approached, a chestnut mare poked her head from a stall. Her sleek coat glistened from a recent grooming and she tossed back her black mane. Johanna leaned over the stall to stroke the horse's forehead. "Is she yours?" She looked at Stephen.

"Yes."

"She is beautiful!"

"Proud, too!" Stephen's hand gripped her wrist like a vise.

Johanna stared at him in complete amazement. The clasp

tightened. "Fiercely independent," he continued, ignoring her look. "Like a certain woman I know."

Wincing with pain, Johanna finally pulled from his grip. "You hurt me."

"I'm sorry."

"This is so unlike you, Stephen!"

He bent his head. "I'm sorry, Johanna, forgive me." The horses fidgeted in their stalls, as if sensing the tension between the couple.

"I certainly hope so." She rubbed her bruised wrist then backed away in sudden wariness and the realization that they were alone. She decided to divert him from his unexpected and annoying attempts at flirtation. She walked past the front of the stalls. "Which one is Father's horse?"

He pointed to the corner stall by the door. "That one."

An enormous black stallion poked its head out and eyed her. She approached the stall with caution, but on closer inspection, she frowned. "Good Lord, he looks like a plow horse."

"He's not a stud anymore, but he'll do." At her scowl, he added quickly, "Oh, forgive me, I didn't mean to shock you. I grew up around horses. With father having bred quite a few of them, I observed nature firsthand." He reached for Johanna, but she stepped back.

"I am not all that naive of horses." *Nor of men.* She gave him a sour look. "I had riding lessons while attending boarding school."

"The horse will serve your father well. He's strong enough for the journey. We got a good price on him, too."

Johanna unexpectedly tripped over a bale of hay, and Stephen seized her about the waist. She gave a startled little yelp when he hauled her closer to him. His kiss came swiftly. Johanna rubbed her mouth in an effort to wipe away the sickening feeling that crept into the pit of her stomach. Stephen held her tight. "What's wrong?" he snarled. "Wasn't it as good as Majors' kiss? Or, should I drag you off on horseback first?"

"Let me go, Stephen!"

"I heard the gossip around town. Word spread of a trapper carrying on with an Eastern lady—a minister's daughter. Johanna, how could you?"

"I was not carrying on with him, nor do I wish to carry on with you." She pushed past Stephen and grabbed the door handle. "Get out of my way!"

A pulse throbbed in his clenched jaw; his hand fisted. A chill gripped Johanna's spine. Suddenly, he released a long sigh and moved aside. "Look, I apologize. I didn't mean for that to happen."

Gone was the once good-natured school-boy companion she knew years ago. The Stephen before her now was someone she didn't know. "What has gotten into you, Stephen? I've never seen you act this way before."

"I am no longer a boy, Johanna. I grew up a great deal when I left for the seminary. But I always thought about you. Even then, I planned our lifetime together."

"I don't know what you're talking about! Let me go!" She pulled the door, only to have Stephen push it shut again.

"It was understandable that you rejected Doctor Watkins in order to join your father's mission." He braced himself against the door, barring her escape. "The mission is more important than anything you can do in Boston. After the settlement, you and I will run it."

She shook her fist. "How dare you speak as if Father were dead."

His lips curled derisively, and he snorted. "He's an old man, Johanna."

"Father is fifty," she protested, reaching towards the door. Stephen pushed her back.

"I'm learning much from him. But one day he will be gone. You will need a man to lead the mission. Who better than I?" He grabbed her by the shoulders and pulled her close. "You know I am right for you," he insisted, lifting her chin. "We can be married before we leave Independence. Then there will be no rumors to hurt your or your father's reputation. I'll even get your father's blessing."

"Never!" Johanna lifted her booted leg and stamped down hard upon Stephen's instep. As he jumped away in pain, grabbing his foot, she escaped through the stable door.

"Come back, Johanna!" Stephen called from behind her. "Let me explain."

Explain, my eye. Tears blinded Johanna as she ran towards the hotel. She ran so fast she fell headlong into the hard, buckskin-clad chest of a trapper. Dazed, she looked up into the questioning gaze of Ryan Majors.

"Of all people to meet," she muttered.

"Hello to you, too!" His smile disappeared as he noticed her tear-streaked face.

"Out of my way. I'm in a hurry." Brushing past him, she moved to the buggy.

He walked alongside her. "I can see that. You look as if you came nose-to-nose with a bobcat." He began taking the bundles from the buggy. She swatted his hands away. "Leave them there."

"Lady, you're more stubborn than ten mules put together!" Ignoring her, he swept up three bundles in his arms. "Go on and open that door for me."

Too tired to argue, Johanna opened the door. She returned to the buggy and took the remaining bundle. Then she marched up the steps behind Ryan. As she reached the landing, a package slipped from her grip. He retrieved the bits of fabric. Her face reddened as he handed her the lace petticoat. She lifted her chin in a gesture of proud determination. "I won't need any more help today! Thank you."

"Wait, we have got to talk."

"I think enough people are talking for the both of us, thank you."

~ * ~

She turned and opened her door. "You can leave those bundles there. I'll bring them in myself."

"Johanna." He touched her shoulder. When she turned to face him, he lowered his voice, "Look, I've come to apologize for acting like a grizzly bear in heat."

Johanna stopped dead in her tracks and looked at him wide-eyed. Taking that as encouragement, Ryan continued, taking off his coonskin cap and twisting it as he spoke. "Honest, ma'am, there'll be no more trouble from me."

"I hope not!" With a shake of her head, Johanna entered the room, slamming the door in Ryan's face.

~ * ~

After a nap, Johanna dressed for supper. She wore an off-the-shoulder, powder blue dress. Simple yet elegant, it revealed a hint of cleavage. The bustle fixed in the back and the skirt circled her narrow waistline. She breathed with a measure of apprehension as she stared at her reflection. With the recent, unwanted attention she received from the young men in her life, she thought she should switch to the dark, more modest gray garment. Her aunt's heavy knock and shrill voice interrupted her thoughts.

"Johanna!"

"Yes, Auntie."

"I will wait for you downstairs."

"Fine."

She heard footsteps pacing the hallway then her aunt saying, "Evening, Mr. Majors."

"Oh, no!" Johanna sighed. Why had Ryan returned?

"I'm glad you will be joining us for supper," she overheard Mabel state.

Supper! Johanna blew out a puff of air, fingering the locket on her bosom. Heavens, no! She glanced down at her dress. Too late to change. Had she known Ryan would be at their table, she might have worn something more modest, like a dress that covered her up to her earlobes. She tried to steady her hand as she brushed her hair, parting it in the center and allowing her thick curls to cascade around the sides. Tiny beads of perspiration broke along her forehead, and she wiped them with a handkerchief. "There's nothing to get nervous about," she told herself. She took two deep breaths then dabbed a bit of lavender toilet water on her wrists. The sweet scent had a way of calming her. When she left her room, Johanna glanced about the hallway and felt relieved to find it empty. Hoping Ryan had left; she descended the hotel steps and headed for the dining room.

Mabel stood outside the dining room waiting for her. Johanna had to raise her voice above the din of pots being banged and plates clattering from the kitchen area. "What are you up to, Auntie?"

"I don't know what you mean, dear." Mabel placed her hand in the crook of Johanna's elbow. "You look quite lovely. It's nice to see you out of those drab, mourning colors and into a more flattering dress."

"Thank you. Now, explain why you invited Ryan to our table for dinner."

"And why not? He's our friend." They entered the dining room and stood by a white-uniformed maitre d', who nodded and smiled at them.

"Evening, ladies. Care for a table?" he asked.

"No, thank you. We're waiting for our friends," Mabel replied.

The maitre d' nodded then went back inside the dining room.

"Ryan Majors is not a friend," Johanna whispered to her. "He's our trail guide."

"Don't tell me you're becoming as stodgy as your father."

As she spied Stephen and her father approaching them, Johanna loosened her aunt's grip. "Shhh, here they are."

Both ministers greeted them.

Reverend Wade's solemn countenance changed to delight. "Johanna, you have your mother's beauty."

Johanna smiled. "Thank you."

"And her father's bullheadedness!" Mabel whispered in her ear.

Johanna smirked at Mabel's remark. She studiously ignored Stephen.

The maitre d' returned to the entryway. "Good evening, folks. Let me show you to a table. Four?"

"Five," Mabel replied.

"Five?" Stephen looked at her.

"This way." The maitre d' led them towards the corner of the room, passing the crowd of well-dressed ladies and gentlemen engaged in conversation or busily eating their meals. Cigar smoke rose up from a table where several men sat drinking port wine and ale. Johanna coughed and waved her hand to fan away the fumes. At that moment, Stephen drew closer to her, whispering in her ear, "You do look radiant this evening." She shook her head, ignoring his remark.

When they reached their table, he pulled a chair out beside his own. "For you."

"No, thank you, Stephen." She chose to sit beside Mabel. Stephen huffed then sat. Reverend Wade sat next to Stephen. Seeing the empty chair across from hers, Johanna wondered if Ryan would appear. The

37

clatter of utensils and dishes and the buzz of nearby conversations drew her attention to the crowded dining room. She focused upon the strangers entering the room then caught her breath as a familiar face glanced her way.

Ryan Majors entered the room as if he owned the hotel. Gone were the familiar rough-hewn buckskin garments. In their place, he wore a grey frock coat that accentuated his trim but muscular build and black trousers covering his long legs. He fingered the knot of his red cravat as he glanced about the room. When his dark eyes sighted their table, he smiled and smoothed back his shoulder-length black hair. As he crossed the crowded room, Johanna noticed that more than one lady's head turned in his direction.

Whether it was the warmth of the room or the effect of her dress, Ryan's blood heated the minute he glanced at Johanna. She looked radiant and tempting. The blue of the garment matched the color of her eyes, and her hair shone like a red rose. He could not help but gaze at her bared shoulders and the lowered neckline of the gown. No other lady in the room could compare to her beauty and charm. She avoided meeting his eyes when he stopped at their table.

"Evening, ladies, Reverend Wade and Reverend Green."

"Mr. Majors!" Mabel exclaimed. "I'm glad you decided to join us."

Tearing his gaze from Johanna, Ryan smiled at Mabel. "Thanks for the invite, Mrs. Foster." Turning a heated gaze on Johanna, he added softly, "And, Miss Wade, you look as pretty as a herd of elk gliding across the tall grasses of the plains."

Suppressing a giggle at his choice of words, Johanna said with a touch of amusement, "My, my—you do know how to turn a lady's head, Mr. Majors." When Ryan flushed, Johanna took pity on him, adding smoothly, "My aunt told me that you were staying at a hotel down the street from ours."

"That's right. It's been my custom to stay there whenever I come to town. Not as fancy as this one." A Negro waiter stepped between them to place a basket of bread on the table and to pour water into their goblets.

"Bring me some Scottish ale," Ryan told the waiter.

"Sure thin'," the waiter replied, leaving them.

"They have good ale and vittles here," Ryan remarked as the waiter returned with the tankard of ale and the plates of food.

Stephen shot him a malignant glance. "Thought you'd be sleeping in the woods, not in a hotel."

Unruffled by the sarcasm, Ryan smiled. "I enjoy the comforts of civilization once in a while." He turned toward Johanna, but her attention remained on the plates of chicken and vegetables.

"Spend a good deal of time in Independence?"

Ryan chose to ignore the young minister. He put his tankard of ale down and watched Johanna. She gracefully dabbed at the curve of her lips with the edge of a napkin between bites. *Those* lips. "Delicious," he said

"What's delicious?" Stephen asked. He glanced at Johanna.

"Why the food here, of course," Ryan muttered. He forked huge chunks of meat and potatoes, eating them in big bites, and pausing to speak. "Got good quail, wild turkey, best thing though is the buffalo meat. It ain't quite as good as it is fresh after the hunt, but best raw."

"Raw meat?" Mabel stared at him in horror.

Noting, the discomfort on Johanna's face, Ryan quickly added, "Forgot ya'll from back East and ya'll wouldn't appreciate such fine delicacies." Lifting his goblet, he took a long drought of ale then smacked his lips as he set the tankard down again.

"We don't believe in drinking spirits," Stephen interjected.

"Oh, no?" Ryan leaned forward, glancing at Reverend Wade. "Is that so?"

Reverend Wade turned to Stephen. "Mr. Majors can have his drink or two as long as he doesn't drink while guiding our wagon train."

"Now wait a cotton pickin' minute." Ryan wiped his lips with the back of his sleeve. "I gave you a condition when I hired on, Reverend. Are you backing out of it?"

Reverend Wade looked at Stephen, Mabel, and Johanna. "No, I'm not."

"Good, didn't think so," Ryan replied. "Ain't another scout around this county would take you folks on who has my experience."

"Is that so?" Stephen challenged him.

Johanna's hand shook as she lifted a cup of tea. "Oh, dear," she stated, spilling half the tea onto the ivory-colored tablecloth. Stephen jerked away from the table. A waiter came by and wiped the mess.

"Heck, that's so," Ryan replied, lending his own napkin to the waiter to help mop up the spill. "I know the territory like the back of my hands." He looked at Johanna. "I came to Missouri every year they had the trappers' rendezvous, gave me a chance to visit my brother's family." Ryan took another gulp of ale then wiped his lips with his hand. "Trapping ain't what it used to be, game is running scarce, that's why I'm leading wagons."

"You have a brother?" Mabel asked.

"Had." A look of pain crossed Ryan's face, but he quickly hid it by lifting up his tankard again.

"Mr. Majors' brother is dead," Reverend Wade explained. "I gave the funeral."

"Oh, I'm so sorry." Mabel patted his hand.

Ryan hated the silence that ensued and the sympathetic glance from Johanna. Hell, he didn't want or need her sympathy. "It's the way of things out here," he stated. "Justice will be done sooner or later."

Johanna too, touched his hand. "I am sorry, Ryan. I, too, have lost a loved one."

Ryan looked at her hand upon his, and when her words finally registered in his head, he looked up in surprise.

"My fiancé died of scarlet fever."

"Oh." Ryan turned his hand and gripped her fingers. For a moment she was tense, but then her hand relaxed. Her father frowned, and Stephen glared, forcing Ryan to remove his hand. *This is business*, he had to remind himself. "Chet died from something more evil than sickness. Greed! He was murdered for money."

Both Mabel and Johanna gasped, looks of horror crossing their faces.

Ryan leaned closer to Johanna. "I didn't mean to upset y'all with my troubles, so it's best I be going."

"Sit a moment longer," Mabel coaxed. "Tell us about your life in the mountains."

Ryan sat back in his seat. Noticing the look of vexation on Stephen's face, he decided to sit a spell. He rather enjoyed irking the young minister. "Ain't much to tell. I was born in British territory. Pa was a merchant for the Hudson Bay. He left England to seek his fortune in America. Papa met my Ma, a Nez Perce. I came along a few years later."

"How romantic!" Mabel sighed, and a dreamy look stole over her eyes.

"Sounds like a fool to me," Stephen huffed. "Marrying Indians!"

It took enormous effort for Ryan to control his temper. When he was able to speak, his voice dripped with sarcasm, "You preach love, Reverend? My parents loved each other though they were different skin colors. My mother became Christian when she was a child— that's how she met my Pa. He visited her tribe with a preacher man. Same fellow later married them."

"Well said, Mr. Majors," Johanna remarked. "We are all the good Lord's children."

"Amen to that," Mabel replied.

Clearly trying to turn the conversation away from Ryan, Stephen snapped out, "Reverend Wade, when do we leave for Oregon?"

"I have twenty families willing to go," Wade replied. "They need time to settle up with the banks and pack up the farm."

"How long will all that take?" Ryan asked.

"Maybe next week," Reverend Wade answered. "I'm calling a meeting on Sunday."

"Don't waste too much time," Ryan warned. "An early snow in the Blues can be hell to contend with. I'd like to meet the folks who've signed on. That way I can check on what they're bringing along, as well."

"We can handle the recruits," Stephen cut in.

"It's my job to make sure the wagons are loaded proper," Ryan insisted. "You can get who you please to join up, but I want to meet each and every one."

"Ryan is our trail guide," Mabel said warningly. "He knows what's best."

Stephen's clenched hand jerked back, knocking a glass onto the floor. It shattered, causing other diners to look their way. "Maybe so, but we don't need his guidance on our work."

"Now who's the fool?" Ryan stood then pushed in his chair.

Stephen rose also. "What's more, you better leave our ladies alone!"

"Hold on a moment." Ryan looked at Johanna. "I have no intention of harming your ladies."

Johanna glanced away from him; crimson tinged her cheekbones.

Reverend Wade stood, cutting the air with a hand. "Enough! It's late and we all have much to do to get ready for this journey. We will be ready by next week, Mr. Majors."

"Good." With a nod to the ladies, Ryan turned and walked briskly from the dining hall.

"Temperamental," Mabel whispered to Johanna. "He'll have to learn to deal with greenhorns like us."

Johanna sighed, nodding her head in agreement. Standing up, she tapped Stephen on the shoulder.

"Yes?"

"I want you to know that I think you're an utter fool to bait Mr. Majors that way. Our very lives depend on him. And for another thing, I am not your property!"

Five

Westward Ho!

Ryan stood by a white picket fence, waiting and watching for the doors of the Methodist church to open. He chewed another wad of tobacco, thinking about how pretty Sara looked in her Sunday finest. Even in black mourning, she had a way of appearing like a ray of sunshine after a fierce storm. He smiled at the image of her sweetness and light. *Good God*, he thought, *what am I thinkin' about? She's Chet's woman—even though he's dead, she belongs to him, not me.* He shook himself, spat out the tobacco and leaned on the fence.

"Hell and damnation, will they ever finish?" An elderly woman in a gray gown glanced at him, and shook her bonnet-covered head in disapproval as she passed by.

"Good afternoon, ma'am," Ryan said, tipping his coonskin cap as he smiled at her. He went back to watching the church.

Finally the doors swung open. Ryan stiffened, and his jaw clenched in agitation as he realized that the minister stepping out was none other than that weasel Reverend Wade and the young pup of a preacher, Reverend Green. The two ministers stood side-by-side as they greeted the exiting congregation.

Reverend Wade's voice carried down to the street below, and Ryan could hear him mention the journey to Oregon and his need for families. When he called out to his daughter, Johanna came forth with a proud tilt of her head and a broad smile that took Ryan's breath away. Compared to the other women, Johanna stood out like a wild blue flower amid ragged weeds. He imagined her sweet scent as she pressed the parishioners' hands, greeting them and thanking them for attending her father's service. Her aunt strode out arrayed in a well-tailored navy gown, which fit her so tightly she looked like a bloated skin about to burst. She held a matching parasol over herself and her niece.

"Come, Johanna, get yourself out of the sun or you'll have a nasty burn," she warned. When she turned, she spotted him and waved. "There's that nice young man, Mr. Majors. Yoo hoo!"

Ryan waved back at Mabel. Johanna peered down at him with a sour look. Then she turned away, continuing to greet the Sunday crowd. Ryan looked for his sister-in-law but could not find her.

Reverend Wade stepped over to a tall oak, a black Bible in one hand, as he called out, "Brothers and sisters in Christ Jesus, I have gathered you here to tell you of the wonders which await you in a new land—Oregon—God's country. A land flowing with milk and honey, a land ripe for the taking, and all free."

This should be good for a laugh, Ryan thought as he watched the crowd stop and listen to the minister. They appeared mesmerized by this gaunt scarecrow of a man who had never been west of Missouri, let alone to Oregon. *What the hell does he know?*

"The Oregon Territory has become the property of the United States government," Reverend Wade continued as the crowd settled down around him, "and it means more land and a new life for many of you. As a minister, it means I have an obligation to bring religion and civilization out there. We have a destiny, brothers and sisters, our destiny to go westward and to settle the lands there."

"Ever see Oregon, Reverend?" a wiry, tall, red-haired farmer in worn denim overalls asked.

Ryan chuckled as he watched Reverend Wade squirm ever so slightly before replying, "No, I have not, but others have gone out there before us, and the reports are all good."

"What have they said?" another man in the crowd asked. His bald head sat like a huge rock upon his square shoulders.

Reverend Wade glanced up to the sky then down at the crowd. "They say that Oregon is a wondrous place—the best place on God's good earth to live. Lots of green, fertile land in the valley, trees that touch the heavens, and good pasture for the animals. It never rains."

Ryan choked on his tobacco, coughed then spat the black substance onto the ground. He swallowed hard, cleared his throat, and called out, "Are ya talking about Oregon or heaven, Reverend?"

A few people in the crowd laughed at that. Ryan went on, "Sure there's land, lots of it, Indian land, too. And weather... why there ain't a place on Earth that ain't had a drop of rain."

Ryan walked up to the tree and stood before the crowd. "You folks gotta know the truth... Oregon is a wondrous sight like the Reverend said, but there's danger, too! Storms so wild they'd blow y'all back to the Kansas River, and wild animals." He scrunched his face, as he looked at them. "Animals that'd rip the flesh off you—mountain lions, wolves, grizzly bears, and vipers."

A ruddy-faced farmer spoke with a thick Scottish brogue. "We've problems a plenty here, too! Last year, the farm grew hardly enough for me ta feed me family. And when the rains come, the river flows near'n the rafters. The cholera killed me poor wife and others here. So, dunna be talkin' on 'bout problems to come when we've problems aplenty here. 'Tis the land we be need'n. I've got six mouths ta feed, an' no wife ta help me." The farmer glanced at Reverend Wade. "Go on, Reverend, tell about dis here Oregon."

"I will, I will." Wade smiled, ruffling the lapels of his frock. "The land is so rich you can grow vegetables three times the size of the ones you grow now. And your cows will have lots of good, green grass to chew, which means plenty of milk. And your young ones will have more than enough elbow room to play in, as will you."

Ryan looked at the crowd whose expressions mirrored their enthusiasm as they warmed to the promises made. They had land fever. They wanted to "see the elephant"—the name given this urgent need to go westward. Ryan understood restlessness, having felt it all his life while he lived a nomadic existence. Yet, he knew the dangers which awaited them, and he wondered if they had it in them, as he did, to face the hardships. He felt a tug on his shirtsleeve and turned to the side.

"What the devil do you think you're doing?" Stephen Green asked him.

"Telling them the truth."

"You are discouraging them and undermining our every effort to organize a settlement party."

"But they've a right to know the truth." Ryan locked gazes with him.

"And what do you know of the truth?" Green poked his shoulder. "A man brought up by heathens with no fear of God."

"Take your hand from me, preacher, or I'll break it!"

Green quickly pulled away, a glimmer of fear lighting his pale blue eyes. "Remember, Majors, you're only a hired guide for our missionary party."

Ryan heard a scuffle of footsteps on the church steps and sighted Johanna coming toward them. She brushed past him and tapped her father's shoulder.

"Father, you must remind them of our plan for the mission. This is the Lord's work."

"Yes," Wade said and nodded, then addressed the crowd again. "Brothers and sisters don't go yet; Mr. Majors is right about there being hardships ahead. The road to paradise will not always be a smooth one, but will test us and our belief in the Lord. For the good Lord will deliver us."

"Amen," someone shouted.

Reverend Wade leaned toward Ryan, whispering, "You take care of the wagons, and leave the people to me." Before Ryan could respond, the minister looked at the crowd and shouted, "And this man, this one who knows full well what to expect, shall be our guide. With his help and the good Lord's, we'll make it to the promised land."

"Amen," Stephen Green stated.

"Mr. Majors is a man of sincerity," Reverend Wade continued, "a good, God-fearing man."

Ryan started to laugh, but stopped when he saw the anger in Johanna's blue eyes.

"Mr. Majors is the man to lead us to Oregon and to help us fulfill our destiny."

"Amen," the lanky farmer replied aloud. A few others echoed him.

"Yes, Amen," Johanna shouted.

Ryan glanced at her, surprised by her sudden smile which vanished all too soon. *This is too much*, he thought, feeling like a piece in a game of checkers. He hated checkers because he lost all the time to his nephew. Samuel waved at him from the front of the crowd.

Ryan nodded then spotted Sara, who frowned and peered off into the distance. Had he embarrassed her? He remembered what a devout Christian she was. *I might as well get the hell out of here.* Ryan moved from the side of the tree. No one paid him any attention as he passed through the crowd. He heard the ministers as they led the crowd in a prayer service. The words "lead us not into temptation" echoed in his mind while he walked.

He thought about the two women who stirred a strong flow of emotions—Sara and Johanna. Both held temptation for him—he could empathize with the Biblical Adam in the garden. All he wanted was to do right by his brother. Suddenly he realized that might be more trouble than he expected.

~ * ~

Dusk settled in crimson tones on the horizon by the time the revival-style meeting ended. A woman in a black dress walked away from the weary crowd. Tendrils of blonde hair escaped the sides of her bonnet. Despite the somber attire, her face radiated health and beauty. She appeared to be but a few years Johanna's senior, yet she managed a brood of children. She held a baby in a white blanket, and smiled as she stepped before Johanna.

"I'm Sara Majors," she said. "I'm sorry for how my brother-in-law acted a while ago. He don't understand the good work y'all are doin'."

"Ryan?" Johanna thought a moment before connecting the woman to the obstinate trail-guide, Ryan Majors. "Mr. Majors has a lot to learn."

Sara glanced in admiration at Johanna's attire. "He ain't had the kind of upbringing someone like you might o' had." The baby cried, and Sara rocked it until it quieted.

"Ryan done grow up as wild as Spanish moss on a cypress tree. Chet, my husband, was his brother. He had the same upbringing, but changed once we was married. I reckon when ya got five young uns, ya got to grow up."

"Yes," Johanna said, staring at the children who gathered around the woman. Their plain coveralls and rompers spoke of a simpler way. They were clean-faced and comely, despite their rough manners, as they poked at one another or pulled each other's hair.

"Settle down, y'all," Sara hollered, "else I'll take a hickory stick to your backsides!"

In an instant her children quieted. The oldest looked at Johanna with a sheepish grin as he shuffled his feet in the dirt. Sara ruffled the boy's black hair.

"He's the man of the family now," Sara said. "He's to help me with the farm and the little ones."

"I'm so sorry for your loss," Johanna said, glancing at the children's sad expressions and wishing she could help. "Perhaps you can come with us to Oregon?"

"No." Sara shook her head. "I'm not about to give up what me and Chet worked so long and hard to build together. It won't be the same but I'm staying on here. And my young uns like it here, too. But, that Ryan, he's a good sort. He'll help us out. Promised us he'd help. And he's good as gold." The baby cried again, and Johanna stood peering down at the blanketed bundle while Sara rocked the tiny child. "Got any young uns of your own?" she asked.

"I'm not married," Johanna said, gazing at the infant's pale pink face and clear blue eyes. "She's beautiful."

"Would you like to hold her?" Sara held out the baby. A strange longing filled Johanna as she reached toward the baby. If Robert McEntee had not died, she might have been married and had her own baby. That dream would never be realized. Releasing a sigh of regret, she shook her head. "No, I have work to do." She glanced at the ground where leaflets from the Sunday service lay like fallen leaves. As she stooped to pick them up, Sara touched her arm.

"Let me help you," Sara said as she handed her baby to her son. "Samuel, take the baby and the others to the buggy."

With Sara's help, the leaflets were quickly gathered.

"Thank you." Johanna smiled at Sara. "I wish there was something

I could do to help you. Please let me know if there is anything you need... food, clothing, whatever. I'll come out and bring it to you. Will you do that?"

Sara sighed deeply. "Oh, you are too kind... but thank ya kindly just the same. I will manage."

They stood a moment staring at one another, and Johanna wondered why on earth Ryan would leave his brother's family in such dire straights when they could use an able-bodied man to help them with the farm. Had he no decency at all? She felt compelled to ask more about Ryan, wondering what kind of relationship might exist between this simple farm girl and the trapper, but she decided not to, saying instead, "Thank you again."

"Oh, I left them waiting. Ryan must be fit to be tied. I must go. Good day, Miss Wade."

"Good day."

Johanna turned at the sound of her father's voice from somewhere inside the church. "If you'll excuse me, I have to help my father. It was nice meeting you."

"Yes. We will see you again."

Johanna found her father and Stephen holed up in the front of the church, talking about the members of the congregation who were joining the wagon train. She listened a while as Stephen told her father about Ryan Majors.

"He's a trouble-maker. I think we should hire someone else. Someone who's with our cause."

"Nonsense, Stephen, the man is an excellent choice despite his view on religion. He has the knowledge to get us west, and that is all that matters."

"Is it?" Stephen raked an impatient hand through his hair. "I think we need someone less likely to incite a mutiny."

"We're not on board a ship, Stephen," Johanna interrupted. "These are families who plan to leave everything they've known for the unknown. And think how frightened they are. We can offer them comfort and knowledge of God's goodness, but they need help in other ways—practical ways which we know nothing of. Isn't that so, Father?"

"Johanna is quite right. She's got a good head on her shoulders." Reverend Wade smiled at her. "She's like her mother that way. She'll make someone a fine wife one day."

"Yes, you're quite right," Stephen agreed.

A vile taste rose in Johanna's mouth at Stephen's impudent, knowing grin. She hated the fact that he thought she would marry him. She had no intention of marrying any man. No, she intended to spend her life teaching children. A spasm of pain crossed her face as she thought of Robert, her dead fiancé. Had he lived... her life would have been far different—but she mustn't think about that now. Now she had other problems to deal with.

"Perhaps, more importantly now is our missionary work," she said, dismissing Stephen's assumptions with her curt remark. "And, Father, I intend to be of service to you, as well as helping these farmers with their school work."

"Isn't anyone hungry?" Mabel asked, poking her head through the church doors.

Johanna chuckled softly, thinking it so like her aunt to bring up food at a time like this. "Yes, I am, and I think Father and Stephen are, too. Shall we return to our hotel?"

"Yes." Reverend Wade nodded. "Come on, Stephen—we can discuss things over supper."

~ * ~

May 30, 1848

Twenty families assembled by their wagons beneath an overcast sky in Independence. Ryan gazed at the livestock—cows, mules, chickens, pigs, goats, and horses—which made for the noisiest and smelliest gathering as farmers brought all they could from their farms. Like those before them, Ryan realized, these pilgrims took all they could for their future lives. The local merchants outfitted the rest. An entire industry grew up around outfitting the pioneers, from saddleries and wagon makers to gunsmiths, general stores, and blacksmiths. The general stores had to replenish their supplies on a regular basis to keep up with the waves of emigrants passing through the town.

Ryan's concern centered on whether the emigrants took the right supplies and not just the family heirlooms. Most of the farmers had a practical bent of mind and took enough flour, grain, dried fruit, and equipment for the journey.

But in a few instances, Ryan had to request that several items be discarded because they made the load too heavy for the oxen or mule team to pull. Most complied with his request, until he came to the McPherson family.

The wagon stood piled high with farming tools, furniture, and six noisy children, who ranged in age from five to fifteen. A red-bearded man, who appeared to be in his early fifties, sat astride a mule. Ryan recognized him as one of the farmers who had attended the revival meeting the week before.

"Your wagon is a mite too heavy!" Ryan pointed within it. "Unload it!"

The farmer scrunched up his features as he peered at Ryan. "Who the heck are you to be givin' me the orders?"

"Ryan Majors, your wagon leader."

"I thought Reverend Wade was in charge."

Ryan began taking a rocking chair off the wagon when a large wooden keg rolled off the wooden bed, crashed to the ground, and gushed like a geyser.

"Me whiskey!" the farmer said, rushing over and plugging the hole with his finger. "Don't go throwing away me precious whiskey!" When Ryan stepped over, the farmer stood and swung at him, and Ryan ducked the blow.

The farmer swung again, and Ryan grabbed his arm. "Hey, let me be!" the farmer shouted. As Ryan loosened his hold, he was knocked down from behind.

He fell in the mud, lifted himself up, and looked at the twin teenage boys who stood pushing up their shirtsleeves, threatening him with their fists. "Leave our Pa alone," one of them said.

Ryan stood and brushed off his clothes. "Don't worry, I intend to." He stared hard at the farmer. "You can call your pups off o' me now. If you know what's best, mister, you'll let down the load or trail behind the rest!"

"Boys, leave 'em. So, you're the fella who done warn us of the dangers ahead."

"Yeah, that's right."

"Ya said your name was Ryan Majors, any relation to Chet Majors?"

Ryan's eyebrows lifted in alarm. "Yep, he was my brother. How'd you know Chet?"

"Me farm was 'bout ten miles east o' his. Decent lad. He sent supplies over one winter when me missus was dying. I'm sorry for the troubles he had, leavin' a widow and young uns and all that. I know first hand of raising children alone. 'Tis a burden. Me and me family will be no trouble to ya." With that, he smiled and extended his hand toward Ryan.

"That's all right." Ryan shook Seamus' hand. He marveled at the strength. A strength from toiling hard in the open fields. He doubted that too many men would try to boss this farmer around. Ryan took an instant liking to this kindred spirit and smiled.

"Ya can keep the whiskey," he said. "I'll get ya another barrel to put it in, but ya gotta get rid of the rocker and anything else of no use."

He followed the farmer to the rear of the wagon. Tied to the wooden frame were plows, axes, bucksaws, and chamber pots. Rocking chairs, feather beds, butter churns, water kegs, cooking utensils, and patchwork quilts lay scrunched in between. "Looks like you're supplying the settlement!" Ryan muttered, as he poked through the wagon. In between the corners, stood stacks of books, wooden toys, a rag doll, a fiddle, and a bag pipe. "You can keep them instruments," Ryan pointed at the fiddle and bag pipe, "Just don't play late at night, or else you'll scare the livestock."

The farmer brought out a portrait of a dark-haired woman.

"My missus," he said.

It reminded Ryan of his mother. "Good lookin' woman."

"Aye that she was." The farmer tucked the portrait into a blanket and stuck it on the side of the wagon.

"What you got there?" Ryan pointed to huge sacks at the bottom of the bed.

"Flour, beans, bacon, bread, dried fruit, and coffee." The farmer chuckled. "Can't live on whiskey alone." He pushed a dresser from the corner of the bed, grunting under its weight. He looked at Ryan. "Can ya not help me?"

"Sure." Ryan took the other end. They lifted it out and placed it on the ground. Ryan glanced around for other furnishings to discard. "Throw that out." He pointed to a walnut grandfather clock.

"But... but that was me wedding gift. It came from Germany." Seamus patted the fine oak base. As if on cue, a tiny wooden bird popped out chiming "Cuckoo, cuckoo."

"Never heard a bird like that before," said Ryan. "But the clock is too damn big. That chest over there, too..."

"Oh, that was me wife's favorite piece... She stored her precious things in it."

"Empty it and put in the food stuff and what ya really need to take."

Sadness crept in the farmer's eyes, "Ach, all right with it then— I'll be emptyin' it... but the wife would turn over in her grave if she knew."

"She'd know you're doin' the right thing," Ryan said as he helped the farmer empty the chest of assorted trinkets—porcelain statues, fine china ware, and a music box. The last item intrigued him. He opened the square mahogany box, and inside stood a wooden dancer who pivoted as the music played a waltz. He watched the ballerina spin twice then shut the lid. "Here," he said, handing it to Seamus. "Keep it for your daughter there."

The teenaged girl gave Ryan a shy grin. "Thank ya kindly, Mr. Majors."

A shopkeeper dashed from the general store. "Hey! I'll buy that." He touched the edge of the cuckoo clock then the mirror. "And those too. I can sell them in my store." He pointed to the rocking chair and the armoire. "Give ya a hundred and fifty dollars for the whole lot"

"Sold!" the farmer said, peering at Ryan.

The eager shopkeeper called out for his assistant, a young teenaged boy. The two began taking the furnishings back to their shop. The shopkeeper returned and paid the farmer.

Ryan watched the farmer count the bills.

Seamus looked up at him, with a grin. "I'm thinkin' the missus would understand." He tucked the money in a leather purse.

"She would." Ryan noticed the assortment of wooden toys in the rear of the wagon—blocks, boats, trains, and animals. He glanced at the McPherson children. The twins looked ready to pounce on him. The youngest, a boy named Jan, pouted. "Heck, ya can keep the toys," Ryan said. "But if push comes to shove, ya gonna have to throw 'em out."

"Thanks," Seamus said.

"Call me Ryan." He shook the farmer's hand then rode out toward the one remaining wagon at the rear. It brimmed with brand new supplies. Ryan glanced in surprise at the occupants seated at the front of the wagon. The fair-skinned, flaxen-haired girl of eighteen held her swollen belly and smiled. The young man, a handsome dark-skinned Creole, held his hand out to him. "I'm Tom Le Fleure." he said with a French accent, "and this is my wife, Megan. We're going to Oregon to raise ourselves a family."

"We come from down New Orleans way," Megan piped in. "Tom is jest itchin' to grab hisself some o' the land the government is promisin'!"

They're so young, Ryan thought—they reminded him of Chet and Sara. He felt concern at Megan's condition. "Looks to me as if you'll have that baby before we reach Oregon! Maybe ya ought to wait it out a few more months."

"No, we must leave here." Tom gazed tenderly at Megan. "We will make a new start."

Ryan felt suspicious of the Creole. "You're not in trouble with the law, or anything like that?"

Tom looked at Megan again. She winced in pain, holding her belly. "Oh, no! It hurt lots this time." Once she got her breath back, she gave Ryan a sheepish look. "It ain't Tom that's in trouble I am."

How could one so young be in trouble? Ryan wondered.

"Hush up." Tom threw her a warning glance.

"No," said Megan. "We can trust him. Can't we, Mr. Majors?"

"Sure, go on tell me why you're runnin'."

"My parents forbid me to see Tom, said he was a no-account

Creole. We seen each other anyways. And this..." she concluded, rubbing her belly, "was the result. Tom planned to wed me before, but my pa wouldn't hear of it. He tried to shoot Tom one day. So we both ran away one night. Reverend Wade done marry us. When he told us of the land in Oregon, we decided to start new. Right, Tom?"

"*Oui, mon cheri.*"

"I'll keep your story to myself." Ryan smiled at them.

"Let me check your load." He looked through the assorted pile of wooden furnishings—a feather bed, stools, table, and a cradle. Then he came to the front again. "Folks, y'all need to buy more supplies of food up ahead at the fort. Need more flour, beans, bacon, and such. Your wagon is plenty light, so don't bother with takin' anything out. Day to ya, now."

"Ryan!" He turned around to face his sister-in-law, shocked by how much Sara and Megan resembled one another.

"Anything wrong?" Sara asked him.

"No." He glanced around. "Where are the young uns?"

"Here's one." Sara showed the baby to Megan.

"Ah! She's a little darling." Megan cooed at the baby then looked over as Sara's other children rushed up. "My, you do have a brood. Hope you get enough help from your husband there." She motioned toward Ryan.

Feeling as if someone had slapped him, he turned away and went to Sara's children. Beth hugged him first, followed by the others. Samuel stood several yards away, like a lone wolf. Ryan ached to ease the boy's pain.

"My husband is dead," Sara told Megan.

"I'm sorry, I thought he was..."

"Ryan is my brother-in-law, but more brother than in-law." Sara cuddled her baby, nodding at Ryan who stood circled by the other children. "He'll make a fine husband and father someday."

That she thought him as only a brother deflated Ryan's hopes to hold that position. He went back to Sara's side. "I'll bring money back to you," he promised, stooping to kiss her forehead.

"Don't worry about them!" a man hollered.

Ryan glanced at the tall, lean figure of Jed Thompkins in a navy frock and grey trousers. Jed came over and offered Ryan a cigar. "No, thanks."

As Jed put an arm around Sara's shoulder, Ryan squirmed in discomfort. "You take care of my kin, Thompkins. And mind yourself where the lady is concerned." He nodded meaningfully at Jed's arm. "She's like a sister to me."

Jed dropped his hand from Sara's shoulder. "Why, Ryan, you know they're like family to me too. You got nothin' to worry about here." He shook hands with Ryan. "Now go on out. Stay safe. Remember what I told ya. Get that reward on Grizzly Dugan." He stood close to Sara again.

The picture of Jed beside Sara made Ryan fume. He didn't like the way she smiled back at Jed, even if they had been neighbors and friends for years. *She's Chet's widow for God's sake, and that makes her off-limits to any other man, including me. Hell, it's better I leave now.*

"I'll be back." He gave Sara one last hug before stepping away. "Now, now, don't cry none." He wiped away her tears. "Soon as I settle a few things. I'll bring back the money I promised. You need not want for anything."

He threw Jed a quick glance. "I will be back to help her. You can depend on that as sure as night follows day."

"Of course, Ryan." Jed clapped his back. "We'll be waiting for you."

Sara hugged him again. As the baby wailed between them, she kissed his cheek. "Come back safe," she whispered.

In that moment, Ryan wanted to sweep her and the children up and haul them clear across to Oregon. *This is plumb crazy*, he thought, pulling from Sara's grasp. "I love y'all," he said gruffly, refusing to yield to that kernel of emotion within himself. He cleared his throat and nodded at Jed. "You take care of 'em until I return. Ya hear?"

"Sure thing," Jed said with a smile.

Ryan looked for Samuel, the only one who did not come to say good-bye. *Stubborn like I was at his age*, Ryan mused. He found Samuel leaning against an oak tree, throwing rocks into a puddle of water.

"Samuel," Ryan called, "come on over here and give your uncle a hug."

"No." Samuel kicked the ground, sending mud into the air. "I ain't comin'."

"Come on, boy. I'm talkin' to ya. It'll be a long time 'til ya have the pleasure of my voice."

Samuel refused to budge.

"Turning into a mule on me now? What would old Aesop say 'bout this?"

"I don't care. It's a silly book, anyways."

"No it ain't, if it learned ya some." Ryan swore beneath his breath. "Hell, I'm a comin' after you if I have to move heaven and earth." In two long-legged strides, he caught up to where Samuel stood with arms crossed over his chest and head bent as he gazed at the ground. Ryan lifted the boy's chin. "What the hell is wrong here?"

Tears streamed down Samuel's face. "Ya promise to kill that man that shot my pa?"

Ryan nodded.

"Swear on your life, and if ya don't ya hope to die."

"What kind o' talk is that? I done told ya I'll try. Damn it, ya don't make this any easier." He brushed the boy's tears and held him close. Samuel sobbed against Ryan's chest.

"Now, now, you gotta be the man for your ma. She needs ya."

"I know." Samuel stood away, sniffled, and wiped his nose on his sleeve, "Sure, Uncle Ryan. You comin' back?"

"Yes." Ryan choked on the rest of his reply, and hugged the boy. "Good-bye, Samuel."

Of all Chet's children, he favored Samuel the most. Ryan released his grip to let the boy shuffle back to his mother. Regret filled him as he watched Sara lead the children away, leaving stirred-up painful memories and a longing he did not want to acknowledge. Despite his reassurances to them, Ryan wondered if he would ever return to Independence. The idea that he might not make it back was a frightening thought as he walked to his horse, mounted, and rode to the front of the wagon train. But it wouldn't be for lack of trying. He sure as hell intended to keep his promise to Samuel.

Reverend Wade rode up to meet him. The sight of the scrawny man in a finely tailored black clergy frock and top hat, astride a giant plow horse, gave him a chuckle. Stephen Green, astride a chestnut mare, rode up and asked in an acid tone. "What's so funny?"

Ryan whistled before lifting the horse's reins. "Oh, nothin', preacher, nothin' at all." He looked at Reverend Wade. "Got everyone ready to move out?"

Reverend Wade nodded, "Yes."

Ryan rode to the front.

"Good morning," a soft voice called from behind the first wagon. Johanna peeked from the wagon cover, tucking her loose strands of auburn air beneath her wide-brimmed bonnet.

Her smile lifted his black mood, and he smiled in return, pulling his coonskin cap down. "Morning, ma'am. That's a good bonnet to be wearing. Sun out here can turn your skin red as a tomato. And the rain can make that fine hair o' yours look like rat's tails. Now, you do know how to drive the wagon? A mule team can be a might cantankerous. Don't be afraid of using that whip in your hands."

Johanna's smile vanished and her gaze held a glimmer of annoyance. "I've no plans to hurt the poor creatures," she said. "As for using the whip, it may come in handy. And for your information, I've driven horses before. After all, we do have horses in Boston, and..."

"Johanna, what's the matter?" Mabel asked as she approached the wagon. "Oh, Mr. Majors." She glanced at the trail guide. "I wondered who my niece was shouting at."

"I was not shouting." Johanna sat on the wooden seat of the wagon. "I was discussing my qualifications for driving the mule team."

"How interesting." Mabel shook her head. "My niece is quite an expert with stubborn creatures; after all, she was a school mistress back in Boston."

That brought the smile back to Johanna's face.

"Would you mind helping me board?" Mabel asked Ryan. "This is a little higher than the usual carriage."

"Certainly, ma'am." Ryan dismounted and helped Mabel clamber onto the wagon. She plopped down beside her niece, clutching a parasol in one hand, and the edge of the seat with the other.

"Thank you, Mr. Majors." Mabel turned to her niece. "See, Johanna, they do have gentlemen in Missouri."

Johanna's face crimsoned as her eyes averted Ryan's gaze. He chuckled then quickly said, "We take care of our women folk, all right, and anything you need... anything at all, I'd be glad to help you with." He winked at Johanna before remounting his horse. "We'll be moving out," he shouted as he motioned his horse to move forward.

Ryan rode on, the vision of Johanna's blushing face still in his mind. *What the devil is wrong with me, flirting shamelessly with a minister's daughter?* Hadn't he done enough damage that day he kissed her by the glen? This would not do, not at all when the need to earn money for his kin depended on this job. Work before pleasure. How the hell could he keep his promise to Chet's family if he couldn't keep his mind from straying to other wants and needs? He had to! He owed it to his dead brother.

The noises from the surrounding crowd broke into his thoughts. Through tears, handshakes, hugs, kisses, and nervous laughter, they bid farewell to friends and relatives aboard the wagon train. A lump rose in his throat as he gazed toward the hillside where Chet's farm stood. In the walls of that little white farmhouse, he'd known many happy moments. He sure as hell hoped he'd one day see it again. He took a deep breath then hollered, "Move 'em out!"

Six

Journey to the Platte River

Two days out from Independence, Ryan peered down at the Kansas River, a dark, turbulent waterway which ran six feet deep. "It's a wide crossing," he told Reverend Wade. "We'll have to float the wagons across."

He pointed out a row of teepees lining the nearby shore. "They can provide dugouts for the wagons, and we'll float 'em across."

Halfway toward the Osage village, he dismounted and met four Osage braves. Johanna observed the exchange between these tattooed, bare-chested Indians in fringed buckskin leggings and Ryan. She gathered from Ryan's sign language that he was attempting to make a deal with them for the use of their dugout canoes.

One brave held up his hands and nodded when Ryan showed them a pouch decorated with peacock feathers. Then he stuck up two fingers and showed Ryan a dollar bill.

"Why, the price has gone up!" Ryan said, glancing over his shoulder at the ministers. "They want two dollars per wagon to get us across."

"That's twenty dollars." Wade looked at the brave.

"I don't think we have much choice, Father," Johanna called.

"We can ford it on our own," Ryan said, putting the feathered pouch back in his satchel.

"Tell them we'll give them the money," Wade said.

After he did so, Ryan rode up to the wagons and ordered that the wheels be removed once they reached the edge of the river. He explained that the wagons had to be unloaded then reloaded once the dugouts were placed beneath the flatbeds. Once on the water, they'd have to use whatever they could to steer the flatbeds. "Use downed branches, shovel handles, or a butter churn if you like," he told Johanna and Mabel. Then he went on to direct each family on what to discard to lighten the wagon beds and how to prepare to ford the river.

"Do we have to do this at every crossing?" Johanna wondered aloud, as she and Mabel removed items in their wagon. "If so, it will take forever."

"Heck, no, ma'am," Seamus said, coming to their wagon. "My guess is this is a wide 'nough crossing to need to float, that's all."

"Let me help you with that," Stephen said, lifting one end of the small chest from the rear of the wagon.

"Thank you, Stephen." With a grunt, he removed the chest and placed it gently on the ground. Fortunately, their wagon didn't have too many bulky items to remove. But it took much longer for the others to unload.

Arguments erupted among families as Ryan told them to discard things in order to fit the passengers. "You've got to fit four young uns in that, mister," Ryan shouted to the McCleary family. "You've got too much. She'll sink!"

"Ryan is right," Johanna intervened. Ryan glanced at her sharply. "If you need something of importance, I'd be happy to take it in my wagon for you."

"That's mighty nice of you, Miss Wade," Mrs. McCleary said, smiling at her. "Would you take these here books and that small chest? It contains the china from my wedding day?"

Carefully balancing the chest topped by books, Johanna carried the load back to her wagon. Just as she was setting the chest down, a hand slammed against its side. She jerked and the books tumbled to the ground.

"And do you plan to take everyone else's possessions, too?" Ryan asked.

"No." She glared at him. "Don't you understand? These people left a great deal behind—loved ones, friends, a life they felt comfortable with—to join us. All they have left now are their memories and a few token reminders—like these books and relics."

"Hell, woman, you pick a strange time to get sentimental. We're about to cross rough water, and you want to hold on to memories!"

A vision of Robert swept through her head—the pain was like a dagger through her heart. She bit her trembling lower lip then held up her head. "Yes, I'll hold onto my memories as long as I like." With that she boarded her wagon, now turned ferry, and began to ford the river. She didn't glance at Mabel but sensed her aunt's apprehension as the river tossed them about.

As a log rammed the side of the wagon bed, Mabel screamed. Johanna did her best to keep them afloat by using the long handle of the butter churn to steer.

"God save us!" Mabel shuddered and gripped the side of her seat.

"We're almost ashore, Auntie."

Soon, the river was filled with a swarm of people, livestock, and wagons. It took half a day to cross under the scorching sun.

One farm boy lost his footing and began to sink beneath swirling water. His scream for help caught Ryan's attention and he quickly dove into the turbulent water. Everyone held their breaths until he emerged with the boy in tow then hauled him to shore where he handed him over to a grateful family. Applause and shouts of glee followed Ryan's wet body as he staggered to a nearby tree to catch his breath. Johanna wanted to go to him, to tell him how proud she was of his bravery, but knew it would cause a stir. He might be uncouth, she thought, but he went up a notch in her estimation. And it gave her some comfort to know he was a man they truly could lean on in times of crises.

Everyone looked wet, tired, hot, and muddy as they stretched out or sat upon the shore. Determined to help, Johanna made the rounds with her father, visiting each family and checking that all had made it safely across. After the Osage reclaimed their canoes, the emigrants fastened the wagon wheels back on the wagon beds. Stephen proved useless at hammering wheels to the board, so Ryan helped her father out. Despite their earlier argument, Johanna couldn't help but respect Ryan's fortitude. The man was amazing. Not only had he delivered them across to safety, but he had saved a child's life. Then he worked non-stop at ensuring that everyone had their wagons intact. To top it off, he built up such a bonfire that its flames rose high up toward the night sky. She soon fell in with the others for a communal supper. As her father gave a prayer of thanksgiving, Johanna stood by his side. She led the women in a hymn then sat beside her aunt.

Seamus McPherson brought a fiddle from his wagon and began to play a lively tune that filled the night air. As Johanna pulled her shawl about her shoulders, her brows rose when her aunt flashed a coy smile at the farmer who gave her a wide grin in response. *Well, well*, she thought, hiding a grin. *Auntie can still work her charms.*

After a supper of fried beans and bread, she and her aunt helped the other women clean while the men sat about the fire and talked of the hardships of traveling across country. "Did you see that man?" Mabel asked.

"See who?" Johanna feigned ignorance.

"That one." Mabel pointed to the ruddy-faced farmer who puffed on a pipe and nodded at something Ryan said.

"The one without teeth?"

"Yes." Mabel placed the cookware into a box at the rear of the wagon. "I heard he's from Scotland. He plays the bagpipes."

Johanna shrugged. "So?"

"Isn't that delightful?" Mabel shifted her gaze to the farmer, and, when he looked her way, she flashed him another coy smile.

"Auntie, the man has no teeth and a wagon filled with children! You couldn't take a fancy to him, could you?"

"Hmm." Mabel sighed. "I think he's rather handsome, with or without all his teeth."

She didn't agree, but there was no accounting for taste when it came to physical attraction. Didn't her heart flutter whenever Ryan came near her? Annoyed by that realization, she snapped. "I think it's time to turn in." She nodded good night to the others. "Let's go,

Auntie. Stephen has set up the tent for us."

Mabel waved over at the farmer as she followed Johanna toward their own camp. Two tents stood beside the wagon. In the two days since they left Independence, they had learned to sleep on a blanket on the hard ground, cook over an open fire, and manage to take care of their toilet needs with as much modesty as possible. "I've got to relieve myself, Auntie. Hold your skirts out, please."

Mabel stood stretching her skirt around Johanna. Johanna squatted, saturating the ground as she relieved her bladder. "Ah, that's better." She wiped herself with an old rag she had tucked in her apron. "Lordy, I do miss Boston at times like this. Never in my wildest dreams had I anticipated such compromises."

"Neither did I, but I think the adventure far outweighs the hardships," Mabel said philosophically. "Hold your skirts for me." Johanna did as told, shielding her aunt from anyone's view. Mabel relieved herself, using another rag. That done, the two women tossed the rags into a pile to be washed by the river. Lowering her head, Johanna entered the tent. She stripped down to her chemise then crawled under her blanket. "Good night."

Mabel undressed and put on her nightgown. "'Night, child. I'll fix breakfast in the morning."

Johanna yawned and turned over. "Good."

~ * ~

As they crossed the open plains, Johanna spotted deer and jackrabbits bounding across the tall grasses. Beavers, busy building dams along sections of the river, took no notice of the wagons. The more skittish chipmunks fled into the gnarled roots of the cottonwood trees that lined the river banks. The sweet fragrance of hyacinths, violets, and white-blossomed primroses permeated the air that Johanna breathed. As her lungs filled with the myriad, strange scents of the earth, she longed to stop and gather a bouquet of wildflowers for her pleasure. But this was not Boston, and this wild, untamed land was not her aunt's carefully cultivated garden back home. With a sigh of resignation, Johanna cracked her whip above the mules' heads, pushing them ever onward toward the unknown.

Another twenty, bone-tiring, miles they had to travel that day following honking geese as they flew in formation above the wagon train, making their way to the river.

Shielding her eyes from the sun, Johanna watched a black hawk circling above. Further on, she spotted a rattlesnake slithering toward the wagon wheels. She tried to veer the wagon from its course, but too late. The wheels had cut the viper in two. She said a quick prayer, hating to see even the lowliest of God's creatures injured in any way.

By the time Ryan ordered a halt to the procession, the sun was sinking like an orange ball of fire over the western horizon. They had reached the lower Platte River.

"We camp here tonight," Ryan told her as she peered at him from the shade of her aunt's parasol. "Circle the wagon with the others and tie up your mules."

"Thank the Lord," Mabel muttered. "My backside is hard as a plank, and my back feels stiff as a rod."

The rolling grass looked to Johanna like a sea about to engulf them in its wake. Shivering at the notion, she climbed down from the wagon seat. "Let's set up for the night," she told her aunt.

As she rounded the corner of the wagon and pulled open the oak storage box, she heard the distinct sound of a rattle. She spun around and froze. Less than twenty feet away, a rattler stuck its head up and flicked its tongue out at her.

"Don't move," Ryan warned from somewhere behind her.

Move? Johanna thought she'd pass out; she felt the earth spin around her. A shotgun blast reverberated in her ears, and smoke clogged her lungs. When she let out a choking gasp, Ryan took her into his arms.

"Johanna? Johanna?" He lifted her chin. "You all right?"

"What?" She felt disoriented. He was holding her close—close enough to kiss. "What happened?"

"Done shot a rattler 'afore he'd time to strike."

She remembered the snake's hideous black eyes and the sounds it made as it curled its way closer. "Oh, my God!" With Ryan's help, she straightened. "Thank you."

"Doin' my duty, that's all."

He ran an appreciative gaze from her head to her toes. Shivers of warmth slithered up and down her spine. She couldn't blame the snake for the tremors she felt now as she stood at arm's length from Ryan. "Well, Mr. Majors, it seems I must thank you for saving my life."

"My pleasure, ma'am," he said tipping his coonskin cap to her, "I assure you." And, with a cocky grin, he sauntered away.

Seven

Stopover on the Plains
June 1848

Johanna thought about Ryan's arms as they held her, and how he saved her from being bitten by a rattlesnake. She had not seen him since then, except as he moved ahead on the trail or occasionally rode by, tipping his cap and giving her a brief smile. She owed her life to the man, and was grateful for his quickness with the gun.

Feeling a desperate need to learn to use the gun she had secreted inside the wagon, Johanna wondered who could teach her. It had to be Ryan! As she drove the mules hard that day, she thought of how to convince him to teach her to shoot.

The miles of yellowish-green grass which spread like an endless sea hypnotized her. At one point, she began slipping from the seat and Mabel yanked her back into place. Her back and legs ached more than ever. At last, Ryan signaled another stopover. Heaving a sigh of relief, she loosened her grip on the reins as she brought the mules to a halt. "I'd thought we'd never stop." She glanced at her blistered and blackened palms. "Auntie, would you give me that rag over there in the wagon bed?" Her aunt handed her a checkered cloth.

"Thanks." She wiped the dirt from her swollen fingers and palms. "Oh." She winced as she touched her skin and moved her arms around. Each movement felt unbearable. She rubbed her aching upper arms and shoulders, rolling her head from side to side to release the tension in her neck.

"I'm so sore." She peered at Mabel, whose nose was covered with a layer of dirt, and laughed.

"What's so hilarious?" Mabel asked.

"You and I. We look like children who've been rolling around in the mud all day."

"It's no wonder you're sore, with the way you yank those reins on the poor mules."

The mules lowered their shaggy heads and grazed on tufts of grass. "I'd better give them water." Johanna went to the rear of the wagon, retrieved a wooden bucket, and filled it from the barrel on the side. She dipped her hands into the water, luxuriating in its cool feel. She splashed some on her face then drank thirstily from the palms of her hands. "Ah," she murmured as it relieved her parched lips and dry mouth.

She filled two buckets with water and carried them to the mules. One dunked his head in and drank quickly. The other shook his head then lowered it and drank.

After filling her canteen with water, she climbed onto the wagon seat, sitting down beside her aunt. "Here, Auntie."

Mabel sipped the water and wiped her lips before handing the canteen back to Johanna. "It's best to conserve water," she said. "There's no telling when we'll get fresh water."

Johanna marveled at her aunt's sudden practicality. "You're absolutely right." She noted how her aunt's white-gloved hands and lace shawl had been caked with the dirt from the trail, and grinned to herself.

The occupants from other wagons began to make camp. Farm animals were tied up to wagon beds or penned in by ropes tied to tree stumps. Dogs yelped as they foraged for scraps of food. Women stirred the contents of cauldrons suspended from tripods or fried food over hot coals. Soon, the aroma of fried bread and bacon filled the air. The men erected tents next to their wagons or hammered loose nails into the wooden floorboards. Johanna's stomach rumbled as she watched tables being set up beside wagons.

"Where's that nice young man, Ryan Majors?" Mabel asked Reverend Wade.

"Out scouting ahead," the minister said, sitting down on a folding stool.

"I'd have cooked him something," Mabel said as she pulled out a small sack of flour. "He looks like he could use a good meal, right Johanna?"

"Majors can fend for himself," Stephen cut in, as he placed a bundle of branches on the ground for a fire. "That man is a trapper, remember, and he's probably out now trapping his dinner."

"You're right, Stephen," Johanna said, "Ryan Majors can fend for himself. If it wasn't for his ability with a gun I might not be cooking your supper, Stephen. He saved my life today."

She helped Mabel with mixing flour. "We can have leftover ham and beans I bought in Missouri."

Mabel pointed a branch at Stephen. "You should have seen it, my boy. Ryan aimed his gun, and boom, he split that rattler straight down the middle."

"Please don't point that stick at me." Stephen brushed the stick away from his shoulder.

"I think we can learn a lot from Mr. Majors," Mabel said, chuckling softly.

Johanna set up a folding table and stools. Then she set out the plates and mugs while Mabel peeled potatoes.

Stephen set up a metal tripod over the bundle of wood. It took a few matches before the bundle of wood caught fire.

Johanna heated a pan filled with ham and beans. Once they had cooked, she used the smoldering fire to brew a pot of coffee.

"We'll eat then hold a prayer meeting," Reverend Wade stated, rubbing his hands together in anticipation of a good meal.

They ate in silence. Johanna felt Stephen's stare as she sipped her coffee. Since the incident in the barn, she'd tried her best to ignore him but it had proven difficult. Her father's paternalistic attitude further annoyed her. He had taken Stephen under his wing, and, for his part, Stephen had stayed close to the elder minister. As thick as molasses, her aunt had said once, of her father and Stephen. She realized it to be true. "I think I'll take a walk," she said, after clearing the dishes. "Want to join me, Auntie?"

"I'll join you." Stephen stood and brushed the dirt from his sleeves. "I need to stretch my legs."

"No," Johanna snapped. "I... I need privacy, too. Mabel will accompany me."

"Oh..." Stephen didn't look too happy, but conceded gracefully. "Very well."

Mabel was busy straining her neck to look at the McPherson wagon. "Sure, dear, I'd love a walk about camp."

"Be careful," Reverend Wade warned. "Don't go too far away."

"Yes, Father." With that, Johanna extended her arm to Mabel, and they walked together from their campsite. Johanna smiled at the families who sat beside their wagons. A small, squarely built, dark-haired woman waved them over.

"I'm Mary O'Dowd," she said as Johanna reached the wagon. "'Tis a pleasure to be meetin' the minister's daughter after I heard so much about ya from the Reverend Wade."

"Please, call me Johanna," she said with a smile, "and this is my aunt, Mabel Foster."

"You're Irish?" Mabel asked.

Mary nodded. "Aye. I come over the first year of the famine. When the potatoes rotted in the fields, me family was starvin' ta death, and we had no choice but to flee. Went to Boston and worked in the factories there. But me wee one got sick, and me husband had a terrible accident at the mill." She paused on a sigh before continuing, "From there we came to Missouri. Me sister lived in Independence. Her husband owned a farm. When she took fever and died, I took her family in with me own. That's her man down there." She nodded toward Seamus McPherson's wagon. "We're all on to Oregon now."

"Ah, I see," Mabel said. "And all those children are yours?" She pointed to the dozen children playing around the wagons, their faces and clothes dirtied as they romped with one another. A dog chased the youngest, who threw sticks for him to fetch.

"Some, and some of them are me sainted sister's. Her husband Seamus McPherson is a decent sort... He's Scottish, not Irish, but at least he's not an Englishman."

"I see." Mabel gazed admiringly at the tall, redheaded farmer, who walked over to them.

"Come along, Seamus, and meet the nice ladies from the minister's wagon."

Seamus came over to Mabel, the smile broadening his narrow, bearded face. "'Tis a sight fer sore eyes ya are, me lassies, to be meetin' the like o' you here."

"And what o' me, please God? Am I a dish rag?" Mary asked, poking his side.

He chuckled. "No, lassie, you're no rag, a fairy's cloth may haps... no rag, though!"

"Ach now, go on... Your children are done tearing the clothes off the line and take that yappin' dog the hell out o' here. He's been more trouble than the six wee ones ya got."

"Now ya donna mean that! Meek as a lamb, he is. A good hunter jest the same. Ach, he served me well all these years. Goes to show age need be no barrier to usefulness."

Seamus winked at Mabel. "Isn't that right?"

Mabel smiled coyly. "I quite agree."

Johanna felt as if she might as well sink into the ground for all the attention they paid her. "It's been nice meeting you, Mary O'Dowd, and Seamus..."

"McPherson," the farmer said. "The pleasure is mine."

"Seamus McPherson, it's my pleasure," Mabel said, lowering her lashes.

"Let's go, Auntie—it's getting late. Father and Stephen will need us for the meeting."

Mabel flashed her niece an annoyed look then, turning back to the lanky farmer, she murmured, "Good day."

"G'd day ta ya now."

Prayer service took place moments later when Reverend Wade called the families to the center of camp. Johanna and Stephen stood on either side of him.

"We must pray!" Reverend Wade bowed his head. "Father, thank you for this bountiful harvest we are about to receive, and thank you for bringing us hence unharmed on these first days on the trail. Protect us on the morrow..."

As her father's voice droned on, Johanna's mind wandered to thoughts of Ryan. She hadn't seen him since they camped by the Platte. To her dismay, Stephen insisted on walking her back to their tents. Try as she might, she could not escape his presence until she spied Mabel beside the McPherson wagon. "Auntie," she called, "I need your assistance with a delicate matter." She glanced sideways at Stephen. "Would you mind leaving us, please? I need to take care of certain... hmm..."

Stephen arched an eyebrow. "You have to relieve yourself, again?"

"Yes." *I need relief from you*, she thought, snapping out, "You don't mind?"

"No... No." Stephen looked abashed. "I, um... I've got to help your father with the horses, anyway."

"Thank you." Johanna walked toward Mabel.

"Yes, Johanna?" Her aunt looked at her with concern.

"Auntie, I need a little privacy."

"There's a bush over there," Seamus pointed out. "Go on an' water it."

Johanna felt her face crimson. "Thank you, Mr. McPherson."

"I'll be by again, Seamus," Mabel said sweetly.

"Seamus?" Johanna looked at her in surprise.

"Yes, nice fellow isn't he?" Mabel said as they walked away from camp to a curtain of wild shrubbery. She held up her skirts, and Johanna relieved herself.

"Oh, it's that time." Johanna took rags from her pocket and placed them between her legs to stop the flow. "That should do for now. But I'll need more rags... and a stream to clean them in."

She straightened, pulled up her pantalets, and dropped her skirt. "Thanks."

"I promised Seamus that I'd bring dry crackers for the children. We have such a large box of them."

"And it gives you a chance to sit with him."

Mabel nodded. "But I'll walk you to the wagon, first."

"Don't be too long," Johanna said when they reached their wagon. "It's getting late, and Ryan said we leave by sunup."

"I won't be long."

After her aunt left, Johanna lit a lantern, placed it beside the wagon then relit the camp fire. The glow provided warmth and enough light for her to read by. Sitting upon the wagon seat, she pulled out a box and opened it. Inside lay a stack of creased, yellowed letters. Removing one from the bundle, she began to read the words Robert had written to her during his illness. The letter spoke of his hopes for them and his love for her. He had even quoted scripture.

Johanna, dearest, he wrote, *my love will last eternally, for, in the end, there are three things that last: faith, hope, and love, and the greatest of these is love.*

Putting the letter aside, she wiped at a stray tear, and peered into the campfire. "Oh, rubbish," she murmured, "Robert is gone. What good do his words do now?" Suddenly, she felt cold—cold and empty. Stepping down from the wagon, she warmed her hands over the fire, feeling the heat touch her palms. She recalled the times she and her friends had built campfires after a sleigh ride on the Commons. It was where she had met Robert McEntee. As the professor crossed over Boston Commons on his way to the university, he had squatted near the fire, glancing through the smoke and haze and into her eyes. He had hummed a tune, and she had repeated it, lost in his dark, somber expression. Envisioning those sad eyes peering at her, she leaned forward to reach him. The sudden heat of the flames made her pull her hands away.

"Johanna?"

She looked through the flames into a pair of dark brown eyes, but the face was different—its contours were harder, its cheeks wider, and its skin darker. Hair as black as night hung about the face. She shook at the realization that the "ghost" of Robert was none other than the very real, very human, Ryan Majors.

"Johanna, what's wrong?" He stood now, drawing close to her. She stepped away.

"I'm going to find Mabel. She might have gotten lost."

"Last time I seen her she was over by the McPherson wagon. Don't reckon she'd get lost comin' across that field, 'less she's as blind as a bat. She ain't batty, is she?"

"No, of course not." Johanna straightened and lifted her chin. "My aunt is as sound as they come."

"Hmpf. Whatever ya say, but I came by to see how ya was doin'." He looked her up and down. "Look fine to me."

"Thank you, I am fine. Excuse me while I fetch my aunt." As she brushed past him, he cornered her by a tree.

"I heard ya hummin' a tune before. I'd like to hear it again. What was it?"

She tingled where his arm brushed against her waist. "Oh it's an Irish tune, one Robert taught me."

He cocked an eyebrow. "Robert?"

"My fiancé... He, um... died several years ago."

"Oh? Ya was thinkin' on him, was ya? I wondered why ya had that dreamy look in your eyes... like ya was in another world."

He lifted her hands, glanced and turned the palms up to look closely at her skin. "They're chapped and near bleedin'. I got gloves ya can borrow."

"Are you this worried about the other women in the wagon train?"

He shook his head. "Farmers' wives are used to the hard toil and grime."

"So, I'll get used to it, too." With a proud tilt of her head, she pulled her hands from his and moved away.

He walked with her. "Ain't safe for a woman to be walkin' alone out here."

"Really?" No wonder, she thought, feeling unsafe from the overwhelming sense of strength and virility he exuded. "Well, it's not seemly for an unmarried woman to be accompanied by an unmarried man."

"Oh yeah? How come I saw you walking with Reverend Green? If ya can consider him a man."

"Stephen, I mean Reverend Green, is a *friend* and a *minister*."

"And a man," Ryan reminded her. He touched her hand lightly, as if not wanting to frighten her. "I thought we were friends."

"Not... not the way you mean." Warmth seeped into her hand and traveled up her arm at his touch. She backed up an arm's distance from him. "Friends can trust one another."

"You can trust me."

"Hah!" She laughed. "And I'm sure you're used to dragging women off on horseback and stealing kisses from them!"

"That was a mistake, and we both know it." Pain swept in and out of his eyes.

Softening toward him, Johanna gently added, "I'd like to trust you, Mr. Majors."

"Ryan."

"Ryan." She smiled tentatively. "Well, we do have a long journey ahead of us, and I'd rather not spend it quarrelling."

"Neither would I."

Johanna sighed with relief, inhaling his scent of leather and soap. Soap? "Mr. Majors..."

"Ryan," he corrected.

"Have you bathed since we arrived?"

"I scouted the area and found a stream to bathe in. I'd be happy to show it to you before we leave."

Johanna longed for a good hot bath. "I'd appreciate that."

When Ryan stepped closer, she stepped back, feeling the urge to escape his strong, masculine presence and its magnetic hold on her. "In the morning, that is."

She glanced sideways, admiring his strong features—the broad cheekbones, the aquiline nose, and the jut of his chin. His dark coloring, no doubt, came from his Nez Perce mother. "What do you remember about your mother?"

Ryan gazed at her in surprise. "Little. A few lullabies she sang and the blackness of her eyes. She died givin' birth to my brother. We grew up among her people. The Indians got a respect for life white folk don't. I don't kill nothin' I won't use. My granddaddy was a tribal leader. He taught me to respect the animals, even goin' so far as to ask for its forgiveness 'fore we kill one." He stared hard at her. "I don't believe in killin' for no reason."

Spirals of warmth went through her hands where he caressed her calloused palms with his fingers. His eyes, unfathomable pools of darkness, gazed through to her soul and she shivered, unable to move from the spot. She had to find her voice or be lost in his magic. At last, she asked, "Was that man that killed your brother arrested?"

He dropped her hands abruptly. His jaw muscle twitched as he spat, "Heck, that rotten, no-good snake-in-the-grass ain't been found. But he will be! Sure as I got breath left in my body, he'll pay for murderin' my brother."

"Ryan, what do you plan to do to him?"

"Miss Wade," Ryan snapped, "this doesn't concern you."

Johanna stiffened. "I beg to differ, Mr. Majors. It most certainly does concern me if it involves this missionary party. My father spent years planning the mission in Oregon. I traveled hundreds of miles to be part of his mission. The last thing we need is a trail guide who'll run out on us."

"I've no intention of running out on you." Ryan's gaze softened a little. "Ever see a grizzly, Johanna?"

She glanced at him in surprise. *What did grizzlies have to do with the matter?* "No," she replied flatly, "but I read about bears in a book."

"Grizzlies are the meanest bears alive, with teeth as long as butchers' knives and claws to match. One clawed at my brother Chet until I shot it dead."

"Good Lord!"

"But there's something meaner than a den of grizzlies."

"What's that?"

"Man. He kills for no damn good reason."

"Is that why you prefer the mountains?"

"Hell yes! The white man came with his religions and his diseases and killed off half the Indians."

They continued on in silence, skirting the rear of wagons whose occupants were either asleep or too preoccupied with their own private conversations to notice the couple. Johanna stopped beneath a thick cottonwood tree. Not since Robert's death had she talked so much to a man. What was it about Ryan Majors, she wondered, that made him easy to talk to? With the exception of Stephen Green, she had no other male acquaintance. Her lonely hours as a governess had been filled with reading books or her father's occasional letter. "I often wish I knew my mother," she sighed sadly. "She died when I was born."

"So, you lived with your pa?"

"Oh, no. Father had to go off to his missionary work. He couldn't take a helpless baby with him. Aunt Mabel raised me."

Ryan scowled. "Hell, it sours my milk to think a man of God, or any man, would haul off and leave his child. If a man has a family, he ought to stay put."

"And what about your brother's children? You left them. Why?"

Johanna sensed his anger as he tensed a moment. Then sadness crossed his gaze.

"I wanted to take 'em with me, but they had other plans. It's better this way. Sara and me... well, we're good friends."

The look in his eyes when he mentioned his sister-in-law's name convinced Johanna that Ryan held more than brotherly feelings for Sara Majors. "Maybe you should have stayed with them. I'm sure my father could have found someone else to lead our wagons."

"Yes, but no one as good as me."

"I can see you like pounding your own drums."

"No reason not to. Why hide 'em under a bush? Besides, I'm honest, and I need the money. So that's why I'm here."

"For money?"

"Sure, why else would I put my butt on the line for a bunch of greenhorns?"

"I thought you did this for the adventure," she said, strangely miffed that he was only interested in the money.

"Yeah—that, too. Tell me, were you lonely growing up?" he asked, smoothly changing the topic and stepping closer. She backed into a tree trunk. The wide branches overhead cast them in its shadow.

"Sometimes, but the Captain had a way of making me laugh, and I made friends at boarding school." He was so close she could see gold flecks in his eyes, despite the darkness surrounding them.

"The Captain?" He braced a hand next to her head upon the tree. Her heart jerked in her chest.

"Mabel's husband. He died in a violent storm at sea—waves swept him over the starboard. He... um... told the best pirate stories and couldn't have been a better father to me." Each breath she took was filled with his clean scent.

"I see." Ryan nodded. "Guess folks have a way of finding what they need." He leaned closer and touched the side of her face. "You had been happy once?"

She gazed everywhere but at him, afraid of showing him how much his touch was affecting her. She had, indeed, been happy with her aunt and uncle. Robert McEntee's entry into her life had only made that small world more perfect. His death had shattered that world and her illusions of a perfect existence. "I'm getting tired." She glanced up at him, afraid of what she'd read in his eyes. She found understanding in his smile as he stepped out of her way. For some strange reason that endeared him to her.

"Auntie?" she called. Mabel waved from the nearby campsite.

"I'll be coming home later. Seamus and Sally will walk me."

"How strange," Johanna said. "Mabel usually doesn't form such quick friendships with men like this."

"Maybe there's more to it than friendship," Ryan said with a grin. "Out here, things happen a lot faster."

Perhaps too fast, Johanna thought, conscious of Ryan's shoulder brushing against hers as they walked. "I must turn in." She faked a yawn.

"Must you?" Ryan whispered, leaning toward her.

A streak of moonlight bathed his head and shoulders, outlining the tight muscles beneath his buckskin jacket. His solid, perfect shape reminded her of a Greek statue. *Oh, he's all too real.* She shut her eyes as he touched her face once more, caressing the curve of her chin and cheekbones. His mustached mouth moved as he whispered her name against her neck, "Johanna."

She looked at him. "Yes?"

"You didn't answer my question? Will you sing for me?" His pleading tone reminded her of a child begging for a sweet.

He stood apart from her, staring into her eyes as if plumbing the depths of her soul. It made her shiver. "Please, Johanna, sing that tune you hummed earlier."

"No, not now—it's too late."

They reached the wagon, the campfire a glimmer above gray ashes and the lantern glowing by the wagon wheels.

In the quiet of the moment, Ryan reached for her and pulled her to him. "Johanna," he whispered, brushing back the stray strands of hair which fell from her bun; then he unloosened the fasteners in her hair, letting it cascade in a soft flow of red tendrils down her shoulders.

Johanna pulled away. "Ryan, don't!"

"Why not?" He smoothed her hair. "Your hair has the glow of a sunset and feels as soft as the morning dew. Johanna," he said meeting her questioning gaze, "you are prettier than any wildflower bloomin' on the prairie in spring."

Her pulse raced, and she pushed her hair back into some kind of neat array, fearful lest someone should spy them together. Ryan remained oblivious of all else, save her, as he captured her hands. He turned them palm-upward then gently touched the sores. "To heal your wounds," he murmured, kissing one palm and then the other. The pressure of his lips heated her from her fingertips upward. *What am I to do?* A sudden tenderness stirred within her.

His lips touched her neck, trailing kisses from the collar to her cheek. "I must have you," he murmured, fumbling with the top button of her dress.

"No!" She pushed him away. "I'm not some strumpet whom you can have your way with."

"No, you're not." He pressed closer until he kissed her lips.

She parted them with a sigh, "Ryan?"

He cupped her breasts as his tongue darted inside her mouth, tasting the sweetness within. She grasped his neck, playing with his black locks of hair.

Deepening the kiss, his legs pressed against hers. She could feel his stiff manhood, evidence of his arousal and need. Through the haze of her own desire, virtue battled and screamed for her not to yield further. Yet, she felt herself moisten deep in her most private area as Ryan caressed her hips and backside through the folds of her skirt.

He opened the buttons of her blouse and fingered through the layers of undergarment to her breasts. When his lips left hers to kiss the peaked nipples, she moaned with pleasure. But when he began to push up her skirts, reality struck her. "No!" she warned as she pushed him away.

He leaned once more, but with every ounce of strength and will, she pushed him back. He stood at a distance, glaring at her with anger and frustration.

She peered at her unbuttoned blouse in disbelief. How had she let this happen? "This can never be," she said aloud, buttoning her blouse and flattening the folds of her skirt. "Never."

"Why not?" Ryan frowned in confusion. "You wanted me."

"I... I... It wouldn't matter if I did or not..." She bit her trembling lip and backed away, lowering her gaze from his. "It's a sin."

She rushed toward her wagon, picking up the small box she had forgotten by the campfire. Her hands shook so much that the box fell open and the contents spilled to the ground.

Ryan retrieved the letters. "What are these?" he asked, handing them to her.

"Rob... Robert... Robert's," she stammered, "poems and letters."

"The dead fiancé?" Ryan crunched the letters in his hand. "Words... words from a dead man... These mean more than mine?"

"I don't really know you," Johanna said, "Give them to me."

"No." With one swift movement, Ryan tossed the wrinkled letters into the dying flames of the campfire.

"Oh, no!" Johanna tried in vain to get the letters, but the flames leaped up and ate them. "Oh, no, you wretched man!" She balled her hand into a fist. "How dare you!" She slapped Ryan hard. "You threw away all I had left of my love... a pure and perfect love."

Ryan rubbed his cheek then took her by the hand. "I'm sorry, Johanna." He rubbed her hand. "I'm so very sorry. I don't know what the hell came over me... I didn't mean to hurt you."

"Go away... Leave me alone." With a choked sob, she ran into the rear of the wagon and she waited until Ryan left before opening the box on the wagon seat. One small piece of paper lay within. She picked it up and carried it with her to the tent. The page contained the gospel quote on love. She folded it and tucked the treasured missive into the top of her garment and lay down, weeping bitter tears. Footsteps and her aunt's laughter disturbed her troubled thoughts.

She sat up, wiped her eyes then tucked the letter under her pillow.

Had they seen her with Ryan? Had they witnessed her shameful act? She had forgotten how close the wagons were. Even in the darkness, they might have been spotted. The last thing she needed now were rumors of her and the trail guide. She wiped her eyes, undressed and put on her nightgown. Her skin still tingled from the heat of his caress. How could she have let him get so close? Had the years of loneliness made her so hungry for a man's touch? She glanced at the simple yellow dress she had worn; two buttons had been torn off at the top. She'd sew them on in the morning. *At least they're easier to mend than a broken heart.*

~ * ~

Ryan sat alone by his campfire—a bedroll beside a tree. He never felt the need for more unless a storm struck. In that case, he had a small tent that he could pitch in a jiffy. He'd had watched the families as they prepared their morning meals. He had his dried jerky and beans long before sunrise. As he sipped his black coffee, he watched Johanna beside her wagon. Thoughts of the night before weighed heavy on his mind. How could he have been so stupid, behaving that way with Johanna? He had to keep his wits about him, especially with so much riding on this job.

Why did he let this flame-haired beauty make him as ornery as a bull moose? *Think, man!* He raked his fingers through his hair. Eyeing the way she swished about in that blue gingham dress, which clung to every supple curve, made his mind fuzzy. Her graceful movements about her campsite, the way she pounded dough for bread then lit kindling wood for a fire, aroused his interest. "Good golly!" he blurted aloud when Johanna accidentally dropped a cauldron of water onto the fire. He rose to assist her, but Stephen Green beat him to her aid.

It jarred Ryan that Johanna acted like a wife with Green. He was green all right, clear down to his under drawers. Ryan despised him more than any preacher he'd ever met. Even the old man, Johanna's father, showed more gumption.

Ryan fumed as Stephen and Johanna prepared breakfast together. Funny, he thought, how the two worked side-by-side without talking or touching. Johanna looked a bit nervous around Green. He wondered why she'd be nervous with such a spineless, whiny, and altogether useless creature.

Johanna's aunt and father joined the duo at the meal. The only one who kept up a semblance of conversation was the aunt. The woman's mouth remained in constant motion. Ryan wondered if she ever shut it. Despite that, he took to the aunt, liking her warm, motherly ways. Hell, if it wasn't for Mabel, he might not have kept this job. Jed Thompkins told him that Mabel had stood up to her brother-in-law on Ryan's behalf. She'd convinced Reverend Wade to hire Ryan despite rumors about his drinking and fornicating. Fornicating? What the hell did that mean anyway? He'd asked Jed. When Jed told him, Ryan took a fit of laughter. He'd never used such a big word for what he did in the brothels of St. Louis or any other place.

Looking at Johanna Wade, Ryan realized that he'd never met anyone like her at a brothel or anywhere else. No, she was special, and he'd better remember that and not let his member do the thinkin' for him. He could already feel it rise with the thought of her and how she felt in his arms last night. He swallowed the now-cold coffee, wishing he could dip himself in an ice-cold stream. The thought intrigued him. *That's what I need.* He took a towel out of his traveling pack and aimed for the stream.

"Day to ya, Majors," Seamus called him over as he passed. "Come and share a wee nip with me."

With the need for someone to talk to, Ryan nodded. "Heck! Why not?" He joined Seamus and sat on a stool beside the wagon. "Thanks."

"Sure 'n it's a grand mornin'," Seamus said, handing Ryan the bottle.

"Dependin' on your point o' view." Ryan sipped the wine then spit it out. "Where'd the heck ya get that stuff?"

"Made it from dandelions growin' on my farm."

"It tastes like mule piss!"

"Shh..." Seamus motioned to the livestock pen. "Betsy there'd get a mite upset if' she heard ya sayin' that."

The mule brayed. Ryan chuckled. "Yeah, you're right." He eyed the Wades' wagon. Johanna and Mabel were clearing the table. The ministers sat side-by-side, bent in conversation. Seamus leaned over as he handed Ryan a flask of whiskey. "Here ya go... are ya thinkin' on those women there with the preachers?"

Ryan nodded, taking a drink from the flask before handing it back to Seamus.

"Me, too," Seamus said then sipped from the flask. "The aunt is the one I'm afta."

Ryan studied him a moment. The children ran wild around them, playing tag or quarrelling with one another. Seamus' oldest, Sally, played mother to them, keeping them in line. "Mrs. Foster would have to take the whole lot of 'em, and you, too."

"I'm hopin' so," Seamus said with a sigh.

They looked at each other a moment then laughed.

~ * ~

Having cleared the table, Johanna felt the need for a walk. She looked over at the McPherson wagon. Ryan Majors sat there staring at her. She dropped her dish towel and felt like running for cover then thought better when she spied the silver flask in Ryan's hand. "Why, they're drinking! Look, Auntie, the farmer and Ryan are over there drinking up a storm."

"A little early to drink." Mabel picked up the dish cloth and put it inside the box on the rear of the wagon where they kept all their cookware and dishes. "Maybe it's only water."

"In a pig's eye. I'm going over there to tell them to stop."

"Now, Johanna, what's the harm of it?"

"Harm? It's against our rules."

Mabel looked contrite. "Right, dear, but surely it won't harm them."

Johanna ignored her aunt's efforts to keep her back. "I must do my civic duty for the benefit of this wagon train."

Once she reached the McPherson wagon, Johanna stopped in her tracks, speechless for the moment as she stared into Ryan's brown gaze. His slow smile made her wonder if he'd forgotten their argument the previous night. When he began to pour the contents of the flask into a mug of coffee, she said, "Mr. Majors, what on God's earth are you doing?"

"Enjoying a bit of Seamus' hospitality." Ryan sipped his coffee, leaned back and stared at her.

Johanna pulled the mug from his hands and quickly sniffed its contents. "Whiskey! I thought as much."

Glaring at Ryan, she emptied the mug on the ground.

A muscle in his jaw twitched, and his hands balled into fists. "What the hell ya do that for?" He jumped up, hands on hips.

"We have a rule, in case you forgot, against drinking any kind of alcohol." She handed the mug back to him.

"It was only a wee nip," defended Seamus, stepping between Johanna and Ryan.

"Whether it's a wee nip or not," Johanna shouted over Seamus' shoulder, "Reverend Wade wants no spirits unless for medicinal purposes!"

"Is that so? Well, I'm not taking orders," Ryan sneered, "'specially from a woman!"

"Now, calm down, the both of you." Seamus grabbed Ryan's arm, whispering to him, "Hush, lad. Ya donna wanna offend the lassie, do ya?"

Ryan scraped a hand through his hair. "Hell, it ain't worth the fuss."

"We won't be drinkin' no more o' it," Seamus said, easing his way from between the couple. "An now ya must apologize to the lassie."

"What for?" Ryan turned his back on her.

"That's all right, Mr. McPherson," Johanna said. "Being part-heathen, himself, Mr. Majors is not used to civilized ways."

Ryan spun around. "See how far your civilized ways will take ya, Miss Wade, if I was to leave right now."

"You wouldn't dare!"

"Oh, wouldn't I?" Ryan picked up his cap and his towel, and stomped off toward the woods.

Johanna rushed after him. "Ryan, I'm sorry."

He stopped abruptly and said, "I'm not a fool, Johanna. You can go on and have that dandy back there." He pointed toward Reverend Green who stood some distance away at another wagon. "If all ya care

about are fancy words and rules that don't mean nothin' out here."
Spinning on his heels, he headed into the wooded area, his buckskin
jacket and leggings blending in with the color of the trees.

"Looks like your sweetheart is a bit miffed," a young voice said,
with amusement.

Startled, Johanna glanced around to find a girl with braided red
hair and cornflower blue eyes. It was the seven-year-old girl who had
greeted her at the church in Independence. She looked around for the
grandmother, but couldn't find her. Instead, she saw a plump woman
in her late thirties, tying an apron around the front of her gray prairie
dress.

"Mind your beeswax, Nelly," the woman said, smiling at Johanna
apologetically.

"Always shootin' off at the mouth, she is. Her grandmother
couldn't make the trip with us. Poor thing got ill the last minute and
stayed behind." She wiped her flour-covered hands on the apron and
shook Johanna's hand, "I'm Nancy Clemens."

"I'm Johanna Wade."

"I know. I met your father at the revival. We signed up at the last
minute. My husband, John, is sick but we came, anyway."

"How is your husband now?"

"Fine. The doc bled him a bit, and he's good as new."

Johanna glanced over at the blue-dyed wagon cover, noticing the
American flag draped on one side.

"John served a while in the war down south. Darn Mexicans shot
him real bad. The army shipped him home to us. He's had pains on
and off since. Don't pay any heed to my daughter. She's too nosy for
her own good. Her grandmother's doing—spoiled her silly. Come
along, girl, we got to go back to the wagon."

Johanna walked over with them. She sighted a grey-haired man,
his face lined and somber. Sadness darkened his blue eyes as he gazed
about. She wondered if the war wounded more than his body, as he
stood there muttering to himself while he hammered away at the
wagon bed. When his wife and daughter approached, he looked up
and smiled at them. Nancy Clemens introduced him to Johanna.

"Good day to ya," John said. "I'm working on this here wagon box 'cause it keeps rattlin' around. We don't want no Mexicans hearing us. They'd blast us to pieces."

Nancy rolled her eyes at that, mouthing to Johanna, "He's been hammering away for hours now. There's nothin' wrong with the wagon bed."

Johanna felt sorry for the family. Nellie leaned against a wagon wheel, staring at Johanna. She twisted a strand of her braid and put the end of it in her mouth.

Nancy yanked her daughter's arm away, "Stop doin' that girl or you'll go bald. Go on and churn the butter like I told ya to."

"Aw, Ma, my hands hurt." Nelly showed Johanna her blisters.

"Your behind will be even sorer if ya don't do your chores."

"I'll help her," Johanna offered.

"Fine," Nancy said. She turned to another redheaded girl who looked about eleven. "Betsy, you take care of the young uns that went into the woods for berries. See to it they don't kill each other."

"Right, Ma!" The girl glanced at Johanna then tugged on her sister's hair.

"Hey, stop that." Nelly slapped Betsy's hand away. As Betsy hurried down the path, she stuck her tongue out at Nelly.

"She's mean, Momma," Nelly said then whispered to Johanna. "Thank you for helping me." Within a few minutes, they finished churning the butter, and Nancy removed the yellow lump of butter from the churn.

"I don't like spoil'n my girls by letting them off to play when there's work to be done," she told Johanna. "It's a hard lot being a woman. A year or two more and my Betsy will be finding herself a husband."

"But, she's so young."

"I was all of sixteen when I married John. We been married twenty years this September, got eight children now."

Good heavens, she's only thirty-six and the mother of eight. "I guess they keep you busy."

"Busy ain't the word for it. They near drive me mad..." She whispered, "Not like him though—the war, ya know." She rolled her eyes toward John Clemens, who was babbling to the air.

Johanna wiped her hands on her apron. "I have to get back to my own wagon. It was nice meeting you and your family. I'll meet the rest of your children later when I start to teach them."

"Sure. If any give ya a hard time, feel free to take a good, hard hickory stick to 'em."

Johanna sighed at that—she disapproved of corporal punishment of any kind. She waved good-bye and headed for her wagon.

She didn't see Ryan until later that afternoon. Perched on the seat of the wagon, she sewed buttons on her dress. Aunt Mabel didn't ask her how the buttons loosened. If she had, Johanna would've told her that they caught on a tree branch while she'd been walking. The dress brought back memories of Ryan's touch. She hadn't even been aware of the buttons coming undone, only the sensation of his hands against her bared shoulder and neck, and the pressure of his lips as he kissed her. She closed her eyes, imagining the kiss and how good it felt.

"Johanna?"

"Stephen!" Flushed with embarrassment, Johanna sat upright then stared down at the garment in her hands. She had managed to rip off the same button that she'd just sewed on. "Darn it!"

"I've been looking for you. I didn't realize you were here the whole time."

"I was busy meeting the families in our party and doing errands." She knotted the thread and bit the ends off before glancing at him.

"You haven't seen Ryan Majors, have you?" he asked, his brows arched above his narrowed gaze.

"No, not since this morning." She put away the dress and took up another garment, one which needed hemming. "This caught on the wagon spokes yesterday," she said unnecessarily. "It's taking me a while to get used to climbing up and down the wagon. I think I may start walking like the others, once Mabel feels that she can manage the mule team."

"Is that wise?" Stephen shot a look at the McPherson wagon, where Mabel stood laughing at something Seamus said to her. "Your aunt is spending a lot of time with the farmer."

"My aunt can do as she pleases, Stephen. And why do you want Ryan, anyway?"

"I want him to scout ahead for us... to check that there are no Indians waiting to ambush us."

"Nonsense, Stephen. Ryan, I mean Mr. Majors, is well-acquainted with the tribes in these parts. From what he's told us, they're all very hospitable."

"Nevertheless, he should check the trail ahead."

"Have you consulted my father on that order?"

Stephen shook his head. "No, I haven't. Your father can be blind to some things."

"That's for sure," Johanna said under her breath.

"What's that?"

"Nothing." She stood. "If you don't mind, Stephen, it's getting late, and I need to start supper... since that's woman's work. I think you should consult my father before you give any orders to Mr. Majors or anyone else."

"I will." Stephen frowned then added, "Someone said they heard a ruckus here last night. Were you arguing with anyone?"

"That is none of your beeswax, Stephen!" She climbed down from the wagon. "If I see Mr. Majors again, I'll tell him that you were looking for him."

"You do that."

She walked away, feeling Stephen's gaze boring holes in her back. She wasn't sure who infuriated her the most—Ryan with his ill manners and surly ways, or Stephen who tried to dominate and control both her and her father. Finding Mabel beside the McPherson wagon was a welcome respite from her cares.

"I'm sorry 'bout the drinkin'," Seamus said.

"I know it won't happen again." Johanna glanced at her aunt. "We must ensure the rules."

Mabel looked at her hands, sighing. "Yes, we must, dear."

"It's time to make supper."

"I'll come back later, Seamus."

"You've become friendly with the Scottish farmer," Johanna said, hooking her arm in the crook of Mabel's elbow.

"He's a fine man. Maybe not as genteel as Captain Foster, but I do like him."

Johanna stopped so abruptly, Mabel was yanked back. "You can't be serious? The man has six children... and no teeth!"

"He has a few teeth... and the children are nice."

Johanna's eyes bulged. "Nice! They're the wildest creatures in the entire wagon party. Only Sally has control of them."

"Poor girl, she has to take her mother's place."

"I caught him drinking!"

"So? The Captain drank enough to fill an ocean. He could hold it, and so can Seamus. They're both good men, good where it counts."

"I can't believe that you're falling for a farmer. You were the one who told me that farmers only paid in pig manure."

Mabel shrugged. "Yes, I did. But Seamus is different. He's kind and genteel in other ways, too. He makes me laugh with his stories of the old country."

Johanna stared at her aunt in disbelief. "You do have feelings toward the man?"

"Yes." Mabel's eyes misted. "It's been a long time since I've felt this way, and it feels good."

"Here, Auntie." Johanna pulled a handkerchief from her apron pocket. "Go on and wipe your eyes."

"Thanks, dear."

~ * ~

After supper, Johanna sat outside the wagon with the ministers and Mabel. A loud blast like air escaping a huge chamber startled them. Johanna looked over at the McPherson's wagon. "Seamus is playing a bagpipe," she said. Wearing a tartan shami with a black feather, Seamus blew into the long polished wood blow stick of the bagpipe. His youngest son, Tommy, beat a drum.

"Oh, I so enjoy Scottish music." Mabel began stamping her feet to the music. "Let's go over to them."

"I can hear them from here," Johanna said.

"Me, too," Stephen said, pushing his stool closer to Johanna's, until his hands touched her arm.

Johanna glared at him. "There's more than enough elbow room, Stephen, without you sidling so close." Her father, she noticed, was staring into space. Deep creases around the corners of his eyes and mouth made him look older than fifty. Old and vulnerable, she thought, and threw a quick glance at Stephen before looking at her father again. "Father, is everything all right?"

The bagpipes drowned out her father's reply. He repeated himself, "Yes, it is. I think I'll turn in for the night. Stephen, what about you?"

Stephen looked at Johanna. She looked away. "Yes, it will be hard to sleep with that infernal noise. Maybe I'll go over and tell that farmer to be quiet."

"You'll do no such thing, Stephen Green," Johanna snapped. "You can't dictate to everyone around here."

"Johanna!" Reverend Wade exclaimed. "Stephen is right— Seamus McPherson can't keep us all awake. We have to rise at dawn. I'll go over and tell him."

"Don't bother, Father." Johanna stood, grateful for any excuse to get away from Stephen. "I'll tell him."

"Fine." Reverend Wade nodded. "Coming, Stephen?"

Stephen stood, glowering at her. "Good night, Johanna, dear."

The music stopped as soon as Johanna crossed the field toward the McPherson wagon. She saw Mabel sitting on a stool with Seamus beside her. They were deep in conversation, and took no notice of her. She decided to leave them alone. Returning to her own wagon, she pulled her diary out from the storage pocket. The page salvaged from the flames slipped out. She reread the words that love lasts above all else then pressed the page against her chest and sighed.

Loud giggling and bouncing noises from a wagon several yards away made her put her diary aside. The wagon contained the newlyweds, the Van Dams—a couple her father had married before the journey began. Gertrude and Hans were second-generation Americans, with parents from Holland. Land must be very important, she thought, for them to leave their parents' homes. The couple had beamed with happiness and love, holding hands and smiling constantly. Now, their forms created a silhouette against the wagon cover, lit from behind by a dwindling campfire.

Eyeing their silhouettes as they embraced one another, Johanna bit back the sour taste of envy. What good were Robert's written words of undying love and devotion compared to the passionate caresses of that couple? She closed her eyes, recalling Ryan's hands upon her bared skin, the taste of his mouth on hers, and the wicked desire he had awakened in her. How many nights had she wanted Robert to hold her, to awaken the woman in her with all the passion he professed in his poetry?

She had wanted to feel that passion burning her. She had wanted to feel his undying love for her. But all she could remember was Robert's pale face against the pillows of his deathbed and the longing she had felt to touch his fevered brow and release him from his misery and her from her misery.

Shame-filled, she buried her face in her hands and fought back the tears. A cold, chilling breeze had her shivering. With a sigh, she tucked the poem away. Pulling the hood of her shawl over her head, she stared for a moment at the newlyweds' wagon and loathed herself for wanting what that couple had. She recalled Ryan's caresses and how his hands had brushed against her breasts. Hugging the shawl about her shoulders, she sighed. For the first time in a long time, she felt totally alone.

Eight

An Evening Vigil's Calamity

Sitting cross-legged by a fire with a well-worn tartan plaid blanket beneath him, Ryan kept evening vigil. A lantern glowed nearby, illuminating the bough of a cottonwood from which a raccoon peered. The scratching sounds of the shaggy animal's claws as it climbed down startled Ryan, and he quickly aimed his gun.

"Hell, only a coon," he muttered, setting aside the rifle. Daisy, tied to another tree, grazed on tufts of grass. The horse's keen sense of hearing could alert Ryan to any danger, whether it walked on all fours, two legs, or slithered on the ground.

Ryan scanned the broad reaches of darkness for signs of such danger. The woods remained still except for the foraging of skunks, raccoons, or field mice. He listened to the wind vibrating the branches overhead and the stirring of leaves. A great horned owl hooted then flew down to the ground, flying up again with a mouse clutched between its claws. The night with its own sights and sounds, held both wonder and terror.

Ryan peered up at the star-filled sky. The one thing he loved most about sleeping in the open was laying back and looking at the pictures the stars made in the blackness. One cluster formed a cup shape, another an arrow, and one a woman's face. "I'm tired, that's all," he muttered. *Tired of being alone.* His eyelids began to droop. He focused his gaze upon the flames of the fire as it licked the crisp air.

Even though the farmers had rifles and their wagons were circled for protection, a sentry had to keep guard while everyone slept. Ryan took turns at guard duty more often than the others, since he didn't have the responsibility of a family or a herd of livestock.

He not only watched for Indians who might pilfer wagon trains for their horses and supplies, but he also watched for renegades from the Mexican War. Rumor spread that these ex-soldiers preyed upon unsuspecting travelers.

Even fellow trappers could be a threat, Ryan knew, heeding Jed Thompkins' warning about rivalry between fur trappers. His thoughts turned to Chet's murder and the need to get the bastard who killed him. "Damn it to hell," he said aloud, kicking a log into the fire. It crackled and split as the flames consumed it.

The shuffle of feet crunching leaves made Ryan grab his rifle. He pointed it at a large bush that shook back and forth before a tall form pushed it aside. "Stop or I'll shoot!" Ryan warned, cocking the trigger.

"Don't shoot!"

"Seamus?"

The farmer's face paled at the sight of Ryan's gun. "Sure 'n it's a sad sight when a man can't take a bit o' relief 'round here without gettin' his head blown off."

When Ryan put down the gun, Seamus joined him by the fire to warm his hands. "For all I knew, you could o' been an Indian or one of them soldiers from the war. Ya got no business sneakin' up like that. Deserved to get your fool head shot off."

"Naw, you donna mean that, do ya? I come to help ya. Fella gets a mite lonesome now an' then." Seamus pulled a silver flask from his pants pocket and passed it to Ryan. "Best Scottish whiskey west of the Missouri. Have a drop."

"Don't mind if I do." Ryan took the flask and turned it over in his hand. "Fancy flask for a farmer." He opened it, took a swig then handed it back. "Thanks." He patted the ground. "Sit a spell, farmer."

"Don't mind if I do." Seamus plopped down beside Ryan. "Think there are any wild Injuns out here?"

"Naw, less'n ya count me." Ryan chuckled. "Hell, I'm part Nez Perce."

Seamus stared at him.

"Don't worry none," Ryan said. "I won't scalp ya, not after redheads, anyway."

"Oh, an' that'd be a lie." Seamus poked Ryan's side, "Ya been aft a that lassie with the red hair. Me own eyes have seen ya gaping at her."

Ryan shook his head. "I got to keep my watch."

"Especially watchin' women folk?"

Ryan ignored him.

"Come on, Ryan." Seamus elbowed him. "I seen ya with that Miss Johanna. A fine and dandy pair you'd make."

Ryan took another swig of whiskey then handed the flask back. "Don't know what the hell you're talkin' 'bout."

"Sweet lassie, she is," Seamus said before sipping more whiskey. "Now the aunt is another thing—she's a looker. Reminds me of me own dear departed missus." He rubbed his eyes. "Me missus was life itself to me. No I donna have her no more. But bein'a bachelor, ya would na understand." He smiled at Ryan. "The lassie took good care of Johanna, made her into a fine lady liken herself, she did. She's a foolish lassie for cryin' so, despite all the good her aunt a done for her."

Seamus grew silent, staring into the fire. *I might as well be on watch alone*, Ryan thought. He stared up at the moon. In a few hours, it would be daybreak. He stretched his legs out, and tried to stay alert. He felt his eyelids get heavier, and he shut them.

"Sure 'n now, Mabel is a wunerful lassie."

Ryan peered at Seamus. "Shh! You're gonna wake the whole camp with your ravin'." Seamus' eyes looked red and swollen. Had he been crying? Ryan sat up, glanced at the flask in Seamus' hand. "You drank enough to kill ten men. Here, give me that." He pulled the flask out of Seamus's hand.

"Don't take me flask! 'Twas a gift from me brother in Edinburgh. Ya've no right ta be takin' it from me." Seamus stood, wobbling as he reached for the flask. He lost his balance and fell into the campfire. "Yeow! Aye! Aye! I'm dyin'!" he screamed, hopping up and down as his clothes caught fire.

Ryan threw Seamus to the ground and rolled him around, snuffing out the fire. "Are you all right?" Ryan touched Seamus' singed pants.

Seamus howled in agony.

Seamus' skin looked swollen and as raw as uncooked meat when Ryan tore off the remaining portion of the pants leg. Ryan wrinkled his nose at the putrid smell of burned flesh. "We gotta get ya cared for," he said, fingering the area around the burn. Seamus jerked his leg in pain. "Hold still," Ryan warned.

"Am I gonna lose it?"

"Heck no," Ryan said. "It's only your leg was burned—you still got your manhood."

"Dunna mean that thing, laddie. Will I lose me leg?"

"No. We gotta get cold water and fix ya up. Come on."

Ryan picked up his lantern with one hand and helped Seamus with the other. He wrapped his arm about Seamus to support him as he led them down the slight incline toward the wagons. "We're close to the Wades' wagon. We'll see if that fine lassie o' yours can help ya."

"Aye, watch it laddie." Seamus yipped with each step they took.

Ryan tried to slow his pace as he helped Seamus. Rocks shot out from under them, and they began to slip, but Ryan put the lantern to the side. "Hell." He supported Seamus using both hands as they managed to walk with only the light of the moon to guide them through the clearing toward the Wades' camp. "We're almost there," Ryan announced when he sighted a sole lantern situated outside the wagon.

"That niece..." Seamus muttered. "She's cause for concern with the aunt. She sits readin' poetry and weepin' into a book."

Ryan felt a lump in his throat and swallowed hard. He knew he had only made matters worse for Johanna. His pride made him unable to admit his wrong to her. Hell, she wouldn't listen to him now, anyway.

"She'd had many suitors in Boston, ya know?" Seamus continued.

"Stop rushing me, lad. It hurts."

"But we're almost there." Ryan waited for Seamus to catch his breath.

"The poor lad wrote poems to her, and she saved every one, her aunt said. She wrote, too. Had a few published in that ladies' magazine back East. Now we Scots got Robbie Burns to thank for poetry."

"Seamus," Ryan said, hauling him up again, "shut up and walk." He grunted and tightened his grasp on the farmer as he led him on in silence.

"But now I think she's havin' a change of heart," Seamus said, glancing at the wagon.

"Oh?" Ryan stood him up against the wagon bed. "Stay put." He walked to Johanna's tent.

"Me thinks the lassie has the eye for ya, too." Seamus' mouth closed with a snap when Ryan glared at him then he muttered, "Sure I'm talkin' to meself."

Rounding the wagon, Ryan lifted the flap of the tent. "Mabel?"

"Who is it?" Fear underscored Johanna's voice.

"'Tis only me and the Majors here!" Seamus shouted.

"Ryan? What do you want?" Johanna's voice sounded sleepy. When she stuck her head out, her long hair swung about her shoulders, reminding him of how she looked the last time he kissed her.

At the sight of her clinging cotton chemise, he grew excited. The soft folds of fabric clung to the curve of her breasts, outlining their pointed nipples.

"What do you want?" she repeated.

Ryan chuckled at the possibilities. But he was brought back to his senses when he heard a thud and Seamus' moan. His gaze shot to the wagon bed, where the farmer now lay on the ground.

"For Christ's sake, isn't there a soul 'round here to give me a hand up?" Seamus lamented.

Rushing to the fallen man, Ryan lifted him. With a deep sigh, Seamus leaned on the wagon. "We need cold water and bandaging,"

Ryan told Johanna when she joined them.

"What's wrong with him?" she asked.

"Seamus burned his leg."

"Seamus?" Mabel poked her head out of the tent flap. "Seamus is hurt?" The flap snapped back as she scrambled out, wrapped in a black silk robe adorned with peacock feathers.

"Is it you, Mabel, or a giant pheasant?" Seamus asked.

"It's me," Mabel said. "What happened?"

"He fell into my fire," Ryan told her. "I need some cold water."

"Oh, dear!" Mabel peered at Seamus' leg. "It looks awful. We need to bandage that as well." She climbed into her wagon, and, after a few minutes, returned with strips of cloth. "These should do."

Johanna took them and ripped them into smaller pieces.

"Where's your water keg?" Ryan asked impatiently.

"Don't shout at me!" Johanna snapped. "You should know where it is—tied to the wagon."

"Get it."

"Get it, yourself." Their gazes locked.

"I would if I didn't have to support the man."

"Stop arguin', and fix me leg." Seamus moaned. "Oh! Oh, the pain grows worse."

With a roll of her eyes, Johanna left to get the water, placing the bucket on the ground.

"Oh, dear." Mabel winced when Johanna poured the water onto the wound and Seamus yelped piteously.

"Hold my hand," Mabel cooed, taking Seamus' hand.

"Ah," Seamus sighed. "I'm feeling better already."

"This'll need liniment too." Seeing her aunt occupied, Johanna went to the wagon and returned with jars of mashed herbs. "This bark root should get rid of his infection," she said, applying the poultice and a wet compress to the burn.

Afterward, with Ryan's help, she bandaged Seamus' leg. Ryan marveled at Johanna's swift, gentle ministrations. Though she wore a stern glance, she gently patted Seamus' leg. "There..." She sniffed his breath. "That's what comes from drinking. You know the rules, and you're very lucky that both Father and Stephen aren't here to see the two of you."

Seamus blushed with embarrassment. "Oh, please don't tell, lassie. For sure 'n now I will drink only tea." He smiled at Mabel then at Johanna. "Sure 'n she's an angel of mercy."

In the glow of the lantern, Johanna appeared to Ryan like an angel with her long, red hair billowing around her in the breeze and with her cheeks flushed from the crisp night air. Her supple curves heated him so, he longed to pull off her garments and caress her bare skin.

"You should be fine." Johanna glanced at the bandage. "I'll check on your leg in the morning."

"And I'll be by to help you, too," Mabel added. "You can't run after your youngsters on a sore leg."

Seamus thanked them both as Ryan helped him stand.

"And, Seamus?" Johanna pointed to his leg. "Keep it raised on a pillow or something."

One last glance at Johanna, and Ryan thought with a smirk, *she could raise something else.*

"Here, take this to guide you back." She handed a lantern to Ryan. As their fingers touched, he smiled.

"Thanks." It wasn't the heat from the lantern that was making him sweat, he thought, knowing her touch could both cool or enflame a man.

Glancing down at her chemise, Johanna blushed and quickly wrapped her arms across her breasts. "I... I'm going back to bed. Good night." She rushed to the tent.

Mabel gazed at Seamus. "Take care, my dear. I'll come by with Johanna in the morning."

"Thank ya, ma'am," Ryan said.

As he walked Seamus back to the McPherson wagon, Ryan wondered how Johanna knew so much about medicines and healing. He had learned about healing from his mother's people, as the use of herbs and incantations was common among the tribe. "Must'a learned it back East," he muttered aloud.

"What's that?" Seamus asked then moaned as Ryan let him off

beside his wagon.

"Aw, nothin'. Go on and rest some. I gotta get back to my watch."

As he turned to go, Ryan glanced over at the tent where Johanna slept. He pictured her again, red hair framing her oval face and her blue eyes staring at him. He had come so close to having her once, and now he wanted her again. As surely as his body throbbed with need, he wanted her. And he wondered if Seamus, crazy drunk as he was, might be right. Perhaps Johanna was having a change of heart. It gave him hope as he kept vigil until the first rays of dawn.

Nine

A Pawnee Village

"Miss Wade?" a young girl called. Johanna turned to spy Seamus' eldest child, half hidden by a tree. "What is it, Sally?"

Sally moved toward her. "Pa is running a fever, and Mabel sent me to ask if you got medicine for it. Do you?"

Johanna nodded. "Yes. Come on. She led Sally toward her wagon then rummaged through the pile of supplies. Finding her medicines, she withdrew jars of camphor and bark root syrup. "This should reduce the fever, and ease the pain." She followed Sally to the McPherson wagon.

Seamus lay on a cot, pale and delirious with fever, rattling incoherently. Mabel knelt beside him and rubbed a damp cloth across his forehead. "Johanna! Thank goodness you're back. Seamus has a fever and chills." She let Johanna get a closer look at Seamus' leg.

"I hope the wound hasn't become infected." She opened the jars of medicine and laid them on the ground. As she removed the old bandaging, Seamus winced with pain. "Hold him steady," she told Mabel and Sally. The wound had blistered, but to Johanna's relief it was not gangrenous. She cleansed it with the rubbing alcohol that Sally found in the wagon bed. Then she applied the camphor.

"Open wide," Mabel ordered, administering the spoonful of bark root syrup.

"Blab!" Seamus exclaimed. "Give me some whiskey."

"Not on your life," Johanna retorted.

"But the whiskey might help him sleep," Mabel whispered to her niece.

"We will see." Johanna tightened the lids on the jars of medicine. She applied fresh bandaging from strips of cloth.

"Rest, dear!" Mabel told him, cradling Seamus' head as she laid him down on the cot. The sun began to sink on the horizon in an orange blaze. "It's near supper time," Johanna announced. "Go ahead," Mabel replied, "and take Seamus' children with you. I'll stay to look after Seamus.

"We'll bring supper for you," Johanna said.

"Eve... Evenin', Miss Wade," Clem Simmons stammered. A slow smile worked on his freckled face. Denim overalls covered his tall, lanky frame. He ran his fingers through his thick red hair.

He's shy; Johanna realized as the fifteen-year-old approached where she sat reading to the McPherson children. "Evening, Clem." He peered at the ground, moving toward her. She gave Clem her prettiest smile. He twisted his cap between his hands. By his nervous movements, she wondered if something happened. "Are you all right?"

"Heck yeah... yes," Clem said, but his reddened face told a different story. "Have, have you seen hide or hair of Sally McPherson? I've been looking for her all day."

"Oh, I saw her a moment ago, Clem." Johanna shrugged. "She had supper with us, but I guess she left."

"Aw, shucks, that's too bad. I was about to show her my dog's litter of pups, knowing how she likes animals and all."

"Pups!" Sally came from behind the wagon. "Did you say your dog had pups?"

"Yeah, Sally." Clem shuffled the dirt with his booted feet. "She'd had a litter of ten pups."

"Ten? My goodness that's a lot," Johanna said.

"You want one, Miss Johanna?" Clem asked.

"Oh, no, I've enough to do without a dog to look after." She winked at Sally, "Maybe you want one, Sally. Do you?"

"Aw, I dun no. Papa would be mad if I take in another animal. I got a pet skunk in the wagon now, plus a bird, and a snake."

"A snake!" Johanna stood and peered intently at the ground. "How did you ever get a snake?"

"Oh, he's all right," Sally said. "He's a plain ole garter snake. He wouldn't hurt ya none."

"That's good," Johanna said with a sigh. "Sally, it's all right if you want to go and see Clem's puppies, but I think we'd better take the other children back. It's getting late."

They glanced at the sleepy faces of Sally's brothers and sisters. Will McPherson had cornered Martha O'Dowd by a tree and whispered in her ear, making her giggle.

"I'd say your cousin Martha is enjoying herself," Johanna whispered to Sally.

"She's teasing the boys, shameless hussy," Sally hissed. She looked over at Clem, giving him a warm smile. "Clem, I'll see to your pups. If that's all right, Miss Wade?"

"Go on, Sally," Johanna told her, feeling that if anyone brought Clem out of his shell, Sally could. The smile that reached his hazel eyes could have lit a Christmas tree. With a sigh, Johanna waved them on. "Be back before nightfall, though!" She shut the book she had been reading.

Jan McPherson took her by the hand. The five-year-old gave her an adoring grin. "Miss Wade, you're a might pretty," he said.

"Why, thanks." She smiled and ruffled Jan's curly, black hair.

"Why didn't ya ever marry?" eight-year-old Bobby asked.

"I almost did," Johanna said.

"Almost don't count," Jamie said.

"Shut up, Jamie," twelve-year-old Jason said. "I think Miss Johanna had so many callers, she couldn't make up her mind."

This made Johanna chuckle. She led the boys back to the wagon. True to her word, Sally met them there. Breathless, she came rushing up holding a brown, furry ball.

"What's that?" Seamus asked, moaning as he leaned up in the wagon bed.

"A puppy, Pa." Sally showed him the dog.

"Uh! Looks like a rat to me." Seamus scowled and then he looked at Johanna. "We've got a damn menagerie here. By the time we get to Oregon, Sally there can open a zoo!"

Will came walking by, hand in hand with Martha. They sat across the fire on a tree stump. Will took out a harmonica and played a tune from "Sweet Betsy from Pike."

"Well, wouldn't ya look at that," Seamus whispered to Mabel, "My son is growing up so fast, ain't he?" He peered over at Sally, "Least one of my children is growing up."

"Aw, Pa," Sally huffed, "Will is the apple of your eye, but he ain't without the worm." She elbowed Mabel who laughed at the joke.

"Children, settle down," Johanna said, "Your father needs his rest. I hope the puppy won't bark the rest of the night, Sally."

"He won't, Miss Johanna. He's gonna sleep with me under the wagon."

"Can I see him, Sally?" Jan asked.

"Oh, all right, don't you hurt her; she's barely six weeks old."

Johanna petted the puppy as well. "She's precious. Do you have a name for her?"

"That's it," Sally said, hugging the puppy. "Precious... you've helped me name her. Thanks, Miss Johanna."

"Good night," Johanna called, walking back to her own campsite with Mabel.

"You did wonders, dear," Mabel told her as they crawled into the tent. "Seamus is resting more comfortably now, thanks to your care."

"I'm glad," Johanna said with a yawn. Once she settled down for the night, her thoughts focused on the events of the day. Despite Ryan's crudeness, his grit and compassion in aiding Seamus made him more endearing to Johanna. However much she tried to ignore it, she couldn't stop her physical attraction to Ryan's raw, virile masculinity. He created such an ache within her to be touched in the most unseemly places. Never in her life had she felt such a stir of need, not even with her beloved Robert. Had the escape from her former life opened her to something so bold? Or had too many months of living in the shadow of a memory with no hope of ever leaving the confines of spinsterhood created such a primitive need?

Peeking out she spied the moonlight as it streaked silver beams along the grass. She recalled a friend whose brother studied medicine talking of the effects of the moon. It could make the sanest man mad. Lunacy they called it. In the glow of its light, Johanna felt a bit touched. What else could she call the longing for a man so ill bred and rough-hewn as Ryan?

The sound of a branch snapping brought her head up. She listened then peered at the trees. Had there been the shadow of a man moving by the cottonwood? Rumors of marauders sneaking into wagon trains to steal supplies, even prey upon unsuspecting females, had been passed around camp ever since they left Independence five days ago. Her pulse quickened in apprehension. She felt for the gun buried beneath a pile of rags. She couldn't find it and feared waking Mabel. She vowed to look for the weapon in the morning. She listened again but heard only the crickets and the hoot of an owl.

~ * ~

By evening the following day, they camped on the open plain. Clouds looked closer as they passed overhead. While the moon made its ascent, Johanna cooked with Mabel. They had a quiet meal with the ministers. Reverend Wade glanced over at Johanna and smiled.

"I've heard talk, my dear," he said.

She paused, holding a spoonful of stew. "Yes?"

"Folks are telling me what a wonderful daughter I have. The way that you're looking after their sick, they've nicknamed you the angel of the prairie. I heard that you brought down Seamus' fever and treated his burns too."

"Yes," Mabel added, "Johanna did fine work on Seamus' leg. He's able to walk with a little help. And there's no scar. That linseed oil remedy really did the trick. She could have been a nurse."

"Thanks," Johanna said, finishing her supper, "but I plan to teach and help Father with his missionary work."

"That's right," Stephen said. "You're a great helper, Johanna."

"These people are grateful to you, Johanna," Reverend Wade said,

"And I'm very proud. You've been an enormous help with the mission."

She beamed with delight. "Thank you, Father. I'll do all I can to help."

~ * ~

At Fort Kearney, a collection of ramshackle buildings made of sod, the families in the wagon train had a chance to purchase supplies, send letters back home, and rest awhile before continuing their sojourn. Soldiers in dragoon uniforms patrolled the fort and offered a semblance of protection. It was at this first outpost that Johanna realized the extent of the influence bred by the belief in the Manifest Destiny as she took in the sight of several hundred covered wagons passing through the fort's grounds, camping nearby and crowding the general store, saddleries, and trading post to stock up before continuing westward. Given the crowded, noisy, and a bit unruly conditions, Johanna rejoiced when Ryan announced they were to move out again.

~ * ~

A week later, they camped along the sandy banks of the Platte River not far from a Pawnee village. A dozen round-shaped lodges constructed of dirt and grass stood amid the flatland while their occupants scurried about. Braves stood tall, regal, and proud in their finery of painted buffalo hides and feathered headdresses. Their women wore beaded leather dresses and worked in the fields, some struggled with papooses strapped on cradleboards. A few of their children, dressed like their parents, came toward the wagons and pointed at the children of the wagon train. "Who do those half naked savages think they are, laughing and ogling us so?" Mabel asked Johanna as they sipped from a canteen.

"I'm sure they're as curious about us as we are about them. Oh, here comes Ryan. He seems to know them."

"He's half savage himself," Stephen snarled.

Ryan communicated with the Pawnee in sign language. Johanna wondered what he told them. When one of the braves pointed at her, she gasped.

Ryan's hearty laugh irked her. Turning around, Ryan rubbed the back of his neck and gave her a grin. "He wants to trade buffalo blankets for my redheaded squaw!"

"How dare he!" Johanna sputtered. "I'm not your redheaded squaw. So you just tell him that, and that I'm not for sale!"

When Ryan spoke to the brave, the brave's dark face twisted into a scowl. His gaze swept the length of the wagon train then returned to Johanna. He pointed at Mabel and gestured wildly with his hands.

"I think he's insulting us." Mabel sniffed the air and held her head high. "What does this dreadful man want?"

Ryan shrugged and said, "He's even willing to take the big mother squaw too as his mother-in-law! Got plenty of room in his lodge for the both of you."

"Well, I never." Mabel wiggled her hip to one side. "This is scandalous!'

Ryan nodded. "I agree he made a truly generous offer. Buffalo are worth a great deal to his tribe."

"Oh, what an insult!" Mabel strutted back to the wagon, muttering, "Never have I been so insulted in my life."

Reverend Wade rode over, dismounted, and stood beside Ryan. "Introduce me as the chief of this wagon party."

Ryan made the introductions.

"Tell him that my daughter and sister-in-law are not for trade. That we come in peace and will stay only to rest before moving on."

The anxious faces of other members of the wagon party spurred Ryan to speak.

After some time where Ryan and the brave engaged in signing, Revered Wade interrupted. "What the devil do they want?"

"They want me to come to their village to meet the chief."

"I intend to come along," Wade insisted.

A few more words were exchanged then the braves rode back toward the village.

Ryan turned to Wade, and said, "It'll be all right. We'll get to their meeting all right. Mind you, you've gotta keep your eyes skinned and your nose open." When the minister looked puzzled, Ryan added,

"Pawnees are known for thieving' horses... it's best to leave a man in charge of the camp whilst you're away."

"Certainly," Wade said.

When the braves rode back to the village, Ryan returned to the Wade's wagon and barked orders. "Corral the wagons round. Use the river for water. But boil it first and steer clear of the Pawnee camp. They're getting ready to go hunting and don't need no other visitors. A few years back, the Blackfeet attacked the village while most of them were away."

"But we're not a tribe," Stephen said.

"No, but we're strangers all the same," Ryan said.

"How can anyone live in mud houses?" Mabel asked.

"Those huts can hold the weight of a hundred Pawnee and stand up to the strongest wind," Ryan said, "a mite stronger than the teepees they use on the hunt."

The sight of the Pawnee men with shaven heads and sharp, angular features made them appear fierce to Johanna. Despite their simple dress of bleached buckskin leggings and animal hides, they held a noble air which she admired. Tall and robust, they strode around the wagons, shaking their heads and uttering in Pawnee. Squaws rushed around, children in tow, eyeing the emigrants with curiosity and trying to trade beaded necklaces and moccasins for clothing and furnishings.

"I think they're frightening some of the families, Father," Johanna said.

"Nonsense, they mean no harm." Ryan gestured to the Pawnee squaws to move back from the wagons. "Simple curiosity, you know. They want to see who's coming through their lands."

"They're heathen savages!" Abigail Emerson hollered from her wagon. "One stole my reticule."

Ryan rushed to the squaw who pulled out an assortment of toiletries, coins, and sweets from Abigail's black reticule. When she saw Ryan, she stuck a piece of rock candy in her mouth, crunched hard on it then handed the reticule to him. Ryan scooped up the discarded items, put them in the reticule then returned to Abigail's wagon.

He scowled as he handed the reticule to Abigail. The red-faced, big-jawed woman grinned and smoothed the reticule between her hands. "How can I thank you?"

"Don't bother," Ryan said, "Quit your yapping, else we'll have the whole Pawnee tribe down on us. Anyway, she didn't mean you no harm."

"Hmpf!" Abigail pulled a handkerchief from her reticule and blew her nose. "We'll see about that! She's a thief."

"Aw, hush!" Ryan sauntered back to the Wade's wagon. "They're harmless," he told the ministers. "As harmless as babes."

As he said that, one of the Pawnee boys ran naked around the side of the wagon and began shooting arrows at something crawling beneath it. The arrow missed its target and sank into the side of a sack of flour.

"Harmless!" Mabel said, "I think not. Johanna, we better stay put if they're as harmless as their babes."

A chill ran through Johanna's back as the Pawnees wandered about the entrance to the village. "I think we'd better camp further away," she suggested to Ryan, "for our own protection."

"Suit yourself. That brave won't bother you again neither."

"I hope not." Johanna's gaze narrowed. *I've had enough trouble with men,* she mused, watching Ryan walk off toward another wagon.

While preparing lunch later that day, Johanna heard the sound of horse's hooves pounding the ground. She looked up at the lone rider, his bare torso covered by a black bear hide. Black eyes stared down at her. She cringed with fright, watching the Pawnee brave who'd tried to trade for her with Ryan. "No!" she screamed as he rode up to her site.

"Aya," he cried, lifting his spear. He muttered to her in Pawnee, and cut a cord that tied a bundle around his waist. The bundle thudded to the ground, splashing blood as it fell to her feet. Johanna jumped back. She opened her mouth to scream, but the Pawnee brave wheeled his horse toward the village.

Johanna stood transfixed, staring after the Pawnee, her hand across her throat.

"Jumpin' jackrabbits," Ryan said. "Heard ya screamin' and I charged over. What's wrong, Johanna?"

Shaking, she pointed to the ground. Ryan's somber expression changed to bemusement as he glanced at the ground and poked the bloodied bundle at her feet. He removed his coonskin cap, scratched his head and said, "There is nothing to fear. That Pawnee brave sure is persistent. He not only brought you one but two gifts. Those jack rabbits make mighty fine fixings if I say so myself."

Finally, Johanna found her voice. "You mean he came back to give me... those?"

"Ya only got to worry if he comes back with a whole damn buffalo... then I'd reckon he was surely after you." Ryan picked up the rabbits, examining each of them in turn. He took out his skinning knife. With a clean slice of the knife, he ripped one rabbit from the middle upward with a single deft move, pulled off the skin then threw it onto the table by the wagon. He did the same with the other rabbit.

Johanna watched and felt like retching. The air became heavy and she began to wobble from side to side. As Ryan wiped his bloodied knife on his trousers and tucked it away, she clutched the sideboard of the wagon.

"Uh, Johanna?" Ryan glanced at her.

Suddenly, her vision blurred and darkened. She regained consciousness in Ryan's arms. He guided her to the stool beside the table. He sat on the opposite stool, patting her hand and touching the side of her face. She stared into his dark eyes, shuddering as they reminded her of the Pawnee's. "Oh," she sighed, "I can't possibly eat those." She felt dizzy staring at the disemboweled rabbits and she grabbed the table for support.

"Johanna," Ryan helped steady her on the stool, "you plumb got to get used to life out here." He took the rabbits away, gutting and cleaning them out of view. The sound of the knife carving the rabbits sickened her. Ryan washed his hands with water from the keg then returned. "The rabbits are ready for stewing or frying. Ain't ya had rabbit before?"

She shook her head.

He stood. "We don't have no fancy shops to buy vittles out here. The Pawnee offered the rabbits in friendship. You'd insult him not to take 'em."

"I know." Johanna wiped her cool, damp forehead with a cloth. "I'm all right. I didn't expect to see the rabbits skinned."

"Ya ain't skinned chicken?" He looked surprised.

"My aunt had a servant who cooked for us. When I worked as a governess, my employer had servants, too. So I guess I have been pampered that way."

Ryan held her hands, rubbing the smooth skin on the knuckles and fingertips. "Ah, the soft, tender hands of a lady." He examined her hands, touching the few blisters and calluses. "But they're hardening. That's good. You best do the same if ya intend to survive."

"Yes, you're right." She pulled her hands away from his grip.

"I'll cook 'em for ya." He picked up the rabbits.

"No," Johanna stood slowly. "I'll do it." She swallowed, fighting an urge to gag as she took the rabbits from him. "Thanks."

"Don't thank me; thank that Pawnee who hunted them." He put on his coonskin cap. "I best be going, let me know how the rabbits taste."

"Why don't you join us for lunch?"

"No, thanks. I got to help Ebenezer fasten a wagon seat. It came loose when we forded the last stream."

After Ryan left, Johanna glanced furtively now and then at the Pawnee village. She felt wary now... afraid the brave would return. She couldn't spot him among the multitudes there. The tribe's women worked like beavers as they hoed the fields, sat tanning hides, or wove baskets. They knew hard work. She studied her slender fingers as she held the rabbits. The rabbits' eyes stared big, round and vacant. She shivered and threw the rabbits on the table. "This is foolish," she told herself, "If Ryan can do it, so can I."

Picking up a carving knife, she began to cut up the rabbit as she'd seen her aunt's cook do with the chickens, halving them and cutting off pieces. She bit back the bile taste in her mouth as she placed the meat into a cauldron.

She diced the stems off the dandelion Jan McPherson gave her, and threw them into the pot. After adding water, bits of onion and bacon, she boiled the stew. Thoughts of Boston flickered through her mind as she stirred the pot with a long ladle.

She missed that earlier time now with its safety and security. At least as a governess, she didn't have to fear Indian braves riding up with dead rabbits or wild animals foraging around as she slept in a canvas tent on the hard ground. Nor did she have to worry about being out on the open plain as lightning lashed from the sky and hail the size of a fist pelted your wagon. Then again, as a governess she wouldn't have met a man like Ryan Majors.

She spied Ryan near the Pawnee village. Beside him stood the brave who delivered the rabbits to her. A tall, slender Pawnee maiden leaned into Ryan's side. He playfully patted her bottom as she led him into the village. The brave followed them. "Hmpf, I see whose wagon you had to fix!" Johanna muttered, stabbing the stew with a spoon. Some juice splattered on the front of her dress. With a yelp, she mopped it with an old cloth. Suddenly depressed, she flopped down on a stool. Hadn't someone told her that Indians loaned their wives and daughters to strangers as a gesture of friendship? The thought irked her more than the gesture of the enamored Pawnee brave.

"Wouldn't it be interesting to convert the Pawnees?" Reverend Wade said while they had lunch. "They seem friendly enough."

Although thoughts of Ryan and the Pawnee squaw walking together in the woods burned Johanna's guts, she saw the merit in her father's suggestion. "I guess so," she said cautiously.

"Friendly, indeed!" Mabel huffed, "They wanted to trade us for blankets... and then one of them took my best parasol."

"They're not to be trusted," Stephen said between mouthfuls of stew. "Indians are heathen."

Well aware that her loss of appetite had nothing to do with the two rabbits she managed to cook, Johanna pushed aside her untouched bowl of stew and said to Stephen, "How do you expect to bring the faith to them if you despise them?"

"With this!" He held up his prayer book.

"Don't be ridiculous, Stephen, it takes more than books to convert the noble savage." She dumped the stew on the ground. "Wouldn't you agree, Father?"

Reverend Wade's stern gaze softened. "You're right. I saw one of those braves leaving our campsite this afternoon. When I saw Ryan coming over afterward I knew that you were all right. But do be careful."

"I'm not afraid of them."

"Not even a brave who'd trade you for buffalo hides?" Mabel asked, helping Johanna clear away the bowls and cookware.

"What was that?" Stephen asked, sniffing his bowl. "It wasn't our usual stew, but it was quite good."

"Rabbit stew," Johanna said. "That Pawnee brave you saw, Father, gave me two rabbits as a gift."

"Beware of Greeks bearing gifts," Stephen said with a sly grin.

"They're not Greeks but Pawnee," Johanna said, "and I think we can trust them. Ryan said we're safe. We need to understand them that's all." Some of the remaining gravy spilled on Stephen's trousers. Johanna threw him a rag to clean his pants then went about serving dessert.

She ladled berries onto china plates and added cream. "These are fresh; I picked them by the river bank yesterday."

"None for me, Johanna," Reverend Wade said, patting his stomach. "Johanna, you must be careful when you're out in the woods. It's not safe for you to be alone."

"Yes, Father." After Johanna handed out the dessert, she sat beside Mabel and ate. The sweet fruit satisfied her hunger pang. When she wiped the juice from her chin, Stephen touched her fingertips.

"Ah, sweets to the sweet," he whispered, stealing a berry from her plate.

Feeling sour, Johanna moved away from the table. When she walked to the back of her wagon, Stephen crept up behind her. She felt his breath along her neck as he whispered. "Johanna, I'll see no harm comes to hide or hair of you. In fact, I'll go with you to the

112

woods to pick berries or do anything else you'd like."

She spun around. "I don't need your kind of help." As he stepped on the other side of her, Johanna slammed the lid of the storage chest nearly catching his hand in the process.

Raking his fingers through his hair, he hissed, "So, if that's how you feel. I'll go where I'm wanted." She watched him walk off to the blue painted wagon where the Emerson sisters would welcome him with idle conversation and fruit pies. "Good riddance," she muttered.

"Johanna! I'm surprised at you!"

She turned, surprised by her father's furious gaze. "Why?"

"You were unkind to Reverend Green. He has your interest at heart."

"My foot." Johanna walked back to the table.

"What did you say?" Her father hounded her. When she didn't reply, he asked. "Why are you fighting with him? Stephen is your friend, my assistant. He's a good man, Johanna. A good Christian man... something rare these days I'm afraid."

"Maybe so, Father. Stephen and I had been friends... childhood friends." Johanna stared at the puffs of clouds rolling by. Years of pent up emotion burst forth like a volcano. "But I'm no longer a child. I'm a grown woman. I can make up my own mind. And if I want to go into the woods to pick berries, I will. If I want to befriend the Pawnee, I will."

"Now, you mustn't yield to immoral acts."

"What on earth is immoral about learning to understand the Pawnee?" She waved her arms about in frustration. "We're on their land. Ryan said so."

"Is Ryan putting ideas into your head?"

"No... I have my own mind."

"Ryan Majors has not had the proper Christian upbringing you had. He's a trapper... a mountain man. He's not used to the refinement of society. Why, I picked him up out of a..." He stopped short.

"A brothel?" Johanna asked. "They exist even in Boston, Father. One of grandfather's mistresses came from there. For all we know, you may have a half-brother somewhere."

"Johanna!" Mabel gasped. "I never thought you'd repeat..."

"Hush up, Mabel," Reverend Wade snapped. "My God, I cannot believe you told the girl about my father's philandering. You had no right to."

"I'm sorry, Howard. I didn't realize that she'd bring it up."

"I'm sorry, Father." Johanna hugged him. "I didn't mean to hurt you. I learned that you ran away when you found out about it and went on to a seminary school. Afterward, you met Mother. I'm sorry."

Reverend Wade stood rigid a moment then fingered the lapels of his frock. "Don't ever breathe a word of my family's scandal to anyone, Johanna. It would do no good, not with these humble farmers. They need a Christian model to look to for sustenance."

She nodded. "I agree, Father. You're the epitome of that model. I don't know why I brought it up." She knew deep down though that the mere mention of Ryan with other women, past and present, stirred anger in her blood she'd never known before. The wounded look on her father's lined face made her want to take back every word. She gently reached for his hand, but he pulled away. "I'm very sorry,"

Shaken and drawn, her father walked away from the wagon. Guilt and worry made Johanna cringe as she watched him. "I had no right," she told Mabel. "Oh, why did I say such hurtful things?"

Mabel looked at her in earnest and patted her hair. "Because, my dear, you're hurt too. Reverend Howard Wade might be the epitome of a good Christian minister, but he's not the best father. I hope time will heal both your wounds."

"It makes my blood boil to think Father falls for Stephen's lies. He really believes that Stephen has my interest at heart. It's absolutely intolerable! He's blind to the man."

"Shh." Mabel took a brush and ran it through Johanna's hair.

"That feels good, Auntie. It reminds me of the times as a little girl that you combed my hair when I felt sad."

Mabel hummed a lullaby. "Remember this one?"

"Yes, you had a way of getting me to sleep."

"Johanna, try to be patient with him. Men don't often understand a woman's heart, my dear."

"I think if I'd been a boy, Father would have taken me with him."

"Now, I'm not suggesting that."

"It's a possibility, Auntie, you can't deny it. What good is a little daughter to a circuit minister?"

"Don't talk nonsense, Johanna, You can't undo the past, all we have is the present. Anyhow, you're here with your father. What more do you want?"

"I want to be respected for who I am."

"And you are, my dear. Come let's sit down and have a sip of that nice tonic Seamus gave us."

"What tonic?" Johanna's brows rose as Mabel held up a bottle.

"This. It will restore your nerves, calm you down."

Johanna took a sip, "Auntie, that's wine!"

"A little dandelion wine, it's for medicinal purpose."

Johanna handed back the bottle. "And now you're drinking spirits? No thanks."

After a sip of the wine, Mabel went back to her knitting. "It eases the pain in the joints, so this work is easier."

Johanna peeked over her shoulder. "What are you knitting?"

"Socks for Seamus. He needs a pair to replace the burned ones."

Ryan suddenly appeared, tipped his coonskin cap and sat. "Ahh... smells like rabbit stew. I hope you enjoyed it."

"Yes," Mabel said. "It was a nice change from the usual fare."

Ryan glanced around. "Where are the ministers? The Pawnee chief wants to smoke the pipe with them."

"Father is over there." Johanna pointed to a clearing where he knelt in prayer. "And Stephen is with the Emerson sisters."

Ryan's brows arched. "Oh, well, we don't need him. I'll go talk to Reverend Wade."

"There, I've finished the pair," Mabel said, holding them up, "How do they look?"

Johanna suppressed a giggle. "Won't they be too big?"

"No, Seamus is a big man with big feet." She put away her knitting. "They'll fit."

As Reverend Wade and Ryan strolled together to the wagon,

Mabel said, "I don't trust the Pawnee, even if Ryan does."

Stephen ambled by, crunching on an apple. He joined the conversation between Ryan and Reverend Wade. "So, you've returned from the village?" he asked Ryan.

"Yes, and the chief wants to smoke the pipe with Reverend Wade."

"I'm coming too," Stephen said, throwing the apple into a bush.

"Me too." Johanna jumped up and moved closer to the men.

Ryan glanced at her. "Womenfolk can't come."

"I'll go if I like." She draped a shawl about her shoulders.

"In a pig's eye," Ryan said.

"I agree with Ryan," Reverend Wade said. "You can't come, Johanna. It could be dangerous. Especially if the Pawnee braves are after red-haired women. We're not in the market for trading our women for any amount of livestock or food."

"But, Father, I could help you."

"You're not coming and that's final."

"I may not this time," she whispered to Mabel as they watched the ministers and Ryan ride off. "But I will the next time."

Ten

Along the Platte River

When her toes touched the frigid water of the Platte River, Johanna shivered. But she was willing to brave anything to bathe off the accumulation of grime and sweat. Fording knee-deep, she stooped to wet her hair. Gritting her teeth, she lathered herself with the hard-milled soap. The water soaked her chemise, making it transparent as it clung to her chilled skin. Secure in the knowledge that the men always bathed downstream from the women, she vigorously cleaned her arms and legs. Her nipples hardened as an image of Ryan washing her suddenly popped into her head. She felt an ache between her legs at the mere thought of Ryan's hands upon her body. The feelings disturbed her so; she quickly splashed her hot loins and reddened face with the cold, bracing water.

When she opened her eyes, she saw through a lush grove of nearby cottonwoods, the silhouette of a rider dismounting. A splash of sunlight revealed a hideous scar along his cheek. He was big and ugly, and when he spotted her, he leered through coal black eyes. His feral grin sent a cold shiver up along her spine and she hastened to cover her semi-nude body. He stood and as she moved toward shore, he mounted his horse again and rode away. Shaken by the intruder, Johanna did not hear her aunt's voice until Mabel threw a stick at the nearby water, yelling, "Watch the water snakes, Johanna."

With utmost speed, Johanna waded ashore. Mabel handed her a

towel. "You're very lucky, my dear. Mary O'Dowd claimed to have seen one of those blasted creatures slithering alongside her."

Draping the towel about her shoulders and stooping to dry her hair, Johanna said, "Thanks for the warning. I'll be more careful next time." Despite the towel's rough warmth, goose bumps tingled her skin as she recalled the vision of the scar-faced man. "Did you see a man by the trees over there?"

"Goodness, no," said Mabel. "The men are supposed to be bathing elsewhere."

"This man, whoever he was, didn't look like any of the men in our wagon party," Johanna said, pulling on her pantalets and dress. Her fingers trembled as she buttoned the front of the dress and tied on an apron. As she walked with Mabel toward camp, she still felt shaken by the sight of the strange man. Even though she had resigned herself to the virtual lack of privacy in the outdoors, she couldn't help but feel as though something was terribly wrong with the presence of the stranger. She wanted to tell her father or Ryan, but since they were already late for service, she decided to tell them later.

"We'll be late for prayer service, Johanna," Mabel said. A commotion from a nearby brush startled them. Fearing the reappearance of the stranger, Johanna moved back. To her relief, the movement was caused by Pawnees—three squaws and their children aged five to twelve. The squaws bowed as they saw her then came forward with ears of corn and yellow squash in red and tan baskets. Mabel clutched Johanna's forearm.

"Don't worry, Auntie," Johanna reassured, "They're not going to attack us unless they plan to stone us with food." A young squaw, whom Johanna guessed to be in her late teens, had lighter skin than the others and pale blue eyes. Her raven black hair was braided and adorned with a colorful beaded band that ran across her forehead. A black and white feather stuck up from the back of the band. She smiled at Johanna and placed her basket of corn in front of her. "For white lady."

Johanna thanked her and picked up one of the baskets. As she did so, an old squaw rushed up and pulled on her topknot. "Ouch!"

Johanna winced in pain, dropping the basket of food. The old squaw stepped away as the younger one yelled at her in Pawnee. Then the younger squaw picked up the food and handed it to Johanna.

"My grandma is sorry for what she do. She thinks you fire-haired spirit with magic power."

"I'm no spirit," Johanna said, rubbing her sore scalp. She fastened her topknot then lifted the basket. "Thank you for the food."

The young squaw approached her again, "Wait! I know you no spirit but missionary who teach. You teach my people."

"What's your name?" Johanna asked.

"Evening Star."

"Where did you learn to speak English?"

"My father was white trapper. He die and Pawnee raise me."

"And the corn and beads are gifts?"

"You trade for teaching us." Evening Star looked at her hopefully. "Trapper Ryan say you teach read and write. Come on." She yanked Johanna's arm.

"Now wait one cotton pickin' moment!" Mabel stood between them. "My niece is not going anywhere with you."

Evening Star held firm to Johanna. "She teacher... so she come teach."

Looking at the eager brown faces of the children, Johanna smiled. How could she let them down? She smiled gently at Evening Star. "I can't go to your village, but you can come to ours."

"Johanna!" Mabel gasped. "Are you out of your mind?"

"How can I refuse them, Auntie?"

"Easy... did you ever hear of the word no?"

Johanna patted the youngest child, a girl of about five whose broad grin lit up her brown eyes. "I'll do it. They can join the children from our wagon party." She glanced at Evening Star. "Bring them to the clearing over there," she pointed to the woods. "tomorrow."

After they left, Mabel stood before Johanna. "You have lost your mind?"

"What harm could there be?" Johanna shrugged, wondering how her father and Stephen would react to the fact that she was bringing the Pawnee into their camp. "Well," she said, "We did plan to convert the noble savages. So, if we're going to camp here for a few days, I can teach the Pawnee's children as surely as I can our own."

"But Johanna, they might be cut-throat savages. There's no telling what they'll do to us."

"Stop it." Johanna sighed. "I refuse to listen. We must learn to live with the Pawnee and the other tribes. After all, we're in their land."

"Very well." Mabel picked up her parasol and began to walk away. "If you need me, I'll be at Seamus' wagon."

"As I expected," Johanna muttered.

~ * ~

"Who are those Injuns?" a hard-edged voice asked. Johanna spun around, glancing at the beet-red face of Molly Fletcher. The heavyset woman struggled to catch her breath, having climbed up the incline from the river. Her stern gaze unnerved Johanna.

"They're from the Pawnee village," Johanna said, looking past Molly to the four dark-haired Fletcher children who climbed one after the other.

"Git yourselves up 'ere right now," Molly called. She turned back to Johanna. "On my way up, I got drift of something ya said. You gonna teach them Injuns?"

"As a matter of fact, yes." Johanna's posture stiffened under Molly's narrowed gaze.

"Lordy, you mean we're gonna have savages coming to our wagons? Bad enough they steal off with horses."

"Nobody stole our horses. And those children are no different from your own." Johanna glanced at the pale, dirty-faced Fletcher boys in their muddied, torn-at-the-knee overalls and berry-stained bibs. The twins, Amos and Andrew, teased their younger brother Jacob, poking him with a stick.

Of the four, the dull-witted Jacob smiled at Johanna. What the eight-year-old lacked in the way of intelligence, he made up for in his kinder, warmer nature. "Here, Miss Johanna," he said, handing her a bouquet of dandelions, "for you."

"Throw those away," Molly said, slapping his hands so the

bouquet fell to the ground in a tumbled heap. Jacob pouted and lowered his head.

"But, Ma, I done pick 'em for my teacher."

"She ain't your teacher no more." Molly glared at Johanna. "And my children don't go running 'round buck naked and smelling like a pile of horse manure."

Johanna picked up the flowers, sniffed them then smiled at Jacob. "Thank you for the flowers."

Zachariah Fletcher, Molly's teenage son, peered at Johanna with contempt. "My ma's right, them Pawnee stink. And there ain't no way I'm gonna sit with 'em."

"Come along boys," Molly said. With a contemptuous glance at Johanna, she added, "And you wait until the other mothers hear of this, you won't have no school!"

Like a mother duck, Molly wobbled and clacked on and on to her children as they followed her in an uneven line. *She's more like a goose then a duck*, Johanna thought, feeling malicious. *But she's got the venom of a snake. I won't pay her no mind*, she told herself, maintaining her cool veneer along with her convictions. Deep down she hoped that the other mothers wouldn't harbor such prejudice.

~ * ~

Reverend Green stepped up to the top of a wooden crate and glanced at the crowd with a look of satisfaction as they gathered in the center of the circled wagons. Johanna sat on a stool beside her father and Mabel. Clean-shaven and wearing a gray waistcoat over his black pants, Stephen cut a handsome figure as he stood with one hand fingering his suspenders and the other clasping a prayer book. He cleared his throat then began, "Brothers and Sisters we gather here in the name of the Lord. He that believeth shall be saved."

"Amen," Reverend Wade said.

"It has come to my attention that some of you lack proper Baptizing. Step forward." He motioned to the Fletchers. Molly pushed her children forward, and other parents came with their children.

"Save us," Molly said, beating her breast. "Oh, save us."

Stephen smiled. "Praise ye Lord." He held his hands over Molly's bowed head. "Woman, will thou be baptized in this faith?" She nodded. "The rest of you come forward, come children." As they gathered around him, Stephen began the baptismal with the words, "Oh, merciful God, grant that the old Adam in these persons may be so buried, that the new man may be raised up in them."

"Amen," Molly said.

"Grant that all carnal affection may die in them." He peered directly at Johanna who flushed under his scrutiny. Lowering her gaze, she pretended to read her prayer book. Stephen continued the baptismal ceremony for another hour. When he finished, he hugged the newly baptized. "Welcome, brothers and sisters to the faith." The crowd applauded.

"We must have faith!" Stephen shouted. "Be saved. Repent ye sinners"

"Praise Jesus," Molly Fletcher said, "Oh, save me, sweet Lord." Stephen placed his hands upon her head. She shook then fell to the ground, writhing like a snake. Others came forward for laying on of hands. They, too, became stricken and rolled or slithered on the ground.

Filled with disgust at the gross display, Johanna pulled on her father's coat sleeve, "What's he up to?"

Reverend Wade looked at her, whispering, "He's got them by golly, and they're taken with the Spirit. Converted to the faith. If his method works, so be it."

"Horse manure if ya ask me!" Ryan sneered, "Hoot'n and holler'n for what?"

This is about power, Johanna thought. *Stephen enjoys mastering these people.* "He's lower than the ground beneath us," she whispered to her father.

"Hush, child," Reverend Wade said, "Stephen is doing the Lord's work."

"An' this is savin' folk?" Ryan said in Johanna's other ear. "Horse whipping' is too good for him. Foolin' folks like he is. I'm sure they'd about give him their last hard earned dollar to be saved."

Noting her father's stern expression, she told Ryan to hush up.

"Maybe he's going about it the wrong way, but he's offering faith to people who need it."

"Don't count me among 'em."

"I won't," Johanna snapped. "Go back to your Pawnee village; I'm sure you're welcome there."

"I know I am." He turned away, leaving her cross and miserable. It took every effort of her will to concentrate on the rest of Stephen's service.

~ * ~

Johanna gathered the children the next morning. True to her threat, Molly Fletcher would not allow her children to join the group. "Ya ain't teaching my young uns with Injuns." She stood beside her wagon, with a rolling pin beneath her folded arms. "We got more important things to be doing." Her husband, Ned, grunted as he lay on the ground greasing an axle wheel.

"That's too bad, Mrs. Fletcher," Johanna said. Jacob Fletcher stuck his tongue out at her making her wonder whether Molly had poisoned him with prejudice and hatred. The thought saddened her. "I think your children could learn a good deal, not only about manners but about being proper Christians."

Molly scrunched her nose, making her face look sour and mean. "We are proper Christians. Reverend Green said so. We've been baptized."

"Very well." Johanna knew it would be futile to argue with this foolish woman. She glanced at the other children behind her, waving them to follow. "Come, children. There are a few people in this world whose words belie their deeds." Turning on her heels, Johanna led them to a grassy meadow and instructed them to be seated beneath a huge oak tree. The girls spread out their dresses and sat; the boys in their buckskin or denim overalls, sat cross-legged. Sally handed out slates and chalk to the children who ranged in age from seven to fifteen.

Lifting the hem of her navy skirt, Johanna sat in the center. Sally sat beside her. "Good day, children." Johanna said with a smile.

"Good day, Miss Wade," they said in unison.

She handed out the readers. "There aren't enough to go around. You'll have to share them." A commotion in the rear of the group, made her look up to see Sally flailing her fist at Joshua.

"Hush up, Joshua," Sally said. "Else I'll box your ears."

"Quiet, please." Johanna waited before beginning to write on her larger slate.

The sharp squeak as the chalk marked the board made the children groan. Johanna ignored this. "We'll begin at the beginning—with the alphabet. Repeat after me." She said each letter, writing it as she said it. The children repeated her words and actions. A flurry of activity made her stop. She saw Seamus' twins pushing Joshua.

"They put a grasshopper down my sister's dress." Joshua pointed to Becky.

The flaxen-haired eight-year-old stuck out her tongue at Will.

"And I ain't letting 'em get away with it." With that Joshua struck Will's chin.

"Stop it!" Johanna pulled the boys apart.

Sally boxed their ears. "Don't be puttin' nothin' down nobody's dress and listen to Miss Wade or ya'll be horse whipped." She pushed them down onto the grass where they rubbed their sore ears and swore beneath their breath. "Hush up, no cussing neither." Sally balled her hand into a fist. "Or I'll give ya more o' the same."

Johanna sighed, and put up her hands. "Hitting begets hitting, Sally. The only lesson to be learned is to hate or fear the one inflicting the punishment. Now everyone settle down, please. Let's get on with this lesson." Having finished the alphabet, she had them print their names on their slates.

Next she led them in a counting exercise. As she neared the end of the time she planned for the lessons, she wondered what had happened to the Pawnees. The sun overhead indicated the noon hour. She read a passage from Genesis. Using the slate to illustrate the idea of creation, she drew a tree. "This is the tree of life," she said, "Here are Adam and Eve at its root. See how it grows big? We are the branches. We're all God's children. We're all brothers and sisters."

At that moment, four Pawnee children ranging in age from six to twelve ventured onto the field, led by Evening Star. They looked fearfully at the emigrant children.

"Injuns!" Tom Henry said, jumping up and pointing.

"Sit down!" Johanna said.

Fearful, Joshua asked, "Are they going to scalp us?"

"No," Johanna said. "Sit down."

When he refused to sit, Sally grabbed his collar and pulled him down beside her. Evening Star motioned to the Pawnee children to sit. She smiled at Johanna, saying, "I tell them what you say."

Studying the fear on the faces of both groups of children, Johanna said, "Let's start again, with introductions." She pointed to the group from the wagon party. "Let's go around the circle, telling everyone our names, shall we? I'll start. I'm Johanna Wade."

Sally stood and curtsied, to the amusement of her younger brothers. "Sally McPherson... and don't mind those two—Will and Jason, they was dropped on their heads when the doctor pulled 'em out... poor Ma didn't realize she'd get double the trouble with 'em and this here's my brother Jamie... and Bobbie... and Jan."

"Thank you, Sally," Johanna said, "Go on... please introduce yourselves."

Thirteen year old Margie O'Dowd stood and curtsied.

"Sit down, Margie," Will yelled. "This here ain't a dance hall or piano recital."

"Oh, hush up," Margie said, stroking her long, braided hair. "Ain't you got no respect for the teacher? I'm glad to meet ya'll."

"Heck, I ain't got respect for them Injuns," Jason shouted. He began to make a whooping sound in mockery of their visitors.

Sally swiftly tapped his arm. "Shut it right now, Jason, or you'll taste my fist in your jaw."

"Children, stop it." Johanna raised her hand, throwing a stern glance at Will and Jason. Becky, Joshua, Tom Henry, and Adam remained seated as they introduced themselves, giggling and poking one another.

"I'm Evening Star," the Pawnee maiden said with a shy smile, "and these are children from my tribe. She spoke to the Pawnee children who remained silent and attentive. Turning back to Johanna, she introduced the children. Pointing to the girls, she said, "Night Sky and White Dove, my sisters. These," she indicated the boys, "are Buffalo Bull and Eagle Flying."

"What kinds of queer names are those?" Will called out, "You name 'em after animals!"

"Hush up, or you'll regret the day you were born!" Sally pinched Will's arm. The other emigrant children began to laugh at them.

Johanna clapped her hands to regain order. "I'm sure our names sound silly to them. We must learn to tolerate each other, Will. Now, let's begin the lesson with the alphabet." Johanna wrote on her slate and showed the Pawnee children then she turned to the group from the wagon. "Children, let's help them by reciting the alphabet."

They did so. "And now," she told Evening Star, "join in with us." As Evening Star began the recitation, the Pawnee children followed in. Johanna gave them each a slate and showed them how to write the letters of their names using Evening Star as an assistant with spelling. One boy refused to do the work, and stared at the white children. The chalk broke in the stubby fingers of a smaller Pawnee child. The youngest drew a white streak along his cheekbone then grinned at the others.

"Aw, those Pawnee are jest plain stupid!" Will shouted. "Miss Wade, ain't no way you gonna teach an Injun nothin'."

Johanna gave a sigh of exasperation then continued, "It's their first time learning our English. Remember how you felt on your first day in school, William." She turned back to her stack of books, looking for the McGuffy readers when a loud scream made her turn around.

"Help, he's got a knife, he's gonna scalp me!"

Johanna looked up as the oldest Pawnee boy brandished a long knife at Will's ear. Fear gripped her inside, yet Johanna knew she must remain calm. She stood, extending her hand. "Give up the knife. We do not use weapons to speak." She prepared to take the knife away if necessary. "Please give the knife to me."

Evening Star spoke in a sharp tone. The boy gaped at her, dropped

126

the knife then sat. Evening Star gave him such a hard slap across the face, a mark appeared where her hand had been.

"Was that necessary?" Johanna asked her.

"Lone Eagle been problem since day he was born," she replied. "Some need to be taught lesson with this, not the book." She held up her hands.

"Now sit down, everyone." Johanna called for order as the children grew noisier. Will stuck his tongue out at Lone Eagle.

"Give me the rod, Miss Wade." Sally stepped forward. "I'll teach them all a lesson."

"We'll use no rods." Johanna sat calmly, "Sit down, everyone please sit down." She glanced at the emigrant children. "The Pawnee can be your friends, if you let them. Sit down!" Finally, they sat. Some continued to eye the Pawnee with apprehension. Evening Star motioned her group to sit. Johanna read an excerpt from the Bible, shut the book then stood. A quick glance at the sky warned her of an approaching storm. "It's time to leave." Johanna motioned to the children and Evening Star. "But before we do, I'd like to lead everyone in the collect."

"Collect?"

"It's a Christian prayer. Oh, you can join in if you'd like or listen to the words."

When the children from the wagon bowed their heads, Evening Star bowed hers too and the children in her care followed suit. Johanna ended the prayer with, "Praise be the word of God. Thank you, children."

"You mention the one God," Evening Star said. "The Pawnee people worship many gods. But we understand the need to praise Tirawa."

Johanna touched Evening Star's arm. "Thank you for bringing the children. I'm sure we'll have no more problems."

Evening Star rounded up her group. A few of the Pawnee children smiled at Johanna and thanked her with a hug. "Wait!" Johanna pulled a bundle from her box of supplies and handed each child a peppermint stick. They waved at her from the edge of the woods, before disappearing into the thicket.

"You look plumb tuckered out, Miss Johanna," Sally said. "I can take the young 'uns back to camp."

"Oh, I'm fine, but for a moment there... I wasn't quite sure what would happen."

"Come on, children." Sally herded them. "Let's get ya'll back to your wagons." Like a shepherdess leading her flock, Sally managed to bring them under control and headed down the path to camp. *She has the makings of a fine teacher*, Johanna thought, *provided she doesn't resort to whips and knuckles to keep order.*

"I see you're making friends?" Ryan's approach startled Johanna. She spun around. He used his coonskin cap to wipe his brow. His hair glistened black and shiny in the sunlight. His gaze lingered on her and his smile warmed her more than the summer sunshine. She returned his smile with a radiant one of her own.

"I hope so."

"I happened to be riding nearby and figured I'd listen in awhile. That was quite a brave thing ya done... trying to get the knife from that boy... he'd have used it too if he felt scared enough."

"Think so?"

"Sure... he's close to manhood and felt threatened by Will. Those young uns aren't shielded from life the way the farm boys are... and the city folk."

"Oh? I suppose I've been shielded, too?"

"Now that ya mention it, reckon so. But ya'll learn sooner or later out here. Hey, that tale ya spun—was Genesis... wasn't it?"

She gaped at him. "Yes. So you do read the Bible?"

His smile collapsed as his gaze narrowed. "Ya don't think a heathen like myself would read the Bible?"

"Maybe not the Bible. You must read something. What do you read?"

He fidgeted with his cap then placed it squarely on his head. "I... I can't."

"You can't read?" Without further thought, Johanna quickly said, "Then I'll teach you to read."

Ryan roared with laughter. "You teach me?"

"And why not me? I'm a teacher."

He shifted his stance, looking ill at ease. "A fella like me ain't cut out for learning. Besides I'm busy. I'm headin' this wagon train, remember?"

"We're all busy. Perhaps you can sit with the children in the afternoon?"

"I ain't about to sit down with no pups." When he stepped closer, she felt the warmth of his breath upon her face. She studied the rigid slope of his shoulders, the way his chest heaved in and out, and how his muscular arms moved beneath the tight weave of his shirt. Her mind began to stray to other thoughts... his hands upon her skin, his lips upon hers. *Stop it before you lose self-control*, she warned herself.

"Maybe you're right, Ryan. If you don't have the time, there's no sense in pursuing the matter. Perhaps you're afraid to learn."

"Hell, woman, I ain't 'fraid of nothin'." His mouth clamped down into a tight line. "I got no more use for reading. That's for dandies like the minister and ladies like yourself. What do I need to read for?"

"Because you want to." She held the slate against her breast like a shield. "And I'd like something in return."

"What?" His gaze raked the length of her as he wet his lips with the tip of his tongue. "I'd be happy to oblige."

Did he take her for a strumpet? *Well*, she thought, *I'm not willing to get his help at any cost.* "I brought my uncle's pistol. I want you to teach me how to use it." When he didn't respond, she said, "I'm serious about this, Ryan. But you mustn't tell anyone. Neither Father nor Mabel know anything about it, and I want to keep it that way because I know they wouldn't approve."

"I'm not sure I do neither. Why would a lady want to learn to shoot?"

"Lots of ladies can shoot. The farmers' wives know how to use their husbands' rifles." Johanna thought of the stranger in the woods. "I feel a need for protection."

Ryan rubbed the stubble on his jaw. "Guess there ain't no harm in it. Wouldn't want ya blasting some poor fool's head off."

"Good. In return, I'll teach you to read?"

"If an' when I get the time." Ryan shrugged.

"Let's shake on it." When Johanna extended her hand to him, Ryan wrapped his large callused fingers around hers, caressing the tips with his thumb.

"We can start today," he said in a husky voice. Heat enveloped her arm at his touch and her thoughts drifted to the moment in the river when she envisioned him there and her own desire.

She shook her head. "Um... oh... no... I can wait."

"I can't." He put his arms about her waist. "It's been too long already." He lowered his face to hers and grazed her lips with his own. A sudden, sharp thrill shot from her mouth down to her core and Johanna pressed into Ryan, deepening the kiss. Ryan responded with a groan as his tongue plunged deeper into her mouth. Raindrops fell upon them as they stood together on the hillside.

"Miss Wade!" a young girl called.

Ryan pulled away from Johanna, muttering, "Sons of bitches! Of all the infernal, confounded..." Ryan glared at Sally McPherson as she rushed up to them. "Is your Pa sick again?" Ryan snarled.

"No." Sally glanced from Ryan to Johanna. "Are you all right, Miss Johanna?"

"Oh... yes..." Johanna wiped her lips. "I'm fine."

"Oh, I heard funny moaning noises and came to find out if you were hurt." Sally glanced from her to Ryan then back again and winked. "But ya look fine to me. It's beginning to rain, Miss Wade."

"Oh, yes." Johanna hadn't noticed, but now the rain fell harder and soaked through her clothing. Flushing a bright red, Johanna wiped her brow with a handkerchief. "Mr. Majors will be joining us for lessons." Ignoring Ryan's groan of protest, Johanna made a big show of gathering her supplies. "Let's get these things packed up." Johanna put the easel and slates in the box along with the books. When she attempted to lift it, Ryan stopped her.

"I'll carry that!" He grabbed the box with such fury that Johanna stumbled back.

"Goodness, you needn't trip me!" Then she chuckled recalling how he had done the same thing back in Independence. *Gosh*, she thought, *that seems like a lifetime ago instead of a few weeks.* When he apologized, she quickly said, "That's all right. I'm sure you're just anxious to get started on your lessons."

"As long as you don't treat me like one of your dang pups!" he snapped, walking ahead with the box tucked under his arm. "It's bad enough," he muttered, "I'm actin' like a bitch in heat."

"What's that you said, Mr. Majors?" Johanna cocked a brow, and bit her lower lip to keep from smiling.

"Aw, nothin', nothin' at all."

Eleven

Pawnee Village

Ryan sniffed the pungent aromas of charred buffalo. "Ah," he said, "Haven't had a thick, juicy hump in a long time.

Reverend Wade threw him a sidelong glance. "Mr. Majors, you're not here to cavort with the women."

Ryan glanced at the Pawnee squaws standing around the open pits, roasting or slicing thick cuts of the meat, then realized what the minister misunderstood. "Heck," he said, "I'm talking about buffalo." Turning around on his horse, he added, "You're in for some fine fixings—fresh buffalo meat is about the tastiest meal you'll ever eat, except for maybe squirrel stew."

Stephen grimaced. "Good heavens, man, do you expect us to eat rodents too?"

Reverend Wade chuckled softly. "If we had no choice but to eat it, Stephen then we would. Buffalo is quite tasty. I once tasted it while visiting a settlement village many years ago. Folks there gave it to me in payment for baptizing their children."

"Buffalo is one critter the Pawnee depend upon," Ryan said. "They use its skin for blankets, robes, and tepees; its hair for rope; its horns for spoons. There ain't nothing on it they don't use."

When the leader of the Pawnee, an aged warrior, came forth from his earth lodge, Ryan dismounted. The ministers dismounted as well.

The chief, wearing a buffalo robe about his hunched, bare shoulders and a beaded and feathered bonnet upon his head, stood with his head back and his heavy-lidded eyes studying them. Suddenly, he addressed Ryan in Pawnee, signing with his hands at the same time.

In Pawnee, Ryan introduced the ministers to the chief then told him, "We come to your village in peace. We go to where the land meets the great waters, Oregon."

As the chief replied, Ryan listened then glanced at the ministers. "He said, welcome. Come and be my honored guests. Sit among my people and smoke the sacred pipe."

They followed the chief and his entourage of bare-chested braves, who wore loincloths or fringed buckskin leggings, to a huge bonfire. Once there, they sat. Ryan sat cross-legged. The ministers sat similarly. Squaws in beaded buckskin dresses served water and cornmeal. The chief spoke again and Ryan translated. "He said that many wagons roll across my people's land. They show no respect for the land, shooting our buffalo, leaving it to rot and only taking the head. This makes the great spirits angry. Tell your people to stop. If buffalo leave hunting grounds, my people will starve."

The chief puffed on a white pipe carved from bark then passed it to Ryan.

"Tell him that his people will not starve," Reverend Wade said.

"Can you promise they won't?" Ryan asked. He took a puff on the pipe and passed it to Reverend Wade.

The minister puffed then coughed. "Tell him we will not kill his buffalo."

"It's not only you," Ryan said. "It's the many who come through the lands. This angers the Pawnee and the other tribes. They take from the land what they need. Can you promise the other settlers will do the same?"

"No, of course I can't," Reverend Wade said, glancing at the chief, "but I know my settlers will not destroy his buffalo nor the sacred land. The land belongs to all of us." Then he passed the pipe to Stephen.

Stephen inhaled the tobacco, choked and coughed. His face turned deathly pale as he gasped for air.

Ryan slapped Stephen's back. "Are you all right?"

"Yes," Stephen grumbled, giving Ryan the pipe.

A squaw in her late teens came into the circle with clay bowls brimming with squash and corn. As she stooped down to lay them on the ground, her feathered headdress brushed Stephen's face. Her blue eyes glanced up and she giggled. "Pardon me." She bowed before hurrying off to join a group of squaws about a bonfire by the chief's lodge.

"She speaks English," Stephen said, picking up an ear of corn.

"She should," Ryan said. "Evening Star's father was a trapper and one of the men with Lewis and Clark."

Stephen kept glancing at the squaw throughout their meal. So much so that Ryan found it mildly amusing. *So, the young buck is after a little doe.*

Ryan ate with gusto, licking his fingers when he finished and sitting back and listening to the old chief tell his tales of the last buffalo hunt and the problems they had been having with the Sioux and Cheyenne. He looked over at Stephen who appeared taken with the squaw who kept refilling his bowl. Stephen didn't even glance at what she gave him; he just ate every morsel and kept smiling at her.

"Ya like the food?" Ryan asked, patting his own belly.

Stephen nodded, his gaze riveted on the squaw. "Not bad, it's a little like rare beef."

"And how 'bout the dog?"

Stephen's head jerked up from the meal. "What? What dog?"

"Why, that young squaw gave you dog. It's an honor since it's her prize pet."

Stephen's hands flew to his mouth. "I think I'm sick."

Ryan looked at the untouched meat in Stephen's dish. "You better finish it or you'll insult the medicine man's granddaughter and he's of a mind to put a curse on you."

"Balderdash! I don't believe such things."

"No?" Ryan leaned over, and whispered, "I heard one fella made him so wrathful, he turned him into that owl over there."

Stephen glanced up at an owl, which winked then spun its head in a circle before lighting from the tree in a flurry of white wings as it pounced on something in the grass. "You don't expect me to believe such utter nonsense?"

"'Course I do," Ryan said with a sly grin, "but a better reason like Reverend Wade here said is to keep the peace. You insult these people and we might as well kiss our scalps good-bye." *Damned fool*, Ryan thought, watching as Stephen gobbled the remainder of the meat.

Reverend Wade, looking stalwart as ever, pulled a small leather book from his pocket and handed it to the chief. "The Good Book."

"A holy book," Ryan said with a shrug.

The chief's mouth became a flat line. "Want guns." He pointed to Ryan's rifle.

Ryan lovingly rubbed the barrel of his gun. "This here's my friend. And I ain't about to part with it, but the farmers might trade a few guns for food and blankets."

"Our mission is to save souls," Reverend Wade snapped, "not to bring guns."

Ryan slapped his knee. "Hell with saving souls!" He leaned toward the minister. "We need to save our hides. If they want to trade a few guns, we get to keep our scalps."

Reverend Wade put his book away, drew a handkerchief from his coat pocket, and mopped the beads of perspiration from his brow.

A stocky squaw snatched the handkerchief from his fingertips. She felt the delicate lace trim then wound the cloth about her wrist, giggling, and showing it off to the other squaws.

"Looks like you pleased the chief's first wife," Ryan said.

"First wife?" Reverend Wade gasped.

"Yeah," Ryan said, "the Pawnee men can have a dozen or so wives. That way the women help each other. Keeps the men busy too," he said, elbowing Stephen and pointing toward a girl rocking a papoose on the ground. "That one there is his wife."

"No!" Stephen's eyes widened in disbelief. "She's but a mere child. She couldn't be more than ten or eleven."

"More like twelve," Ryan said.

Reverend Wade glanced at Stephen. "You see they do need some religion, more than guns."

"They want guns more than your religion." Ryan stood and spoke in Pawnee to the chief, asking him how many guns. Then Ryan told the two ministers, "He said the village has been raided over and over again. The old, the sick, the very young—who cannot go hunting—are victims to the raids by neighboring tribes. He wants guns to defend his people."

"And what if they use the guns on us?" Stephen asked.

"Trust me," Ryan said with a nod toward the chief, "they're harmless 'less you make 'em mad. And in return they offered to lead us across the river a bit. That squaw you've been gawking at all night, Green, is going to guide us. She and her brothers are coming with us awhile."

Stephen's face lit up as he glanced over at the squaw. "Maybe Ryan is right," he said to Reverend Wade. "We don't want trouble with these people. They do seem friendly enough."

"Very well," Reverend Wade said. "To keep peace I'll ask the farmers if they can spare some guns."

"Good." Ryan told the chief what the ministers had agreed on. The chief nodded and stood with his arms clasped across his chest. His braves stood also. They bid farewell to Ryan and the ministers as they left the village. Evening Star hid behind a tall oak tree and waved at them before going back to the village. Ryan untied his horse and mounted, noting Stephen's slow movement and somber expression.

For all the dandy's schoolin', Ryan mused, *he's got neither grit nor sense. He wouldn't have given the guns up except for that squaw, so much for his preaching on sin.* In all his years, Ryan knew enough preachers who'd bed a squaw or any other woman as much as look at her. The thought that the young minister tried to keep company with Johanna only inflamed Ryan's contempt. "What's a matter, preacher?" he asked as Stephen leaned to one side of his chestnut mare.

"I'm sick!" Stephen's face turned ashen in the moonlight as he held his belly.

Yanking the reins of his own horse, Ryan rode to Stephen's mount and grabbed the reins from Stephen's hand. Leaning to one side, Stephen upchucked his supper. As soon as he came back up, Ryan returned the horse's reins. "That wasn't dog meat but buffalo tongue."

Stephen looked ill again. "Hold on a moment." Ryan steadied Stephen's horse.

When Stephen finished vomiting, he wiped his mouth. "Let's get the hell out of here."

"That was a foolish trick to play, Mr. Majors." Reverend Wade gave Ryan a sharp glance. "Stephen gave you no cause for trickery."

"Only having a bit o' fun." Ryan peered at Stephen. "Don't worry, Reverend Green, you'll live."

~ * ~

In a dream, Ryan saw Chet's lifeless body lying in a pool of blood. As he bent to peer at Chet's face, the eyes opened and the mouth spoke. "What did you say?" Ryan asked the corpse. A thunderous laugh rumbled from behind him. Ryan turned to face the soulless black gaze of Grizzly Dugan.

"Ryan! You boys left me to die... remember the grizzly and remember me... I ain't done yet." A giant brown bear stood behind Dugan. Its claws cut across Dugan's face. This time, Dugan struck back with a hunting knife. He slashed the bear's throat, and it fell with blood gurgling from its open mouth. Ryan stared at the grizzly's face. The thick shag of fur changed to creamy soft skin and the bear's features became that of a woman's—Johanna Wade. Her eyelids opened and she stared at him through teary eyes. Her eyes shut and her head tilted to one side. He lifted her up, calling her name over and over. "Come back, Johanna."

"Ryan?"

Lilacs, the scent of lilacs filled his nostrils as he awoke. Johanna leaned over gaping at him.

"Ryan... what do you want?"

"I was dreamin'." He grabbed her hands. "You're all right!"

"Of course, I'm all right." She pulled her hands away. "Why shouldn't I be?"

"Uh? I had the queerest dream." He pulled the blanket to his waist then stood. "You were in it."

Johanna arched an eyebrow. "I was?" A crimson tinge edged up her cheeks.

It dawned on him that she had not seen him without his shirt on and his pants lay in a heap on the ground.

"Excuse me," he said, reaching for them. The blanket slipped a bit revealing his flat middle and hips.

"Oh, dear." Johanna spun on her heels. "I thought you called me for a reason, that you wanted me for something."

I certainly do, he thought, admiring the swish of her hips as she turned around again and the slight swell of her breasts as they strained against the gingham dress. If she knew her effect upon him, she'd blush a shade redder or faint.

"Naw, I called your name in my dreams." Not wanting to reveal the true contents of the dream, he said, "It was a silly dream something about meeting a bear." He buttoned his cloth shirt. "It's going to be a hot one today."

"Don't let the heat keep you from your lessons."

What the hell is she clucking about? "Lessons?"

"Yes, I'm calling the children for their lessons after our noon stopover. I'll expect you there."

Ryan rolled his eyes. "Heck, I got more important stuff to do... I got to clean my gun, fix the Johnson's wagon, and go back to the Pawnee with rifles..."

"Rifles? Is that wise?"

"Whatta ya know of trading?" He rolled his blanket and packed it on his horse.

"Nothing really—but it seems unwise to give rifles to the Indians."

"As I told your Pa and the preacher, we have to trade with the Pawnees. They're giving us blankets. Evening Star, the medicine man's granddaughter, and a couple of braves are coming with us."

At the mention of the young squaw whom she'd befriended, a light blinked on in Johanna's mind. Evening Star's youthfulness and attractiveness must have caught Ryan's attention. How could it not? Hadn't Evening Star mentioned Ryan as the trapper who suggested that she teach the Pawnee children? *So, that's it.* Johanna put two and two together.

"Ah... now I see why you're trading. It's a ruse to bring squaws with us on the trail." Acid dripped off each word.

"Heck, no. They're guides, Johanna, that's all. They want to help us; it's a gesture of friendship."

"Oh, go on." She twisted the hem of her apron. "Go on back to the Pawnee village. Forget about the lesson." She started walking away but he caught up with her.

"Johanna, listen to me. I'll meet you and the children later."

"Don't be too late or we won't be there."

Ryan watched her determined stride and the rhythmic sway of her hips as she headed back toward the center of the circled wagons. *Sure is gonna be a hot one today*, he thought, pleased by Johanna's show of jealousy. "Reckon we can all use a cool dip in the river."

~ * ~

Hours later, Ryan stripped naked and dove into the chilly river. After a brisk swim, he floated on his back and took in the serenity of the green hillside. White and yellow daisies, Black Eyed Susan, and wild violets dotted it. Glancing up at the sky, he thought of the blue in Johanna's eyes. The sudden heat in his loins had him rolling over into the chilling water again to ease his discomfort. Later, he sat on the sandy banks and studied the lush plant life. He compared Johanna to a wildflower, beautiful on the outside yet stubborn enough to root in the wilderness. She has to be stubborn, he realized, to get through times ahead. When he held her, he sensed that like a wildflower, she longed to grow freely, and that aroused a certain desire in him. More than the carnal one, he wanted to free her from the constraints she placed on herself.

He recalled his last time when he came here as a trapper. A lot had changed since then. His only kinfolk, Chet, had been murdered and the burden of caring for Chet's family fell upon him. He had sworn to right the wrong. *Vengeance is mine.* He swore it to his nephew Samuel and he felt it in his heart.

Once he was dressed, Ryan removed a razor, mirror, and soap from his satchel. He put the mirror on top of a huge rock, lathered his face then began to shave. His whiskers pulled and hurt as he ran the blade across his face, and he nicked himself.

"Damn it!" He wiped the blood with his fingertip then shaved around his mustache. Pleased with how he looked, he splashed off the lather at the water's edge.

He stared at his reflection. He did look like Chet, he realized, though he had a few years on him and a few wrinkles around the eyes; still, they could have passed for twins. The familiar lump rose in his throat as he thought of the last time he and Chet went hunting. The very last time... ten years before... the time he met up with John Dugan.

John Dugan came out of Canada like a storm front, blowing things his way. He spoke French and English and got around real well with the Indians. Except for his gruffness, Dugan appealed to women with his dark looks and strength. An excellent hunter, Dugan hauled in more beaver hides than any other trapper west of Missouri. He enjoyed brawling and drinking as much as Ryan did at twenty-five, but to brawl with Dugan meant to risk losing your eyes, ears, and teeth.

Until that summer so long ago, Ryan realized, Dugan had been a half-way decent sort. Odd how men change. Ryan and Chet had set their traps along a stream and waited while Dugan sat back at camp. The next thing, they heard Dugan's screams. When they rushed back they found a grizzly bear twice the size of a man ripping Dugan. Dugan fought him off then lost consciousness. Ryan shot at the bear a split second too late. The bear took a second victim—Dugan's wife— a Bannock squaw. They found her mauled, half-eaten body floating in the stream the next day. Dugan was left with his face hideously scarred. Unable to deal with the loss of his squaw, he took to hard drinking, telling all who'd listen that the two Majors brothers were to blame for not doing more to save him and his squaw. Few believed the half-crazed man. Ryan and Chet had a fair reputation among their fellow trappers.

"Dang it, all," Ryan muttered. "He's gotten rid of Chet. He wants me dead, too. But why now? Why after all these years?"

I should have been there to save Chet. The pain welled within Ryan, gnawing at his marrow. *Chet should have lived. He had a family. What have I got?* He tucked the toiletries back into his satchel, picked up his rifle, and set back to camp.

~ * ~

Johanna sat beneath a willow tree with the children circled around her. Despite her wide-brimmed bonnet, her fair face burned from the strong sunlight. As a rider came toward them, she squinted up through her hand. Ryan sat astride his horse, peering down at her. He pulled off his coonskin cap and tucked it into his belt. "Thought I heard singing," he muttered, getting down and walking closer. He tied his horse to the tree and sat.

"This is for you." She handed him one of the McGuffy readers then glanced at the cut on his chin. "You're hurt!"

He rubbed his chin a little too hard, causing the wound to bleed. "Ain't nothin', just nicked myself shaving, that's all."

"Here." She handed him an embroidered handkerchief. "Wipe your cut. It looks painful."

"Thanks." He peered at the monograms on the cloth, and wondered what they stood for. He was about to ask when Sally McPherson called Johanna. "Here's your hanky," he said, handing it back to her.

They listened to Sally reading aloud. When she finished the passage, Johanna turned to him. "It's your turn." She held the book out to him. He touched her hand and held it in his as he leaned close to her ear.

"You'll have to help me," he explained. Slowly, Ryan read the words on the page with Johanna correcting his effort. Once he paused, a look of annoyance crossing his eyes, then he continued as she nodded for him to go on reading. "This is harder than wrangling with a mad bull," he said when he finished the page.

"Ah," Johanna said with an encouraging smile, "but so much the better. You learn quickly, Mr. Majors."

"Yes, he does." They both looked over at Evening Star.

The admiration in her eyes as she stared openly at Ryan irritated Johanna.

"Thanks," he said. "I don't want to read no more, you finish it." He handed the book to Johanna.

Fanning her warmed face a moment, she sighed. "Very well." She continued the passage. Having finished, she dipped into her leather satchel and brought out several slates. "This time we'll have no face drawings," she announced.

Sally giggled at this. "Here, let me help you." She distributed the slates to the children. Since there were not enough, they had to share with a partner. Evening Star quickly came to Ryan's side to be his partner.

"Hmpf!" Johanna fumed inwardly, but remained calm on the outside as she continued the lesson. "Let's try copying these letters." She showed them the alphabet.

Ryan appeared oblivious to the young Pawnee squaw's flirtations as she brushed her arm against him in attempts to write on the slate board. Smiling up and fluttering her dark lashes, Evening Star 'oohed' and 'ahhed' at every attempt Ryan made with writing words and sentences.

By the end of the lesson, Johanna felt fit to be tied. She snapped her lesson book shut. "Class is dismissed," she announced in her sharpest tone. The children looked a bit taken back. Even Will's eyebrows arched in surprise.

"Aw shucks, we was havin' fun."

When Johanna glançed at his slate board, she knew why. Will had sketched a drawing of the Pawnee brave, Lone Eagle, falling from a horse after an axe had been planted in his skull. In a small corner, he drew a girl's face. The girl had ponytails like his cousin Martha. *So, that's what's in the little ruffian's mind*, Johanna thought. She pulled the slate from his hands. "This is for writing, not drawing, Will. If you want sketch material, tell me so. I'd be happy to provide a budding artist with tools for pursuing his or her career."

"Aw hell, who needs this," Will said. He stood, hands on hips. "I ain't comin' back." He ran off, leaving Johanna flustered.

She shook her head. "That was unkind of me," she said to Sally.

"It ain't a loss, Miss Wade," Sally said. "I'll take the young uns back for you."

"Thank you." Johanna watched her walk away. Evening Star had gathered her group and headed off, leaving her alone with Ryan—the source of her aggravation.

"I behaved dreadfully with Will," Johanna told him. "I don't know what got into me. I usually have more patience with the children."

"Don't worry, woman," Ryan said, gently taking her by the shoulders. "Seems to me you've got more than enough to do around here. Let me help you."

Johanna packed up the supplies in the carton. "I will talk to Will again; I don't want him to give up. And Ryan, the same goes for you. Don't give up, you did fine today."

"Having a teacher like you helps." He gave her a smile that lifted her spirits. "Teaching heathen and pups like Will can't be easy. I'd rather be skinning cougar hides than dealing with that band."

Johanna packed up the supplies in her satchel and the small wooden carton. She thought of reminding Ryan of his pledge to help teach her to shoot. "Ryan, when can we..." A loud rustle from the nearby bush interrupted her. "I see you have an admirer."

Evening Star stood, partially hidden by the leafy branches.

Ryan shrugged. "Pesky little thing! Why, she's young enough to be my daughter!" He laughed aloud, but Johanna simply scowled. "Don't tell me you think she'd mean anything to me?"

She peered down at her hands. "I suppose I shouldn't care."

"But you do." He pressed her hands in his. "And that gladdens my soul." A loud bang resounded nearby. Evening Star kicked the side of a tree trunk, tears in her eyes, and ran off.

"Evening Star," Johanna called after her.

"Let her go," Ryan said, pulling Johanna closer. He massaged her tense shoulders and kissed the top of her hair.

"Wait a moment," Ryan said, breaking away. A frown creased his forehead.

"What?"

"I've no secrets from you," he said, "but tell me yours... who is RM?"

"Who?"

"You know damn well who. The R M right here on this cloth." He pulled the fabric from the top of the carton of supplies. "You carry this everywhere you go... like a trophy."

"R M." Johanna sighed. "Robert McEntee? I've told you about him. He was my fiancé back in Boston. He died of scarlet fever. It's been a few years now." She stood, leaning against a tree. "I can't seem to part with the wretched piece of cloth; it's like a part of the past."

"God, you are beautiful." Ryan cupped her chin.

"Not like Evening Star."

Ryan lifted her chin. "More beautiful than a thousand evening stars... more than a field of wildflowers on a summer's day... more..."

She held up her hand. "Stop, Mr. Majors," she said, with a soft chuckle. "Your words are kind, but..."

"True. Oh, I can't write fancy poetry like RM did. But tell me, Miss Wade, did your RM make you feel this way." He kissed her. A long, full-mouthed kiss that sent her head spinning, her heart racing, and left her breathless when his lips left hers.

No, she knew the truth; Robert McEntee loved her but never made her feel the way she did at this moment in Ryan's arms. She leaned against his chest for support, lest her own legs give way and she fall.

Ryan studied her a moment. "For all his learning, your precious RM must have been a damn fool! Yankees!" He shook his head. "Maybe we both learned some lessons today." He turned, lifted the carton, and headed down the path toward camp with a very puzzled and flustered Johanna trailing in his wake, her lips still damp from his kiss.

Twelve

A Lesson at Scott's Bluff

"What's wrong, Johanna, you look upset? Are you ill?"

Johanna shook her head. "Tired, that's all. How about you?" Slowing up the mule team, she glanced at Mabel's face. Fine lines around Mabel's upturned mouth and round eyes testified to her age. Cutbacks in food rations caused a loss in her weight. Swollen hands and reddened skin told of the effects of the sun and the harshness of weeks of travel in a wagon. Despite these, Mabel kept up her spirits. The physical change shadowed in comparison to that of the spirit. Johanna realized that her aunt, whom she once considered eccentric and delicate in nature, could be a woman as strong and resilient as herself—a woman who'd weather whatever came along. Perhaps the years of living in wait for a sea-faring husband had toughened Mabel. Then again, she reasoned, the new interest in Seamus McPherson, a rugged farmer, brought out another side of her aunt. Mabel's sudden coughing fit made Johanna ask again, "Are you all right, Auntie?"

Mabel breathed more easily, and mopped beads of perspiration from her brow with a fringed handkerchief. "I'm fine, dear, just a tad sore from all this sitting." She put a hand on her niece's knee. "And the knocking about on this hard wooden seat doesn't help matters. My bottom feels as hard as a rock."

"Good day, Johanna," Ryan called as he rode alongside their wagon. "And Mrs. Foster, how are you?"

"Fine and dandy, Mr. Majors." Mabel waved back. "Thank you."

"Good, see ya'll later." Ryan spurred his horse onward.

Mabel tapped Johanna's arm. "So, you're on friendly terms with Mr. Majors?"

"I don't know what you mean." Johanna yanked back on the reins, averting a ditch.

The last thing she needed was for the wagon to get stuck in the mire. *Oh, why can't I concentrate today?* With a harsh crack of the whip above their heads, Johanna spurred the mule team onward.

"I think you do," Mabel said, "I'm not blind, Johanna. I've seen the way you look at him. As your aunt and the chaperone for this journey, I feel I have a say in who you court."

"Then you have nothing to say," Johanna snapped, "because I'm courting no one. Furthermore, you have no..."

The sound of splitting wood interrupted the rest of what she was about to say. Startled, she glanced at the side of the wagon, praying it wasn't coming from the axles. "It's not ours," she said with a sigh.

"Look! Over there." Mabel pointed to the McCrorys' wagon as it swerved and heaved toward one side. One wheel rolled right off the wagon bed and careened down a gully. Even from where they sat, Johanna could hear the occupants screaming for their lives.

"My dear God!" Johanna screamed. "They need help." She cracked the whip over the mule team, sending them at lightning speed toward the lone rider poised beside a stream. As she drew alongside him, she handed the reins to Mabel and stood. "Ryan!" she shouted. "Come quick, the McCrorys are in trouble... their axle broke!"

The McCrorys' four-mule team dragged their prairie schooner along on three wheels. Cargo fell out the rear, crashing and splitting as soon as it hit the ground.

"Damn it!" Ryan slapped his horse's side and galloped to catch up with the McCrorys' runaway wagon. Frank McCrory was wrestling with his wife for the reins.

Within arm's length of the wagon, Ryan grabbed the sideboard, launched himself off Daisy, and climbed onto the wagon. He quickly moved to the seat, grabbed the reins from Ellie's hands and pulled the mule team to a stop. Ellie and Ryan flew to one side of the seat. Ryan held Ellie by the waist. "Are ya all right?" he asked.

She nodded, shaken and crying, then glanced about. "Where's Frank?"

Ryan looked over at the river's edge. His horse nuzzled the limp body of a man lying face down in the dirt. "Frank?" Ryan jumped down and ran over to the prone man.

Ellie climbed down and rushed to her husband's side. As Ryan turned him around, she gasped. "Oh, no, Frank! Frank!" she screamed, fingering the bloody gash on his head.

Fourteen-year-old Jason McCrory ran over, followed by his six-year-old sister, Peggy Sue, and their eight-year-old brother Jed. "Is Pa alive?" Jason asked.

A quick glance showed Ryan that Frank's neck had not been broken. *Thank God for small miracles*, he thought. He felt for a pulse and heaved a sigh of relief. "Frank's injured bad, but he's alive."

The other wagons halted. People streamed out, gathering around the McCrory family. Johanna, carrying her bag of medicinals, hurried over with Mabel following behind her.

Johanna patted Ellie's shoulder. "I'll do what I can, Mrs. McCrory," she said. She checked on Frank's wounds. The torn pants revealed an ugly and deep gash along his thigh. Blood spurted profusely from the wound. Johanna tried not to vomit as she ripped up the hem of her skirt and applied pressure to the gaping wound. *Be strong*, she told herself. "Here, hold this awhile," she ordered Mabel as she searched for some salves.

"Please save my Frank," Ellie begged.

"Pa's gonna be all right, Ma," Jason said. "Ain't he, Mr. Majors?"

"Yeah, he's breathing," Ryan said.

The McCrory wagon crashed to one side.

"Oh, my God!" Ellie screamed. "The baby!"

The cries of an infant mobilized both Ryan and Johanna who rushed to the wagon. In a cradle tied to the backboard, an infant kicked furiously and cried at the top of its lungs.

As soon as Johanna lifted the baby, it stopped crying. With a deep sigh, Johanna snuggled the baby, checking it for any injury. Miraculously, the child appeared unhurt and smiled at her. "Praise the Lord," Johanna said to Ellie, "your child is safe."

"It's a miracle." Mabel cooed at the infant.

Ellie sobbed as Johanna handed the baby to her. "We could've all been killed. I don't know what got into me... I lost control of them mules and that wagon... good Lord... we paid a fortune for it. It should've held up better." She glanced at Ryan. "Thank you."

"I'm glad I reached you in time," he said, wiping his brow with his sleeve. "Your big boys can help me fix the axle and put on the spare wheel."

The children, their faces clouded with horror, peered up from their father's broken body to Ryan. "He'll be fine," he told them. "Miss Wade will patch him up."

"First, help me with Frank," Johanna said. "He needs to be carefully lifted out of this heat and dirt. Don't jostle him too much; he may have other broken bones."

Ryan picked up two branches then took a large blanket from the rear of the wagon. He folded it in half over one branch. He put the other branch on top of the blanket and folded it again. "You've got your stretcher," Ryan said. "Let's get your Pa on it, boys."

When Frank lay unconscious upon the makeshift stretcher, they moved him to a shady spot. Ryan made a lean-to with a sheet from the wagon bed, covering Frank further as Johanna knelt to tend the wounded man's injuries.

Johanna ripped off her apron, shredded it into strips, and used it to apply pressure to the gaping wound, careful not to damage the bone beneath. Ellie stood sobbing behind Mabel. "Auntie," Johanna called, "please get some water to clean Frank's wounds."

Ellie rushed for the bucket on the backboard of the wagon, quickly filled it then handed it to Johanna. Some sloshed to the ground. "Oh, how stupid of me!" Ellie said through tears.

Mabel touched Ellie's shoulders. "Calm down, you're not helping matters." They watched as Johanna wet an apron and used the damp cloth to clean Frank's wounds.

"More bandaging," Johanna said in exasperation. "There's too much blood here."

Both Mabel and Ellie tore off their aprons, ripped them and gave the strips to her.

"Get me those smaller branches over there," she told Ryan. "I'll need to make a splint around this leg." Ryan handed her the branches.

"Come on, Ellie." Mabel hugged Ellie's shoulders. "There's nothing more you can do here. Johanna will tend to Frank. Ryan and the boys will fix the wagon. Your baby is fine, thank the Lord. I'm sure Frank will be fine too. Come on to my wagon, I'll fix us a spot of tea."

Grim-faced and clutching her baby, Ellie followed Mabel through the thinning crowd of on-lookers. The ministers met them halfway there.

"Are you all right?" Reverend Wade asked Ellie. "It's a blessing you and your man survived." He nodded to the sleepy-looking baby. "And by God, she's alive too. We've much to be grateful for."

"Yes," Ellie said. "Thanks to Mr. Majors and your daughter." She sobbed into the baby's blanket. Reverend Wade put a comforting arm about Ellie.

"Now, now, it'll be all right, you'll see." He glanced at the crowd of on-lookers. "Go on back to your wagons, folks," he said. "There's nothing more to be done. Be sure your own wagons have no loose joints or nails. And mind yourselves well."

~ * ~

The fact that Stephen Green had remained silent to one side, his hands in his pockets, didn't go unnoticed by Ryan as he gathered the tools to work on the wagon.

Finally, Stephen took his hands out of his pockets, walked over to Ryan, and asked, "What can I do to help?"

Ryan glanced at Stephen's hands, the kind of hands that had never known hard, physical work, and said, "Ain't much you can do now. Me and the boys here are going to fix up the wagon like new. I wouldn't want you to muss up that fine black suit of yours."

Stephen flushed as he eyed Reverend Wade sitting with Mabel and

Ellie McCrory. "You did a fine job, Ryan," he sneered. "You earned your pay today." He turned on his booted heel and stopped mid-stride as someone called him.

"Oh, Stephen, we need you a second."

Ryan peered at Abigail Emerson who sat on a wagon seat, fanning herself. The middle-aged widow's ash blonde hair looked frumpish beneath a pea green bonnet. Too much red on her lips and cheeks made her pock-marked face look dreadful in the full sunlight. "Well, Green, I guess someone needs you."

Since the trip began, Stephen had been at the beck and call of Abigail and her sister Charlotte. Ryan guessed the fact that the widows inherited so much money and donated so much to the mission board played a factor in Stephen's behavior.

The sun heated him as he worked. He pulled off his leather shirt. Beads of perspiration formed upon his muscled torso and ran down his face. So intent upon his work, Ryan failed to hear Johanna's voice as she came up to him. A tap on his shoulder made him gaze down into her eyes that mirrored the blue of the sky.

"Where'd you learn to ride so well?" she asked him.

"I've been riding ponies since I stood as tall as a gopher," he said, "Indian boys learn to ride as soon as they can walk... learn to ride bareback, to hunt on ponies, and to swoop down low from the saddle." He hammered away at the wood, trying to keep a steady grip on the hammer as Johanna watched him work. Even now, her lilac scent filled his nostrils and fired his imagination with the possibilities of what he'd do if they didn't have a crowd of people gathered about. He missed a nail, cursing as the hammer smashed against his thumb. He growled, threw a sharp glance at Johanna, realizing that he'd scared her a little. He put the axle in place with Sam McCrory's help. Then he wiped his grease-covered hands on his pants.

"Those hands need bandaging." She touched his bloodied fingers. "Come," she said. "Sit down on that stump over there and I'll bandage them."

He sat, grinning at her. "Guess I tore them up good rescuing the wagon. No one said it'd be easy leading this bunch of greenhorns."

"Hold them steady." Gripping his hand, she cleansed the wounds with a salve of witch hazel on a sheet of cotton, rubbing the palms on up to the fingertips. He bit his lower lip as the medicine stung his cuts. Her touch soothed him as she gently wrapped a bandage around the palm of one hand, crossing in the middle and tying it around at the wrist.

"If you made it any tighter," he snapped, holding the hand within his other, "I couldn't move my hands at all. Why I wouldn't be able to take a piss neither."

"At least they won't get infected," Johanna said, closing her medical bag with a snap. She knew what those hands could do... gentle touches that sent her soaring or firm, strong hands which could overpower a runaway wagon. "I'm glad you're all right," she added with a smile.

Frank's moan made them gaze around at the tree. They ran to the lean-to. Frank's eyes opened as he stared around. "What happened? Where am I? Where's Ellie?"

"Don't move," Johanna warned him. "You've been hurt. I took care of you but your leg is broken." She turned to Ryan. "I'm going to get his wife. Ellie would want to be here with him now."

"Ellie! Ellie, leave go the reins!" Frank shouted.

Ryan knelt down beside him. "You're all right. Ellie, you, the baby... are all right."

"Thank the Lord," Frank said then shut his eyes again, moaning incoherently.

"It's all my fault," Ellie muttered as she sat and kept vigil by her husband. "I had to be so stubborn and insist on driving the team. Frank had been complainin' all day of tummy troubles. He drank some of that bad water."

Johanna patted Ellie's back. "Don't torture yourself. You did what you thought was best. Trust in the Lord."

"Amen." Ellie clutched Johanna's hand then went back to tending her husband. "You're an angel, Miss Johanna. You've been so good and kind, like that man of yours—Ryan Majors. That's a good man ya got."

"He's not my man," Johanna snapped then added softly, "We're nothing more than friends." She lowered her gaze, fearing that her eyes would belie her remark.

"Oh, I see," Ellie said. "Shame, he's a good man though. Hard to find the likes of him round these parts. I have a sister in her forties who's still looking for the perfect man... ain't no such critter. My other sister worried all three of her husbands into an early grave, now she's looking for her fourth. I lucked out with Frank; he's one in a million, yes sir."

Ellie's endless chatter made Johanna's head throb. She rubbed her temples and tried to be patient with the woman; after all, she'd almost lost her husband and her child. Having finished with Frank's bandaging, she looked up and patted Ellie's hands. "I'll be by in the morning, Mrs. McCrory." She stood, wiped the salve from her fingers on her dress and walked to her wagon.

She hadn't walked twenty feet when she overheard an argument between Ryan and Stephen. *What's the problem now?*

"And I say you're pushing us too hard, Mr. Majors. Look what happened here!" He pointed to the McCrory wagon.

Ryan looked up from applying grease to the mended axle. "I ain't responsible for the roughness of the trail. Wagons gotta be looked after." Ryan stood, facing Stephen. "From now on, I'll be sure everyone takes care of their wagons. Lot o' mules need to be reshoed."

"Thought you knew this territory," Stephen said, "like the back of your hand."

Ryan felt tempted to use his hammer to pound a bit of sense into Stephen's head.

"Damn it." He put the hammer down. "This here was an accident. If you're gonna be a yellow-bellied tenderfoot, ya ain't gonna get out o' here alive."

"Is that a threat?" Stephen stiffened. "Because if it is, I can see to it that you're let go from your duties with us."

"Oh, yeah... and who the hell will lead these people?"

"I will," Stephen snapped.

"Stop it!" Johanna ran up to them and glared at Stephen. "Stop fighting like a bunch of school boys. We need Ryan more than he needs us. There's no way we'll make it to Oregon without him. Frank McCrory will come around soon and his family will be fine. We can't stop for every sick or injured person, or we'll never make it to the Willamette."

"Well put, Johanna," Reverend Wade said, joining them. "I knew there was a lot of sense in your head." He turned to Stephen. "She's right, we move on in the morning as Ryan suggested."

"Good." Ryan put down the hammer. "It's been a long day. My sore hands are beginning to ache." He turned and walked off without looking back.

"Wait!" Johanna called after him. "Wait for me. I'd like to check those bandages again."

"Johanna..." Stephen held his hand out, trying to stop her, but she ran past him.

Ryan peered at Johanna in surprise. "You needn't follow me, I'll be fine. You patched my hands up too tight; I got to remove this bandage."

"Let me." Unwrapping the cloth, she poked at the dry wounds. "At least there's no pus, no sign of infection. You'll live. I only hope Frank McCrory will. He ran a fever tonight and he drifts in and out of consciousness. Poor Ellie has her hands filled with the children."

"It must be tough on them. The McCrorys are good folks. They were neighbors to my brother Chet and his family. In fact, they raised a heap of money to bury Chet. I hate to see bad things happening to good folks."

"So do I," Johanna murmured, leaning closer as she tied up the bandaging. "Is that too tight?"

"No, but it's a dang nuisance holding the reins with these on." As his gaze swept the length of her, he smiled. "You're an angel of mercy, all right. It's amazing what your touch can do to a man."

A small sigh escaped her lips as all thought of remaining detached collapsed like the bed of a broken wagon. "Uh, yes, well... I try to help where I can."

"Why, Johanna, your face is as red as a ripe strawberry. But those lips are sweeter than any fruit I ever tasted." He leaned forward.

She felt his bandaged hands grabbing her about the waist. "Now, Ryan, you should take care with those hands..." As his lips met hers, her pulse thudded wildly in her ears. The sound grew louder as he deepened their kiss. When he stopped, holding her at arm's length, she sighed and gave him a dreamy smile.

What was it she came to ask him about? She couldn't remember. The pistol. That's it; she recalled that she wanted him to help her learn to use a gun. *God, am I crazy? I can't even spend a minute in this man's presence without yielding to his touch.* But who else would teach her to shoot a gun. She wiped her lips then stepped away. "I've something to ask you..." she began.

A devilish grin lit his face. "Anything... I'd move mountains for you."

"I'm not asking for that much," she said with a soft chuckle. "Um... Ryan, will you..." Her voice trailed off as she thought she heard her aunt calling her.

Ryan pulled her closer. "That was a fine speech you gave on my behalf."

"Stephen has a lot to learn. And you do know a great deal more about the wilderness then he does."

"I especially liked the part about needin' me."

"It's true." She felt heated again as his chest grazed her tautened nipples.

"You need me?" He stroked her cheek with his thumb and she felt herself trembling from head to toe.

"Cold?" he asked.

Not in the least, she thought; on the contrary she felt hot enough to explode. She glanced away at the river; its calm dark waters rolled on, gurgling over the rocky bed. She felt like that river, changing and moving onward in life despite the pain of the past. A quick glance back at Ryan's dark gaze filled her with the realization that yes, she did need him, in more ways than one. In her heart, she knew he was more than a trail guide, a hired hand, as her father and Stephen referred to him. He was so much more.

"I... I... I need to ask a favor from you, Ryan."

"Yes?" His face mirrored her desire. "What do you want of me?"

Another kiss, she thought, answering instead, "Remember our deal? You agreed to teach me to shoot."

Ryan playfully smacked his forehead. "Darn it, I plumb forgot." His brows creased in a frown. "What about your Aunt Mabel and the ministers? Would they approve?"

"For your information, I'm not a child..."

"And well I know," he said, grabbing her by the waist.

"Ryan, I'm serious."

"So am I."

She pried his fingers loose, noting the agony on his face as her nails accidentally dug below the bandaging. "Oh, I'm sorry, Ryan. I didn't mean to hurt you."

He straightened up, letting his arms hang at his sides. "All right, Johanna. I'll keep my promise and teach you as soon as we reach Scott's Bluff."

"That won't be for weeks!" she protested. When he didn't respond, she added, "Oh, I'll wait. But I'll hold you to your promise." With that, she left him, fearful that she'd lose her self-control if he kissed her again yet wishing she could stay and savor the taste and feel of him once more.

~ * ~

August 1848

Six weeks later the wagons reached the red sandstone outcropping known as Scott's Bluff, having traveled several hundred miles alongside the Platte River and passing unusual geological marvels named after what some thought that they resembled. Courthouse Rock and Chimney Rock with their sandstone spires had been camp stopovers. When they at last reached Scott's Bluff, they had grown less enamored of the hillside.

By late afternoon, Johanna sat in the shade with the children. They had ended their lessons with Ryan's account of how the rock formation received its name. Johanna admired the way Ryan captivated the children with his tall tales of life in the wilderness and the myths his mother's tribe told to explain things. But the story of a man named Scott who took ill and had been left to die while his companions headed westward was one Johanna disapproved of. Ryan told the children that a search party came for Scott a year later only to find his bones on the bluff. "Wolves ate up his flesh," Ryan said. The wide-eyed children glanced at one another.

A little girl cried, "I'm not gonna die out here and be left for wolves, am I?"

"Naw," Ryan reassured, patting her head. "Not with me to guide ya."

"Anyway," he continued the story, "Scott was so mad after he died, that his ghost haunts the hillside. Folks seen him wandering around looking for that search party and coming into camps, begging for food."

"Stop it!" Johanna stood. "That's enough. You're frightening the youngsters, Ryan."

"It's the honest truth." Ryan crossed his chest with his fingers as children often did to prove the merit of their words.

"Are ghosts real?" Jan asked.

"No, honey," Johanna said, "but when someone dies, their soul goes onto heaven if they led a good life and to hell with the devil if they didn't."

She elbowed Ryan, "Now see what you've done. How will their parents ever get them to sleep tonight? They'll be petrified of ghosts and wolves and..." The howl of a coyote made everyone jump.

The smaller children ran to Johanna's outstretched arms. She hugged them, scolding Ryan. "Don't ever scare them like that again. There's enough to worry a body without talking about ghouls and ghosts."

"Ghouls?" Ryan looked puzzled. "Ya mean girls?"

"No, ghouls..." Johanna laughed at him, "Ghouls are like monsters."

"Monsters?" Jed gasped. "My Pa said that he'd seen something called a Loch Ness monster back in the Highlands."

"Children, there are no ghosts nor are there monsters," Johanna said, trying her best to calm everyone down. "Let's get you back to your parents before they get scared."

"Aw heck," Will McPherson said. "We'll tell 'em that old Scott's ghost done got us and we had a heck of a time gettin' away."

"Hush up," Sally snapped, poking his side with her elbow.

Will pulled her hair and they began rolling around, wrestling one another.

"Children! Children!" Johanna held her hands up for silence. "Don't fight. It's getting very late. We must get back."

After they had dropped off the last child, Ryan continued to walk Johanna about camp. She admired the wide-planed features of his handsome profile, the strong jut of his chin, and the way the light of the moon bathed his head and shoulders in its silver glow. She thought about his family, his brother's widow and children, whom he left in Missouri. Then she wondered why Ryan had never settled down. He would have been a good father; the children warmed to him and welcomed the opportunities when he joined them for lessons. He proved to be a quick learner. She felt proud that she'd helped him in some way. Ellie McCrory's words haunted her now. You can't find men like him anymore. Was it true? From the rumors she'd heard about him, Ryan didn't seem likely to settle down with any woman. Yet, why did he bother with her? She knew that he thought she was beautiful, she read the longing in his eyes whenever he came near her. Deep down, she wanted him to want her the way she had come to want him. Rumors aside, she felt Ryan was the most courageous and kindest man she'd ever met.

When they reached her wagon, she leaned against it a moment and looked up into his dark eyes and smiled. "You've come a long way with the reading, Ryan. In fact, I'd say you're one of the best pupils."

He grimaced a moment then smiled back. "Well with you as my teacher..."

His hands came toward her, but she moved away. "And I've waited over a month for you to keep your promise." She glanced about, secure that no one else would hear them. "You will teach me to use the pistol?"

"Yes, I will, soon as I get time. If you hadn't noticed, I've been busy."

I have noticed, and I've missed your company. "Yes, I know. We're all busy. Well, goodnight." She felt him lean over, close enough for a kiss. He backed away suddenly at the sounds of footsteps. Mabel approached and gave them a broad smile.

"Goodnight, Mr. Majors," Mabel chirped. "I guess we'll be up bright and early."

"Yes," he said with a nod toward Johanna.

~ * ~

"Are you off to see Mr. Majors?"

Johanna dropped her tin mug, which clanked loudly as it hit the ground. Could Mabel read minds as well as tea leaves? "What makes you think that, Auntie?"

"Oh, a guess, that's all. I've noticed the way you smile a lot more lately whenever Ryan Majors rides by our wagon. And I did see you talking to him last night after you brought the children back. In the past two months there's been a spark in you I've never seen, not even with your precious Robert. I can tell you're getting fond of the trail guide."

"Oh, you can? Well, as a matter of fact, I'm going over to lend Ryan a book. I've been teaching him to read. With the other children, of course, and he's doing quite well."

"Other children?" Mabel tapped her niece's wrist. "My dear girl, Ryan is no child."

"I'm well aware of that. And neither am I, so if you'll excuse me." She brushed past Mabel and went to the wagon. Rummaging inside the blankets, she found a small cloth-bound book then lifted the lid of a tiny walnut box. She took out the pistol inside, dusting off the barrel with a rag, then stuck it into her apron pocket along with some bullets.

Ryan lay curled in a heap beneath a dust-covered blanket. He had such a serene look on his face, Johanna hated to wake him. She stood a moment studying his wide-planed features and the strong, broad expanse of his shoulders. As he turned in his sleep, she could see the wisps of black hair along his muscular chest. He grinned even in his sleep and she wondered what or whom he dreamt about. Putting those thoughts aside, she bent down slowly and tapped his shoulder.

Ryan's eyelids snapped open, and in one smooth move, he rolled over, grabbed his rifle and crouched, aiming it ahead. When he saw it was Johanna, he lowered his gun and said, "What the devil do ya think you're doin'?"

"Good morning to you too."

"That's another thing ya gotta learn. Don't go sneakin up on a fella when he's sleepin'." He stood.

"Why? What would you do, shoot me?"

"No, not you." In one quick move, he pulled her close and touched the curve of her face, traced the top of her lips and smiled down on her. "Never. Pretty as a wildflower."

Half expecting a kiss, Johanna felt a pang of disappointment. "Mr. Majors, I'll get to the point."

"Which is?"

Johanna pulled the pistol from her pocket and held it up for him to see.

Ryan snatched the gun away. "Don't... don't ever go pointing that thing at me!"

"You promised to take me for target practice when we arrived at Scott's Bluff. We're here now, so let's go." She put her hand out for the gun.

Ryan examined it a moment. "Fancy one at that. Where'd ya get it?" He handed it to her then quickly pulled on his leggings and his buckskin shirt. He followed her down the dirt trail as she explained.

"It's a Colt revolver. It belonged to my uncle, Captain Foster. He bought it years ago from a man who lived in Patterson, New Jersey. Back in Boston there seemed little need for it, but out here. You understand."

Ryan led them to a grove of walnut trees. "There's a spot over there. We can use the walnuts for targets."

When they reached the trees, Ryan stopped. "Watch me." He loaded his rifle, aimed then shot a walnut clear off the branch. He reloaded and shot again. "Let me try your pistol." Using her gun, he shot again. This time he knocked several nuts from the tree. "Your turn," he said, handing the pistol to her.

"It's too difficult." Johanna gazed at the tree. "How can I ever hit anything so far away?"

"That gun o' yours can reach a couple o' hundred feet. Ya got to train your eye to see them nuts."

As he placed his arms around her shoulders, she could feel her heart racing. Then his cheek grazed against her own, tingling her soft skin. She concentrated as best she could until his legs got closer to her own. She felt his arms brush against the sides of her breasts as he helped her get a steady grip on the revolver. "Now cock it," he said.

"What?" She tried to remember where she was as she eyed the nuts in the tree and aimed the gun.

"Hold it up higher." He moved her hand. "That's good. Now relax." He massaged the ridge along her shoulders.

Relax? How could she as his fingers worked their magic on her back and shoulders? Spirals of warmth moved along her spine. She steadied her hands, and aimed at a thick black walnut. Ryan placed her fingers on the trigger. "Ya got to pull this back when I say so."

He waited a moment then said, "Now pull!"

As she pulled the trigger the gun went off, sending her backward. Ryan caught her before she could hit the ground. With his hand resting on her hip, he said, "Let's try again."

She moved from his grasp. "Darn it! I told you they're too far. It's too difficult for me."

"I thought readin' was difficult too." Ryan helped her steady her aim. "But you taught me otherwise. Now if I kin learn to read, you kin learn to shoot."

He had a point, Johanna thought, and tried harder to concentrate, though it wasn't easy with him hanging all over her, making her nervous. Ryan helped her to reload the pistol. It took several more tries before Johanna finally shot one walnut. She shot a few more times and felt so excited she jumped up and down with the pistol in her hand.

"Hey! Watch where ya aim that thing." Ryan grabbed the gun. "Ya done all right today. We'll come back tomorrow afternoon."

They walked and talked under a canopy of leaves from the trees edging the dirt path. Fleet-footed squirrels scurried out of their way, racing up the trunks after one another. A brown bear sat scooping honey from a bough, ignorant of the couple's presence.

"He's harmless," Ryan reassured Johanna as she braced herself against a tree with the pistol pointed at the shaggy carnivore. "It's grizzlies that ya gotta watch for."

Johanna caught her breath as she tucked the pistol back in her apron pocket. "I hope we don't meet any." She continued to walk. "I feared the shadows outside my tent, that's why I wanted to learn to use this gun. Mabel wouldn't understand."

"You're wise to learn."

He stood in front of her now. "You done good, Johanna." He held her hands in his for a moment. She felt as though she could spend all day staring into his warm brown eyes.

"Thank you for the lesson, Ryan." She dropped her hands from his.

"You're welcome. We'll meet again tomorrow."

Tomorrow! She could hardly wait until then. She felt feather-light as she headed toward camp with the image of Ryan's smiling face in her mind.

The next day, as Johanna walked to the meadow, she thought there was something exciting about the forbidden. She knew her father would not approve of her being alone with the trail guide, let alone being taught to use a weapon. Given her provincial upbringing, she knew full well that meeting a man in the woods, no matter how innocent the matter, would have been frowned upon in polite society. But Ryan was no ordinary man. Nevertheless, she quickened her pace and headed to the area where she had her lesson the day before. This time she packed a picnic lunch in a basket.

When Ryan spotted the basket, he smiled. "Ah, food. The way to a man's heart... and I'm hungry as a bear."

"Now wait a moment." Johanna shooed his hands away from the

basket. "You have to work with me first, the target practice, remember?"

"You won't let me forget," he said with a laugh. He rubbed his hands together. "Come on, woman, we'll go shoot a few nuts."

As they walked into the meadow, Johanna noticed how the trees cast them in their shadows; sunlight filtering through the leaves painted patterns on the ground and on Ryan's buckskin garments. She inhaled his scent of leather along with that of the damp earth. She longed to run barefoot through the field of buttercups. Now was not the time, she told herself. Instead, she went on to the place they had visited the day before. A bee hovered near her arm, and in shooing it away, she lost her balance and stumbled over a log. Ryan caught her before she landed face down, but her basket overturned, spilling the contents. She retrieved most of the food, but Ryan picked up the red apples and kept one for himself. "Are you all right?" he asked.

She nodded. They continued walking.

Between mouthfuls of the crunchy apple, Ryan said, "Tasty... Are you tempting me, Eve? Is this the forbidden fruit?"

"No, you silly goose," Johanna said with a soft chuckle. "One of the farmers gave me a barrel of apples for helping his children with their school work. I didn't want to take it, but he insisted, he said he grew them himself."

When they came to another downed log. Ryan helped Johanna over it. "A storm must have knocked down trees," he said. "There's a walnut tree over there. Why don't we practice?"

"Sure," Johanna said, placing her basket on the ground.

A few shots later, Johanna managed to knock down a handful of walnuts. She felt proud of her accomplishment as she tucked the gun in her basket. Yet she knew the thrill that coursed up and down her spine had less to do with marksmanship and more to do with the admiration in Ryan's eyes and the way his hands clasped hers as they walked. *I must be nuttier than the trees*, she mused, returning his smile. The very air charged with the intensity of his heated gaze; Johanna felt she'd melt in it.

"You'll make a sharpshooter yet," he said. "Now I'm starved, woman. Let's have our lunch over there."

Johanna stretched the blanket beneath the shade of a gnarled aspen. She lifted the hem of her skirt and sat. Ryan sat opposite, watching her as she removed the food. "Ah, a loaf of bread I fried this morning," she said, breaking it in two and handing him half. "I would have brought a jug of cider but my aunt gave it to Ellie McCrory. Since some of their food fell out of the wagon, we're supplying them with the necessities. I've given them enough apples to make half a dozen pies."

Ryan pulled his canteen out of his leather satchel and handed it to her. "I've got plenty of water and we're near enough to a clear stream to refill our supply."

Johanna unscrewed the cap then drank greedily before handing it back to him. "Thanks." She pulled an apple from the basket and began nibbling on it. Juice dribbled down her chin. When she started to wipe it with a cloth, Ryan took the cloth away from her.

"Allow me." With his index finger, he wiped the juice then outlined her lips.

Passion glimmered in his eyes as he brought his face closer to hers. A lark sung cheerily above them, causing her to look away and sigh contentedly. "It's so pretty out here."

"Sure is," Ryan whispered. "As fair of face as ever there be." He stroked her cheekbones and the bridge of her nose. "Freckled from the sun, prettier still." He kissed her forehead. "In all my years in the mountains, I ain't seen nothin' as pretty as you."

Johanna sighed as he kissed her cheek, her shut eyelids then her nose. Her lids fluttered open and she smiled. "You do have a way with words," she murmured against his chest, leaning into him and listening to the steady beat of his heart.

He sat back a moment, a frown creasing his features. "I don't have fancy words to tell you how I feel," he began, "not like that poet of yours."

"No," she said, leaning against his chest and listening to the steady beat of his heart, "you're not like Robert at all. You're so very... real."

"I am real, Johanna. Come... feel me." He turned her around so they faced one another.

She touched his arms and shoulders then put her hands about his neck and felt the softness of the black tendrils of hair along the back of his head. "Oh, so real."

He kissed her cheek then lifted her chin up and brushed her lips with his.

Swept along by a tidal wave of primal desire, heat coursed up and down Johanna's spine. She wanted nothing more than the touch and feel of him. His name resounded in her head as his tongue darted between her parted lips and entered the cavern of her mouth, exploring it and savoring her. She tightened her grip upon his neck, pulling closer.

Ryan loosened the ties that held her hair in a prim knot. She caught his look of admiration as she shook loose the strands of red hair, letting it cascade down her shoulders and around her face. He sat back, looking at her. Then he plucked several daisies and laced them through her hair. At that moment, she felt like a garden nymph. She giggled at the thought, but Ryan's heated gaze sobered her. He held her hands, kissing them. He tugged on the strands of her hair, sniffing the flowers and sighing. His breath tickled the nape of her neck.

"This is how you should wear your hair—free and flowing—my wildflower."

His lips claimed hers. When she sighed out a breath, his lips trailed kisses along the curve of her throat. Wherever he kissed her, she shivered with excitement. He teasingly nibbled her earlobe, murmuring her name. Then he brought her to a kneeling position, faced her and caressed the swell of her breasts through the cotton fabric.

She willed his fingers to work more magic and moaned when he at last freed the buttons and felt between the clothing to her bare skin. He lightly rubbed the top of her breasts, lowering to the nipples and squeezing ever so gently until they peaked with arousal.

He pulled the top of her dress down, baring her shoulders and breasts. She felt like a goddess being worshipped as he praised her with his kisses and his touch. He suckled each breast as she held him to her.

"Ryan!" she sighed, her mind reeling with the very want of him.

"Here," he said, lowering her hand until it reached between his legs. "Feel what you do to me."

When she felt the hardness between his legs, she drew back in sudden shock. But her curiosity overrode her shock and she touched him again. When he moaned with pleasure as she stroked him, she smiled to herself. "Johanna," he whispered, "I want you. Do you want me?"

"Yes," she rasped, thrilling to his every touch. He unbuttoned her dress then sat back as she stood and slipped it over her head, revealing her chemise and pantalets. He watched with admiration as she undid the chemise, untying the laces before pulling it off. She stood scared yet emboldened as she removed the pantalets.

That done, she stood, naked and heated under his gaze.

She watched in awe as he pulled off his shirt, revealing his tanned, broad, muscular expanse of shoulders, his tight stomach and chest. Then she gasped as he undid the leggings. He stood, tall and regal in his nakedness. Timidly, she averted her gaze from the swollen manhood she had felt and given rise to. He came to her then, holding her and kissing her with more force than she'd ever imagined. He kissed her and caressed her flat belly, massaging and kneading it like dough. Then he touched the soft down between her legs. To her surprise and delight, he began to rub the mound; his fingers moved in and out of her most sensitive spot, sending hot spirals of heat along her abdomen and down to her curling toes. "Oh, Ryan!" she moaned.

Then his lips left hers and he laid her flat as he stretched alongside her. He began kissing her abdomen then moved further down. She arched as he kissed her between her legs. His tongue circled around the mound and then in and out. "Ryan." She bucked in shock then moaned with pleasure and arched her back as his expert touches made her tremble with delight. Wave upon wave of heat coiled up from the point where he licked her.

Suddenly she felt about to explode but he moved away. She cried out in frustration, but he began to caress her again, kissing her belly then on up to her breasts. She clung to him, urging him on. When he moved to her mouth, he parted her thighs with his knees and straddled her. "Oh, my Johanna," his voice came hoarse but husky. "Come with me."

She opened to him willingly. He entered her with a quick and hard thrust. She winced with sudden pain but his lips came down upon hers, silencing her soft sob. He moved back and forth within, making her moan from pleasure as he rocked with her. Tightening below, she clutched him hard and fierce with a crazed desire to keep him inside her. He plunged faster and deeper, groaning her name; an explosion of white stars suddenly burst behind her eyelids.

Together, they rose upward, to the very peak, then came down slowly. Only then did she realize how sore she felt. Opening her eyes, she squirmed slightly, and he moved from her.

His eyes mirrored concern. "Did I hurt you?"

Yes, it did hurt, she thought, but shook her head no as she leaned into him, preferring to savor the pleasure rather than dwell on the soreness. He threw the tail end of the blanket about them then wrapped his arms around her. Filled with a sense of wonder and peace, Johanna snuggled against the damp, muscular contours of his chest. A breeze stirred the branches overhead as she wondered if this was the Garden of Eden and if this was how Eve felt that first time?

Thirteen

An Act of Self Defense

Johanna awoke to the tingle of raindrops on her naked skin. She should feel shock and shame, she thought, as she glanced at Ryan's arm draped about her shoulders, pinning her down, but oddly all she felt was a sense of peace. Even now her body ached to be held once more by her lover. All the puritanical notions she held evaporated in the heat of passion. "Good Lord," she murmured, "I'm a wanton woman!"

Ryan opened one eye then another. He smiled lazily, leaned over and brushed a lock of red hair from her forehead. "Guess we fell asleep." He chuckled as she attempted to pull the blanket over her breasts.

"Don't do that," he said, "I like you buck naked and natural." He caressed the mounds of her breasts, nuzzled each one and suckled on the nipples until they peaked.

Even as the soft drops of rain fell upon her fevered skin, Johanna felt hotter still. When his fingers kneaded her taut stomach and abdomen, she thrilled in anticipation. His lips came down upon hers and she grew heady from his kiss. She felt him playing with the tufts of hair between her legs, once again probing within her, which aroused and moistened her. She parted her thighs as he hovered above her, opening herself to his deep, penetrating thrusts toward her womb. Hot spirals coiled up and down her back and made her quiver as he plunged deeper. She rode on a wave of passion, cresting higher and higher until she felt the roar in her ears and saw the explosion of lights behind her tightly closed eyelids. She spiraled down with him then she lay, satiated, in his arms.

When she opened her eyes, she smiled at the realization of what their bodies could do to each other. She hated to move, but the heaviness of his thigh against hers propelled her to do so. Immediately, the cool air and wet grass around her brought her back to a sense of where they were. *Ah, the meadows...* their spot looked like a garden with white butterflies fluttering amid the daisies and violets. Orange tiger lilies stood like trumpets in the grass. Birds chirped from the boughs of aspens and pines further away. The blue grass had cushioned them. She angled to sit up.

"Where are you going?" he asked, cocking an eyebrow yet smiling.

"Nowhere," she whispered as his lips crushed down upon hers in a swift kiss. She snuggled into his warm, damp chest, allowing the feel of him to envelope her every sense. Daisies tickled her between her breasts, and she laughed, recalling how Ryan had woven the wildflowers through her hair. *I'm a mess, but oh, how wonderful it feels.* As he lay there gazing at her with sweet desire, she stroked his shoulders and arms, feeling the hard musculature beneath the tanned flesh. She kissed his shoulders. Impulse made her run her tongue up and down his arm, then she nibbled on his earlobe.

"Ah, my wildflower," he said, cupping her buttocks and rolling her on top of him. "You've not had enough of me?"

She shook her head, marveling at how well they fit together as he entered her. She moved up and down, feeling him within her and gasping from the heady sensation as he swirled inside her. "Oh, my gosh," she murmured. He caressed her breasts as she arched her back, rocking and riding him to the very precipice of erotic bliss before plummeting slowly back. She collapsed on him, spent at last.

"Oh, sweet love," he said, hugging her and angling her to lie beside him.

Love. The word struck her like a rock. Had he admitted that he loved her? So soon? What had they done? While her body thrilled at his every touch and the rain of kisses upon her face and hair, her mind fought for a sense of decency. "No," she said, pushing herself from his hold. "We must get back to camp."

"Must we? We're not leaving today. Why not stay awhile longer?"

"No. It's nearly suppertime, Mabel will be missing me—surely, you understand." She stood, and glanced down at her clothing, averting the heated stare Ryan threw her way. Despite the fact that they'd become lovers, shyness overcame her and she scooped up the garments and hid behind the nearest tree to dress. As she put on the pantalets, she noted the undergarment had torn—evidence of her carelessness in her hurry to undress. *No matter, I'll fix it once we get back to the wagon. The wagon—oh, what shall I tell everyone?*

Dressing quickly, her mind raced with excuses for their long absence from the wagon party. "I must be getting back... it's indecent..." She rambled on, "no respectable woman would be out in the woods for hours on end... and what would they think of me being here alone with..." She threw him a frantic glance.

"With me?" A scowl darkened his face. "Don't worry, you'll think of something. Why shouldn't you be with me?"

"I know," she said, buttoning up her dress. "I'll tell them we got lost."

Ryan stood, dressed quickly, and rolled up the blanket. He held her hands and stared at her. "Do you think folks are stupid? Who's gonna believe you got lost with the trail guide?" He rubbed the back of his neck. "Naw, if you're gonna fib, make it a big one. Tell 'em that a bunch of Sioux came by and tried to kidnap you. They do that sometimes with white women. 'Course I got here and rescued you." He chuckled at his own joke. "And then, you looked at me as your hero and threw yourself at me."

"I didn't throw myself at you!" she snapped, removing the few daisies from her hair and fingering her hair into some semblance of order. She twisted it into a knot and fastened the length with a ribbon from her pocket. "Ryan," she said, peering over at him as he picked up the forgotten picnic basket. "We can't meet like this again."

Had she struck him with a rock, he wouldn't have looked more pained. "I was afraid you'd say that. Didn't you want me?"

"Yes." She sighed. "Oh, yes, but it's not meant to be."

"Johanna," he said, taking her by the hand, "marry me... we don't have to separate at the end of the trail. I want you."

Taken back by the sudden proposal, she shook her head in disbelief.

"I'll do my damnedest to make a good husband... we can be wed by your father."

"Father!" Johanna said, fingering the top buttons of her dress. In all this time, she hadn't given a single thought to how her father would feel about her with Ryan. No, she had allowed her body to dictate to her. She knew full well that her father would rather see her dead and in a grave than married to this rough-hewn trapper. No, Father wouldn't approve. She already felt condemned as she glanced over at the spot where they had made love. She walked in a daze, clinging to Ryan's hand as they moved down the path. "My father mustn't know about us."

Ryan stopped in his tracks. "So that's it. I'm not good enough for him. And I guess I'm not good enough for you either."

"No, Ryan, that's not true." She gazed into his eyes, stricken by the sorrow she caused him. "Maybe I'm not right for you."

"It's easy for you to hurt me, isn't it? Maybe you should settle down with that young minister. He'll provide the kind of life you want. Not me... I'm a worthless trapper... lived alone so long, I don't know what I'd do with someone like you."

"No, Ryan, don't say that." She was about to admit that she loved him but stopped. She feared what such revelation would do, quickly recalling how Ryan had spent his life up until now. Hadn't Father said he'd found Ryan once in a brothel... that's where he cornered him about leading the wagon party. Some dance hall singer named Molly lived there. How many other women did he have waiting somewhere? He seemed awfully friendly with the Pawnee and Bannock squaws. *Stop it*, she told herself, *that was before... before he made love to me.* "Ryan," she said, coming back to the present moment. "I have to think about it."

"Do so." He went on ahead of her, leaving her feeling cross and miserable.

~ * ~

Back in camp, Stephen met Johanna as she walked behind Ryan. He stared at her as if she wore the loss of her innocence like a badge on her soiled garment.

"What happened to you?" he asked, shooting a glare at Ryan who stopped beside her wagon.

"Nothing, Stephen. I got lost and fell over a log. Ryan helped me up. We had been out walking for awhile. That's all." When Stephen eyed her skeptically, Johanna feared her lie hadn't gone over too well.

"You needn't escort Miss Wade," Stephen said to Ryan. "She's not one of those farm girls or heathen women you're fond of, she's a missionary. Furthermore, she's engaged to be my wife."

"What!" Johanna screeched. "How dare you suggest such a thing, Stephen?" She didn't have to look at Ryan to sense his anger. "Stephen is lying."

Ryan reached Stephen in two strides, pulled him up by the collar. "I ought to crush your bones to a pulp, preacher!"

"Johanna and I go a long way back," Stephen continued, "and you're not about to come between us. So, let go of me or I'll have you packing."

Johanna shook Ryan's arm. "Let him go, Ryan. He's a liar but he's not going to send you away. He can't. We need you here."

Ryan opened his fist and released Stephen. "Get the hell out of my sight."

"Come, Johanna," Stephen called, "Your father has been looking for you all morning. Don't pay any attention to Mr. Majors. He's not worthy of you. He's probably got a bunch of half-breed bastards in every corner of the territory."

"Why, you no-good, yellow-bellied pup!" Ryan slammed his fist so hard into Stephen's chin, he fell against a rock. Stephen lay still, blood trickling from a gash on his temple.

"Oh, now you've done it!" Johanna went to Stephen's side. "Good heavens, Ryan, you didn't have to hit him!"

"He got what he deserved." Ryan glared at Stephen, who began to moan and rub his sore head.

"I'll clean you up," Johanna said, helping Stephen to stand.

She mopped his wound with a rag and made him sit down on the wagon seat. "Will you tell my father that I'm back, Ryan?"

Looking like a dismissed and belittled servant, Ryan backed away from her. "Yes, Ma'am." But before he left her side, he snapped at Stephen, "Miss Wade wants nothing to do with you neither or haven't you learned your lesson yet?" He rubbed the back of his neck. "Aw, heck, I've got my work to do 'round camp."

Johanna's thoughts returned to her moment with Ryan, and she fingered Stephen's wound a little too roughly.

He winced in pain. "Easy there, I've only one head."

"Maybe Ryan knocked some sense into it."

Stephen grabbed her fingers as they probed at his scalp. "You don't mean that, Johanna. What have you got in common with that lout? I meant what I said, he's not worthy of you!"

"But you are?"

"Yes. What's more, it works according to the divine plan. Can't you see us together, working side by side in the settlement? Our children growing up like a well-cultivated garden?"

Garden. The word stuck in her thoughts as she imagined the wildflowers in the meadow where she lay with Ryan, spent and yearning for more of his tender lovemaking. She shook her head. "No, Stephen, I can't. I can't because I don't love you. Surely, you must know that by now." She applied a poultice to his wound then bandaged it with thick wads of cotton. When she finished, he looked as if he wore a turban and she laughed.

"Don't mock me, woman." He climbed off the wagon. "In time you may come to love me. We have more in common, Johanna, then you and that half-breed savage. Furthermore, when he gets what he came for, he'll leave you. Mark my words. A man like Ryan has no use for a lady reared in a proper Christian society."

"Leave me, Stephen." Johanna snapped the closure on her medicinal bag. Her heart sank at his words and she wanted with all her might not to believe them.

~ * ~

"But, Father," Johanna said over supper that night, "I had been walking with the trail guide only because he wanted to show me a few of the edible herbs... he helped me find some for our supper. Didn't you like the gooseberry pie and the prickly pear salad?"

"I'm not interested in your culinary skills, my dear," Reverend Wade said, glaring at her with that look which had made her cringe as a child. He had never struck her as some parents did to their children; it only took that look—that murderous, dark gaze—to make her contrite and well-mannered again. "I'm worried about your being out in the woods with all kinds of dangers and being with a man alone, especially one as contemptible as Ryan, who has no respect for ladies."

"If he's so contemptible, Father then why did you hire him?"

"He came highly recommended as a trail guide, that's why." Reverend Wade scowled and waved his hand as if dismissing further thought on the matter. "Enough about him. Johanna, I needed you today. The McCrorys needed you; the Thompsons with their sick child... all needed you. And what on earth did you do? Take off to pick gooseberries and walnuts with the hired help. Where on earth did you get the walnuts? Surely, you didn't climb up the trees."

Uh, oh, Johanna thought, *now how do I explain the nuts?* "Um, they were a gift," she said, "from Ryan. He shot them down for me." She smiled weakly, hoping to win her father over as she once did in childhood with that please, don't be mad at me expression. It didn't work; her father's face remained a thin, lined granite-like mask.

"Now, Green here," Reverend Wade gestured to Stephen. "...is a fine young man. I wouldn't mind it if you had been out walking alone with him, Johanna. At least, you can trust him."

Johanna choked on a piece of pie. Lord, if he only knew. She peered at Stephen's smug expression.

"And one day, Stephen will take over the missionary work."

Her throat constricted as she gasped for air.

"Johanna, dear, are you all right?" Mabel asked, patting her back.

"Water... please..." Johanna pointed to the bucket on the wagon side.

Stephen stood and dipped a tin mug into the bucket then brought it to her. "Here, Johanna, there's nothing to get choked up about."

Had she a sharp stick, she would have loved to beat that silly expression off his face. She drank the water, feeling better again. "No, I suppose not." She peered at the three people around her. Father could be so blind where Stephen was concerned. Auntie Mabel still pampered her like a child. If only her aunt knew that she'd grown up so much in the last few weeks. She wished she could confide to her aunt about Ryan. She wanted Mabel to know her dilemma, yet she feared that when it came down to it, her aunt would not approve either. Hadn't Auntie been the one to chase away the so-called ragamuffin suitors the Captain brought home for her? Oh, she thought, such misery. Then an even more dreadful thought loomed before her. What of the consequences of what Ryan and she had done? Having thrown caution to the wind in the passion of the moment, she might find herself in a hotter pickle. She could be with child. "Oh, my!" she cried.

"What's wrong?" her father asked.

"My stomach, that's all. I think I ate too much pie. I feel ill."

It gave her an excuse to get away from their stares and their questions. Most of all she needed to think... to think of Ryan's offer.

~ * ~

Johanna couldn't run fast enough. The scar-faced man ran after her. She could feel his hot, reeking breath upon her neck as she stumbled through the brambles scratching her legs and arms. She pushed away the thorny branches, but tripped over a log and hit her head on something hard. She lay dazed and shaken until strong hands pulled her up. Ryan whispered in her ear. Relieved it was him, she turned toward his voice. She screamed. It wasn't Ryan, but the scar-faced man who held her. "No, let me go!" She cried out. "Let me go! Don't touch me!"

"Johanna!"

Mabel shook Johanna's shoulders, waking her from the terrible nightmare and the hideous image. "What?" She gazed around wildly. Her racing heart slowed as she focused on Mabel's concerned expression. "I must have been dreaming."

"What about?" Mabel asked, sitting beside her in the tent.

"That man I saw down by the stream—the one with the scar. I dreamed about him. He chased me through the woods. He tried to attack me." Johanna wiped her forehead. "It was horrid."

"And you fear this man?"

"Yes, I meant to tell Ryan about him but we were so busy."

"Ah, Ryan." Mabel studied her face a moment. "How *do* you feel about Ryan Majors?"

Johanna swallowed, wanting to tell her everything, yet afraid of what her aunt would think or do. Instead, she simply said, "I like him a great deal. I've never met anyone like him before. Even if he's gruff on the outside, he's warm and gentle inside."

"Hmm," Mabel said with a smile, "I thought so. I've been watching you lately, Johanna. You have every sign of falling in love—the glassy look in your eyes, the way you watch Ryan's movement about camp, and the way you've defended him to your father and Stephen."

"Oh, Stephen," Johanna said with a sigh. "He's another matter. I don't love him at all, yet he took it into his head that I would. He wants to marry me."

Mabel shook her head. "That would be your greatest mistake." She patted Johanna's hands. "But you know that."

"Father is so blind to him, thinks Stephen could do no wrong."

Mabel cocked an eyebrow. "Has he?"

"He's tried to corner me a few times, grabbing me in a barn and by the brook we passed. I've told him over and over that I want no part of him, yet he persists. Ever since Robert's death, Stephen has pestered me with letters about the mission. I thought he really wanted to work as a team with my father and me. But now, having seen how he works, I know he's out to run things. But, by golly, he's not going to run my life for me!"

"That's the girl." Mabel hugged her. "Go back to sleep. The sun will be up before we know it."

Johanna yawned and lay down again. "Goodnight, Auntie." It took a long time to fall back to sleep. She listened to Mabel's snores, the hooting owl, and the movement of other nocturnal creatures outside the tent. Raccoons made weird, cat-like hissing sounds as they skirmished with each other. Sally told her they sometimes made the same sounds when they mated. Mated—the word coming from Sally's mouth struck Johanna as odd until she realized that Sally had grown up on a farm. Children on farms saw life close-up, the rivalry between animals as well as the mating. Sally said she enjoyed helping her father with the birth of the calves and sheep. Mating—it sounded so mature coming from the young teenager's mouth.

Mating is what she and Ryan did in the meadow. Now she feared the outcome. She would count the days again until her menses flow, frantic and worried with each passing day. Had Ryan offered her marriage from a chivalrous sense of duty? If so, she wanted no part of his offer. She sensed that he'd marry her if she was pregnant. Her pride would stand in the way of a shotgun wedding. Shotgun—that's what got her into trouble. Slowly, her eyelids grew heavier and she caved into the need for sleep.

~ * ~

The next day, Mabel found the gun. Johanna had been cleaning her clothes by the stream when she heard Mabel calling her. Running to the wagon, she glanced at the pistol in Mabel's hand.

"Forget something?" Mabel asked.

"Where'd you find it?"

"Same place you put it, in the small box. Johanna, I thought you got rid of your uncle's pistol. I know I put it in a box for donation to the seamans' charity. They needed to raise money and could have sold it."

"But I needed it more, Auntie." Johanna took the gun from her aunt. "The Captain wanted me to learn to use it. He said I'd need it in case pirates raided our home on the Cape. I kept it by my bed at night until you packed it away."

Mabel shrugged. "It should have gone to the charity. What does a lady need with a gun?"

"It's for protection."

"From pirates?"

"No, from anyone who threatens my life or the life of my family. I take it with me when I go off with the children."

"And did you learn to use it?"

Johanna nodded. "Ryan taught me. I've got a pretty good aim."

"Ah, Ryan, you couldn't have chosen a better teacher." Mabel smiled to herself as if enjoying a private joke. "I'm sure he'll teach you a good deal."

He already has, Johanna thought. Feeling flushed and worried about what Mabel might read in her eyes, Johanna pocketed the pistol. She picked up a large woven basket. "I promised to take the children berry picking."

"Berries again, I thought you made enough pies to last the rest of the trip."

Johanna chuckled. "No, not all that many. Anyway, we're getting blackberries. Maybe you and I can make a nice jam. Want to join us?"

Mabel shook her head. "I've got to finish mending my garments then I promised to read a little to Seamus and Jan. I'll meet you later, though."

"Very well, it should be fun." With that, Johanna headed off, making the rounds of camp as she called upon the children for their field trip. Eager young faces greeted her at each wagon. Only Molly Fletcher kept her children away, glancing with that haughty look as if Johanna had the plague.

As they made their way to the berry patch, Johanna warned the children not to eat too many berries but save them for pie. "Or else you'll all get terrific tummy aches."

The sun warmed her face and arms as she gathered the berries. The purple juice stained her sleeves. She licked her sticky fingers, thinking about yesterday and how she had boldly tasted Ryan. Honeybees buzzed around the group, sending children into a panic as Johanna shooed the insects away with a flap of her arms.

"Goodness," she said, "there are an awful lot of bees today."

Sally looked at her a moment. "Were you here before, Miss Johanna?"

Realizing what she said, Johanna added, "I scouted the area for the best berries before bringing us here." Since yesterday, she felt she'd told enough lies to suffer eternal damnation, that along with her other sins. "It's beautiful though, isn't it?" She peered at the striped butterflies lighting among the purple-blossomed pinecone flowers. Not far from them stood the aspen where she and Ryan had picnicked. Her skin warmed at the mere thought of how they had lain in the short grass.

She watched Sally leading the smallest children around the berry bushes, and thought she'd be a fine teacher someday. At fifteen, Sally towered over most of the children, even the oldest boy. Despite her tomboy manner, she had blossomed into a young woman. Johanna guessed that Sally's bowed hair and clean attire had something to do with Aunt Mabel.

"That pink ribbon looks most becoming," she told Sally, who smiled.

"Thanks. Mabel gave it to me and said I should act a little more like a lady."

Johanna chuckled. "That's my aunt for you."

Sally began to hum a tune, an Irish melody of some sort that Johanna had heard the workers in the factories back home singing. She smiled then held her breath. Not ten yards away, a young Indian brave, painted black and white on his arms and chest and crowned with a wolf's skull, rode an Appaloosa around in a circle. He appeared to be looking for something, pointing a spear at the ground.

"Miss Johanna!" A small boy hollered, oblivious to the lone rider who suddenly took notice of him and began to shift in his saddle.

"My God, it's Jan!" Sally cried. "He'll get killed. We got to do something."

Without a single word, Johanna felt for the pistol in her apron. "Stay here," she told Sally. She began to move, snake-like along the grass, praying she'd not get Jan's attention too early. As she reached close enough, she saw with horror that the Indian warrior held his bow in one hand and an arrow in the other.

Heart pounding, Johanna jumped up and aimed her pistol on the warrior. "Get down, Jan!" she shouted. The boy glanced at her then began to rush over. "No, get down." She motioned to the ground. Jan lay flat. The warrior took aim at her, his arrow steadied in one hand and the bow in the other. Without another thought, Johanna pulled the trigger. Something cut across her ribcage and she fell backwards in utter pain, then blackness filled her vision.

"Miss Johanna!" Sally cried, shaking her.

Johanna stared at the clouds, wondering if she'd gone to heaven, but at the frightened voice, she turned her head. "Sally?"

The other children crowded around her.

"Miss Johanna, are you all right?" Jason asked.

"Jan? Where's Jan?" Johanna bolted up, sudden pain shot through her and she grabbed her side, fingering a gash. Blood dripped onto her fingertips. "Oh, my gosh."

"You're hurt, Miss Johanna," Sally said, helping Johanna to sit up. "It looks like that arrow cut you a bit."

Johanna touched the wound. It hurt like hell but didn't run too deep. "I'm all right," she mumbled. She looked around at the children, mentally accounting for each one. "Oh, thank the Lord. You're all safe." She got up with Sally and Jason's help, feeling dizzy as she wobbled. "The arrow didn't go into me."

"We've got to get you to the wagon," Sally said.

"Let's go." Johanna leaned on her and Jason as the children followed them. They passed the fallen warrior on the way. Horrified by the sight of the wide hole in his chest, Johanna screamed, "I killed him." She stared at the painted, youthful face. "Why, he's only a boy. I killed a boy."

"Ya killed an Injun," Jason said, "You killed a no good, rotten Injun. I'm glad he's dead." Jason began kicking the body.

"Stop it!" Johanna pulled on Jason's arm. "I... I didn't want to kill him but I had to. He'd have killed us."

"Listen," Sally said, "I hear someone coming."

"Get down by the bushes there," Johanna told the children. "It might be another warrior looking for this one."

Ryan rode up wearing a puzzled expression as he spied the children peeking from behind bushes. He dismounted and walked over, almost tripping over the Indian warrior's body. He looked at Johanna as she came out, supported by Sally.

"What happened to the Blackfoot warrior?" he asked.

"I killed him, Ryan. I killed him." Johanna collapsed in Ryan's arms.

He felt the blood on her dress. "Johanna! You're hurt." He tore off the piece of cloth covering her wound and glanced at the cut. He heaved a sigh of relief. "The arrow didn't cut to the bone, but a few more inches and it would have pierced her heart."

Thanking God he hadn't lost her, Ryan cradled her against himself as he mopped the blood with his scarf. Using her apron, he fastened it into a bandage around her middle to stem any further flow of blood. "You'll be all right," he murmured against her flushed face. Despite her mild protest, he scooped her up in his arms and carried her back to camp.

~ * ~

Hunched over a roaring campfire, Grizzly Dugan stared at the soured expression on the Blackfoot chief's face. Smoke curled up between them as the chief fingered the chain of a pocket watch. Its gold case reflected the flames and the young Pawnee squaw who sat tied beside the chief. She threw a furtive glance Dugan's way then looked back at the chief. John Dugan hadn't had a woman in quite some time, especially one as pretty as the slender, blue-eyed, black haired maiden before him. Her dark, youthful looks reminded him of the squaw he wed so long ago. He needed a woman—too many moons spent alone made him as wild as a moose in heat. The whiskey made him bold. He snatched the watch from the chief's fingers. "Trade ya this watch for that squaw over there."

"Hmm... where you get watch?" The chief asked.

Dugan felt hopeful, lust got the better of him tonight—along with a pint of good whiskey. The latter loosened his lips as he began telling the chief how he robbed a warehouse in Independence, shot the clerk, and took off with the watch, too. "Dang fool got in the way of me and money. Anyone get in the way of what I want deserves to die." He looked over at the squaw again, licking his lips as he rubbed his belly. "Yes, siree, old Grizzly got a way of gettin' what he wants." The chief pushed the watch away. "No want it, want the whiskey and that there." He pointed to the pistol in Grizzly's belt. "You trade 'em and take her." He nodded toward the squaw. "She's too much work. I got plenty wives."

"First the girl goes with me, then ya get the pistol," Grizzly said, standing.

The chief signaled to his braves. Two of them shoved the squaw, pulled her up then untied the rope on her wrist. She spit at one who quickly slapped her.

"Whoa!" Grizzly said, grabbing the girl by the waist. "Don't go hurtin' the merchandise fellas, she's mine now." He pointed the pistol at the chief as he quickly backed away from the two warriors. They followed him to a tall pine where he untied his horse. He mounted the horse and pulled the squaw up behind him. "Here ya go." He tossed down the pistol. As one of the warriors bent down to pick it up, Dugan fired another gun, shooting him in the head. He fired a shot at the second warrior, who fell alongside the first. "Let's get the hell out o' here." Dugan quickly retrieved his pistol then struck the horse's flank, making it gallop at top speed with the Pawnee squaw clinging to Dugan.

~ * ~

It took an hour to reach his hideaway, far enough away he hoped from the Blackfoot and the Pawnee. He yanked the reins, halting his horse. Dismounting, he glanced at the squaw who looked about to bolt. "Ya ain't going nowhere now, sister."

Pulling her down, he held her a moment, feeling her buttocks. She pushed him away, but he caught her by the throat. "Don't go getting no foolish notion that ya gonna git away, cause ya ain't." He brandished a scalping knife by her face. "Understand?"

She nodded.

"You speak English, the chief said so, so speak to me. What's your name?"

Sitting cross-legged on the ground, she lifted her chin defiantly.

"What's wrong? Cat got your tongue?" Dugan made a fire and sat across from the squaw. "Woman like you must have given those Blackfoot a hell of a good time."

She remained silent, averting her gaze from his.

"Hungry? I got a squirrel this morning. I'm willing to share him with ya." He held up the decapitated body of the squirrel, slit the skin from top to bottom, pulled it off then ripped out the guts. That done, he put the mutilated carcass in a pan and roasted it over the flames. "Hmm... smells mighty good don't it?"

"Evening Star," the squaw whispered.

"What's that?" Dugan took the half-cooked meat off the flame and put it on a plate. He sliced it and handed her a piece. She pushed his hand away. "Suit yourself." He chewed the meat, licking his fingers and eyeing the squaw up and down. "You're awful thin, should eat more... but you're all right in the right places." It had been a long time since he felt the tender skin of a young squaw like this. His groin ached with need, but he'd wait a bit. The night was young, and so was she.

He opened his satchel and counted the money from the robbery. "The company don't need to know how much I got here. Right, honey?"

The squaw stared at his scar, shuddering. Women either showed revulsion or pity toward him. "Grizzly bear done this to me," Dugan said, rubbing the scar. "Don't seem right though. My friends left me and my squaw in the woods to die, but I fooled 'em. I killed that bear and cut out his heart. It tasted good." He licked his lips, glancing at the line of cleavage revealed by her buckskin dress. Ripe for the picking, he thought with a sly grin. "Yep, I'd do the same to anybody who crosses me. Aw, don't look away, honey," he cooed, coming across to her and cupping her chin. "I got the grizzly bear in me now... that's how come I got the name Grizzly Dugan. Come on, hon, give us a little kiss."

He lunged for Evening Star, toppling her to the ground. She kicked him in the groin. Screaming, he rolled to one side. She stood, facing him with a defiant look and his scalping knife.

"Why you... How the hell did ya get it?" He backed away from her as she flailed her arms in the air, trying to stab him. "Now, you don't want to get hurt, do you?"

She struck his arm. "Yeow!" he cried. "Don't make me mad." He grabbed the knife away and tumbled her to the ground. She struggled beneath him as his head lowered toward hers. "Kind of remind me of that bear... only friskier." He licked her face like a cat. "You taste good, honey." She scratched him and tore at his hair. He pinned her hands back with his fists. "Got ya now. Ain't no escaping from the Grizzly. Grrrr!" He nuzzled her neck, nipping at her earlobes.

The more she struggled beneath him as he ripped off her tunic, the more excited he became. He squeezed her bared breasts, forced his mouth into hers then splayed her legs apart with his knees. Her naked body squirming beneath him hardened him. He fumbled with the buttons on his pants, kneeling above her. Loosened, he felt ready to charge into blissful release.

Suddenly he felt a blinding pain in his head. "What the...?" Blood filled his vision as he glanced at the rock in Evening Star's hands. "Why you little whore!" He shifted his weight and she squeezed out from under him.

She hit him several more times, all the while, screaming, "Don't touch me... let me alone!"

"You bitch!" He stumbled forward, but he couldn't reach her; his vision blurred then he fell like a stone beside the fire.

When Dugan came to, moonlight had cast a glow on the log where the squaw had been sitting. There lay his satchel. He picked it up and roared with rage. "Gone! She took my money and the watch. Damn the bitch!" He peered at the woods, shouting, "You won't get far, Evening Star. You won't get far with my money. I'll find you. And I'll get even or my name ain't John Grizzly Dugan!"

~ * ~

A black hawk circled the sky. Johanna couldn't help notice that the bird held the same course. She'd been listening to the children's recitation of the multiplication table, and as they droned on, she daydreamed. Not since the incident in the woods had she dared to take them there alone. But today, Mabel accompanied her.

"How do you feel, Johanna?" Mabel asked.

"Fine, Auntie. It only hurts when I laugh."

"I haven't heard you laugh in awhile."

"Hmmm." Johanna hadn't had anything to laugh about in a long while, not since her moment with Ryan. Although she had garnered the respect of the children for her bravery in defending them against an Indian attack, it cost her in that her father no longer trusted her. She recalled the sadness in his brown eyes, the hurt in his voice.

"Had you come to me with the matter of learning to shoot, Johanna," he had said, "I'd have seen that you got lessons. You didn't have to sneak off with the likes of Ryan Majors to learn how to shoot."

Any pleading she did on Ryan's behalf went in one ear and out the other. Even though Ryan had seen to her care after she came in wounded, he hadn't measured up to what her father wanted for her.

She peered at the sky again. "That bird's been circling for some time, I wonder what's there?"

"Stay put, Johanna," Mabel said, patting her hand. "It might be a sorry sight, like the shallow graves ripped apart by wolves."

Curiosity got the better of her. "Stay with the children, Auntie. I'm going to see what's there." She picked up her pistol and moved slowly toward the undergrowth. Thorny branches scratched her hands as she parted them.

"Oh, my gosh!" Johanna bit her lower lip. A woman lay face down on the ground. Her torn garments, covered with dirt and blood, exposed her bruised shoulders and arms.

Johanna walked over to the woman, knelt down and felt for a pulse. *She's alive. Thank God!* She turned her over and gasped. "Evening Star!"

Black-and-blue splotches on the squaw's face angered Johanna. "Who did this to you?"

"White trapper," Evening Star said as Johanna lifted the squaw up and brought her toward the clearing where Mabel led the children in a rowdy sea chantey. They stopped singing when Johanna stopped before them. The young Pawnee woman collapsed at their feet.

Fourteen

Evening Star's Return

"What the hell happened to her?" Ryan asked, eyeing Evening Star's bruised arms and legs and the blood-stained knife in her hand. "Who'd she kill?"

"I don't know. She needs our help," Johanna answered. "Someone tried to kill her."

"Evening Star?" Mabel gasped, shaking her head. "She looks like she's escaped from the devil himself."

"That may be, she's been beaten and battered by some brute no doubt." Johanna helped steady Evening Star, who looked about to collapse.

The Pawnee squaw leaned onto her, whispering in Johanna's ear. "Blackfoot ambush us at the river. They killed the warriors. They will raid our village."

"What did she say?" Ryan asked.

"She said she'd been ambushed by the Blackfoot. The Pawnee guides must have been attacked after they left us. She's worried about her village."

"But the Pawnee went on their buffalo hunts."

"Some stay behind," Evening Star said before collapsing against Johanna.

"Help me get her to the wagon," Johanna directed Ryan. " I must tend to her wounds."

"The Blackfoot must have killed her brothers and the elders,"

Ryan said, as he lifted Evening Star up and carried her to the Wade wagon. "But I don't think they'd let her go like this. She must have fought 'em tooth and claw." He set her down on the ground.

Mabel put smelling salts in front of Evening Star's nose. She came to, staring wild-eyed as she jerked from side to side. "Shhh, child, it's all right," Mabel whispered and cradled her like a child until she calmed down and the light of recognition lit her eyes.

"He beat me," Evening Star said. "But I got 'em." She held up a bloodied knife, which Ryan gently took from her hands. "And got this." She pulled a pouch from her belt, but dropped its contents on the ground. The gold watch glittered in the sun.

Ryan snatched it up. His mouth formed a thin line and his eyes darkened. He rubbed his fingers in the engraving on the case. "CM... Chet Majors." He snapped the case open. "Chet must have dropped it when the shots hit him. He died at noon." He showed Johanna the watch. "See, that's when it stopped."

"Oh, my God!" She took the watch in trembling fingers, noticing a look in Ryan's eyes which she'd never seen before—a look of pure hatred. She snapped the watch case shut then handed it to him. "It's Dugan, isn't it? He's the man you're after."

Ryan rocked on his heels, uttering an incoherent curse before taking the watch.

"He's probably long gone, Ryan." She glanced at Evening Star. "Did you kill him?"

"Cut him good," she said with a wide grin, "He cannot live..." She lost consciousness as Johanna washed her wounds with alcohol.

~ * ~

Reverend Wade visited Ryan's camp site. "Evening Star said a trapper beat her up. A man with a scar along his face. You know anyone like that?"

"Yep, Grizzly Dugan. He's the man done killed my brother and stole from a warehouse back in Missouri. He's the man I'm after, and if he's close by I'm gonna git him."

Reverend Wade held his hand out against Ryan's shoulder. "Now, hold on a moment. Your duty is to our wagon train."

"And to Evening Star," Johanna said, coming up behind her

father. "She's so young and in need of our help. We must return her to her people."

"No," Ryan snapped. "Heck, that's the last place she ought to go. She suspects the Blackfoot of raiding her village. It's too dangerous. Besides, if Grizzly is alive, he's sure to look for her there. No, I'll go to the village before we head out to Fort Laramie."

"Ryan." Johanna touched his arm. "Don't go to the village alone." His dark gaze mirrored the hatred brewing in his soul and poisoning him with the thirst for vengeance. "It could be dangerous."

His gaze softened and a smile curled his lips. "I'll be careful. I'm from the backwoods, remember?"

How could she forget? She lowered her hand.

"I'm glad you still care about me, Johanna," he whispered

Giving her father a furtive glance, she said aloud, "Of course, Mr. Majors, I don't want to lose our trail guide. This wagon party depends on you to make the journey safely."

So, that's how it is, Ryan thought. "Fine, worry about yourselves. I can handle myself and be back sooner than you can skin two jackrabbits."

This reference to her earlier incident with the gift from one tribe quieted Johanna. She put her arm through the crook in her father's elbow. "Come, Father, we've work to do here. I'm sure Mr. Majors will be true to his word."

~ * ~

"So, Ryan is off with that Pawnee maiden again." Stephen chided as they watched Ryan leave camp with Evening Star who had insisted on returning to her village. The sight of the young squaw sitting behind Ryan, her legs parted on the back of the horse the way a man would ride, irked Johanna to no end. She balled her hands into fists at her side.

"It's time to move out, folks," Stephen said, with a glee in his voice. He rode up and down the line of wagons, calling them to move on.

Mabel clutched the side of the seat as they rattled along the trail. "Don't you worry about him... Stephen's pea green with jealousy, dear. Ryan will be back. Have faith in him."

"I do, Auntie. I do." Johanna clutched the reins as tightly as she clutched onto the hope in her heart that Ryan would return. Since their time together in the meadows, she had not had her menses. Not that she was late but it worried her. She prayed her flow would come soon and that she'd not suffer the shame and humiliation of a pregnancy. She counted the days since their coupling as she would now count the hours until Ryan came back to her. *Oh, my love, come back soon.*

~ * ~

Three days had passed since Ryan left the wagon train. Johanna had no interest in the passing scenery, nor did she join the others who went off to look at the natural wonders. All she could think of was Ryan. She sat tense, her spine rigid as a board as she peered out at the unusual landscape. Then she peered up at the sky where ashen clouds threatened another storm. The last one proved so vicious, lightning struck several cows and sent everyone running for cover beneath a rocky ledge. Lightning came in great bolts cracking the sky wide open as sheets of rain fell, forming pools about the wagon train and soaking everyone to the bone. Johanna sniffled with a cold. Mabel complained of an ache in her back and legs.

The children jumped in and out of the puddles, despite the stern warnings from their tired parents. Mud caked everything. Although the women walked with their hems tied to one side, they couldn't avoid the mire nor the manure from the animals. Johanna had her share of muddied skirts each time they broke camp along this part of the trail. They had moved so far from fresh water, supplies had to be rationed. Somehow they had ventured off course. Reverend Wade blamed the storm and held a prayer meeting for guidance. Stephen told Johanna it was all Ryan's fault for abandoning them.

"He'll come back," she said with a cough. "You wait and see." She shivered despite the campfire, warming her cold fingers over the dwindling flames. Her head ached and she excused herself from the others gathered there to rest awhile. Mabel gave up her blanket to keep Johanna warm in the tent. Even so, Johanna shivered beneath the blankets.

The next day, Johanna gave up her seat on the wagon when her father complained of stomach cramps. He sat beside Mabel, who drove the team. Reverend Wade's horse had been tied to the backboard. Johanna walked the trail with Sally. She listened to the talk of the other women who complained about the food and how they couldn't manage to eat another ration of bacon, beans, and fried bread.

"Be glad we've enough to eat," Mary O'Dowd said.

The cry from a baby in a backboard cradle sent a dark-haired mother to the wagon. "I've got to nurse her, we've gone so far and she needs to feed."

"She'll be all right, Kathleen," Mary O'Dowd shouted above the clamor of the wagon wheels. "A mile or so won't hurt."

Johanna listened to the chattering, thinking how burdensome children and babies could be on the trail and wondering how she'd manage if she had a child. They had passed a few wooden markers, symbols of men, women, and children who died along the way. A few graves, dug up by wolves, revealed fragments of bone, clothing, even ribbons from hair. The most disturbing, though, was that of a young child. The grave had been ripped asunder with no remains except for a soiled bonnet and a rag doll. Johanna sobbed at the sight and the thought of the dead who had to be left behind.

What if something had happened to Ryan? The thought that he might have met an awful fate at the hands of warring Indians chilled her to the marrow. She'd prefer to think that he had been held up by the storm. Or, maybe as Stephen said and she hated to think, he'd gone off for good with that Pawnee maiden.

Suddenly she smacked the side of a wagon that passed her. "Damn it, Ryan!"

Sally threw her a shocked look. "What's wrong, Miss Johanna?"

She lowered her gaze then cleared her throat. It hurt a lot and she felt feverish. She held her sides as she stood erect. "I have to sit somewhere."

"Over there." Sally pointed to a fallen tree trunk. "You look so pale, Miss Johanna." She massaged Johanna's hands. "And you're awfully cold."

"I'll be fine." She clutched her abdomen. "It will pass and we'll go on."

But as she said that, rain fell in torrents. Thunder rolled and lightning flashed in brilliant streaks against the charcoal sky. Pieces of ice smacked Johanna's head and sides. "Ouch!" She rubbed her cheek.

"It's hail!" Sally said, "It's a hail storm. We best be getting away from the trees."

The wind picked up a furious speed, blowing the wagon covers like bits of thin paper.

"Stop the wagons!" Reverend Wade ordered, raising his hand high over his head.

"We can't continue in this downpour," he told Stephen. "Prepare everyone to camp and seek shelter beneath their wagons and away from the river. We don't want to be caught in a flood."

Johanna walked with her father from one wagon to another to see that everyone was all right. Most people piled their families under the wagon, hidden from the full lashing of the storm. Others squeezed inside their wagon bed, pushing out supplies in their way. A few daring souls stood and watched in awe as nature put on a dazzling display with bolts of lightning striking distant hilltops and searing trees in half. "It's like the fireworks on the Commons," Mabel quipped as Johanna snuggled inside the wagon bed. She peered down at her niece, and her jaw dropped.

Bundled in every available quilt she could scrounge up, Johanna shivered and clutched the wagon board. "Auntie," she coughed, "I'm... I'm sick."

"Oh, where for heaven's sake is that Ryan Majors? He'd get us to that fort," Mabel said, touching her niece's brow. "My Lord, Johanna, you're burning up. We've got to get you to a doctor."

Fifteen

Pawnee Massacre

Lodges lay in mounds of ash and smoldering rubble. The enemy left bloodied corpses—people and animals lay scattered on the ground, surprised victims of the attack. Bile rose in Ryan's mouth as he witnessed the aftermath of the raid—skulls bared by scalpers, limbs torn off, disemboweled bodies, others hit by arrows through their vital organs. Blood drenched the ground.

Evening Star choked on a sob, her body shaking as she sat behind Ryan. He pulled the reins on the horse, veering away from the stench and sight of mutilation and destruction. His own stomach lurched as they passed a blood-spattered earth lodge where two women stood, mouths agape in a silenced scream from the spear which pierced their mid-section, pinning them to the mud walls. In all his years traveling the wilderness among the native people, he'd never seen so much carnage as that inflicted by the raiding tribe on the Pawnee. He thought of the young girl clinging to him as they rode.

"We can return to the wagon party," he suggested, feeling it safer than leaving her here where she'd be preyed upon by an enemy tribe.

"No," she protested. When he stopped his horse, she jumped down and ran through the village, stumbling over the dead, crying, "Atias! Atias!"

An old man shuffled out from one lodge, dragging a leg behind him. A gaping sore on his thigh oozed with pus. He stumbled over a dead brave whose scalp had been ripped open, landing beside the corpse, with hands outstretched toward the maiden.

"Atias!" Evening Star rushed to the old man's aid. She held him, sobbing into his long white hair. "Oh, great father, what have they done to us?"

"Your grandfather?" Ryan asked.

"Yes," Evening Star said.

Ryan stooped and examined the crust of pus on the old man's wound. "Might be infected." He opened his leather satchel and pulled out a bag of herbs. He sniffed them, satisfied that they had not lost their potency, and placed them on a rock. Using the handle of his Green River knife he crushed the herbs into a fine powder then placed them into the cloth bag. Evening Star stopped Ryan's hand. "Atias will not trust white man's medicine."

"You forget that I am part Nez Perce." Ryan pushed her hand away and laid the powders down. "I learned much from my mother's people." Over her objections and the old man's feeble complaints, Ryan examined the gash, which stretched from the knee on up to the groin. "Looks like a spear slashed him." Ryan glanced at Evening Star.

"Let's get him out of this sun." With the granddaughter's help, Ryan lifted the medicine man and carried him back into the lodge.

They placed him on buffalo hide blankets. The old man lurched and struggled as Ryan cleaned the wound. His incoherent scream of pain echoed in the woods. "Hush, old man, you'll bring a raid on us all."

Evening Star brought an earthen jar filled with chia seeds. Ryan mashed them, mixed them with water to form a paste, and placed the poultice on the old man's sore. The howl of the man filled Ryan's ears as he tried to concentrate on bandaging the leg with the strips of deer hide. Evening Star watched from the corner. Her face was drawn and peaked; Ryan half-wondered if it best to take them both from the place.

He looked over his handiwork then at the squaw. "Your grandfather will be fine, but he must rest. I'll stay tonight. You both come back to the wagon train. I'll make a pallet to drag Atias behind my horse."

"No." Evening Star's jaw set as she lifted her chin in defiance. "We're staying here!"

"Suit yourself." Ryan covered the old man with the blanket. "But he's too weak and you're a woman... how can you fight off anymore raids?"

"I take chance. We take care of the Blackfoot and anyone else who come." Evening Star stood and opened the flap of the lodge.

"You've got true grit, Evening Star. But I ain't about to leave you and your grandfather to fight off the Blackfoot single-handed."

"We'll be fine." Evening Star walked outside the lodge.

Knowing he couldn't change her mind, Ryan followed her outside. Clouds gathered like gray curtains in the sky, and a strong breeze ruffled the air. The stench of death hung everywhere. "Let's bury them," Ryan muttered, looking at the bodies. Flies buzzed and buzzards circled overhead. "They'll only bring the wolves and vermin... and maybe scalpers lookin' for trophy. Best to bury 'em." With that, he covered his mouth with a bandana and took to the grim task of a mass burial. Evening Star mourned these elders and the weak left behind who now lay in shallow graves. After several hours of backbreaking toil, Ryan wiped the dirt and blood off his hands. Evening Star leaned against him, sobbing, and he held her a moment, rubbing her shoulders. She stood away, wailing and flailing her arms.

"Shh." He sighed against her dark hair, feeling like an older brother as he tried to comfort her. Nothing would ever erase the sight of the onslaught, the stench of rotting corpses, and the sharp pain of loss felt by an adolescent girl. *She's so young*, Ryan thought, *yet she's seen the cruelty of men.*

Ryan rested outside, guarding the girl and her grandfather as they slept in their lodge. Somewhere before dawn, he gave into exhaustion and nodded off to sleep.

On the second day, the old man could just about sit up with his granddaughter's help. She gave him the wild berries she'd collected that morning. Ryan changed the bandaging, then he went hunting. It felt good to escape the odor of decay and destruction, to be in the fresh air of the woods. Rabbits and squirrels scurried through the underbrush. A woodchuck sat up, paws in the air, and eyed him with curiosity. *Small game*, Ryan thought, *not enough for an old man and a young girl.* A deer ran past him into the thicket. With sure, quiet movements, Ryan pursued. He had taken the bow and arrow, a gift from Evening Star for helping her grandfather. Now he crouched behind a tree, arrow poised. The deer turned, her dark eyes watching, her ears pointed in alertness. Ryan swallowed the lump in his throat, feeling suddenly sorry for this wild creature. Yet he knew the rules of survival. With the quickness of a skilled hunter, he fired the arrow and struck his mark. The deer fell with a thud. Ryan ran to her, sighed heavily then pulled the arrow from the heart. He stooped and hauled the deer over his shoulders and headed back to the village. Evening Star greeted him with a smile and delight at the fresh kill.

"You'll have enough to eat for some time, at least until Atias is well and you can provide for yourselves."

"My people will return in three moons," Evening Star said. "I have much to do till then. Atias and I will rebuild the village. I can hunt too."

The medicine man stared at Ryan.

"I've got to get back to the wagons." Ryan told them.

"Go," the medicine man replied.

"Well, I'll be danged!" Ryan scratched his head. "You do speak English."

"We wait for our people," the old man said. "Evening Star strong, she get away from trapper and from Blackfoot."

Ryan turned to the girl. "Don't worry none about that white trapper... Dugan. He won't get far from me. If I have to come back and scout every inch of these here woods to find him, if I have to look under every rock, I will turn up that no good for nothing snake! And when I do, by golly, he'll get his just desserts."

"Here." The medicine man pushed a cold clay piece into Ryan's hand.

Ryan glanced in surprise at the eagle fetish then at the man.

"Spirit of eagle guide and protect," the medicine man said before shutting his eyes. His head nodded to one side as he sat rigid, barely breathing.

The old coot died, Ryan thought and shook him. When the

medicine man startled and stared up at him. Ryan sighed. Later, he told Evening Star that he'd leave at first light.

At dawn, Ryan prepared to leave the village. The medicine man stood, supported by both a thick tree branch and Evening Star. She appeared sad as she walked with Ryan. "You'll do fine," Ryan said, and patted her shoulder.

"Stay," Evening Star pleaded and threw her arms about his neck. The supple curves of her breasts pressed against his chest. And he had thought her a mere girl? Another time he'd have thought nothing of accepting her tempting offer. Not now. Not when the woman he wanted waited miles ahead.

"No, I must go." He gently pulled away then patted her head. "It's a might tempting, I must admit, but no. Go get yourself a young buck and make a bunch of papooses. Stay with Atias. I'll send help."

He untied his horse, tightened the saddle then mounted.

"Redheaded squaw is yours?" Evening Star asked.

Ryan chuckled. "Ya mean Johanna Wade?"

Evening Star nodded.

"Don't think so," Ryan said, moving the horse out toward the dirt path.

"You stay." Her voice grew desperate. "Help Atias with medicine. Need more braves. We rebuild village."

Ryan sighed, wishing he had the time to help them and knowing it was better that he leave while he could. "I can't," he said, stopping the horse as she stood beside him. "And the old coot will do jest fine without me. I'll get one of your people to check on you. There has to be some kin at the fort up ahead."

She bowed her head then stepped away. "Go, Ryan Majors. Go with the spirit of the eagle. May you see many moons before meeting the Great Spirit. And never forget this Evening Star."

"I'll never forget." Ryan tipped his coonskin cap then kicked Daisy's flank, sending her into a gallop westward.

As he rode over the dusty terrain and through the gullies, he smiled at the thought of Evening Star's willingness to keep him there. *Gosh, she can't be more than sixteen*, Ryan guessed, *yet she's friskier than a bobcat for a mate*. But he had no need for a quick tryst when the only woman he hungered for rode miles ahead in a covered wagon and God, how he longed for her now. His need for her spurred him onward. He rode through the day and into the night, following the trail of animal droppings and the dry ruts of wagon wheels as they moved along toward the banks of the Platte River.

Fort Laramie towered like a wooden sentinel above the Platte River. There were unpainted wooden houses and two dozen long, adobe buildings. The outpost of the frontier stood as protector and place of trade for emigrants heading west. Ryan sensed the Wades' wagons would have come through the fort, like so many others had done. He rode up then dismounted and walked through the gates. Soldiers in dragoon uniforms paraded in an open square. Their crisp dark jackets and white pants contrasted with the soiled and ragged attire of the emigrants passing through. Ryan scanned each face— looking for the one which haunted his dreams and waking hours. Dirty-faced children in ragged clothes, men and women whose faces mirrored fatigue and trepidation, gawky adolescents who giggled among themselves... young and old, fair and homely—yet none the one he wanted to find. The fair redhead was nowhere to be seen.

Discouraged, he approached the officers' quarters then stopped midway when he spied two black-clad figures in animated conversation with the commanding officer, a heavyset man in a dark, brass-trimmed uniform. Reverends Wade and Green nodded at something the officer said. A familiar face peeked over Green's shoulder. Mabel Foster waved Ryan over. At that moment Stephen turned around, casting a look of utter contempt at him. Ignoring Stephen, Ryan smiled at Mabel and at the Pawnee scout.

"Tom Knifechief," Ryan shouted, rushing forward. He slapped the scout on the back. "You were knee-high to a grasshopper last I seen ya, now you're a handsome ole devil!"

A wide grin of recognition split Tom's face. "Ryan!"

They bear-hugged each other.

"You know this clod?" Stephen asked Knifechief.

"Sure do," Tom said. "He took me hunting with him when I was a boy." He turned to Ryan again. "I'm sorry to hear 'bout Chet. Word spread like wildfire on a dry prairie... hear tell it was some no-account white trapper who shot him."

Ryan sighed. "Yes indeed. A trapper... John Dugan... Grizzly Dugan."

Tom Knifechief's brow knitted before he shook his head. "Dugan, never heard of him."

Reverend Wade stepped between them. "Well, Mr. Majors, it seems you owe us an explanation for being gone so long."

"That can wait, Howard," Mabel interrupted. "Johanna is burning up with fever."

Ryan's jaw dropped. "She's sick?"

Mabel sniffled and wrung her hands as she spoke. "Yes, the commander was kind enough to let her stay here at the fort's hospital. But the doctor can't help her."

Ryan put his arm about Mabel's shoulders. "Take me to Johanna."

"We don't need your help, Mr. Majors." Stephen snorted, poking him in the chest. "You ran off on the wagon train. We managed without you. Knifechief will act as our guide now. Johanna doesn't need your help either. Give her time and she'll get well again."

Ryan glanced from Stephen to the minister. "I can help your daughter, at least I'll try."

Reverend Wade's gaze scanned the sky as he fingered the brim of his hat. "It's in God's hands, Ryan. The doctors did all they could for my daughter."

"They didn't do enough." Ryan pushed past Stephen. "Come on, Tom." He signaled to the scout. "We know remedies these folks don't."

A sheepish look came over Knifechief as he walked with Ryan toward the adobe building which housed the infirmary. "They said you took off on them," Tom said.

"I had to take Evening Star back to her village," Ryan explained. "She'd been attacked by Grizzly Dugan. When we got to the Pawnee village, we found it had been raided. I stayed to bury bodies and help her grandfather, the medicine man."

"The maiden and the old man need help. I must go to them," Knifechief said. Loud footsteps followed him and he turned to find a red-faced Stephen behind him.

"I go back to Pawnee village," Tom said. "My people need me."

"Now wait a moment," Stephen said, blocking his path. "You were hired to work for us. We paid you twenty-five dollars."

Knifechief opened his leather satchel and pulled out a wad of bills. "Here, take it. Don't want your money. I go help my people." He glanced over Stephen's shoulder at Ryan. "You got him. Ryan Majors is best scout west of Mississippi. No need me now."

"I insist Knifechief lead." Stephen shoved the bills back into the scout's hands.

"You insist on nothing," Reverend Wade blasted back. "If it hadn't been for your driving us all day through that wretched storm, my daughter might not have gotten so sick."

The scout tried to return the money to Stephen.

"Keep it," Reverend Wade said, "Go buy supplies for your people."

Tom Knifechief thanked the minister.

"Damn you!" Ryan rushed toward Stephen. Tom blocked him, holding him back as Ryan fought the fierce impulse to break every bone in Stephen's body. Johanna lay sick or worse in the walls within the adobe fortress because of Stephen. *She needs my help now*, Ryan thought. He hoped it wasn't too late.

"Ryan," Knifechief pleaded, "if your woman is sick, let's go to her. Fighting won't do her any good."

Ryan nodded at his old friend. "You're right." He turned to Mabel. "We need onions, lots of them."

She gave Ryan a puzzled glance. "Onions?"

"It's an old Indian remedy," Ryan explained. "And some sage tea might help."

"Johanna doesn't need your heathen cures," Stephen said.

Reverend Wade's hand clamped down hard on his shoulder. "Leave him, Stephen. If Johanna fares from simple remedies, so much the better... it's in the good Lord's hands. Come away now."

Reluctantly, Stephen turned and walked away with the elder minister as Ryan and Knifechief entered the infirmary. Ryan inhaled the scents of rubbing alcohol as his eyes adjusted to the dimness of the log-hewn room.

A lone candle flickered on a table by a small cot. Beneath the sheets lay a woman whose features appeared as pale as the cotton bedding. Her breath came worn and ragged from her pinched features as she lay still. Red hair framed her oval face, providing the only color to the alabaster skin soaked with perspiration. Her hands clutched a small gold cross. Had he not known better, Ryan would have thought she lay absorbed in prayer.

The sight of Johanna's weakened condition made him stumble backward against the door. He, a man who'd seen the remains of an Indian massacre and who'd buried those brutalized victims, could not feel more of a shock at the sight and the thought that Johanna might be dying.

Dying?

"No!"

Ryan bent down and grasped her hands. "She's on fire," he said to Tom Knifechief. "She's burning up with fever. We got to work fast. Blasted, where is that aunt? Go out back, Tom, gather up the onions and herbs then bring them here." Ryan threw the bed sheet off then lifted Johanna from the bed. She hung like a rag doll in his arms as he carried her to the door.

"Where ya going?" Knifechief asked, holding the door for them.

"To the river." Ryan walked out, ignoring the stares and murmurs of soldiers and civilians as he made his way through the fort. *Let them think what they will.* He continued on to the Platte.

Once he reached the river, Ryan laid Johanna down on the grass. She didn't stir as he removed her nightgown. Taking one quick, admiring glance at her smooth breasts, he gently touched her face. Then he pulled off his shirt and trousers. He lifted her again. He waded with her into the ice-cold waters of the Platte. She moaned and shivered in his arms; her eyelids fluttered open as her gaze focused on his. "Ryan?"

"Shh!" he said, holding her close and splashing the water on her fevered body. "I'm here to bring you back to health." She shut her eyes, and nestled her head against his chest until he returned to shore. In her weakened state, she did not resist as he dried and dressed her again. This time, she clung to him as they made their way back to the fort. By the time they reached the fort, she was fast asleep.

Mabel met them at the infirmary. "My dear Johanna." She clasped her niece's hands. "Why, they're like ice."

Mabel followed Ryan to the bed as he placed Johanna in it and covered her with a single sheet. Tom Knifechief came in with a basket of onions. "Mabel, would you boil them for her?" Ryan asked.

"I'll do anything for my niece, Mr. Majors. I do hope you know what you're doing." With that, Mabel left the room, Knifechief following in her wake.

Ryan massaged Johanna's feet and hands. Moments later Tom Knifechief returned with a bushel of leaves. "Sage, will help her." He laid them down on the bed.

"Thanks, Knifechief." Ryan crushed the leaves. When Mabel returned with the boiled onions, he created a mixture of herbs and onions.

"Phew! It smells absolutely dreadful!" Mabel exclaimed.

Ryan listened to Mabel's tale about the misadventures of the wagon train under Stephen Green's lead. He prepared a poultice and smeared it onto a damp cloth.

"So, as you can imagine," Mabel went on, watching him closely as she spoke, "several of the wagons were stuck in the mud from that downpour. And Green, who fits his name, suggested they take off the wheels and carry the flatbeds. How ridiculous! Oh, my." She cocked her head in bemusement as Ryan smeared the cloth onto the soles of Johanna's feet and the palms of her hands. "What will that do?"

"Kill poisons, bring down fever," Knifechief explained for Ryan.

"Oh," Mabel mouthed. "Can I get you some coffee, Ryan? You look tired."

"No, thanks," he said, wiping the mixture from his hands. "I'm fine. I want to stay awhile by Johanna's side. See if there's a change. You go get some rest. Knifechief, take Mrs. Foster back to the wagon train. Some of the men round here can get unruly."

"You're quite a gentleman, Mr. Majors. I mean that in the truest sense of the word. I hope my niece appreciates you." With that, Mabel kissed Johanna's forehead then gave Ryan a peck on the cheek. "Thank you for all you've done for us. We might not show it, but we do so appreciate your help."

A grin tugged at the corners of Ryan's mustached mouth. Days of neglecting to shave showed on the facial stubble he rubbed as he nodded. "Thanks, ma'am." As the door shut behind them, Ryan leaned forward in his chair and grasped Johanna's hands. Her long, delicate fingers, now hardened and callused, fit well in his own. How he loved the woman, he sighed to himself. "Stay with me, don't die," he said softly. At that moment, he became aware of someone in the cot across the way—a soldier.

"Woman dying?" the stranger asked.

"Don't say that," Ryan snapped, then guilt jabbed him as he noticed the man's face had been completely bandaged. A nurse, the first Ryan noticed since arriving, came in and ministered to the soldier.

"He was hit by gunshot," she told Ryan. "Near lost his sight. Thank God, he'll heal."

"Glad to hear that." Ryan dropped his hold on Johanna's hands.

"Your missus should be all right," the nurse said, creasing the white folds of fabric of her dress. She stood tall, round and smiling at him. "Doctor bled her before."

"What?" Ryan stood and cursed aloud, "Don't let any bastard touch her. She's going to heal... without leeches or any white man's medicine."

The nurse shrunk back from his verbal tirade. "Oh, anything you say mister." She rushed from the room.

Hours passed with little change. The soldier in the cot spoke to him, but Ryan paid little attention to him. His sole concern lay before him. For her part, Johanna drifted in and out of sleep.

Exhaustion from the ride overtook Ryan. He caved in to the need for sleep.

Sometime later, the door creaked, waking Ryan. The minister stood, a frown on his face as he glanced in. Mabel came in with him, a kettle in her hands. "Brought some food for you, Ryan." She ladled stew from the kettle into a bowl and handed it to him. "You haven't eaten since you came in, which was hours ago. We've had our supper and wanted to spend time with Johanna."

The aroma of boiled meat aroused his appetite. After he checked Johanna and saw she was no worse, he sat by the table and dug into the stew.

"Thanks," he said with a smile when he finished. The stew tasted good to his empty stomach. He recalled the last time he'd eaten a beef stew—the day he visited his sister-in-law. He wondered how Sara Majors was faring. He owed it to Sara and the children to finish the job so he could send some money home to them. His unresolved feelings toward Sara had suddenly been resolved when he met Johanna. What was it about this New England school mistress, who made him want to hang around and see this journey to its conclusion? She, more than his honor-bound sense of duty to kin, kept him to the course.

Mabel sat on a stool on the opposite end of the bed, took up a skein of yarn from a basket and began to knit. "I told her not to give up hope."

Ryan nodded. "I said I'd return."

"Mr. Majors," Reverend Wade said, sitting opposite them. "I hope this will be the last deviation from our course—you were hired to lead us to the valley." To Ryan's surprise the minister smiled at him. "And we depend on you to do just that."

"I swear," Ryan said as he crossed his chest, "to bring you there. To see that Johanna gets there safely." He looked at the bed.

Reverend Wade stood then glanced at his daughter. "Johanna is stubborn. She looked after everyone else except herself."

"Ryan?" Johanna called weakly.

Surprised, he sat up and held her hands. She tried to sit up but Mabel scolded her. "You're too weak to be up and about. Rest."

"I've rested enough for a month, Auntie." Forcing herself up to a sitting position, Johanna smiled at Ryan. When a coughing fit racked her, Ryan patted her back.

"Your aunt is right," he said. "You gotta rest. Drink some of that broth she boiled for you. It'll help with your cough."

When Mabel handed her a cup, Johanna sipped the tea. "Mmm... it's good." She drained the contents then lay against the pillow. "So, Mr. Majors, you've returned to us like the prodigal son returned to his father."

"The what?"

"Never mind, it's from the Bible. I must help you to read it someday." She looked at the minister. "Isn't that right, Father?"

"Yes, my dear." Tears welled in the old man's eyes. He rubbed his daughter's hands and smiled. "Johanna will make a Christian of you yet."

"Yeah." Ryan smirked. "I'd o' returned sooner but there was a bit of trouble at the Pawnee camp... Blackfoot raiding party wiped out a number of Evening Star's people."

"Oh, good heavens!" Johanna bolted upright. "And what's to become of her?"

"Beats me... she and her grandfather wanted to stay put... rebuild the village. The rest of the tribe is due back in another month or so... but don't fret none. Tom Knifechief is going to check on 'em. I'm sure he'll notify the other Pawnee villages and they'll be fine."

He took the empty cup from Johanna's hand and placed it on the table. He told her how he had found the Pawnee village in ruins and had to bury the dead then tend to the medicine man's wounds. He hoped she'd understand. Finally, he added, "You scared me, Johanna. I thought you was at death's door. But thank goodness, you rejoined the living. We won't pull out for another day or two." He glanced at Reverend Wade. "Give her more time to rest up."

"I've come to check on Johanna," Stephen mumbled as he entered the scene. His smile faded as his gaze focused on Ryan holding Johanna's hands.

"Majors, haven't you done enough harm?" He glanced at Johanna. "Looks like you're better, my dear. But no thanks to that no-account scoundrel."

"Stephen, you're wrong about Ryan." Johanna sat up and glared at him. "He did what he had to do."

"Yes." Ryan tightened his grip on her hand, sensing her need for reassurance.

"Don't tell me that," Stephen snapped. "I learned in Independence you're after a bounty reward for the trapper who killed your brother."

Ryan let go of Johanna's hands and stood, towering over the

minister. He placed his hands on Stephen's shoulders with the uncontrollable urge to crush the bones beneath them, but Johanna's disapproving stare made him back away from the man. "Aw, the hell with you, preacher! I don't need to explain to nobody. I returned and I'm ready to lead ya all to Oregon Territory."

"We can manage on our own," Stephen challenged.

"Now, Stephen," Reverend Wade interrupted. "Thanks to Ryan, Johanna is on the mend."

"She would have mended in God's good time," Stephen said, "with or without that man's medicine."

"Fine job you did without me, Green," Ryan 's voice thundered, waking a few of the sleeping patients in the other cots. Ignoring their groans, he continued, "Hear tell you were the one who insisted the wagons move on through a storm. Two men were struck dead by lightening. Cattle ran off and it took a night to find them. And Johanna here caught a fever so bad she'd nearly died.

Heard you let folks drink from the stream and they got sick. No, you need me, but I sure as hell don't need you. And yes, I do want my brother's murderer. I want justice. And in time, I'll get it." Ryan pushed past Green as he stormed out the door.

The night air chilled him as he stumbled in the darkness. He peered up at the moon. The shadowy features of a grin mocked him. The full moon could make men mad, he'd heard that dozens of times. So could a grizzly bear ripping open a man's face. The image of John Dugan clawed by the huge brown beast lingered in Ryan's mind. He didn't have time to save Dugan from his fate that awful night. He didn't save Chet from Dugan's shotgun. But at least he had saved a lovely schoolmistress and an injured old man.

Nothing would bring his brother back. Nothing. But he'd get his revenge. The reward was for Chet's family. That much of what Green said was true. He wanted the bounty, but not for himself. "Aw hell," Ryan swore aloud. Moonlight cut a path across the palisades, lighting up the gallery where a lone sentry walked. In the distance, wolves howled at the moon. He wanted to howl, too.

His throat felt dry and his temper needed cooling. *Whiskey! That's what I need.* Ryan glanced about the barricade for Tom Knifechief.

He didn't want to sleep yet as too many ghosts of the past haunted his dreams lately. And he didn't want to drink alone. Trappers roamed the fort, a few drunk or carousing with the squaws outside their cabins. *Whiskey loosens the tongue,* Ryan thought as he listened to their singing and chattering. *Before this night is out, I'll learn more about John Dugan's whereabouts and how to find him.* "Vengeance is mine!" Opening his satchel, he pulled out a bottle of whiskey. Holding it up to the moon, he let out a fierce howl.

Sixteen

Fort Laramie

A bugle blasted near Ryan's ear. He jumped up, bumping his head on a wooden post. "Gosh darn it!" He rubbed his head, blinked then recognized where he was: Fort Laramie. As he lifted his blanket, an empty whiskey bottle rolled forth into the dirt path. An elderly woman from another wagon party crunched it under her booted heel then threw Ryan a look of admonishment before going about her business.

"Oh, my achin' head," Ryan lamented as he stood. He grabbed the reins on Daisy then led her out to pasture. He didn't remember having fallen asleep outside the general store. He barely remembered last night, except for Tom Knifechief's dance on the long table in the bar and a scuffle that had broken out between two soldiers. Ryan broke it up but not without having taken a blow on his chin. Danged if he knew why on earth he challenged the men to a drinking contest. He won, of course. The pounding in his head and his queasy stomach proved a hefty price for his foolishness.

Through bloodshot eyes he gazed around the fort. Emigrant men and women were haggling over prices on supplies. Pawnees traded buffalo blankets and beaded necklaces for tobacco or "fire water". Last thing he needed now was "fire water". He swore off drinking for the rest of this trip; he couldn't stand the pain.

"Shoot," he said aloud. A quick glance at Johanna who traded with the Pawnee reminded him of the unwritten rule against alcohol. Last thing he needed was a lecture. He turned around, but it was too late. He heard her call his name.

To his surprise, Johanna grabbed his hand and smiled. "Thank you, Ryan, thank you for saving my life. I heard all about what you did—the concoction and the river. You're a saint."

If she knew the ache in his throbbing temples, she'd think something else. His breath smelled rancid too. He swallowed, before replying, "Aw, shucks, it was nothing."

He waited for the lecture, but instead, Johanna went on in an apologetic voice, "I'm sorry for not trusting you." She released her grip on his hands. "I never believed a single word Stephen said against you."

"I'm glad 'bout that." Ryan huffed, unhitching his horse. "And I'm glad you're feeling better. You had me worried."

Johanna positively glowed with health. A tinge of pink on her cheeks and eyes, which sparkled like sapphires, reminded him how she had changed. Sunlight brought out the gold-highlights in her red hair. It spilled in waves from under her saffron colored bonnet. "My, you look pretty as a picture."

"Thank you." She smoothed the collar of her calico dress. Without a bustle, the simple cotton garment clung to every curve before reaching the top of her booted feet. "I must go now. Father expects me to help with the Sunday service. Won't you join us?"

"No, thanks. Ah, here's the man, himself." He greeted Tom Knifechief.

Tom tipped his cap toward Johanna. "Miss Johanna." He winked at Ryan. "Looks like the preacher's daughter is better."

"Yes, Mr. Knifechief," Johanna said with a radiant smile. "And thank you for your help too."

"My privilege. Now, I go on to Pawnee village. Help my people there."

"Good," Ryan said. "Evening Star could use your help." He shook Knifechief's hand. Ryan watched the scout walk to a tall oak and untie a dapple gray mare then ride off through the trees. He turned back to Johanna. "I've got a favor to ask you. I need to send a letter to my sister-in-law. Would you help me write it? One of the trappers is heading to Missouri and offered to take it for me."

"After all you did for me, I'd be happy to help you," Johanna said, "and I intend to continue to teach you how to read and write."

Ryan sighed. "Aw, heck. When I got time for it, not today." He sniffed the air, seized by the awareness that he needed to bathe, and he bid Johanna good-bye. He might not be a dandy like Reverend Green, he thought, but heck, he sure as hell could smell better than cow dung.

Johanna watched Ryan's tall, lean figure shuffle off to the trading post. *What a strange man he can be! One moment, he's hard as granite, the next gentle as a lamb.* His desire to contact his sister-in-law left her puzzling again over the kind of relationship that might have existed between them. Sara Majors had been no bawdy saloon singer, but simple and of a plain kind of beauty. Perhaps Ryan loved her beyond the way a brother-in-law should love his sister-in-law?

Did it matter? Yes, Johanna realized, it did matter. Like it or not, she had feelings for the man her father had hired... the man who nursed her to health... the man who lit a fire in her very soul.

"I thought that I'd find you around here."

Stephen's voice startled and annoyed her.

"What do *you* want?"

"Your father and I decided the wagons are moving out tomorrow now that the farmers have stocked up and the livestock have had time to graze. You look well enough for travel, so does Sally McPherson."

"Sally McPherson?"

"Yes, she came close to dying."

Johanna lifted the hem of her skirt. "I must go to her."

"Wait." Stephen grasped her forearm. "Your Aunt Mabel did a fine job nursing Sally and the old man. She practically moved into their wagon. Now that would be a scandal. The old widow and the widower."

"Stephen Green!" Johanna pulled from his grasp. "What my Aunt Mabel does is none of your concern."

"This wagon train is my business."

"You're not the leader. From what we've seen, you can barely lead your own horse!"

He pulled on her wrist. "Think, Johanna."

She pulled from his grasp. "Stop your infernal clawing of me."

"Your father is getting old, Johanna. We've got another two months of travel through miles and miles of a lot of desert, prairie, Indian country, and the mountains. Do you think he can survive?"

"You wish my father dead!"

He gave her a sour grin. "No, but I'm prepared for the inevitable. The strong shall overcome."

"You're wrong, Stephen. So very wrong." Johanna swung away. "I'll see to Sally now."

Mabel gazed up as Johanna entered the dimly lit tent. "You're out of bed too soon, Johanna."

Johanna looked past her aunt to the young girl propped on a buffalo blanket, her face contorted with pain and her skin beaded with sweat. "How is Sally?"

"You shouldn't be out of bed," Mabel insisted.

"Auntie, I'm fine. Ryan's remedy cured me." Johanna bent down and felt Sally's forehead. "She's burning up. How long has she been this way?"

"A few days," Seamus answered as he sat in a corner. Worry creased his brow and he sighed. "The mud hole back yonder made her sick, she took with the fever. I don't understand, I skimmed the water for bugs, just the same she got sick."

"Diarrhea," Mabel whispered. "Sally had a terrible case of it. She's weakened from it."

"Johanna!" Sally mumbled as she held out her hands. "I'm dying."

"Nonsense, I need my girl, Sally." Johanna patted Sally's hands. "You'll get better. Who else can I get to help me with the new school? I will make sure you are up and about in no time." Johanna forced back the tears, swallowed hard then turned to Mabel and whispered, "She could have dysentery."

"I gave her bitters and herbal tea and a good broth," Mabel said, "but nothing helped. She couldn't keep anything inside."

"Perhaps Ryan can help her." Johanna smoothed back Sally's hair and whispered, "Don't worry. You'll be better." She nodded to Mabel then left the tent. She'd heard enough tales about travelers coming down with such illnesses as dysentery and fever from mosquitoes that she feared the worst, but she was not about to give into fear. Not when she felt sure that Ryan could help them. If only she could find him. She asked the other emigrants and the captain who stood talking to her father.

"Johanna, you're out of bed?"

She spun around. "See, I'm perfectly fine now. It's Sally who's sick. Have you seen Ryan? He cured me, surely he'll do the same for Sally."

"Oh, well, Ryan is with the Jones's wagon." He gave her hand a squeeze. "Glad you're better, my dear. I'll come by and see the McPhersons in a short while."

Johanna followed the sound of hammering and a man whistling as he struck blow after blow on a piece of wood. Shirtless, with his naked back toward her, Ryan hammered upon a wooden axle.

"Ryan?" Her voice came small beneath the heavy blows of the hammer. She continued to stare at him. Perspiration beaded Ryan's broad, muscular chest and arms. A leather rope bound his black hair at the nape. Observing how his clothes clung to his solid form, outlining the smooth curve of his buttocks and thighs, she thought of what lay beneath the leather material. In a flash, she saw him raw, virile, and masculine as when he caressed her naked body and kissed her in the most private places. Places which throbbed even now at the memory. Her pulse hammered as rapidly as his calloused hands did. Inhaling and exhaling deeply, she finally found her voice again. "Ryan!"

Her shout caught his attention. He wiped his sweated brow with the back of his hand. Gold flecks of light danced in his brown eyes as he peered at her then a grin broke across his face. He put down the hammer and held her by the waist. "What's wrong, are you ill, your face is pale?"

She shook her head. "No, but Sally McPherson took ill."

"What?" Ryan looked puzzled.

"Diarrhea. She's racked with fever and has been bedridden. Auntie's medicinal didn't cure her. A doctor at the fort wants to bleed her."

"Don't let him." Ryan glanced beneath the wagon bed. "That about does it for the axle, Joe."

Joe Walters, a burly, bearded farmer, slid out from underneath and shook Ryan's hand. "Thanks."

Without further word, Ryan followed Johanna through camp. They found Sally propped up on a pillow, a damp rag across her forehead, and Mabel by her side. Ryan instructed Johanna on the treatment—onions and sage mixture for a poultice—then applied it to Sally's hands and feet.

"All we can do," he said at last, "is wait. Time will help."

"And prayer," Johanna said, kneeling down and praying for Sally.

They left Sally in Mabel's care, walking from the wagon toward Johanna's campsite.

"Your cures work wonders," Johanna said, smiling at him. "Sally's on the mend and I feel fit as a fiddle. By the way, I'll write that letter for you."

"Speaking of fiddle, there's a dance tonight at the fort." Anticipation lit his eyes. He stopped her mid-stride, caressing the knuckles of her hands. "Come with me."

"Hmm." Johanna lowered her gaze, warmed by his tender touch as her pulse raced with excitement and the prospect of attending a dance with him. "I don't know." She suddenly remembered her father's warnings and the fact that she would be needed at camp. "There's a revival tonight. I'll have to stay to help father and Stephen."

Ryan squeezed her hand, "Surely, you can sneak time away for me?"

Why not? Her heart asked as she felt its quickening beat. She hadn't been prepared for such a public occasion as a dance. *Yet, there's no harm in going to a dance*, she silently told herself. She'd overheard Mabel telling Seamus about it. They could all go together, that is if Sally could be left in her brothers' care for a short while. "I'll let you know." She gave Ryan a promising smile.

~ * ~

Johanna used the excuse of a headache to get away from one of Stephen's long revival meetings. The whole event of his striking down believers with the spirit made her nauseous. She met up with Mabel and Seamus at the McPherson wagon. Sally sat on the wagon seat with a blanket wrapped around her shoulders. She barked orders to her younger brothers.

"I see you're feeling better," Johanna said.

"Oh, yes, Miss Johanna," Sally called down. "Pa and Mabel are off to listen to the fiddler at the fort. I'm keeping the young uns in line here."

"I see." Johanna chuckled, watching how the boys ignored Sally as they played tag or wrestled on the ground.

"You listen to your sister," Seamus warned Will and the others. "She's got orders to hit ya on the noggin' otherwise."

"Aw, Pa," Will protested, "She's a pain in the..."

"Hush up." Seamus pinched Will's shoulder, "Mind your tongue in front of the ladies, son. And mind your manners too, else you'll have me switch to answer to. Ya understand?"

Will shook his head. "Yes, sir."

Seamus let go of the boy then motioned to Mabel. "Come on, lassie. We've a dance to go to."

"Come on with us, Johanna," Mabel begged.

It didn't take much convincing. Johanna nodded then ran off to her wagon. She changed into a pale blue dress with a green sash and pinned her hair up into a tight knot, allowing loose curls to cascade around the sides.

When she returned to the McPherson wagon, Sally grinned. "You look so pretty, Miss Johanna. Don't she, Will?"

Will gave her a shy smile and shrugged. "Yep, you do."

"It'd be an honor to accompany two lovely ladies," Seamus said, taking Johanna's elbow in one arm and Mabel's in the other. He led them from the circled wagons toward the fort.

"Wait up, folks," Ryan called.

Johanna turned around, stunned momentarily by the sight of Ryan wearing a crisp, white shirt beneath his buckskin jacket. A silver clasp held a string tie around his neck. His dark, shoulder-length hair had been combed back and framed his tawny, chiseled features. Desire lit his eyes as he beheld her.

"You look might pretty, Johanna," he whispered, taking her hand and moving her away from Seamus. "Hey, you got your own gal," he quipped.

They made their way up the slope to the brightly lit cabin that housed the dining hall. The strains of fiddles and a harmonica filled the air with the tunes "Buffalo Gal" and "Turkey in the Straw".

The dining hall held its fill of uniformed soldiers dancing with their wives or girlfriends. A few emigrants danced, and recognizing Johanna and Ryan, they waved. With her aunt as a chaperone, Johanna didn't have to worry about her reputation nor a word about her being unescorted to the fort. She hadn't expected to meet her father and Stephen at a banquet table. The two ministers stood talking to the fort's captain and only took notice of her as she went for a cup of punch.

"That's not a fit drink for a lady," Stephen said, cupping her elbow and moving her away from the table. "I thought you remained back at camp. You said you were ill."

"I had been. I'm sick of your brand of ministry, Stephen. And who are you to fault me? You've come to this dance as well."

"That's different, I'm here on business with the Captain." Stephen dropped his hold on her and stood back.

"I'm sure you are." Johanna sighed. "I came to be with friends. Mabel and Seamus accompanied us."

"Us?" Stephen looked past her to where Ryan stood, leaning against a doorjamb, with his arms folded. "You and Ryan?"

"Yes, we came together."

"Have you no sense of decency, Johanna?" Stephen hissed. "The man is immoral and you'll become one of his many whores. Look at how he favors the captain's wife and those others." He pointed to the three women in full bustled gowns circling around Ryan like moths to a flame. They appeared to be drawing him into their conversation. Ryan chuckled at something the captain's wife said then he looked over at Johanna and gave her a sheepish grin.

She felt her cheeks burn as she turned back to Stephen. "How dare you!" She held her hands to suppress the itch to strike Stephen's face. Taking a deep breath to calm her anger, Johanna walked over to her father. "Sally is on the mend," she announced.

"Good." Reverend Wade nodded. "The captain assured me that his men would help our wagon train through the Indian territory. He'd send a few scouts behind us." He gazed at her dress and smiled. "You do look beautiful, my dear." The music changed to a slow waltz and her father held out his hands. "I'd be honored if my lovely daughter would dance with me."

"It's an honor." Johanna smiled, relieved that her father hadn't been angry about her being there. She held his hands as they approached the dance floor. A surge of pride lit her father's eyes as he gazed down at her. She recalled a time when as a little girl he held her and danced a slow waltz on her aunt's porch. It had been the only time she recalled him smiling.

When the waltz ended, he looked at her and smiled with that same sad smile.

"The music reminded me of your mother." He cleared his throat, tears wet his hooded eyes and he stared away.

"May I?" Ryan asked, coming up to them and peering at Johanna.

Reverend Wade threw Ryan such a fierce look, she feared he'd say no, but to her surprise, her father's face softened into a small grin. "We are indebted to you, Mr. Majors. For what you've done, we're grateful. Yes, you may dance with my daughter, but do be careful. After all Johanna is still recovering from what ailed her." He stepped away, leaving Ryan standing before Johanna.

The fiddler picked up a lively beat. Ryan pulled her into a reel. The wooden floor creaked as dancers clicked their heels and stomped booted feet on its dust covered surface. From the corner of her eyes, Johanna knew one face didn't smile at them. Stephen Green scowled as he lifted a cup of punch to his pursed lips. The liquid spilled onto the lapels of his frock as he drank from the tin cup.

Johanna ignored Stephen's daunting stares, concentrating on Ryan's attempts to teach her to jig. Back in Boston, she'd learned to waltz. It had been years since she'd had a chance to dance. In fact, her last dance had been the night of her engagement to Robert McEntee. Her friends threw a party in her honor. The sudden flash of memory brought tears to her eyes; she blinked them away before Ryan could see them.

"It's warm in here," Ryan said, leading her to the gingham-covered table for cider. He poured two cupfuls, handed her one then led her outside. In the circle of moonlight, they sipped the cider. Johanna choked on her sip. Ryan patted her back. "It's got John Barleycorn in it."

"What?" She put the cup down.

"Whiskey." He winked and held her hands a moment. Rubbing the palms, he asked, "Are you feelin' it?"

She stared into his eyes, feeling lightheaded and knowing full well that the whiskey had nothing to do with the sudden dizziness nor the heat in her shoulders and arms as Ryan caressed them. He looped his arm about her waist and walked with her a distance to a cottonwood tree. There they could still see the fort lit up by lanterns. Yet, they had a measure of privacy. "Ryan, don't trick me anymore. I want to have faith in you."

He looked down at his feet a moment, shamed by her words. "I'm sorry, it won't happen again."

"I've heard that before," she said with a mild laugh.

"I mean it," Ryan said, gripping her close to him. "I won't do anything to you that you don't want me to do. By the way, thanks for writing the letter to my sister-in-law. I couldn't say what I wanted to say, you helped me."

"For some people it's easier to write what they feel inside then say it. I guess I'm that way." When Ryan's face turned serious, she asked, "Sara means a lot to you, doesn't she?"

"Yes, she's like a sister."

"Hmm." She watched his smile return. "No, I think there's more to it than that. Come now, Ryan. You did love her, didn't you?"

"Yes, I did, a long time ago."

"But no more?" She searched his face for clues to his true feelings.

He shook his head. "Not that way. I had asked her to come west, to get away from the farm. She'd have nothing to do with it. She loved Chet, not me."

"Oh." Johanna leaned against the tree, remembering her meeting with the pretty blonde mother and her defense of Ryan at church. "I understand." Deep down, though, Johanna realized that she didn't understand how any woman could turn away Ryan.

"I hope so. You need not worry about me and Sara... what had been is long in the past." He toyed with the curls of Johanna's hair. "I'm no poet, not like that fiancé you knew in Boston. But ever since I set eyes on ya, I'd felt such a stirring down to my very soul. I've never felt this way for any other woman, not even Sara. I swear it." He pulled her to his chest, and freed the knot of hair atop her head.

She felt a hot shiver as she stared into his heated gaze. Pressed tight against him, she listened to the thud of his heart as it pounded within his ribcage. Her own pulse matched the quick tempo when his hands cupped the curve of her breasts. As he fingered the folds of material, her nipples hardened and strained in response. She peered up at him, reading the desire in his face. Moonlight haloed him, making him appear otherworldly as his lips curled into a feral grin. "Johanna," he murmured. "I want you."

She stood transfixed, feeling as if every nerve in her body had been charged. He blazed a trail of kisses along the soft curve of her neck then up to her chin and her forehead. She leaned back until his lips crashed down upon hers.

Her mouth opened to his. Their tongues danced and tasted as their hands explored through the folds of their clothing. "Ryan," she murmured, feeling frustrated by the buttons and ties that came between them. He gazed at her questioningly.

She stepped back, undoing the infernal buttons and ties of her dress. Beneath the cottonwood and moonlight, she pushed off her pantalets, unfastened the buttons of her chemise then stood, bold and wanton, in the shadows watching Ryan. He unbuttoned his white shirt and opened his pants. As he stood partially naked and erect, desire ripped her to the core. He brought her to him. She wrapped herself around him, her nipples grazing the wisps of hair on his chest. She felt his hardness against her thighs and quivered with anticipation.

Ryan massaged each breast then took turns licking each, making the nipples peak in response. She moaned as he licked her shoulders and neck then leaned back against the soft grass. He stretched alongside her, kissing her face and her lips in a frenzy of pent-up need. His fingers played upon her taut abdomen, entwining in the down of hair on her mound before thrusting into her. She arched, opening wider and moistening at his expert caress. "Oh, Ryan," she moaned, pulling his arms so that he hovered over her. "Please don't torture me."

"Only if you want me..." His voice came husky and warm upon her face.

"Oh, yes. I want you!"

With a soft chuckle he leaned over, parted her thighs and entered her. His hard shaft thrust deep but slow in circling motions, which caused her to feel peaks of ecstasy. She felt the tightness of his buttocks as she pushed him deeper still, hearing his groan of pleasure as he rode with her on a wave and rocked with her in that timeless dance. White-hot sparks burst in her mind's eye then she lay still, spent and satisfied. Too soon he moved from her. They lay awhile listening to the sounds of the woods: the crickets, the peepers, an owl's hoot, and the howl of a lone coyote. The howl rattled Johanna. "Don't fear," Ryan said, easing her back to the blanket of grass. "She's looking for her mate, asking the moon to help her find him."

"I hope she does," Johanna said with a dreamy smile as she snuggled against Ryan.

"That's the great bear." Ryan pointed out the constellations. "And the little bear is over there."

"Ursa Major and Ursa Minor," Johanna said. "My uncle taught me about the constellations. He used the stars to guide his ship. Over there is the North Star. You see how it forms a tip at the handle of the Little Dipper." A devilish urge made her run her fingers along him, feeling the hard contours of his abdomen and his member still damp from their lovemaking.

"Woman," he growled, "keep that up and I'll have you again."

She giggled, warming to the notion of causing such arousal in a man. She lay back, allowing him to caress her breasts and trace kisses along her shoulders. "It's so peaceful here," she said, glancing around at the silver sheen of moonlight along the woods. "I can understand why you love it so much."

"That I do. There's nothing better than sleeping beneath a blanket of stars on a clear night." He kissed her lips, while his fingers did marvelous things to her. When the kiss ended, he straddled her. "I can only take so much," he growled. He entered her and she was ready for the charge as she widened for him. Warm and wet, she moved with him this time. A rocking to and fro, up and down, and whispering his name over and over until the trembling stopped.

When he slid from her, she felt sated like a peasant who had been granted the finest from a feast. "Oh, my love," she cried aloud. He smiled and held her to him. Never had she felt such peace. Nestled beside him, she slept.

The sound of leaves being crushed awoke Johanna to a new day. Dawn, a crimson ribbon on a gray sky, brought the cold light of reality. She glanced at Ryan who looked so peaceful asleep with his arm wrapped about her waist. She nudged him, but he didn't waken. For the first time she marveled at his mustache, dark and thick above his lips. Those lips did wondrous deeds, she thought in amusement. She shivered, grateful that some time during the night, Ryan had placed his thick buckskin jacket over her... so thoughtful of him. She pulled it up to her chin and nestled again for awhile. The sound of people talking startled her. Then she realized it must be later than she suspected. "Ryan," she said more loudly, "please get up, we must leave."

A branch snapped in the distance, followed by footsteps. Was someone coming? Johanna rose and dressed quickly. She nudged Ryan's shoulder. "Wake up."

"Uh?" He rubbed his eyes, smiled at her then pulled her down.

"No, we can't do this now. Someone is coming."

Ryan bolted upright. As he scanned the woods he adjusted his clothing. That done, he lifted his rifle then took Johanna's hand. "Let's get the hell out of here."

"Ryan, I've been gone all night. What will people think?"

"Tell 'em the truth, tell 'em you were here with me."

She shook her head. "I can't do that."

He held her. "God, Johanna, I've wanted you. Even now I want you. I want you forever."

"Forever... that's a very long time."

"For this life. Marry me."

She stiffened, dropping hold of his hand. "Marry?"

"Yes." He gazed at her lovingly and patted her belly. "For all we know, you could be carrying my seed. I'll leave no bastard behind me."

"No." Johanna brushed his hand away. "I won't marry a man because he feels it's his duty to marry me."

"I don't see it that way. I want you." He gripped her hand. "For always."

"I'm not some kind of wildflower you can pick in the woods, Ryan. I want more from marriage than that."

A pained expression crept on his face. "Guess after all is said and done, I'm not good enough for you! Maybe you deserve that dandy, Stephen Green. He's had his sights set on ya long before we met. Why don't you go on and marry him?"

"I would rather die than do that!" Johanna threw her arms about Ryan's chest. "Don't ever, ever think that you're not good enough for me."

He held her so tight, Johanna felt she'd melt into him. "Marry me! As soon as we get to the next fort."

She pulled away. "No, that's too soon. I need time."

"Don't take too much time, Johanna. A man can only wait so long." With that, he helped her pick up their things and led her back to camp.

She felt like a thief in the night, stealing into the tent. Mabel lay curled to one side, snoring loudly. Had she faced the opening, she might have caught Johanna sliding beneath the quilt and pretending to sleep. Thank goodness, Johanna thought with a sigh, that her aunt was a heavy sleeper. She'd have to make a good excuse later, but at least she could pretend to have come in late. Closing her eyes to the memory of Ryan's hurt gaze as she rejected his proposal, she tried to rest. Her thoughts raced to the events leading up to their lovemaking. Nothing could alter what had happened.

She touched her abdomen. Suppose Ryan were right? Suppose his seed had taken root? She hated to think it possible, not now. Not when she had so much to do. She couldn't become a disgraced woman. Then again, Ryan offered her a solution when he wanted to marry her. He loved her. He'd even wait for her to decide. She had to decide soon. Did she love him?

Oh, yes, I love him, her heart told her.

You can't, her mind screamed back.

Why not? She rolled to and fro under the quilt, tugged by conflicting feelings and thoughts. She recalled a maid named Mary whom her aunt hired years ago. The shy, young emigrant from Ireland had dated one of the sailors under Captain Foster. In a short time, Mary became pregnant by the sailor. The Captain pressured the couple to marry, but the sailor took off for the South Seas before the wedding could take place. Poor Mary returned to her native County Meath, broken-hearted and six months pregnant. Through letters to her aunt, Johanna learned that Mary met another man in Ireland and wed him. So things had turned out for the best.

Would things turn out so well for me? Johanna wondered. She opened her eyes and stared at the walls of the tent. Light penetrated the canvas, making her more aware of the hour. Mabel stirred then woke up and yawned.

"Johanna! You're back. Oh, thank heavens. You had us worried. We sent some men to scour the woods for you. Where did you go with Ryan?"

Johanna hoped her face wouldn't give away her guilt. "Oh, we went for a walk. We fell asleep and I came in much later, after you were asleep." She breathed a sigh of relief when Mabel accepted her explanation, part of which was true.

"Please do be careful, dear. The woods are filled with fearsome creatures. Even though Ryan is an expert on such things, it's dangerous."

Johanna stifled a laugh at the irony in her aunt's words. Ryan, an expert on such things. Dangerous. "Yes," she stammered, "I suppose it could be dangerous." She sat. Realizing that her dress might give her away, she said, "I came back too tired to change into my nightgown, Auntie. I will be careful." She averted her eyes from her aunt's bewildered stare, fearful of saying anymore that might trigger her aunt's suspicions. As they exited the tent, Mabel's sharp gaze met hers.

"Why, my dear, you've popped a button on that dress."

Johanna glanced down, noticing with horror that the two top buttons had popped. Her fingers trembled as she touched the material. In her haste to dress and return to camp, she'd popped them. "I'll sew them later. I think I'll go change into a more comfortable dress anyway." Before Mabel could make further inquiries, Johanna hurried to their wagon. On the way, Stephen stopped her.

"Johanna, you had us all worried about you. Where'd you go with that woodsman?"

"We walked about the camp, around the meadow, and a little beyond." She pointed to the distant trees. "I'm fine, I came back a little late but I'm a big girl, Stephen. I can take care of myself."

"Can you? That wasn't what worried me."

"Oh." She cocked her head to one side. "Well, you've no need to worry about me at all." She leaned over the backboard of the wagon and threw open the trunk. Folds of fabric lay sandwiched between china dishes and blankets. She removed a beige prairie dress then folded it over her arms as she walked past Stephen's daunting stare. "I need to change, please excuse me."

"I think you've changed already." His hands clenched at his sides.

She stared at his narrowed gaze, nonplused. "What do you mean?"

"I think you know, Johanna. Don't play coy with me. I've seen how you and he look at each other—it disgusts me! I know your little secret, and I hope he has enough honor to do his duty to you."

"Out of my way, Stephen, now!"

He stepped aside as she glided by. Fear gripped her at the thought that Stephen knew about her and Ryan. Could he have seen them? She recalled the footsteps which woke her from Ryan's arms. Did he know that she had lain with Ryan? *Oh, God, I'm ruined!*

It took every effort to remain calm through a simple breakfast. Reverend Wade peered over his mug at her. She imagined how devastated he'd be if he knew her sin. He mustn't know. She spent the last few months trying to prove herself as a missionary, to get into his graces, and to please him.

In her childhood, she often felt that if only she'd been a more dutiful daughter, he wouldn't have left her. She had been an adolescent before she realized the foolishness of that notion. Her father couldn't take her on his ministry circuit and that was that, but he came back every so many years. Those remained bittersweet memories... times spent trying to know one another and to forget the pain of parting. She knew he'd leave each time and vowed one day to join him. Now, that she had, she vowed not to disgrace him—if she could prevent it. But what if it all came down to a choice: Ryan or her father? She'd think on that after she talked to Ryan; she needed time to decide.

Ryan didn't come by at all that morning. He rode ahead, telling the ministers he had to scout the trail. At one point, Johanna thought she saw him riding up to her wagon as she loaded it, but it turned out to be Seamus on his mule. "Thanks for the help you give me and my kin," Seamus said. "Oh, and thank Ryan too. I haven't seen hair or hide o' him. Think he went on ahead to scout... do you know?"

Johanna shook her head, a small lump rose in her throat as she fought back a sob.

"'Day to ya," Seamus called then rode off again.

The strain of the days began to take its toll as her mind became beset with new worries. Could she be with child? Fear and shame flooded her, and she had to steady herself a moment before gripping the reins on the mules. Blinking back tears, she lifted her chin high and clicked her tongue to get the mules to move.

"Are you all right, Johanna?" Mabel asked, hanging on tightly to the seat beside her.

"Yes." *There's no use in crying over spilled milk*, she told herself. Like the path ahead, she'd have to go on. After several miles, she decided to get out of the wagon. "I think I'll walk today." Handing the reins to Mabel, she added, "Can you manage the team?"

"Certainly," Mabel said. "You don't mind the mud?"

"I'll walk like everyone else." She climbed down from the seat. In a way, walking helped her to avoid her aunt's interrogation about last night. She didn't want to discuss Ryan. "I'm in good health," she said over her shoulder. "I can walk and the boots will keep my feet dry."

Taking long-legged strides, Johanna realized that it felt good to walk compared to the constant jolts of the wagon seat. She hiked her skirt up like the other women did, tying it to one side to avoid trailing it in the still wet, odorous animal droppings. In a short time, her hem became worn and soiled anyway. *It's like me*, she thought bitterly. Sally McPherson joined her as they walked alongside the wagons.

"I feel good, Miss Wade," Sally said with a grin, "but that brew you gave me sure tasted awful. It made my tongue as fuzzy as cat fur."

"Medicine isn't supposed to taste good, Sally." Johanna stopped a moment, leaning on a downed tree. Lightning from an earlier storm had split and blackened the trunk. Even now it felt warm and Johanna pulled her hand away. She continued on with Sally by her side, talking non-stop whenever they paused in their race to keep pace with the wagons. She didn't mind the chatter; it kept her from dwelling on her own fears and worries.

They plodded through the dust-covered trail, along the muddy riverbanks and past mile after mile of endless prairie. At times, Johanna felt swallowed by a sea of grass. The breeze created an illusion of waves breaking beneath the wagon wheels. The sun scorched her face and hands. Despite Ryan's warnings, several farmers let their cows drink the brackish water from the Platte. As a result, the cows became sick and started vomiting in the grass. A few times, the wagons halted so that farmers could regroup their livestock.

Tiny islands, thirty feet to a half mile wide, dotted a shallow river. Fleet-footed antelope romped through the green grass of the valley, avoiding the oncoming wagons and the intruders who marched and made tracks. Johanna recalled Ryan telling her that they had entered the land belonging to the Pawnee, Cheyenne, and Arapahoe tribes. She saw members of one of the tribes—she didn't know which one—wave as they passed by. She waved back. Once more, dugout canoes provided by a tribe of Pawnee helped them ford the wide Platte River.

It took two hours to cross, but by midday, the entire wagon party had forded the Platte. Once ashore, people left their wet belongings on the ground to dry in the warm sunshine. Johanna peered at the harried, exhausted faces of the emigrants. She didn't find Ryan anywhere. She followed Seamus and Mabel to the riverbank's edge. Seamus, like the other men and boys, used a makeshift fishing pole and a bucket to catch the catfish and bass that propagated the waters.

Supper meant a fire by the river, grilled fish, baked bread, and beans. Famished, Johanna didn't mind the undercooked, doughy bread nor the blackened fish. She ate with relish then sat listening to the chatter around her. A couple in their late teens appeared totally absorbed in each other's company. The young woman's belly protruded like a ripe watermelon. Her unborn child would be birthed on the trail. The woman's face radiated happiness as she tossed her blonde hair back and laughed at her husband's antics as he rubbed fish bones together. Their obvious happiness gave Johanna a pang of jealousy.

"Miss Wade," the woman called over.

Johanna tried to remember her name then said, "Um, yes, Megan?"

"Is it true you're starting a school in Oregon?"

"Yes," Johanna said, "I intend to establish a missionary school. We need to educate our youth on proper morals."

The couple gave her a blank stare.

"That's a good thing," the husband said, patting his wife's belly. "We want him to have good schooling."

"It may be a she," Megan said with a wry grin, "Tom here thinks we're gonna have a boy, but a gypsy in N'Orleans said different."

"Don't believe gypsies," Johanna said. "Whatever you have, you can rest assured the child will be educated." She turned away from the couple, feeling miserable. She thought of the tea leaves her aunt read in Missouri. Mabel foretold how she'd meet a man who'd change her life forever. Forever... Ryan's words to her. He'd love her forever.

That night, Johanna wrote out her feelings in her journal. It helped to put down those emotions she kept pent inside. She shut the book and took up her quilt making. The rags of discarded material were beginning to take form in shades of peach, navy, green, and yellow. *It has no pattern*, she thought, *like my life now*. "I talk of dreams, which are the children of an idle brain, begot of nothing but vain fantasy," she said aloud.

"Romeo and Juliet," Stephen said, coming up beside her. "How appropriate for us."

Startled, Johanna dropped her work. Stephen picked up the pile of rags and handed them to her, touching her fingertips.

"You near caused the death of me, Stephen," she chided, "sneaking up on me like an Indian."

"I'm no Indian, not even half. Perhaps that's my trouble." He leaned back, rubbing his chin with one hand. "It's the savage that lures you. Doesn't it?"

"No." She lowered her gaze and resumed work on the quilt.

"She is woman, therefore may she be wooed." He placed his hand on her knee. "She is woman, therefore may be won."

Johanna pushed his hand away. "Titus and Andronicus. No more Shakespeare, please, and leave me to my work."

"Who should I quote, dear Johanna? What will spark that fire in your soul? What poetry... that of Robert McEntee or that of a coarse, rough trapper who has no more manner than a jackass?"

"Enough!" She stood and planted her hands on her hips. "Why aren't you with Father, Stephen?"

"He's talking with Majors, that's why."

"And you're here to annoy me?"

"Ouch!" He soothed an imaginary wound on his chest. "You wound me to the quick, Johanna. I came back to guard the fine ladies of Camelot. You're in the thick of Indian territory. I'd hate to see those beautiful tresses of yours cut from that fine and noble head."

She met his stony stare with an angry tone. "Thank you for your honorable intentions, Reverend Green, but I'll do fine with or without you."

"Oh, the pistol, I forgot. You are an armed and dangerous damsel. You killed a savage and saved the entire camp."

"I saved myself and the children."

"Bravo for you and a lucky shot too." He stepped off the wagon and unrolled a sleeping bag. "Nevertheless, I intend to sleep here tonight, beneath the wagon. I'll keep away anyone who might harm hide or hair of you or your aunt." The bushes rustled as Mabel stepped between them. She held a clay jug in one hand and her parasol in the other.

"Why, Reverend Green, it's nice of you to think of our protection! I carry my parasol in the event that I'd have to clobber a marauding

Indian or two." She grinned at Johanna, before turning to Stephen again. "It seems as if you and Howard have been a busy pair. Care for a cup of this chamomile tea?" She held the jug up.

"No, thanks." Stephen grimaced as Mabel sat on the wagon seat.

"How about you, Johanna? Can I interest you in a cup of tea?"

"No, thank you. I plan to turn in for the night." She leaned over, whispering to Mabel, "Cramps are bothering me."

Mabel's brows lifted. "That time?"

"I think so." Johanna nodded. *I hope so*, she thought. "I need to change and rest up."

"The chamomile tea will relieve those cramps."

"One cup then." Johanna took a china cup from within the wagon and held it out to her aunt. Mabel filled the cup with the greenish yellow tea. Johanna spooned honey into it, then sipped the tea. Her brows lifted when she detected a slight trace of dandelion wine.

"Shh!" Mabel whispered. "Our little secret... and Seamus' addition to the brew."

Reverend Wade approached looking older than his fifty years. Johanna recalled how his somber countenance had remained unchanged over the years, only a few lines creasing the skin beneath his dark eyes. A sprinkle of gray tinged his black hair. He looked gaunter now, unhealthily so. "Father are you ill?" She touched his shoulder as he stood next to her.

"No, I'm fine, child." The grimness remained in his expression. "I'm a little tired. I haven't slept too well lately. The other night when you didn't come to the wagons after the dance left me worried. I guess being a father carries great burdens. I hadn't realized how much in those years when I left you in your aunt's care, but you're back and safe. Don't ever run off without telling us where or when you'll return."

"I suppose I could say the same for you." She chuckled softly. "All those years I worried about you and if you'd ever return to visit me."

"I'm sorry about them, Johanna. You must understand." He sat, looking like a rail against the thick trunk of the tree. "Riding the circuit left no time for me to care for a small child. It's hard enough being a circuit rider without a wife and child to worry about. It held dangers too, running about the backwoods and mountains around Missouri." He shook his head as if clearing his thoughts. "No... no place for a child, especially a girl."

"I imagined you were too busy, Father. Too busy for me."

"Back then, I was young and eager like Reverend Green here." He clapped Stephen's shoulder. "I could take on any obstacle. And believe me, with families scattered about the river area, there were many obstacles. Yet, I managed to deliver the Lord's message. Many a home welcomed me. I acted as a doctor to some folks, bringing home remedies for colds and fevers. I helped deliver a few children too."

But you forgot the one you left in Boston, Johanna thought, fighting back the urge to lash out at the father she loved.

"A regular saint he was." Mabel's sarcasm dripped like melted wax on fine paper. "Off to save the heathens when his own wife lay at death's door."

"It wasn't my fault," Wade snapped back, "the Lord called your mother back." He gazed at Johanna. "It wasn't my fault that I could not be there for her or for you." He covered his face with his hands. To Johanna's surprise, he began to sob. "I loved her. I did love her."

Johanna threw the tea from her cup, laid it down then rushed to her father's side. *He needs me*, she realized, *as I've needed him*. She gently hugged him about the shoulders. "Don't cry so, Father. I believe you loved Mother."

His slow, sad smile tugged at her heartstrings. "You're so much like her. She'd have been your age when she gave birth to you. Too young to die, oh my precious." He glanced at the sky, extending his arms upward. "God, you should've taken me, not her. You left me alone."

"No, Father." Johanna held him. "You're not alone."

Stephen yawned. "I guess we all should get some rest."

Reverend Wade's mouth became a thin line, his gaze hard as granite as it met the young minister's. "You're absolutely right, Stephen. There's no time for sentimentality. There's work ahead of us." He looked at Johanna, his gaze softening, and smiled. "We should turn in for the night."

Mabel climbed down from the wagon seat. "Come on, Johanna, let's get some rest."

Johanna let go of her father's drooping shoulders. In all her life, she'd never seen him cry for her mother. The show of emotion moved her. She wanted to comfort him but he turned away. The slight glimpse of the man behind the somber mask touched her to the core. "Sleep well, Father," she whispered, watching him walk with Stephen as the men prepared to camp by the wagon.

~ * ~

Conditions on the open plain meant little privacy for one's toilet. Johanna thought of her times in Boston now as days spent in great luxury compared to everyday existence on the prairie. At times, she thought she'd do anything for a nice, hot bath instead of scrubbing the dust from her body in bone-chilling streams. Gnats, mosquitoes, flies and other pests further aggravated conditions. *Thank goodness for the witch hazel rubs and ointments from back East,* Johanna thought as she soothed the itches from insect bites.

One morning she had to walk around with a swollen eyelid from an insect sting. Mabel told her to apply a cold compress of baking soda. By evening, she felt fine.

"We shouldn't complain," Johanna told Mabel. "At least we've food enough and the fresh meat and fish Ryan and the farmers provide has added to our cuisine."

She found that the days melted into one another as she marked them in her diary. Ryan remained aloof during stopovers, causing her to feel lonely and cross. She taught the emigrant children during the stopovers. Ryan never returned for his lessons.

Her father appeared to grow weaker, and this worried her. She spoke once to Mabel then to Stephen about it. They said she worried too much. Reverend Wade looked as stalwart as ever. He delivered his weekly sermons and camp prayers with his usual fire and brimstone style. She assisted him in distributing prayer books and leading the chorus of songs.

By their second week out from Fort Laramie, Johanna found to her delight that she didn't have to fear being pregnant. With the coming of her menses, she rejoiced as she cleaned off in the stream, stemming the flow of blood with rags. She finished dressing then peered at the landscape with its sagebrush and gentle hills. Grateful for the pangs of womanhood, she felt she could bear her backaches and cramps with relief for a change. This, she reasoned, she could live with as she washed the bloodied rags with the rest of her laundry in the river's icy waters. She piled her laundered clothing into a basket then collected gooseberries along the riverbank. She added the bunch to the basket. Feeling giddy, she plucked a few wildflowers—daisies, marsh marigolds, and blue brookline. She threaded them through her hair and shut her eyes as a warm breeze caressed her face.

"Don't you look just like a forest nymph," said Stephen with contempt.

Alarmed, she spun around, overturning the basket.

"Here, let me help you." Ryan came forward, gathering up the berries and wet clothing.

"Johanna and I need to talk," he told Stephen. Without further word, he took Johanna by the hand and led her the remaining way toward the wagon.

Seventeen

Along the North Platte River

Grizzly Dugan tracked the footsteps of the Pawnee squaw to a mud-caked field churned by wagon wheels. He scratched his head, figuring that the little bitch had been picked up by one of the wagons. With hundreds of wagons heading west, he feared he'd never find her. Not finding her meant he'd never get the money back. His boss would take his hide for losing that money, and he'd be out of his cut. He sneered then spat tobacco on the ground. Crouching down, he lit a branch to start a campfire as dusk settled around him.

Tuned as he was to the natural sounds of the night, Grizzly's ears picked up the stealthy sound of footsteps. Grabbing his knife, he crouched behind a sagebrush and waited. If it were an enemy intruder, he'd slit the bastard's throat from ear to ear, he thought, eager to take out his frustrations on someone. Within seconds, a Pawnee brave, clad in buckskin, inched closer to his campsite.

"What ya want, stranger?" Grizzly asked, springing up and brandishing the knife in the man's face.

The brave's eyes widened. "I mean no harm, mister," he assured him, holding out his hands. "Jest saw your campfire and thought I'd like a bit of company. I got me a flask of whiskey to share."

"Always willing to share a pint or two. Set a spell." Grizzly put away the knife and pointed to the ground. He relit the fire, eyeing the scout. "You Pawnee?"

The scout nodded, taking out his flask and handing it to Grizzly.

"I'm Tom Knifechief."

Grizzly took the flask, pulled the cork out and toasted, "Here's luck, Tom." As he held the bottle, he watched the scout fidgeting as he sat cross-legged beside him. *Fella got something to hide*, Grizzly thought, taking a swig of whiskey. The taste made him gag; he spat it out. "Ya call this whiskey? I tasted better horse piss than this. Here." He handed the flask back. "What ya doin' in these here parts?"

"I go back to my people." Tom Knifechief drained the rest of the whiskey before continuing. "I led white folk across prairie. Come now in hundred or more wagons, they give me whiskey and guns, money, too. Ryan Majors lead missionaries."

"Looks like them whites got the better of the deal, giving ya piss water like that." Grizzly poked the fire with a stick and sat back. "I had a good bottle of Scotch whiskey. I sold it to a Blackfoot chief for a squaw. The Pawnee bitch run off on me, damn bitch took off with my money. Maybe you seen her... name of Evenin' Star. She went on one of 'em wagons. She won't get far though." He noted how the scout looked away, and how a muscle twitched in his cheek. "Hey, bet you knew her... bein' a Pawnee ya'self."

The scout dropped the whiskey bottle, shattering it on the hard ground.

Something ain't right, Grizzly thought as he leaned toward the scout. "You do know the bitch, don't ya?" He slipped his knife from its sheath, turning it round and round in his hand.

Tom Knifechief eyed the knife nervously. "No, I don't."

"You're lying... I can tell it in your eyes." Grizzly stood and grabbed the scout by the collar. "Tell me where to find her."

Knifechief reached into his pocket but it was too late. Grizzly slammed his hand back and pinned him to the ground. "Tell me," Grizzly shouted, "or else." He pointed the knife against Knifechief's throat.

"I don't know."

"You do so." When Grizzly lifted the weapon, Knifechief rolled under him. Grizzly grabbed Knifechief's feet, and the two men wrestled on the ground. Grizzly landed atop the scout, resting the weight of his legs on Knifechief's chest. "You done tell me where she is, or I'll pluck out dem two eyeballs."

Knifechief moaned under the assault as Grizzly struck his face. Somehow he wriggled free, and once more the two rolled on the ground. Again Grizzly got the better of him and held his knife poised at Knifechief's jugular vein. "Tell me now!"

"No!" Knifechief moved slightly and Grizzly slashed deep into his shoulder.

Blood gushed out onto Grizzly's face. Knifechief cried in agony.

"Talk." Grizzly slashed Knifechief's face. "Tell me where the bitch is."

Knifechief shook his head, and made a final attempt to push Grizzly off his chest.

Grizzly grabbed Knifechief's throat. "Tell me now or I'll cut you from ear to ear."

Knifechief spit in his face.

Grizzly slashed again, cutting the high cheekbone. "You want to live then tell me, Injun. Your life or the girl's."

The color drained from Knifechief's face as he gasped, "She's with the damn missionaries."

Grizzly brought the blade across Knifechief's throat, slashing a bright red ribbon of blood. He howled in victory as blood gurgled from Knifechief's mouth. The scout went rigid. His eyes, widened by terror, now held no life.

With his bloodied knife, Grizzly sliced off the top of Knifechief's scalp and placed it on his leather belt. "Teach ya for lying to me." He kicked the body downhill into the river, listening with satisfaction as it splashed and sank. Returning to his camp, he wiped his hand, saddled his horse and rode on in search of a wagon train with missionaries. *Shouldn't be too hard to find*, he thought. That name Ryan Majors rang a bell... the man he shot had the same last name.

He recalled a young trapper he met at a rendezvous years ago. Trapper named Ryan and his younger brother. They left him in the woods the day he got mauled by the grizzly bear. "So," he said aloud, rubbing his face, "if it's the same fella who left me to be scarred, I'll have the privilege of seeing him dead." Bloodlust and greed spurned him onward.

~ * ~

Ryan had cursed himself all morning for acting stupidly with Johanna. *What gave me the idea that she'd ever marry me? Of all the stupid notions I've had, that had to be the most foolish,* he thought. As days ran into weeks, it became apparent to him that she'd had a change of heart. That she'd never be his wounded him like no other pain in his life. He had to get over it soon, but he knew he'd never be rid of the love he felt for her. Watching her with Stephen only made him angrier. He wanted to crush them both with his bare hands like a wild animal.

Is this what love did to a man? No, he knew better. He'd seen how love had molded his brother, making him a respectable farmer and trader in Missouri. He'd seen the love between his parents. Even at six years of age, he knew his mother suffered the humiliation of the whites to be with her Englishman trapper. It wasn't love, it was the notion of rejection, which hurt. His way of dealing with it was to confront it head-on. "Johanna," he said, glancing at her sad expression as she peered up at him.

"Yes, Ryan?"

"Johanna, I was worried about you. I feared you might be in a family way."

She shook her head and wildflowers she so deftly wove in her hair tumbled down around her shoulders. "No, I'm not pregnant. You needn't worry."

"You know for certain?"

She held her breath a moment then nodded. "Yes, I know."

A pang of disappointment struck Ryan. For an instant he felt a sense of loss, and he realized that he wanted to father a child, especially one carried by Johanna. But now they could start fresh, no embarrassment, no shame, and he felt hopeful. "Johanna, I meant what I said two weeks ago. I want to marry you. We're right for each other. You know it. I know it."

Her lips trembled, opening as if to speak then closing in a tight, sad line. He continued, "Think about it. If you don't want to marry me when we get to the valley, I'll leave. You won't see my face ever again."

She lowered her gaze, dropped his hand then whispered, "I have been thinking about it. It's all I think about." She twisted the hem of her apron. "I think we shouldn't meet alone anymore. Father is growing worn and frail; I need to care for him. If he knew, the shock would kill him."

Her father must be special to her, Ryan thought. *I won't push her further.* It would be better to go slow, to wait for her to come to him. If need be he'd wait it out in the valley too, but he hoped she'd decide sooner. He touched her chin, cradling her face in his hands. "Don't wait too long, Johanna. Think of what we had, what we can have together." He wanted to say more, but their talk was interrupted by a group of emigrants—the Jones, Montgomery and O'Dowd families gathering buffalo chips for their campfires. Ryan released a frustrated sigh and dropped his hands to his sides.

"I promised to check on Megan LeFleure. She's due any day now."

"Oh, all right," he snapped, rubbing the sweat from the back of his neck. "Go on then, but think about what I said."

~ * ~

As Johanna walked back to camp, she thought about Ryan's proposal. Now that she didn't have to marry him, did she want to? He had been her lover. Could he be her husband? Nothing in her strict, Bostonian upbringing had prepared her for the likes of him. His touch melted her reserve and fired her own passion. But could that passion meet the demands of a marriage? She wanted desperately to believe so. At twenty-four, she felt more than ready for marriage. She'd had her chance once with Robert. Oh, how different the two were. Robert wooed her with poetry and gallant ways. Ryan wooed her with his lips, his touch, and a passion she'd only read about. He was willing even to take in her father and her aunt.

The desolation of sandy hills and scraggly green brush spread before her. She stood like a lost lamb unaware of its direction. The sun beat down on her. No longer feeling lighthearted, she pulled the wildflowers from her hair and tossed them on the mud-colored earth. Parched and heated, she licked her dry lips and thought of the clear waters of the stream which rambled by the camp. When she reached her wagon, she withdrew her toiletries: lavender soap, scrub brush, and clean clothing. "I'm going to the stream to bathe, Auntie, want to come?"

"No, dear. I'm too tired. I think I'll take a nap."

Moments later, Johanna peered into the pebbly bottom of the stream. Grateful for the curtain of bushes that allowed a measure of privacy, Johanna stripped down to her chemise. She took brush and soap and waded into the water, startled at first by its chill then delighted by its coolness. The harsh, quacking of Canada geese flying overhead pierced the quiet. She shielded her eyes with her fingers and watched them fly off into the clear blue sky.

The scent of lavender lifted her spirits as she lathered her skin and hair. Wicked delight from the sensation of bathing filled her. She sank deeper, up to the collarbone. The seclusion of the surroundings and the still waters freed her inhibitions. Opening the buttons of her chemise, she bared her breasts, massaging them liberally with the soap. Her nipples tingled and peaked. She smiled at the thought of Ryan's tongue licking them. "Stop it," she told herself, shaking the water from her body and pulling up the top of her chemise. Had a man's loving made her so wanton? She buttoned her chemise then waded ashore. She slowly dried off with a rough cloth and dressed. Since learning that she wasn't pregnant, Johanna wanted to restrain her impulses with Ryan. But the very thought of him made her quake with heated desire. She could finally admit, here in the open, she wanted him as much as he did her.

~ * ~

Yellow wasps, black flies, mosquitoes, and gnats buzzed around the emigrants walking through the waving fields of grass. Johanna swatted the pests away, more fearful of the snakes slithering near the rocks and grateful for the breeze which caressed her heated face. "My God, I hope we're going to stop soon," she hollered to Mabel who drove the wagon beside her. They had walked twenty miles since dawn, rounding the bends and skirting the thorny plants, which sprang up along the way. The Platte River meandered northward with isolated islands and streams that veined the drier land.

At midday, Ryan ordered the stopover beside one of the streams.

Bone-weary and heated so that her face looked like a ripe strawberry, Johanna fanned herself with her bonnet before sitting to take lunch. Mabel poured honey-laced tea for her and the ministers. They ate a modest meal beside the wagon. The heat made Johanna want to doze. She shut her eyes as the flies buzzed around the mule droppings.

Something buzzed in her ear, waking her as she swatted it.

Stephen glared at her. "Johanna, you haven't heard a thing I've said."

She shrugged and rubbed her eyes. "I guess I fell asleep. I was tired."

"Aren't we all," Mabel said. "This sea of green grass can drive a soul mad."

"Ah," said Reverend Wade, "wait until we enter the fertile Willamette. There'll be milk and honey for all."

"I hope there's more than milk and honey," Johanna mocked, "for these farmers will be sorely disappointed for their troubles."

Ryan came over to their table, glanced at Johanna then at Reverend Wade.

"We got ten more miles to Independence Rock. I think we best get a move on before those thunder clouds come our way." He pointed to the large, gray mass of clouds moving in a westerly direction. "We need to camp somewhere else."

"I agree." Reverend Wade said. "After the prayer meeting, we'll move along."

"No," Ryan said, "we don't have time for prayers. We got to get out of the open field or else we'll be fried by lightning."

"Now hold on a minute." Stephen stood with his hands on his hips. "We're going to have our prayer meeting."

Reverend Wade interrupted impatiently. "Ryan is right. Reverend Green, calm yourself. We'll wait."

"But..." Stephen muttered.

"But nothin'." Ryan glared at him. "I won't risk families and the cattle in a thunder clap so you can pray. That's your trouble, Green, you got your head in the clouds. Mine is down here on the ground, right where it belongs. We move out now or we'll get cooked by lightning. Whether you like it or not, I'm in charge. So when I say move out—we move!" With that he stomped off.

"Bully for you!" Mabel shouted after him. Leaning close to her niece, she whispered, "Now that's what I like in a man, my dear. He knows when and how to take charge of the situation. And he has our interest at heart."

Especially mine, Johanna thought with a sigh.

~ * ~

"You'll do fine, honey," Tom Le Fleure said as he held his wife's hand.

Johanna worriedly gazed at the drawn features and pale face of the pregnant woman who lay nestled in the wagon. Megan looked frightened to death. The thunderstorm Ryan predicted had unleashed its fury before the wagon train had time to move out. Hail and driving rain pelted the tarpaulin cover. Wind whipped at the sides. The sudden downpour and intermittent lightning had sent frightened children rushing to their parents, and farmers running after spooked livestock.

Megan Le Fleure looked like a child herself as her husband cuddled her. *They're so young*, Johanna thought. All she could do was cook a quick meal for them from leftovers and reassure them that the midwife in the wagon party would come around to check on her condition. The meal lay uneaten on the blanket.

"You've nothing to fear, Megan." Johanna reached in and patted the woman's swollen hands. "Mary O'Dowd has had lots of experience delivering babies. She'd been a nurse back in Ireland, too. I'm sure she'll see you through when the time comes."

"Thank you, Miss Johanna," Megan whispered, leaning back against her husband's chest. "It's Tom here that I'm worried about. He's been as sick as me."

Johanna looked at the Creole's dark face and read the worry in his eyes. Circles beneath them testified to his lack of sleep. Concerned, she asked, "Are you sick?"

"No, mademoiselle. I've got a cold, nothing more. *Mon cheri*, Megan, is the one to watch. It is still too soon for the baby. Please, help care for her. I know your reputation for helping the sick. See no harm comes to her or our baby."

"Now, we'll do our best," Molly said. Her plump figure shook the wagon as she climbed inside with the couple. She glanced at Megan. "It's not your time, child. But we'll see you and the babe get good care."

Johanna left them, planning to return later. Rain pelted her face as she ducked into the tent that her father and Stephen had quickly erected beside the wagon. Pools of water filled the corners where Mabel sat. "Where's Father and Stephen?" she asked.

"They're helping round up the livestock. Where have you been?"

"I visited the Le Fleure couple. Megan's frightened as is her husband. The midwife says it's not time for the baby. She looks close to delivering it, though, and of all times to do it... in the middle of a storm."

Mabel sighed. "Your mother gave birth to you in a snow storm. I blamed the storm for her death... the doctor showed up so late that evening because of the snow and ice. He blamed it on complications, but I blamed the winter."

"Hopefully, Megan's baby will be delivered safely. Auntie, they're so young. Had Mother been that young?"

"A few years older than Megan. She had her pick of young men, but she chose your father. Why? God only knows. At least, they produced something of great worth... you."

Johanna kissed her aunt's forehead. "I think they loved each other very much. Things just didn't work out for them."

"No, it didn't. Ah, let's not go on about the past. We must live for tomorrow. Isn't that why we're here, after all? Children are the future... they make us young, you know." She stared pointedly at Johanna. "Maybe someday you'll have your own baby. At least I got to feel like a mother, caring for you. I'd have given anything to have my sister alive but..." Mabel wiped a tear. "Then again, she gave me something more precious by giving birth to you."

"Listen, Auntie." Johanna looked up at the tent ceiling. "It sounds like the rain stopped." She peeked out of the tent. "I'm right. It's not raining." Stepping outside, she gazed about and saw a rainbow stretched between the slopes of two hills. Taking it as a good luck sign, she smiled. She wondered if anyone else spotted it, but everyone had settled in. Even Ryan lay curled up in a lean-to. *He needs to rest now, but soon I'll have my answer for him.*

At supper that evening, as Johanna watched her father munch on a dry crust of stale bread, Johanna tried to imagine him younger and fueled by the fire of love. Perhaps her mother could have married someone handsomer and richer, but she chose this stalwart figure in black threads who offered a humble parsonage off the Commons. Maybe they had a great love that had countered their lack of money and her mother's loss of a privileged status. Maybe a love so strong could overcome their differences. As the thought occurred to her, she peered up at the figure of Ryan leaning against a tree. He looked at the moon shining between the clouds as he played on a harmonica. The tune sounded sad and wistful.

"I didn't know Ryan could play the harmonica," Mabel said to her as they cleared away the dishes.

"He can," Johanna said. *There's a lot he can do. He can name every wildflower and bird in the woods, pick out the edible plants from the inedible, and speak in several tribal languages. There's a lot he can do. He can make me feel things I've never felt before... a passion I've never known.* "Yes," she murmured, "Ryan can do a lot."

"You had such a funny look on your face now," Mabel said, gripping the dish from Johanna's hands before she dropped it.

"I think I'm in love."

Mabel dropped the dish. It shattered the silence between them.

"Well," Mabel huffed, hugging Johanna. "It's about time!"

~ * ~

Ryan knew he owed Johanna an apology. But every time he saw her, she was surrounded by others... the children, the ministers, or her aunt. He couldn't get her alone and he figured that she wanted it that way. Frustrated and hurt, he sat. When he landed on a prickly cactus, he howled with pain. After removing the spines, he sat again and thought about what he could do to right the wrong.

Maybe he could write to her? She respected a man of words. Yes, he decided.

He'd write her a letter. As he thought about the words he'd write, he couldn't help but notice the constant attention the Reverend Green paid her... bringing her wildflowers from the fields as they drove along, reading passages and quoting Scripture. Words. Damn words. That damn minister had a gift for words.

Ryan witnessed with disgust how Stephen garnered converts to his revivalism method of ministry. Stricken by the spirit, they claimed to be saved from damnation. *Bunch of foolhardy greenhorns.* Thank goodness, Johanna didn't show signs of following Stephen's sheep to the slaughter. *That's where they're heading if they follow the likes of him*, he figured.

Sitting beneath a ponderosa tree, Ryan began to write the letter. With a lantern to light the darkness, he printed word after word of what he couldn't speak to Johanna. His calloused fingers gripped the pencil like a hammer. How could he tell her of the longing he felt each time he saw her and the loneliness he suffered without her? He wrote how sorry he felt for acting like a jackass then ended it with the words "Johanna, forgive me. I'm sorry. Ryan." He wanted to say more but felt it too humiliating to express the words which remained welled within him.

When he finished writing, he glanced at the awkward printing. "Heck, it'll just have to do." Then he folded the sheet in half and strode with determined steps to deliver his message.

Johanna sat on a huge log, stitching patches into the quilt. Upon Ryan's approach, she folded up the quilt she'd begun for her father and smiled. "Hello, Ryan."

He placed the note in her hands then stood back.

She glanced at the note, opened it, and read silently. He had expected an argument, or her refusal, but this was worse—she began to laugh. He cursed himself for being such a fool and walked off.

"Ryan!" Johanna shouted as she ran after him.

When he paused, she stopped and stood looking up at him. A solemn expression with a glint of humor in her azure eyes held his attention. "I'm dreadfully sorry, I didn't mean to laugh. Actually, I'm proud of your writing. It's the first time you've written a letter. I know it wasn't easy for you. Except for printing the 'S' and the 'P' backwards," she continued, unaware of his bunched eyebrows and the tight clench of his jaw, "it's a perfect note. I'll treasure it forever.

Thank you." She pressed it to her breast.

"Is that all you've got to say? Don't you believe me?"

"Yes." Her gaze softened as did her voice. She touched the back of his hand. "I believe you're sorry. So was I. We've got to get to know one another, Ryan. I still need time to give you your answer."

"I see." It wasn't what he wanted to hear, not by a long shot. He combed his hair with his fingertips and turned to go, but she held his hand.

"Wait a moment," she said, "I've got something for you." Dropping her hold, she ran to the wagon. She returned with a leather purse and handed it to him.

He stared at the bulging purse with its string binding. When he moved his hand, something within it jangled. "Money?"

"I should have given it to you sooner," Johanna said. "Inside is the money belonging to your brother. The money stolen from the trappers."

"How do you know that?" He gripped the purse.

"Evening Star gave it to me as payment for the care I gave her when she came to our wagon. She had no idea what the money was only that it meant something of value. And she felt grateful for my help. I didn't make the connection with your brother until later on."

Ryan opened the purse and peered in at the wads of bills coiled up like a snake. Coins weighted the bottom of it. "Blood money," he said, shaking the purse. "My brother Chet died because of this!"

Johanna touched Ryan's clenched fist and massaged the hard, white knuckles. "I'm so sorry, Ryan."

A flood of emotions coursed through him—anger over Chet's murder, relief over getting the money back, and gratefulness that this money could help Chet's family.

"I'm sorry I didn't trust you before, Ryan. After you left the wagon train to return Evening Star to her people, I thought you wouldn't return to us. You were gone so many days, that I feared you had deserted us. So, I kept the money. But when you returned, I intended to give it to you. Then I was so ill at the fort, and we were so busy. And then..." Her voice became a whisper. "Our time together made me forget everything else. They were the most beautiful times

I've ever known."

"Do you trust me now?" He touched her cheek and pulled her close to him. He felt the tension leave her as she sighed against him.

"Yes," she said. "I trust you. I know you're a good man." She stood back; her eyes mirrored his own feelings of want and need, and more importantly, love.

He wanted to sweep her off the ground then and there and take her in an all-consuming embrace. Instead, he hugged her close again, murmuring into her hair, "Thank you." Once more they parted as the ministers and Mabel returned to the campsite. Mabel invited Ryan to join them for supper but he refused. Food was the last thing on his mind. Being so close to Johanna without touching her proved more frustrating than ever. "No thanks, Ma'am," he said with a smile and nodded to Johanna. "I've got a few chores to do."

As he returned to his own campfire, he envisioned the radiance on Johanna's face as she told him how she felt. *She loves me*. Right now, that mattered more than all the money in the world. He tucked the purse in his satchel, vowing to send it back to Missouri with a letter to Chet's widow.

Eighteen

Buffalo Stampedes

After traveling three months, Johanna suffered the physical pangs of the journey. Her back and legs ached with stiffness, her muscles cramped up on her, and her feet throbbed and swelled. When she felt a cramp coming on, she leaned against a tree. Her long-legged, rapid strides to keep pace with the wagon train had hardened her calf and thigh muscles. Despite the discomforts, she preferred walking to driving the wagon with its constant bumps and jolts. Besides, Mabel proved a good driver, keeping a firm grasp on the reins and directing the mule team along the dusty trail. Father and Stephen rode close to Ryan.

Shielding her eyes from the blinding sunlight, she observed them. A kind of peace had settled between them and she felt glad. Stephen had given up pestering her and turned his attention to the Emerson sisters. At least ten years his senior, Abigail and Charlotte delighted in having the young minister visit them and they often provided him with fresh pies and bread. The two women had quite a bit of money between them, an inheritance left by their father who had been involved with the railroads.

In their lace-trimmed, cream-colored silk gowns the sisters looked prepared for a ballroom. Johanna stifled a chuckle as she recalled her own aunt's inappropriate attire at the start of the trip. It hadn't taken a

243

week until Mabel along with Johanna had resorted to wearing more practical dresses of cotton and calico with a sunbonnet. These held up, and shielded them from the effects of the endless miles of dust, mud, and dirt-covered trail. Somehow the Emersons managed to have enough in their trunk to attire in more extravagant fashions despite the adversity they all faced.

Johanna turned from the sisters back to the changing scenery. Grassland had given way to dry land where prickly pear cactus and purple coneflowers competed for moisture. Every so often along the way, the most amazing creatures would pop up from the ground. These prairie dogs as someone called them never ceased to amaze Johanna. They amused her with their antics as they sniffed the air, clasped their paws in prayer-like fashion and bobbed from side to side. While the children watched and applauded the creatures, their elders shouted warnings not to get close, lest they be bitten. Johanna had no intention of getting too close to the wildlife.

Gray owls with black-circled eyes hooted down from scraggly tree branches. Checkered snakes basked in the sun. Having had one experience with snakes, Johanna treaded with caution and glanced at every rock and brush to avoid them. Grasshoppers sprang up from underfoot. Tired of being startled by them, Johanna learned to listen for their buzzing among the weeds. As she scanned the horizon, she saw a brown cloud rising up into the air.

"Cover up!" Ryan shouted as he rode by the wagons. "Duster is comin'."

Johanna dashed for her wagon, climbed aboard, and covered herself and Mabel with a blanket. The wind picked up speed, ruffling the blanket. Johanna coughed as particles of dust flew into her face. When she heard her aunt begin to wheeze, she slapped her on the back. The dust storm passed as quickly as it came, leaving dust-coated wagons in its wake.

"All's clear!" Ryan shouted as he rode past their wagon.

Johanna yanked off the blanket and took a deep breath. "Father, is that you?" she called after the gaunt figure riding an old stallion. Dust covered him from head to toe, but a red handkerchief protected his face.

The man tried to speak but a coughing fit racked his body. He pulled off the handkerchief. "Yes, Johanna, it's me." He coughed again. "I need water," he gasped. He slid off his horse, ladled out water from the keg on the sideboard, and drank deeply.

Johanna went to him. "Father, you look ill."

He coughed then shook his head. "I'm fine. Go on back to the wagon. Don't worry about me. I've been through dust storms before."

With a sigh, Johanna returned to Mabel. They cleaned the dust from inside the wagon bed. "Luckily, it didn't get into the food." She showed Johanna a sack of flour, "but these did."

"Ants!" Johanna peered at the black creatures running through the flour. "Is it ruined?"

"Would you eat them?" Mabel lifted the sack and began dumping the flour.

"I wouldn't throw out food," Ryan said, pulling his horse over to their wagon.

He glanced in at the sack of flour. "What's wrong with it?"

"Ants got into it." Johanna pointed them out.

Ryan shrugged his shoulders. "Sift it. Ants won't harm it. Thing to watch are those flies. They can make you sick." With that, he slapped the side of his horse and rode to the front.

"I suppose it won't harm us," Mabel said. "I hate to throw food out."

"Especially when we don't know how long it will last us out here," Johanna said, realizing for the first time how long the trip would take. "Ryan said we had another two months of travel. We'll need to ration our food."

"Good idea." Mabel pulled a colander from the chest and began sifting the flour for ants. With Johanna's help, she cleaned out the sack and the rest of the wagon.

"At least we'll stock up again at Fort Platte," Johanna said when they finished the chore. "Those mules need to be shoed too. Our wash load has piled up."

"The work never ceases," Mabel said, "but it will be good to stop at a fort again."

Johanna mulled this over. Had it been so long now since she and Ryan made love? It had been two weeks since they left Scotts Bluff. The months stretched before them and she had to decide sooner or later what to tell Ryan.

~ * ~

On a stopover, Megan Le Fleur gave birth to a baby girl. Mary O'Dowd acted as midwife. Johanna heard the cries of the infant as she passed the wagon. "Megan?"

She rushed to the rear and peeked inside. Megan sat, pale faced, and perspiring, with the blanketed bundle tucked near her breasts. A small black-haired newborn nursed as Megan smiled up at Johanna.

"What is it?" Johanna asked Mary.

"She's Hanna Mary Le Fleure," Tom said, "We named her Hanna after you and after Mrs. O'Dowd here."

"Oh." Overcome with emotion, Johanna could hardly say more. Tears filled her eyes. "She's so beautiful!"

"Ouch!" Megan winced and held the baby to the midwife. "I'm sore, please take her."

"Yes, child, rest," Mary took the infant, placing the baby in a wooden cradle attached to the backboard. "How's your head, Megan?"

"I feel so cold." Megan shivered despite being wrapped in a heavy quilt.

Mary touched Megan's hands then felt her forehead. "You've got a fever. We'll see if we can bring it down." Mary glanced at Johanna. "I'll need your help."

Johanna followed Mary to her wagon. The big woman leaned to one side, weariness and concern creasing her brow.

"What's wrong with Megan?" Johanna asked, fearing the worst.

"She's got childbed fever. It doesn't look good. Poor lass, I'll do what I can." She nodded toward Tom Le Fleure, who stepped from the wagon and walked over to a tree and sat, hiding his face in his hands. "He's not too well himself. If anything happens to the wife, it's sure to kill him, too."

"Oh, dear." Johanna gripped Mary's arm. "There's got to be something we can do for them." She glanced around for the one man she'd come to rely on more than anyone else. "Ryan, he'll help them. Come, quick, Mary. We've not a moment to lose."

~ * ~

Johanna peered up at the two brass cannons above the gate of Fort Platte.

A navy uniformed guard stopped her. "Day, Ma'am." He tipped his cap. "Can I help you?"

"The trail guide for my wagon party is inside," she said. "I must find him."

The guard waved her through. As she rushed by, her gaze scanned the adobe structure for Ryan. She passed lock houses and a series of cabins housing a blacksmith, harness maker, and trading post. A half dozen fur trappers milled about the post to sell off their beaver or otter pellets. Beside them Sioux braves in fringed buckskin leggings traded buffalo blankets for weapons. No Ryan! Gasping for breath from her run, Johanna pushed her way through a crowd of settlers. Finally, at the log-hewn barrack, stood Ryan. He seemed completely engaged in conversation with the fort's factor—a bearded man in his early sixties who maintained the fort.

"Ryan!" As she rushed over, the reed-thin, pock-faced factor eyed her from head to toe.

"Well, what have we here?" His predatory smile sent a shiver up Johanna's back.

Ryan's eyes widened with surprise then narrowed with concern. "Johanna! Is something wrong?"

"Yes... Megan Le Fleure had her baby early this morning."

"Lots of women have babies," the factor interrupted.

"You don't understand... she's ill and so is her husband Tom. I think they have the flux." She tugged Ryan's arm. "Please, hurry, we have no time to lose."

"Don't tell me you brought cholera with you?" The captain scowled at Ryan.

Ryan's brows drew together sharply as he looked at Johanna. "Are you sure it's the flux?"

She ran an impatient hand threw her hair. "Oh, I don't know. All I know is that they've been ill for three days now. After Megan's delivery, she grew weaker. Mary O'Dowd dosed her with castor oil. We used the onion syrup to bring down the fever, but nothing helped. We must help them."

"I agree," the fort's factor said. "Bring them to the back of the fort. I'll talk to my scout master. His people, the Oneida, survived an epidemic of cholera. They used a cure made with blackberries."

"Oh, we'll do anything," Johanna said, giving him a small smile of appreciation. "Thank you, sir."

Ryan followed her to the gate then grasped her shoulders. "Not a word to anyone, Johanna. Not until we're sure it's cholera. From now on, make sure everyone boils water before they drink it and make sure the Le Fleure wagon is thoroughly cleaned.

~ * ~

By the time Johanna reached camp, she found Mary weeping outside of the Le Fleure wagon. "Mercy no!" Johanna whispered. *Don't tell me the baby died.* She bit back a sob and touched Mary's shoulder. "What's wrong?"

"Megan, poor thing." Mary sobbed. "She died holding the baby to her breasts."

"No!" Johanna screamed and rushed to the rear of the wagon. Bile rose in her throat at the sight of the young mother lying still with her hair plastered against the pillow and her face as white as the sheet.

The baby kicked and wailed beneath the blanket. "Oh, God... the poor thing."

Johanna lifted the baby from the cradle and held it close. "Oh, you poor child," Johanna sobbed against the infant's black hair. "You poor, poor motherless child." She moved slowly from the wagon, careful not to stumble with the delicate bundle in her arms. She rocked the infant awhile, and when the infant quieted, she placed her back in the cradle. Johanna leaned her aching head against the bow of the wagon, tears blinding her vision as her sobs racked her shoulders. "Oh, it's unfair!" She stood away and shook her fist at the gray clouds. "Damn you," she shouted at the heavens. "You've created one life and ended another! Oh, and so young, so terribly young."

"With one hand, He gives," Mary muttered, "and with the other, He takes away."

Johanna went to Mary. "But why?"

"Don't be asking the likes of me, Miss Johanna. I'm but a simple woman. You've got schooling and are a minister's daughter. Go ask your father. He might know."

"No, none of us knows the answer to that. Life is unfair, but the Lord has His reasons, I suppose." Johanna wiped her tears away. "We've got to prepare a burial." After a deep sigh, she asked, "Where's Tom Le Fleure?"

"I don't know," Mary said, wiping her face with a crumpled handkerchief and blowing her nose. "He ran out after Megan breathed her last. He couldn't bear it and cursed the baby. I had to stop him from throwing the child out of the wagon. I think he went that way." She pointed to a grove of alders.

"Mary, see to the baby's care for now, please. I'll go find him." With that, Johanna followed the narrow, dirt path that led through the trees. Sunlight penetrated the dense growth, outlining a man with a rope in his hand.

Johanna watched in horror as Tom Le Fleure stood beside a thick birch tree. He threw the rope up to the lowest branch, caught the other end of it and began to tie it around his neck.

"No!" Johanna screamed and ran. "Don't do it, Tom."

Agony contorted his face; pain shadowed his eyes. "Why not? I've nothing to live for now. *Mon cheri*, my one and only love, my Megan is gone!"

With more strength than she imagined she had, Johanna pulled the rope from Tom's hands. He was weeping so hard his body shook. "My Megan is dead."

"I know... I know." Johanna held Tom, rubbing her hands along his back. "But you have to live for your child, Tom. Your little Hanna Mary needs you. With her momma gone, she has no one else. You have to think of that poor, defenseless baby, Tom. Megan would expect you to."

Her words must have penetrated because Tom stopped crying. "You're right," he said with a sigh. "The child needs me." He smoothed back his hair. "Thank you for reminding me."

He's young and he'll survive. "And the first thing you have to do is to get her to the fort. You and little Hanna need medical care."

"What?" He looked puzzled.

"I think you've both got the flux. For that matter, anyone in our wagon train may have it, but you and Hanna must get cared for, now!"

Though he was emotionally spent, Tom followed Johanna to camp then on to the fort. A doctor from a nearby wagon train examined both Tom and the infant, Mary O'Dowd, Mabel, and Johanna. They didn't have cholera as suspected. Tom had dysentery.

Johanna recalled how weak her father had been and asked the doctor to come to camp and check on him. Reverend Wade became a difficult patient for the doctor. He was grumpy and impatient, but he agreed to take the doses of castor oil and the herbal remedies prescribed. Fortunately, Mabel and Johanna had nothing to worry about. The doctor sent them off, telling them all they needed was a little rest from their journey. Rest. Johanna laughed at the word.

"Is the man serious?" Mabel asked. "We won't rest until we reach the Willamette."

At sunset, Megan Le Fleure was laid to rest in a small plot beside the fort. Reverend Wade gave a brief eulogy. Tom, too ill to attend his wife's funeral, lay in the rear of his wagon. Johanna had scoured the wagon bed before allowing him to rest inside.

She held little Hanna in her arms as she watched Seamus throw the last shovelful of dirt on Megan's grave. Sally McPherson led a small band of children to the grave. They threw a handful of wildflowers—daisies, violets, and primroses—on top of the grave. "Your mommy's in good care. She's in heaven now," Johanna whispered to soothe the crying baby. *It's as if she senses the loss*, she thought, glancing at the hungry baby. "I can't help you there," she said, observing how the baby's mouth smacked in a sucking motion. Johanna nudged Mary O'Dowd, who stood beside her, rubbing her eyes with a lace cloth.

"We've got to find a way of feeding her," Johanna said.

"April Jones may help. She gave birth right before coming aboard the wagon train. She's a nursing mother. Would Tom mind?"

"It doesn't matter whether he does, does it?" Johanna said, rocking the baby and glad that Hanna had stopped crying. "If she doesn't get nursed, she'll die, too."

"Megan liked daisies the best," Sally told Johanna as they walked downhill to camp. "We picked them together one time. I'm going to miss her." Sally leaned against Johanna and wept.

"Shh! I know." Johanna pulled Sally close as she balanced the baby in her other arm. "We all will. It's a shame this child won't know her." She looked at Sally a moment.

"Would you help me care for her while her father's sick?"

Sally smiled. "Oh, yes. I'd do that for Megan and Tom. They were good to me."

"Thanks, Sally. I know Tom will appreciate the help."

Johanna walked over to the Jones family. April Jones looked busy enough with her brood of five children and the one nursing at her breast. Yet, she had a smile for Johanna when she approached. "Hello, Miss Johanna."

"April, how are you feeling?"

"Tired but rightly so. The young uns keep me going. What's that you got there?"

"Hanna Mary Le Fleure," Johanna held up the baby to show her.

"Oh, is she the prettiest child on earth!"

"I've got a favor to ask." Johanna felt a flush of embarrassment.

"I heard about poor Megan," April said, "I'm so sorry. But truth is, we've got to take care of the living. And if that baby needs nursing, I'd be right happy to do it." She handed her own baby to her husband Dan. "Take her to the cradle."

"Thank you so much," Joanna said, handing Hanna over to April. "I knew you'd understand. I hope it won't be too much for you."

"Nonsense, girl, I've reared bigger ones than this."

"I'll help take care of her, too," Sally offered with a shy smile.

"Now, I'm going to check on the father," Johanna said. "He's been very ill."

"Go on then," April said, "Sally and I will look after this child. She's in good hands."

"Thanks again." Johanna felt a pang of envy as she watched April Jones holding the baby close and nursing her. A part of her wanted to take on the maternal role, too. Yet, she knew she must do what was best for the baby. In time, Tom Le Fleure would heal both physically and emotionally too, but would take a long, long time to come to terms with the loss of Megan.

"Megan Le Fleure's death is the first on our trip, Father," Johanna said that evening over supper. Taking in his tired face and sad brown eyes, she covered his bony hand with hers. "Are you well? Have you taken all the medicine the doctor ordered you to?"

"Yes and yes," he said. "Don't worry so over me."

"You're my father, I will worry over you." She released his hand

and sat back.

"I know you're upset about poor Megan," he said, lightly taking her hand in his. "I pray Megan's death is the only one. But the Lord giveth us Hanna and the Lord taketh away Megan. We've been lucky. For miles now, we've seen the graves of those who'd not continue onward. It's sad but they remind us of our own mortality. We're in God's hands."

She pulled from his grasp and made coffee. As she boiled the water, she said, "Not all will make it to the promised land, Father." The image of a grave they passed along the trailside haunted her. The sight of gnawed body limbs covered by a torn dress had made her sick to her stomach. As she retched on the side of her wagon, she'd heard Ryan explaining to the ministers that wolves dug up shallow graves. He stopped long enough to bury the remains and allowed Reverend Wade to say a brief prayer for the woman's soul.

Bad enough to die and leave loved ones, but to be eaten by wild animals had to be a worse fate. She tried to think of pleasanter things as she poured her father a cup of coffee. "How much longer until we reach the valley, Father?"

He sat back, sipped his coffee, then said, "If all goes well, about two more months. Ryan told me of a new cut-off that will save time. We might try it."

"I'm going to get supplies at the fort tomorrow," Johanna told Mabel as she joined them by the fire. "We need to restock and get some fabric while we're here."

"Good idea." Sitting down on a stool, Mabel leaned over and whispered to Johanna, "Sally is taking good care of that Le Fleure baby. She's treating it like her own child. April Jones nurses the infant then turns her over to Sally. How's Tom?"

Johanna stirred the fire with a stick. "His fever broke. So I guess he's getting better. But he kept calling out his wife's name in his sleep. Ryan is with him now."

"It will be hard for Tom." Mabel looked over at the Le Fleure wagon. "The hardest part will come later, when he's well again. Young as they were, the Le Fleures were very much in love."

"How I know," Johanna sighed. She stood, wiped the supper dishes with a wet rag then put them in the chest. "I'm exhausted, Auntie, it's been a long day. Good night."

Half way to the tent, she bumped into Ryan as he rounded the corner of the Le Fleure wagon. "Johanna," he whispered, taking hold of her hands.

"Ryan, how's Tom?"

"Getting stronger everyday—I reckon he'll soon be fit as a fiddle. I guess nothing will cure the ache in his heart." Ryan glanced at Johanna's hands then added, "Nothing but time, that is. Anyway, Captain Greysmith's chief scout gave me a heap of brews to bring down Tom's fever. He should rest another day before we move out."

"So soon?"

"We can't wait too much longer, we got to move out again." He clasped her shoulder, "Tom will be all right. How do you feel?"

"Fine, why?"

He studied her face. "You'd been sick before, remember, and I worry about you."

"I'm fine, Ryan, really I am." She leaned against his chest and collapsed.

"Johanna!"

~ * ~

"The doctor at the fort said it was exhaustion," Johanna told Mabel the next day. "Ryan wasted no time in carrying me over there."

"And that's all?" Mabel looked at her suspiciously. "You faint in a man's arms and it's only exhaustion?"

"Yes," Johanna said. "Oh, let's go over there." She pointed to the cabin housing the trading post. "We need to restock our supplies."

"Certainly." Mabel followed her inside the cramped, crowded and dimly lit interior. Sacks of flour, rice, beans, and sugar lined one wall. Bolts of fabric lay on a table and black cookware was suspended from the ceiling by the counter. Emigrant men and women shuffled through the narrow aisles and pulled at the piles of assorted notions and farming implements scattered about.

"What a mess," Mabel said, glancing at the assortment.

Johanna listened to a woman bickering over prices with the shop owner.

"You call this silk from China?" she screeched, holding up a raggedy looking fabric. "It looks like cotton to me."

The man behind the counter rolled up his shirtsleeves and glared at the woman. "It's silk, come all the way from the Orient, and it'll cost ya more than cotton. If ya want it, take it. If ya don't, put it down."

"Snippety little man," Mabel whispered to Johanna.

Johanna glanced up from a rack of beef jerky; the dry brown meat held little appeal to her. Yet in times of dire need, it could be precious. She decided to buy some. "Prices are certainly dearer here than back in Missouri," she muttered after paying for her purchases. She realized that being so far from civilization allowed a merchant a monopoly on trading. This one was obviously taking advantage of it.

"Do you believe the cost of this?" Mabel asked, fingering some lace. "Five whole dollars? For this dreadful scrap."

"Put it back then, we won't need it."

"Hmpf!" Mabel sniffed, eyeing the irate shop owner. "I'll take these." She placed several bags of flour and sugar on the counter. When the clerk rang up the sale, she fumed. "You, sir, are a crook!"

"And you, Ma'am, are a royal pain in the buttocks!"

"My word, not even the ruffians on my captain's ship used such vulgarity!"

Mabel clasped her purchases and stormed from the store. Johanna trailed behind, armed with another bundle. Outside in the open courtyard, Mabel sat on a bench and began to cry.

Johanna sat next to her. The trip had worn everyone down, she thought. She handed Mabel a handkerchief. "Oh, Auntie, don't cry.

Things will get better."

Mabel wiped her eyes and blew her nose. "I surely hope so, Johanna."

~ * ~

Grizzly Dugan picked up the trail again, having lost it during a dust storm. He camped a few miles down from Fort Platte. A fellow trapper named Jeremiah Atkins informed him earlier that a wagon train filled with missionaries headed for the Willamette had recently passed by. One of their members died from the flux. Dugan hoped it wasn't that bastard Majors. He wanted his chance to put the skunk in his grave.

Jeremiah accompanied Grizzly to a Sioux encampment on the river. There they met a group of braves with a grudge against the encroachment of whites on their land. This gave Grizzly an idea. As they sat over a campfire, sharing the leftovers of a buffalo hunt with him, he persuaded them to form an alliance against one of the wagons heading west. He told them missionaries were planning to settle upon their land and bring more whites which would destroy their people. He then bribed them with the chance to get guns, horses, and money—the booty from the wagons—for their efforts to join forces with him.

"Hey, hear tell there's a reward for ya," Jeremiah told Grizzly as they settled down for the night.

"Yeah, I seen posters. They got a reward for bringing me back alive!" Grizzly chuckled. "I don't reckon on going back to no Missouri courthouse to stand trial."

"Hard to see ya in any kind o' jail," Jeremiah said, snuffing out the fire. "Ain't no jail big enough to hold the likes of you."

"That's for damn sure." Grizzly cleaned his teeth with his knife before settling down on his blanket. "And these braves will do my work for me." He motioned to the Sioux who slept nearby. "What they say?"

Jeremiah leaned closer, and chuckled before responding with,

"That ya finished off a man with your teeth? Hey tell, is it true?"

"Bloody lot of 'em, I done clawed and chewed my way out o' many a fight, and would do so again if it means getting what's coming to me. Yep, I done my share of killin', all right."

Jeremiah's laughter cut the still night air. When he finished, he flashed a smile at his companion. "I guess ain't no one gonna mess with you."

"Nope, they sure ain't." Grizzly stuck his knife in the ground beside him. The blade glowed in the dwindling flame of a lantern.

~ * ~

A china teacup flew off the table as the ground shook beneath Johanna's feet. She picked up the broken pieces then glanced across at Mabel, who stood beside the jockey box.

"Goodness," Mabel said, "What could it be?"

"There's about a thousand of 'em heading this way," Ryan shouted, riding by their wagon. "Circle round," he called, gesturing to the others to make the camp circle with their wagons.

"A thousand what?" Johanna stared after him. When he rode up to her, and loaded his rifle, she asked him again then followed his gaze to a black cloud on the horizon.

"Buffalo." He pointed to the cloud. "I saw them this morning. They're heading this way."

The rumbling drowned out the shouts of people who ran for cover as the black cloud moved ever closer, raising dust in its wake.

Johanna stood in awe and terror as the army of shaggy horned beasts became evident. The youngest children hid behind their parents. Johanna comforted a little girl who ran to her side. "We'll be all right, Melissa," she said.

"Get back to the wagons," Ryan told the families. "Men, ready your rifles and shoot any beast comes near your wagon." He rode off, rifle poised in one hand.

Johanna helped Mabel drive the mule team into the circle of wagons. She peered out from behind the side of it. As instructed, the farmers stood with rifles poised at the approaching herd. Their women and children stood nearby.

"Charlene!" A dark-haired woman shouted above the din and dust. "Oh, where on earth is that child?"

Johanna turned around to spy Viola Wilkins walking between two wagons.

"Get back," Johanna called. "You'll be trampled."

"I've got to find my child, Miss Wade. She stood here a minute ago." Tears welled in the woman's gray eyes. "Please," she began, wringing her hands, "please help me find her."

Johanna put her arms about the mother's shoulders. "She must be here. Let's look around, perhaps she's hiding in the wagon. Children sometimes hide when they're afraid."

Johanna peered in the wagon and underneath its bed as she shouted, "Charlene!"

Viola echoed the plaintiff cry. "Charlene! Come to Mommy."

"Mommy!" The high-pitched cry from outside the circled wagons sent shivers up Johanna's spine. She looked out at the open field. A small shape huddled on the ground. In one hand, the pigtailed girl held a cornhusk doll. She sucked her thumb then cried, "Mommy!"

"There she is." With a cry of relief, Viola rushed toward her child. "I'm coming, Charlene!" Johanna grabbed Viola's arm, but was shaken away. "I got to get my little girl."

"No, you'll be killed. I'll go." Johanna stepped forward.

"Johanna, no don't go." Mabel rushed to her side. They both stopped, stricken by the sight of an uncountable number of buffalo rushing forward like a black cloud to the river.

"My baby!" Viola sobbed, trying to push Johanna out of the way.

"Hold her back, Auntie. I'll get the child."

"I don't think you have to," Mabel said "There's Ryan."

~ * ~

Like a man possessed, Ryan rode with more speed than he'd ever ridden. Years of living among the Nez Perce gave him the skill to ride like one with his horse. Charlene's cries sounded pitiful and low beneath the rumble coming their way. She walked directly in the path of the stampede. "Good Lord," Ryan shouted. "Stay there. I'm coming."

Charlene glanced at the herd of buffalo heading toward her and screamed for her mother.

Viola stood, with open arms and a face twisted in fear. "Baby, baby," she shouted, "My baby girl, come to Mamma."

Ryan could almost feel the hot, fetid breath of the frantic buffalo. "Stay there," he told Charlene, hoping beyond hope that she'd listen. Suddenly the child stopped walking, stooped and picked up a small yellow flower in the field. It gave Ryan enough time to swoop down on his horse and scoop her up. The cornhusk doll fell to the ground.

"Dolly!" Charlene reached out for the doll.

Ryan pulled her up before she had a chance to topple off the horse. He spurred the horse on and cut a path clear across the field as the buffalo herd split in two directions running parallel to the wagon train. With heart pounding and sweat pouring from his brow, Ryan reached the wagon train. Shaken and worn, he managed to hand Charlene over to her frightened mother before sliding down to the ground. He rubbed his horse's side, leaned against her. "Thanks, Daisy," he whispered.

"Thank you, Mr. Majors." Viola sobbed, clutching her daughter to her side.

"Thanks." Her husband Dan grabbed Ryan's hand, nearly breaking the bones with his strong grip. "If there is anything I can ever do for you."

Ryan grinned as he eased his hand from the man's death grip. "Naw, forget it. Getting your daughter back alive, that's good enough."

"Good work." Reverend Wade clapped Ryan on the back.

Ryan shrugged as if it was all in a day's work. He glanced over at Johanna, and basked in the warmth of her smile.

"You are quite the hero, Mr. Majors," Johanna told him later as he groomed his horse, removing the dust from Daisy's hide. "I'd say the Lord provided us with a miracle."

"The Lord?" Ryan huffed. "Is that what you think? Hell, the Lord had nothing to do with saving Charlene. I rode out and grabbed her in time."

"But the Lord does work in mysterious ways. He cleared a path for you among the hundreds of buffalo who might otherwise have crushed you both to death."

"I see," Ryan snapped back. "Maybe your Lord will clear a path from here to Oregon for us while He's at it... a clear, straight, clean path through the mountains, maybe."

"Maybe." Johanna chuckled.

"Bah!" Ryan turned away. What was the use of arguing? She had him pegged as a heathen; he was not about to change her mind on that. "I did what I had to do, that's all."

"But you saved the child's life." She touched his hand and smiled. Ignoring the whisperings around them, Johanna kissed Ryan's cheek.

"Well, well, well," Stephen interrupted. "You're quite a hero, Mr. Majors."

Startled, Johanna spun around to face Stephen's narrowed gaze. She stood beside Ryan, their hands lightly touching. "Yes, Ryan is heroic. He rode out to save the child. He proved fearless. It's a miracle he survived. The Lord sent him to us."

Stephen grimaced. "It's more like money sent him." He turned to Johanna. "Do you really think Ryan came back for the sake of the wagon train? He's here for the money... and maybe something else." He pushed his way between Ryan and Johanna. "She's too fine a lady for you, Majors."

Ryan shoved Stephen aside, causing him to stumble and fall over a log. "Says who?"

"Stop it." Johanna bent to help Stephen stand. "Stop it, both of you. Quit locking horns like two rams." She turned to Stephen.

"Father hired Ryan. He's being paid to lead us. But no amount of money could make him run amid wild beasts to save Charlene."

"Ryan is as wild as the beasts."

"You don't know him."

"And you do?" He studied Johanna's face then shook his head, "I feared as much. Your eyes give you away, Johanna. I know that look, it's the same one you held for your fiancé, Robert McEntee. Has following the wake of this dust-clad trapper made you forgot him already?"

She clenched her hands at her side, reining in the desire to slap his face. "Never, I could never forget Robert, but Robert is dead."

"Dead and forgotten," Stephen snapped. His half-hearted laughter irked Ryan.

"Johanna, if you need me, I'll be by my campsite." Ryan walked away. He had his fill of excitement for the day and felt drawn and in need of rest. He smiled at the thought of how Johanna held his hand and kissed him before the others. At the sound of a hard slap, he glanced over his shoulder. He grinned with satisfaction at the sight of Stephen rubbing his face and Johanna rushing to her wagon. The young pup finally got what was coming to him.

~ * ~

"And I say, let's go after the buffalo," Amos Jones shouted, twisting his grey beard as he did so. "We could use the fresh meat."

"No, you don't know how to hunt down these animals." Ryan tightened the reins on Daisy as he sat back on the saddle. "I'm going alone."

"We'll come," Seamus said. "We want a bit of fun hunting these critters. We could sure use the meat too."

Ryan relented at the glimmer in Seamus' eyes and the growing excitement written on the faces of the farmers gathering near his campsite. He had barely had an hour's sleep when they rushed over to him, rifles in hand, demanding to go hunting. "Oh, all right." Smiles split the faces of the young and old men. Ryan wondered if they knew

261

what they were in for. "But if you're gonna hunt buffalo, you need a fast horse and a trusty rifle."

"I got my mule," Seamus said. "She's trusty as they come."

"No mule." Ryan shook his head. "It'd panic first time a buffalo got close."

Hearing the men, Johanna nudged her father's arm. "Can you lend them your horse?"

Reverend Wade glanced at her then at Seamus. "Sure... go on and borrow the stallion. He's quick enough for one put out to pasture. Had him shoed and got a good saddle."

"Thanks," said Seamus.

A few of the farmers drifted off, telling Ryan their horses probably wouldn't make the hunt. In the end, he led Seamus, John O'Dowd, Tom Le Fleure, and Amos Jones. The five men rode out at first light.

They rode mile upon mile of semi-arid land, along sloping hillsides, past prairie dog towns and a pack of wolves feasting on antelope. The wolves growled at the men on horseback. Ryan shot his rifle into the air, chasing them away. The buffalo trail led the men to a ravine, where dozens of buffalo grazed in the tall grass.

The huge, shaggy black beasts moved slowly. One calf, legs still bowed and shaking, nursed from his mother. Ryan sensed his horse's trepidation as she moved in on the herd. Daisy slowed. One of the largest buffalo lifted his head, sniffed the air then let out a loud snort. The rest of the herd stopped grazing, and looked up at the men.

As if on cue, the large animals started to run in unison. Once more the ground quaked with their heavy hoof beats. "Let's go," Ryan called and led the farmers in hot pursuit. Their horses kicked up dust and stones in their wake.

With lightning speed, Ryan galloped onward, skirting bushes and willows. Seamus kept up with him; the other riders fell behind. They rode up and down hills, over grass and sandy riverbanks. The buffalo broke into several small groups at a large stream, scattering the herd. "Follow me," Ryan hollered.

Only yards away, the buffalo they pursued paused. Splashes of mud matted its shaggy hair and traces of last winter's hair covered its back in uneven shreds and patches. It sniffed the air. As the riders approached it ran. Ryan's horse held back despite his attempt to spurn her onward. The buffalo got away. Ryan fired from a distance but missed. Seamus took aim and missed too as the buffalo ran by him.

Undaunted, Ryan took off after the animal until he came abreast of the buffalo. The bull, cornered by the slope of a ridge, slowed his gallop and turned toward Ryan. He lowered his huge, shaggy head, stamped the ground, and prepared to charge. With a snort, Daisy leaped aside in terror, throwing Ryan to the ground. Stunned, Ryan lay a moment then fired at the bull. His shot missed, but it did send the buffalo running in the opposite direction. As he stood, Ryan spotted Seamus chasing the buffalo. "Seamus!" Both disappeared beyond a hillock. Mounting the horse, Ryan rode out again. A shot rang out over the sound of the wild hoof beats.

Wasting no time, Ryan galloped onward. Standing before a dead buffalo, Seamus beamed with pride as he held his rifle aloft. "I done killed me a buffalo!" he shouted to Ryan.

Glancing at the blood spouting from the animal's head, Ryan nodded. "You sure did. Get some rope."

John O'Dowd and Tom Le Fleure rode up. "Ya got one!" Tom shouted.

"Darn herd outran us," John piped in.

"Well, let's get him tied up." In a short while they had hitched the carcass to two of the horses.

Suddenly it dawned on Ryan that one of the hunting party hadn't returned yet. "Where's Amos?" Ryan asked.

Tom shrugged. "He must of gone the other way when we came over."

"We better find him before dark, he could get lost out there." Ryan shielded his eyes from the sun as he scanned the horizon. "John, Tom, take this carcass back to the wagons. Seamus and I will find Amos.

We'll meet you at camp."

Half an hour later, Seamus called Ryan over to dense underbrush. "Ya, hear that?"

A deep-pitched moan, followed by a string of foul utterances, came from somewhere in the overgrowth. "Damn it to hell, the pain is killin' me!"

They found Amos, bloodied, dust-covered, and crumpled on his side, clutching his right leg and moaning.

"Amos?" As soon as Ryan saw the man on the ground, he jumped down from his horse and rushed over to him. Seamus followed.

In the twilight, Ryan could only discern the bloodstain on Amos' leg. "Looks like he's hurt pretty bad. We've got to stop the bleedin'."

"Here." Seamus handed Ryan his neck scarf. "Wrap it round the leg."

"Almost got the bastard," Amos moaned. "Damn bull spun round and gored me."

"Hold still, Amos." Ryan wrapped the scarf around Amos' leg. With Seamus' help he lifted Amos up and placed him behind the pommel of his horse. He held the reins and led the horse toward camp. Although Ryan walked slowly downhill, Amos moaned with each bounce and sway of the horse.

"It's going to be all right," Ryan reassured him, "you'll live."

~ * ~

Back at camp, Johanna tended to Amos' wounds. Afterward, she joined everyone at the camp as they feasted on the buffalo Seamus shot. Mabel looked wide-eyed as Seamus recounted how he cornered the huge buffalo and shot him. Ryan chuckled to himself as he listened to Seamus' exaggeration.

"Amos has an infection, Ryan," Johanna said, sitting next to him. "I've done all I could for him."

"The bleeding stopped, didn't it?"

"Yes, but he lost a lot of blood, and his fever is high." The bonfire crackled and spit as they both sat staring into the flames. The strains of a fiddle broke the stillness. The lively tune did little to relieve her mood. All day she'd been battling with herself over the cutting remarks Stephen threw at her. She regretted slapping him when he told her she behaved like a whore in front of everyone. It only made her feel guilt-ridden. She became impatient as Seamus went on and on about the hunt. "Is that all men can think of?" she asked Mabel on the side. "The hunt... the killing of an innocent animal."

"They didn't look so innocent to me when they tried to trample Ryan and Charlene this morning. And didn't one gore Amos Jones?"

"You're right." Johanna stood, crossing her arms in front of her chest. "I guess I'm just tired. It's been a long day. I'll pray for Amos. He's so weak."

"So will I," Mabel said.

"There's talk of a celebration when we reach Independence Rock," Sally said. "We're halfway to Oregon. Will you help bake some pies?"

"Certainly." Mabel smiled. "We'll have a real celebration, right, dear, like we did back in Boston on the Fourth of July?"

"I suppose so." Johanna mumbled, feeling cross as she poked a stick into the ashes from the fire. Halfway there meant they still had half the trail to travel. Only God knew what else lay in wait for them. As the flames dwindled, the families began dispersing to their wagons.

~ * ~

Amos Jones made a slow recovery from his wounds. By the time the wagon party reached Independence Rock, he could manage sitting up in the rear of his wagon. Johanna waved to him as she walked by. She spotted his wife nursing Hanna Le Fleure and smiled. Little Hanna looked plumper and healthier each day. For that, she felt grateful to the Jones' family. After their one expedition, the farmers didn't bother to venture too far from the wagons.

As she walked the sandy trail, Johanna breathed in the scents of the wildflowers... sweetpeas, wild roses, and yellow-flowered cactuses growing alongside the North Platte River. She stretched her arms and shoulders, releasing the strained tension in their muscles. On the brief stopover, the men fished, using sticks for poles and leftover bread for bait. A lucky few caught catfish and perch. Seamus showed off his catch.

"Mind yourself," he told her as she touched the slimy fish. "He's got razor sharp teeth that one. He'd cut off your fingers."

She quickly pulled her hand away. "Thanks for warning me."

At the base of Independence Rock, Johanna pulled off her boots and rubbed her feet. Calluses had formed on the soles, blisters bled, and the stench of sweat sickened her. "I need a good bath," she told Mabel, who came to sit down on the ground beside her.

"We'll have one soon," Mabel said, rubbing her sore hands. "Mules have been pulling so hard lately, I thought my arms would be wrenched off."

"I can take the lead for awhile," Johanna offered.

"What are they doing?" Mabel pointed to the people who stood in front of a towering sandstone formation.

Several people began to carve their names into the rock using a hammer or a small chisel. Johanna ventured over to read the long list of names inscribed by earlier travelers. "They're just making their mark like all the settlers who came through before us," she told Mabel. "It's like what Longfellow once wrote, 'leaving behind us footprints on the sands of time.'"

Mabel gave her a puzzled look then followed Johanna over to the sandstone formation.

"Don't you think it's fitting that these people long to be remembered in time?"

Taking out a small knife, Johanna dug into the stone and inscribed her own name. She handed the knife to Mabel and waited while she carved her name on the rock. "There," Mabel said, handing the knife back and wiping the dust from her hands. "Now our footsteps are there for all time, too."

"Yes," Johanna said with a giggle. "Or until a rainstorm washes the marks off."

~ * ~

To celebrate their mid-way passage, the women in the party made a feast. Johanna baked an apple and a blackberry pie. Ryan brought the carcasses of an antelope and a turkey he shot during his forays into the wilderness. A communal fire raged in the evening as everyone sat to enjoy the bountiful feast of roasted meat and baked goods. Amid the lively chatter as people passed wooden bowls of food, Seamus played his bagpipes. Stephen Green covered his ears as he strolled with the Emerson sisters. Later, all joined in a circle around Reverend Wade for a thanksgiving prayer service.

Johanna left as soon as she could. She found Ryan alone, deep in thought at the base of the clay structure nick-named Independence Rock. "Lovely night," she said, reaching out to clasp his hand.

Ryan spun around and pulled her to him. "Yes," he murmured, outlining her lips with his thumb. "Sure is a lovely night and a lovelier woman."

Johanna's pulse raced with his touch. Their kiss in the shadows was slow and needy. Johanna clung to Ryan, letting the wind whip her hair from its fastenings. She felt warm and wanting as Ryan held her in his tight embrace. This had been the moment they'd waited for, having been unable to be alone in a long time.

"Johanna, I—"

They turned around and saw that there was a commotion back in camp with people running and shouting. "Something is wrong! I see Seamus standing there with his gun."

"Let's go back." Ryan took her by the hand and led the way.

Fear gripped Johanna when she saw Mabel leaning on the side of a wagon holding her hand to her shoulder. Blood stained the top of her dress.

"No!" she screamed, running to her aunt.

"My God, I've been shot," Mabel said, grabbing onto Johanna.

"'Twas an accident," Seamus mumbled over and over. "Me gun went off as I was polishin' it. My poor lassie, will she be all right?" He stared wide-eyed at Ryan.

"Oh, please God, I hope so." Johanna sobbed. Ryan scooped Mabel into his arms.

As they passed Stephen, he snickered, "Hmpf, I can smell the whiskey on him. Seamus McPherson was so drunk he shot Mabel."

"Shut up," Johanna shouted, but gaped in horror when she noticed the empty flask of whiskey lying on the ground beside Seamus. She shook her head. "No, it can't be true."

"Johanna, please, I'm in such pain," Mabel moaned, twisting back and forth in Ryan's arms.

"I'm sorry, Auntie. Hurry, Ryan, I have to help her."

He placed Mabel within the wagon bed and Johanna quickly stripped off Mabel's dress. "I'll get my knife," Ryan said, "I'll have to cut that bullet out of her shoulder."

Johanna grabbed his hand. "Ryan, do you think Seamus meant to shoot her?"

"Not on your life. Now hold her steady."

Mabel screamed as Ryan brought the knife to her arm then thankfully she fell unconscious.

Nineteen

Marauders Attack

Rocks plummeted down to the ravine. Grizzly Dugan dashed between them, flinching and cursing as marble-size chunks pelted him. He hurried back to the cave where his men greeted him with a chorus of grunts and nods. Their campfire cast their giant-size shadows on the limestone walls. Fruit bats swooped low, circling Dugan's head. He swung at them. "Stay away, ya slippery varmints."

"Afraid of bats, are ya?" Jeremiah asked with a wry grin.

Dugan scowled. "I ain't afeared of nothin'." He rubbed his scalp, fingering the blood from a small cut. He sat in the somber circle licking the blood off his fingers then he stretched his legs out. "After five days, we found 'em," he said. Noting the stiff postures and indifferent expressions on the Sioux warriors, he realized that they didn't understand a word. Grunting, he leaned toward his old trapping friend.

"Hey, Jeremiah," he whispered, "There's about a hundred pilgrims down there and there's only eight of us. We're gonna have to surprise 'em. Maybe go at night. What do ya think?"

Jeremiah spat his tobacco on the ground. "Sounds good to me, boss. We go in when they're sleepin' and cut their bloody throats. Right?"

"Right."

"And maybe take a few women. I heard tell the minister got a daughter. A trapper at Fort Laramie said she's some punkins."

"A beauty, eh?" Dugan's gaze narrowed. "You leave her to me," he sneered. "Take one of them farm girls. Since I'm running this show, I get the golden egg."

Jeremiah cocked his head to one side. "The what?"

"Nothin'." Dugan rubbed his bearded chin. "Ah, it's a dumb story my ma told me. Ya see this man's wife was real greedy. The man got a goose as a reward for helping a fairy."

"A what?"

"Fairy... they got wings and fly about."

"Oh, like bats?"

"No, you jackass, they're little people with wings," Dugan said. "Anyways, this goose laid so many gold eggs, it made the man rich. Then he did a dumb thing. His wife wanted him to kill the goose. He did and they became poor cause they had no more golden eggs. Yep." Dugan sighed, stirring the fire. "Sure was one dumb fella." He stared into the flames, thinking about how his mother told him stories, the only time she coddled him as a youngster. The years had been unkind to his mother, Marie Du Bonnet. "Yep." He spoke his thoughts aloud. "My ma thought she'd end up on a sugar plantation. Hell, he left her high and dry with a bastard. She had to whore for her supper until her dying day."

"Here." Jeremiah handed him a flask. "Ya look like a man in bad need of a drink."

"Thanks." Dugan took a swig, wiped his mouth on his sleeve then stared into the fire. The golden flames licked the chilled air. Thoughts of his past raced through his mind as he drank. He recalled the grizzly bear mauling and the two men who left him. He never expected their paths to cross. Doing the dirty work for the Pacific Fur Trapping Company led him to one brother. Following the Oregon Trail would lead him to the other. "I'm going back out," he announced.

Dugan felt his way along the guano-covered walls. "Dang bats," he muttered, wiping the excrement from his hands as he exited the cave. As he leaned on a tree, he spied a black-frocked man and a woman in a calico dress. "Well, I'll be damned," he muttered to himself, "if it ain't that woman I seen at the lake. She's a beaut all right."

The woman rushed away from the grove, leaving the young minister sitting on a stump. The wagon camp lay about a half mile west. Like a snake slithering after its prey, Dugan stepped slowly down the dirt path that led from the mouth of the cave to the base of the hill. Occasionally, the young preacher would stir and glance up from his black prayer book at the curtain of pine trees. Dugan hid against a trunk. Small rocks flew from under his feet as he stepped away. The man looked through the trees again, shielding his eyes from the sun.

When Dugan reached the base, he stepped with the stealthy grace of an antelope. As soon as the minister turned away, Dugan crept up and brandished his knife. "Hey, pilgrim, what ya reading?"

Stephen's eyes widened as he took in the sight of the burly, scar-faced trapper wielding a long knife. He dropped the Bible. "Who... who... the devil are you?"

Dugan picked up the book, read the cover then sneered. "Save our souls, if you ain't a right good minister?"

Stephen fingered his stiff collar. "I'm Reverend Green."

"Here, Reverend." Dugan handed him the book. As Stephen reached for it, Dugan pulled him closer and pinned one arm behind his back before pressing the flat edge of the knife against Stephen's chin. "Say a word, and I'll cut your damn tongue out!"

"What do you want?" Stephen rasped.

"Not a word, preacher." Dugan tightened his grip. "We're gonna have us a little walk up that hill." He nodded toward the cavern. "Move it."

He dropped his grip on Stephen's arm, and shoved him. "Move it, I said."

Stephen stumbled up the hillside with Dugan's knife poised inches away from his back. "Do anything foolish," Dugan warned with cold menace, "and I'll crush your skull with my bare hands."

Stephen's breath came ragged as they struggled uphill. He stumbled on a fallen tree limb. Dugan pushed him forward. "Keep going."

"What do you want with me?"

"Never you mind. You do as I say, or else."

They climbed several yards further, scattering a herd of mountain goats. They'd reached the mouth of a cave; a lantern lit the way toward level ground. Stephen slid on a layer of bat guano. Dugan hauled him to his feet then shoved him inside.

"Look, boys, we got us a preacher man." Dugan pushed Stephen so hard his Bible flew into the fire. "Get the book, Jeremiah," Grizzly growled.

Jeremiah grasped the book, screaming as the flames scorched his hand. "Damn it, Grizzly. I ain't your serving boy."

"No, but you're working for me. Ya'll working for me," he told the Sioux. "And remember that this here's a preacher. He's with that wagon train I told ya about."

Jeremiah handed the Bible to Dugan, who stared at it a moment before ripping out a few pages.

Shock and anger lit Stephen's eyes. He rushed to stop Grizzly. "That's a holy book."

"Your holy book won't save you." Dugan blocked him with one hand and held the book up with his other. "But your helping us will. Here." He handed the book to Stephen, who frowned at the singed and torn pages.

"What... what do you want me to do?"

"Where's Ryan Majors?"

"Ryan Majors? What do you want with him?"

"None of your damned business, Yankee. Just tell me and you'll go free."

Stephen stood stone silent.

"I cut up a fella who refused to talk to me, Tom Knifechief."

"The scout from Fort Laramie?"

"You knew him, eh?"

"Yes." Stephen frowned. "He would have been our guide, but Ryan came back."

"Ya mean Ryan Majors?"

"Yes." Stephen sniffed the air, grimacing at the sight of the painted warriors roasting skewered bats. "Why'd you kill the scout?"

"I told ya, he wouldn't talk." Dugan brought the knife closer to Stephen's head and cut off a lock of ash blonde hair. "But I know you'll be different. You'll help me, right?" He tore off another chunk of hair.

"Yeow!" Stephen winced.

"Ya see," Dugan said, releasing his hold on Stephen, "it's like this—a Pawnee named Evening Star stole my money and ran off to a wagon train. I'm looking for her, the money, and the no-good bastard Majors."

Stephen stood mute. "Damn it, pretty boy. You don't have to die for Ryan Majors. Now do ya?" Dugan snapped.

"No," Stephen mumbled. "The squaw's gone."

Dugan cupped his hand to his ear. "What's that? You squeak like a mouse."

Stephen's voice echoed in the cave. "Evening Star isn't with us."

"She ain't?" Dugan tucked his knife in his belt. "Well then..." He rubbed his beard. "I'm after the other one. Tell me where I can find Ryan Majors." He shook Stephen. "Tell me or both you and your pretty missus will die."

"What?" Stephen stumbled back.

"The pretty missus I seen ya with. She's a beaut. I seen her at the lake... watched how she rubbed the soap up and down her arms and along here." He touched his crotch. "I can't say I wouldn't have my fun with her 'fore I kill her. Does she smell as sweet as she looks... soft, pink, and wet from head to toe?"

"You bastard!" Stephen lunged for Dugan's throat. "You won't lay a hand on Johanna Wade."

Dugan struck him hard across the face.

As Stephen lay moaning, wiping his bloody lip, Dugan towered over him.

"I can kill you as much as look at you. Do as I say, and you and the girl go free."

"I don't believe you."

"You got no other choice, except to die."

"I'll do what you want." Stephen sat and hung his head. "But don't hurt Johanna."

"Got a soft spot for her, don't ya? Good, then me and the boys here will follow you to them wagons. If you say so much as a peep and give us away, both you and the girl will die, and it won't be a pretty death neither. Them Sioux killed a man once by burying him chin deep in a mound full of fire ants, and as the ants ate him alive, the Sioux took turns shooting arrows at his head. Vultures finished him off." Dugan nodded toward a row of stalagmites. "Go sit over there."

With a defeated sigh, Stephen slumped into the corner, shivering as his back touched a frigid spiral. He hugged his chest, peered up and locked gazes with the warriors. Jeremiah Atkins came over and handed him a bowl of food. Stephen wrinkled his nose at its foul smell.

"Dog," Jeremiah said, pulling the bowl away. "Fella don't like our hospitality, Dugan. What ya reckon we do to him?"

Dugan held up the roasted dog leg and ate, crunching hard on the bone. "What's a matter, pilgrim," he muttered between mouthfuls. "Ain't ya had dog meat before? It's mighty fine fixins."

Dugan threw the bone into the fire then stood next to Jeremiah. "At last, I've got 'em. I'm gonna get that money and make up for this." He touched the scar. He had blamed it for his years of loneliness. He cleaned his teeth with the blade of his hunting knife, all the while watching the minister's face grow pale and worried.

What a dandy! Dugan thought with utter contempt. *Fair of face and hair, the minister's looks could win any woman. Damn his blue eyes and smooth skin. Damn his youth too!*

Dugan watched Stephen's delicate hands as they clutched the holy book like a shield. When Stephen's gaze met his, he snarled. "What ya staring at?"

"I'm not staring."

"Uh." Dugan chortled. "Ain't you an honest preacher? I know sure as hell you was staring at this." He touched his scar. "A beaut, ain't she? I got my name Grizzly from the bear that mauled me. I killed it and ate it, hair and all."

"Dugan got the har of the bar in him," Jeremiah said to Stephen. "Nobody but nobody messes with Grizzly Dugan."

Dugan poked Stephen's shoulder blades with the knife handle. "Yep, siree. I'm part bear now." He ran the handle along Stephen's right arm, turned the blade on his hand and lightly rubbed the smooth palm. "Eh, maybe that fine redheaded woman would like a man like me instead of a dandy with golden locks and useless hands."

Stephen pulled away.

Dugan tucked the knife in his belt. "Mind the time, Jeremiah, when I caught a preacher sneakin' off with my woman. He said he was gonna save her soul. He saved it all right. He hauled off with her in the night. I caught 'em naked in each other's arms by the creek, and he wasn't using no Bible neither. It still sours my milk to think on it." He drank a sip of whiskey from Jeremiah's flask.

"Yep, my woman got a beatin' and after tearing off the preacher's topknot, blonde as yours, I done tore out his eyes. Guess, you can say an eye for an eye." Dugan guffawed at his own joke. He clapped Stephen on the back. "Now ain't that funny, boy?"

"You sure are funny, boss." Jeremiah gave him a lopsided grin.

"Damn it!" Dugan smacked his forehead. "I plumb forgot my manners." He offered the flask to Stephen. "This here's the best John Barleycorn west of the Mississippi."

Stephen shook his head in refusal.

"Aw, a little of the devil's brew won't harm ya none."

"No, thanks."

"Hey, he's got manners, boys. My ma liked a man with fine manners. I never had no use for 'em, though." Dugan handed the flask to Jeremiah. The two sat staring into the flames and poking fun at the minister.

"Since we got us a minister," Dugan slurred, "how about a few prayers for these poor forgotten souls?" He pointed past Stephen to the rear of the cave where a skeleton lay in scattered pieces on the ground. The skull bore a macabre grin. Dugan walked over and picked up the skull. He held it in his palms. "Alas," he said with dramatic inflection, "alas, poor Yorick, I knew him."

Jeremiah and the Sioux laughed at his shenanigans. Dugan threw the skull at Stephen's feet.

Stephen jumped back. "My God," he gasped, "You're mad!"

Dugan laughed, slapping Stephen's knee. "Eh, maybe you're right, boy. I'm plumb out of my skull." He pointed at the skull as it rolled into the fire, chuckling as flames shot up through its hollows.

"You... you know Hamlet?" Stephen asked.

"Naw, can't say I do," Dugan said with a sly grin, "but my ma had a fella who quoted Shakespeare to the whores before bedding 'em."

Stephen's face mirrored interest, so Dugan continued, "Yep. The first words I remember was 'Oh, my God!'" He winked at Jeremiah.

"Those were the men plowing the fields. One seeded my ma and I come along nine months later. I learned a lot about women."

Stephen made a pitying noise. Dugan hated pity more than anything; it made him furious.

"Hey, Reverend, know anything about women? Naw, I bet ya don't, except for that one in the wagon. She's a redhead, like my mother. My mother could o' been a preacher's wife. Ummm..." He paused, rubbing his grizzled chin. "Ya mentioned Wade... He was the actor from Boston. He sure had my mother fooled. Randolph Wade was his name. Ma said after him, she'd never fall for another actor. Then this fella come, drunk and angry at my ma. He pulls a knife on her because he thinks she cheated him. I wrestled the knife out of his hand but he knocks me out. Next thing, I wake up and there's my ma with a broken neck. Well, I run after that bastard with his own knife and cut him good. I didn't know he was the marshal's son. I had the whole damn town coming for me. I was twelve but they'd have hung me anyway. I ran off on a steamboat heading to Missouri. I learned how to steal and cheat at cards. And I won quite a bit before losing it all to a French trapper named Jaffrenau. Fella took a liking to me 'cause I was full of spitfire. He took me on as a trapping partner. We headed to Vancouver and worked for the same fur company. Then I married that Bannock squaw. She was more of a whore than my own ma, laying it out for any man who came her way. Whores! The whole damn world is full of 'em. And they ain't all women neither, lots of men sell their souls for things. Yep, siree."

He shoved Stephen's hand away from his face. "Of course, you wouldn't know such things—you with your fancy frocks and pretty face." Dugan rubbed his scar. "Back before this, I could have had my pick of women." He peered outside as the rays of light dwindled. "It'd be about supper time in those wagons, boys," he told his men. "As soon as it gets dark, we'll go on down there." He stood, blocking Stephen's view.

"Ya look scared, Reverend. I thought you believed in a heaven. If ya die, you go to God. Where do folk like me go? Eh? I reckon I got more to be scared of than you. But I reckon I'm gonna fight my way out of this world and with the devil himself in the next one. But I'd sure like to have a pretty girl like that Johanna before I die."

"Don't you dare touch her," Stephen sputtered, standing up like a David before Goliath, and meeting Dugan's dark gaze.

"What's that you say, Reverend?" He squeezed Stephen's shoulders in a bone-crushing grip.

"Ouch!" Stephen winced. "Do what you want, but don't touch Johanna."

"Don't tell me what to do." Dugan slapped Stephen's face. "Look here, boy, you're lucky you're getting away with your life. Go on and sit down." He shoved Stephen to the ground. "You better rest before nightfall. This here's gonna be one hell of a night."

~ * ~

"I wonder what on earth is keeping Stephen." Johanna finished applying the poultice to Mabel's wound. Fortunately the bullet didn't cut deep, and Ryan had removed the slug with only a slight loss of blood.

"He's probably off with those two sisters again!" Mabel winced in discomfort as the bandage made from old bed sheets was tied tightly around her shoulder and arm.

"There, it will do." Johanna admired the sling she made for her aunt. "The poultice from the chia seeds should help with the healing."

"He didn't mean to shoot me, Johanna." Mabel sniffled.

"I know, it was an accident. But still, you're very lucky. If it had gone any deeper or hit your chest, you wouldn't have lived." She plumped a pillow and brought it over to her aunt then wiped beads of perspiration from Mabel's brow. "You're warm, I'll bring you sage tea. It will restore your strength and lower the fever. Rest awhile now."

Mabel clasped her hand. "Thank goodness, Johanna. You've been an angel of mercy caring for me and the rest in the wagon train. Your father told me that he's quite proud of you." She studied Johanna's face. "You could use some rest too. You look as if you're about to drop from exhaustion. We don't want that to happen again."

"You're right." Johanna stood and wiped the poultice off her hands. "I had a fight with Stephen. He's become so adamant about changing our course. He said that the factor at Fort Laramie told him of a better trail than the one we're on. He said Ryan is leading us the wrong way."

Mabel sat up, groaning with the sudden movement. "Do you believe Stephen?"

"Of course not." Johanna shrugged, changing into her nightgown. "I think Ryan knows more than anyone else what's best."

"I'm glad that you're getting on with Ryan. You'll both be in my wedding party."

"What?"

Mabel smiled through tears. "Yes, I know it's sudden, but Seamus and I are getting married as soon as we reach the Willamette Valley. I want you to believe that Seamus McPherson is a good and honest man. I love him."

Johanna hugged her, careful not to hurt her shoulder. "I'm so happy for you." Tears of joy ran down her cheeks.

"Yes." Mabel wiped away her own tears then blew her nose on a handkerchief. "This is ridiculous, isn't it," she said with a wave of her hands. "Here we are two grown women with much to be happy over... and we're both crying."

They laughed. Johanna brushed the hair from her aunt's forehead and kissed it. "Goodnight, Auntie. I love you, too." She blew out the lantern then stretched out on the blanket.

~ * ~

Nighttime ushered in with the chirping of crickets and the movement of nocturnal prowlers—skunks, raccoons, and deer foraging for food. Johanna squeezed her eyes shut but couldn't sleep. She knew her father and Stephen would be sleeping nearby. She peered out at the sky through a slit in the tent. Stars glimmered in the blackness. She shivered and pulled the blanket to her chin. A mosquito buzzed in her face; she swatted it. Yet the persistent buzzer didn't quit until she squashed it with the heel of her boot. Aside from the low braying of the mule team, all remained quiet. Images of marauders lurking in the brush ran through her mind. *Stop it!* she told herself. *Ryan is keeping guard, he'll protect us.*

As she thought that, she heard a branch snap and she peeked out of the tent flap. A family of raccoons rushed by, toppling piles of discarded rubbish. They nibbled on fish bones, half-eaten corncobs, and burned bread. "Silly me," she whispered, "afraid of a few raccoons."

She lay down and shut her eyes. Flashes of scenes, like pictures from a book, skittered through her mind. There was Robert, lying pale and drawn, reaching for her hand. As she took it, his face changed to Ryan's. He came closer and kissed her. As she drew back, Ryan's face changed. His wide-planed features became rotund, the nose thick and straight, and a scar ran down one cheek into a bearded chin. The thick lips curled into a hideous grin. "No!" she lashed out as the face approached. Hot, rancid breath licked her skin. Johanna twisted her head away. Her eyelids fluttered open. She stared into the soulless, haunting eyes of the face in her nightmare.

"You!" She cringed beneath her covers. "You're the man from the lake!"

"That's right, I'm Grizzly Dugan. We meet at last, sweetheart." The man's thick, hairy hand cut off her scream.

"Don't harm my—" A loud thwack silenced the rest of Mabel's words.

"Aunt Mabel, are you all right?"

"Shut up!" the man snarled and yanked her out of bed. He held her against him, covering her mouth with one hand as he dragged her from the tent.

"Please," Stephen begged, "leave her alone. If you want Ryan, I'll take you to him. He's not here."

"No, Stephen! How could you? Don't tell—" The man's hand clamped over her mouth again, choking off her air. She felt dizzy.

"Say a word or make a move," Dugan hissed, "and I'll kill you and the reverend there." Stephen cowered behind a group of warriors with painted faces. Dugan took his hand away from her mouth, allowing her to catch her breath. She greedily gulped in air and grimaced at the man's foul stench.

"Stephen, you're worse than a snake in the grass!" Johanna spat out. Dugan's coarse, thick hands pinned her arms behind her back.

"Tie her up," he ordered Stephen.

"No." The rope dangled from Stephen's hands.

"You will," Dugan sneered. "Now do it."

Releasing a sigh, Stephen hung his head. "It wasn't my idea," he said as he tied the rope about Johanna's wrists. He whispered in her ear. "They're loose enough, escape when you can."

Stepping back to Dugan, he said, "Please believe me, Johanna. This fiend forced me to do this."

Dugan grabbed Johanna's shoulders; the blade of his knife caught on the top of her nightgown and ripped at the sleeve, baring her shoulders and the top of her breast. He cupped one breast between the folds of cotton and molded the supple flesh in his hand. "Ah, it's aching to be touched, ain't it?" He leered at her. "She's a whore like the rest," he told Stephen. "See how she aches for it... right, honey?"

Johanna spat at his feet. She swallowed back the bile rising in her throat as Dugan's hands fumbled with her other breast and he rubbed his jutting belly against her. She worked her hands free while Dugan licked her neck, and quickly reached for his knife. As she lifted the handle, Stephen rushed forward, knocking Dugan away.

Trembling, Johanna held her torn garments with one hand and the knife with the other and watched in horror as Dugan smashed Stephen against a tree. He fell unconscious to the ground.

"No!" Johanna screamed, charging at Dugan with the knife. He ducked and yanked on her hair. "It's not a boy you want, Missie." Dugan sneered, grabbing the knife away. "Not at all, but me and her will have our fun later. Right now, I want Ryan Majors."

Johanna tried to squirm loose, but Dugan pulled harder on her hair. She yelped. He turned her around and lifted her chin, forcing her to stare into his fierce, lust-filled eyes. "Take me to Ryan, now!" he demanded.

One of the warriors kicked Stephen who was starting to regain consciousness.

"You'll not have me or Ryan."

"Johanna!"

"Father." Her cry caught in her throat. "Go back."

Dugan grinned wickedly at the elder minister. "Ah... what have we here? Reverend Wade? Any relation to Randolph Wade?"

"Randolph was my half-brother," Reverend Wade stated. "What has he got to do with this?"

"Well, howdy, Uncle." Grizzly Dugan nuzzled Johanna's neck. "That kind of makes us cousins, Missy. Give your cous' a kiss."

The minister's face turned as pale as his nightgown. "Now, see here, leave my daughter alone." He rushed toward Johanna's aide, but a Sioux brave followed behind him.

"Watch out, Father!" Johanna tried to lunge forward to shield her father, but Dugan tightened his hold and she was brought up short.

With a blood-curdling whoop, the brave sprang on top of the minister. They wrestled on the ground, and the minister tried to push off the heavier brave. Johanna continued to fight Dugan's grip, but by the time she sprang free it was too late for her father. The Sioux had lifted his hatchet. In one swift move, he brought the axe down on Reverend Wade's head.

"No!" Johanna's scream pierced the night air.

Blood and pieces of brain splattered on the ground. Johanna wailed as she stared at her father's head. Blood gushed from the open wound. Shaking, she stood and lunged for the brave's throat. "You've killed him. You killed him!" The brave grabbed her by the hair and held up his axe.

"Johanna!" Ryan shouted. With lightning speed, he aimed and fired his rifle at the brave. The warrior fell with a crash as Dugan lunged into the nearby brushes. His men followed him. Johanna ran to her father's side. She knelt, clutching his lifeless body to her. Tears blinded her eyes. "Oh, no, Father, you can't be dead." She cradled his head, and his blood covered her arms and shoulders as she rocked on her heels and sobbed. "No! No! No!"

Ryan called over to her from the side of a wagon. "What the hell happened?" He saw her father. "Is he... dead?"

"Yes," she mouthed. Hearing Dugan edging his way toward Ryan, she waved her bloodstained hands. "Run, Ryan! It's a trap. These men came for you."

In one leap, Ryan jumped for cover behind another wagon. "Get down behind your wagons," he hollered to the farmers. They hid, rifles ready to fight Dugan and his men.

Dugan lunged for Johanna, yanking her to her feet. He poised his knife against her throat and called out. "Kill me and she dies, too."

"Let her go," Ryan shouted, his rifle still aimed at Dugan's head. "What do you want?"

"You," Dugan snarled. "Come on out."

"No, Ryan, don't," Johanna begged with tear-filled eyes. "I lost my father. I'll not lose you too." She grabbed her captor's hand and bit hard. With a curse, Dugan released his grip and rubbed his sore hand. Johanna ran to Ryan's outstretched arms. He pulled her to safety behind a wagon bed.

Shots rang back and forth. Cries of women and children pierced the night along with the loud booming sounds of the guns. Johanna found her pistol and hid behind a backboard. A rush of adrenaline gave her the strength to stop her shaking hand and shoot with deadly aim at Dugan's gang. Killing the other trapper felt like a bitter victory as she watched him clutch his chest from the fatal wound and fall dead in front of her. She sat, pistol in her hand, weeping into the folds of her apron.

The acrid smell of gunpowder permeated the air, creating clouds of smoke. The cries of terror and moans of human suffering terrified Johanna. She feared there'd be other casualties. But an hour or so later, quiet descended as the air cleared of smoke. Thinking the battle had ended, Johanna stood. Her heart skipped a beat when she saw Dugan slinking around the corner of a wagon, knife in hand, as he edged toward Ryan.

Johanna cocked the trigger of her pistol. "Mister," she said, steadying her hand, "surrender now or say your prayers."

Dugan turned around. "Hell, lady, I don't believe in no God. You can put your gun away." He stepped forward. "Cause I know you ain't gonna use it on me. You're too much of a lady for—"

Johanna pulled the trigger, firing a bullet into Dugan's leg. He fell with a thud and a cry of anguish as he clutched his thigh. "Damn it, she shot me!"

"Serves you right," Stephen said through bruised, bloodied lips. "You're not worth saving."

"Aw shucks, Reverend, ain't every soul worth saving?" Dugan crawled toward his knife, but Stephen kicked it away. Ryan came forward and pulled Dugan to his feet.

"I'm bleedin', man, ain't ya got some compassion?"

Shoving Dugan to the ground again, Ryan loaded his rifle and aimed it at Dugan's head. "I've put wild creatures out of their misery, and I can do the same for you."

"No!" Johanna stopped him from firing. "I've as much reason to want him dead as anyone." She stared around at the growing gathering of people from the wagon train. "But this is not the way. Justice must prevail."

"Let's hang 'em." Seamus said, holding his arm. Blood caked the sleeve of his shirt as he shoved a Sioux brave toward Ryan. "Hang 'em both."

"Seamus, you're wounded!" Mabel rushed to his side.

"It's nothing, lassie, not a thing." Seamus shrugged. "Compared with what happened to our poor minister."

"Oh, no, Howard!" Mabel screamed. She stared in horror at her brother-in-law's bloodied face then knelt to touch his cheek. "Poor Howard." She shut his eyelids then stood beside Johanna. The two women wept in each other's arms.

"Fort Bridger is coming up after South Pass," Ryan said, "We'll bring them in, and I'll get that reward that's on your head, Dugan." He directed John and Clem to get some rope. "There'll be no hanging. Like Miss Wade said, justice will prevail."

Having tied up the prisoners—Dugan and two of his men—Ryan went to comfort Johanna, who sat crying beside her father.

"We'll have to bury him here," he said softly. He smoothed back the locks of hair which covered her face. "I'm sorry."

"Oh, it's unfair, after so many years apart, we became close." She leaned into Ryan. "It hurts, Ryan. It hurts so much." Deep sobs racked her insides as he held her.

"Shh, I know." He smoothed back her hair, kissed her forehead and held her tighter while Mabel clung to Seamus. Others in the wagon party wept for their minister. Some resorted to name calling and slinging rocks at the prisoners. Ryan left Johanna's side, shouting at them to stop. "We'll deal with them later. Right now, we must care for our wounded and our dead."

"Did anyone else die?" Johanna asked Seamus.

"No, child." He held her hand. "A few injuries... but nothing serious. Johanna, your father may be gone, but you still have me and Mabel. Think of us as parents."

"Thank you." She gave them a slow, sad smile before bursting into tears.

"We've got work to do," Mabel said, sniffling and blowing her nose on a torn handkerchief. "Howard, more than anyone else, deserves a good Christian burial."

~ * ~

In the early gray dawn, Ryan shoveled the last of the dirt for the minister's grave. Tom Le Fleure helped him carry Reverend Wade in a shroud—the quilt Johanna had made. It would have been a birthday gift for her father, a testimony to her affection for him.

"He shouldn't have died this way," Stephen muttered, removing his hat as he stood waiting for everyone to attend the service.

Johanna stood, stiff and silent; her lip quivered as she choked back a sob as they lowered her father's body into the earth. "From dust ye come, to dust ye return," she mumbled with Stephen then prayed silently. She had steeled herself to be strong, asking for the strength only her faith could provide. She felt Mabel's worried gaze upon her, but held up her head. Somehow the burial made it all too real.

"Oh, Auntie," she said, touching Mabel's hand as she tried to deal with her grief. "I'll never see his sweet smile again nor hear his voice. We had barely enough time to get to know each other... and now he's gone." Through blurry eyes she read the inscription on a wooden cross. Ryan had carved her father's name and the date he died, inverting the letter 'd' in Wade. She smiled, despite the heavy weight of sorrow that sliced her like a knife.

As the farmers gathered to pay their respects, Johanna summoned up her strength, fighting back tears to thank them for their kindness and consolation. The O'Dowd and the Jones families offered to help her and Mabel. Tom Le Fleure pressed her hand.

"Reverend Wade's kindness to me and my child will not go unforgotten. I didn't get to thank him. Please take these." He handed her a bag of apples.

Stephen stood, and somberly stared into his battered prayer book. Pages flew out and scattered around his feet. He shut the book then recited the twenty-third Psalm. As he sprinkled flower petals on the shroud, he concluded with, "We bid farewell to a great man, Reverend Wade, who goes to the good Lord. May his soul rest in peace."

"Goodbye, Father," Johanna whispered. She trembled at the sound of dirt being shoveled and thrown into the open grave. Ryan came over to her. She clasped his hand tightly, and leaned into him when he put his arm about her.

"What do we do with the rest of 'em?" Mary O'Dowd asked Ryan as they returned to the wagons.

"Let's kill 'em," her husband said.

"Hang'n is too good for the likes of 'em," Will McPherson said.

"We can't kill them," Ryan said, speaking in a reasonable tone. "Or else we'll have the whole Sioux nation after us. Besides, I know their chief. He'll deal with his men."

~ * ~

The next evening Johanna sat listlessly on her wagon seat, staring bleakly at the prayer book she held in her hands.

"Johanna isn't quite right, Ryan," Mabel said, "Last night, she talked to her father as if he were alive, and today she sits like a stone statue. I'm afraid the strain of losing her father is too much."

"That's natural." Ryan patted Mabel's shoulder, "She needs time, but if it'll help I'll talk to her." He took a sip of the coffee Mabel poured for him then went to the front of the wagon.

"I'm sorry, Johanna."

Shutting her prayer book, she gazed up at him through bloodshot eyes. "I'm trying to find comfort in the words Father read to his congregation, but I can't. His words comforted so many people, Ryan, but they're lost on me. Why?"

"There are times when words just ain't enough." Ryan stroked the curve of her face then lifted her chin. "This is one of those times."

"Father died trying to save me." Her voice faltered. "I don't understand. It doesn't make any sense."

Ryan climbed onto the seat and covered her hands with his own. "None of it does."

"I didn't even get the chance to tell him how much I loved him."

Ryan slipped an arm about her shoulder. Laying her head upon his broad chest, Johanna began to sob. He rubbed her back and gripped her hand until she stopped. He smoothed back the strands of hair from her blotched face and kissed her forehead, murmuring, "I think he knew."

Twenty

Devil's Gate

The wagon train kept moving along the course of the Sweetwater River. At midday they stopped at Devil's Gate, a narrow gorge cut by the river. As the wild current crashed into the granite walls of the canyon, it reminded Johanna of the rough tides lapping the shore on Cape Cod. The name itself held a sinister ring, and she kept away from the riverbank as she watered the mules from the barrel on the sideboard. Mabel cooked a light supper of leftover stew and bread. Johanna nibbled on the bread but left the stew on her plate.

"You must eat, Johanna, if you're to stay strong and healthy."

"I can't, Auntie, please bring some over to the McPhersons or Tom Le Fleure. They could use extra food."

Ryan passed by. Noticing the untouched food on her plate, he scowled. "Many is the time I went hungry in the wilderness, Johanna, while hunting for beaver. I'd have given my good arm to have such a fine and splendiferous meal as the one your aunt cooked."

Johanna handed him the plate. "Here, you eat it then."

"Don't mind if I do." Sitting by the wagon, Ryan dug into the stew with a chunk of day-old bread.

Mabel sat beside him, a worried crease on her brow. "What am I to do with that girl?"

Ryan heaved a heavy sigh. "She's about as stubborn as a mule when she's in such a state. She's pining over her Pa and only time will heal her wound."

"No, I think she's upset because of him." She nodded toward Grizzly Dugan who sat with his back turned from them, arms and legs shackled to a cart. "Sure she's grieving the loss of her father but then on top of it, she has to look at the face of the man responsible for his death. It's too much, Ryan. How much longer is it to Fort Bridger? This is an awful burden for her to bear."

"As soon as we can get 'em in there, we'll get justice. I've as much cause to want Dugan dead as anyone else here, but there's a reward on his hide. I mean to get it, as well as see that he stands trial for killing my brother even if this means riding a few more weeks to bring him in."

"I see." Mabel took the empty plate from Ryan's hands. "So, in the meantime, we have to put up with that man and the constant threat of his presence in our midst."

"I'll be sure nothing happens." Ryan stood. "I'll keep guard and so will some of the other men. When we get to the Valley, I'll take Dugan back to Jackson County."

"And what about those Indians?"

"The Sioux? I'm bringing them to their tribe tonight. The chief is sure to deal with them in his own way. We don't want no trouble with the Sioux."

"What will you do about my niece? Will you return to her?"

Ryan gave her a warm smile. "Don't you worry none about Johanna. I've asked her to marry me."

Mabel clapped her hands in approval. "You did!"

"I'm giving her ample time to decide if she'll have me. G'd day to ya, Mrs. Foster."

"And good luck to you," Mabel called after, a pleased grin on her round face.

~ * ~

"Reverend Wade might not be with us anymore, Mr. Majors, but I am. As presiding minister and leader of this party, I insist on a semblance of order and civility. There must be no carousing among the unmarried people here and no drinking."

Ryan's gaze narrowed as he stood facing this young upstart. "I'd be careful what you say, Green. We're not done with this trip, not by a long shot. As far as I'm concerned, you have no say in what we do."

"Is that true, Johanna?" Stephen asked, standing in front of her.

"Yes," she said with a weary sigh. It had been one of those odd moments; Ryan insisted on walking her to the stream to clean dishes. Can't be too careful, he warned. How well she knew! Cross and heated, she turned on the children who fidgeted and teased one another around a tree. "Children, settle down. Go back to your wagons and eat your supper."

"It's that man over there," Sally said pointing to the cart where Grizzly Dugan sat, tied at the feet, eating his meal. "He's staring at us. It gives me the willies." Her brother threw a rock in the man's direction; he growled in response sending the smallest children dashing off.

When Johanna stared at Dugan, he pursed his lips in a mock kiss. "Oh," she sighed, shrugging her shoulders, "the man's a friend and an abomination."

"More like the devil's kin, than human," Stephen added.

Johanna reminded herself that Dugan couldn't harm her. Ryan went to him, loosening the ropes on his hands so that he could eat his supper. He ate like a vulture, nose down in the food. Gravy covered his bearded mouth. He swallowed whole chunks of meat then licked the plate. He sucked the gravy off his fingers. "Want some?" he asked her. When she turned away, she heard his wild laughter. It chilled her to the marrow. Her cheeks scorched crimson with humiliation.

"How much longer must we put up with this savage?" Mabel asked Ryan.

"Until we get to the Valley, then you folks are free of him. Remember, I plan to get the reward as well as take Dugan off our hands."

"Ya'll never make it!" Dugan shouted. "Not while I got breath left in me body. Your uncle, Missy, created this bastard you see before you. Come on, give us a kiss!"

"Shut your trap," Ryan shouted, striking him on the head with the butt of his rifle. "Don't ever speak to her like a cheap whore, Dugan."

Stephen clasped Johanna's trembling hands. "We need to talk," he looked at Mabel who stood. "Alone. There's something I need to explain to Johanna."

"Very well," Johanna agreed, removing her hands from his and keeping her distance as she walked with him to the top of the ridge called Devil's Gate. As she stood, staring down into the abyss at the swirling dark waters, she sensed the appropriateness of the name. Then she turned on Stephen, eyes ablaze with her fury. "You... you brought that devil here... you're responsible for my father's death!"

"You think I'm a coward, don't you?" Stephen demanded to know. "Don't you?"

She flailed her arms and pummeled him with her fists. "It's all your fault, Stephen!"

He grabbed her by the wrists. "I did it for you," he said.

She met the somber glint in his blue eyes. "That's a damn lie. How could you be so cruel? Father respected you, Stephen, more than I ever could. He planned the missionary for you, not me." It became clear to her now, clear as the sky overhead. All her pent-up frustration, her jealous rage, had been over feelings of inadequacy. Yes, she knew deep inside her father loved her. But she hadn't gained the same measure of respect that a man, that Stephen Green, had gained. "Damn you to hell!" she shouted at him then ran, sliding halfway back down the hillside to camp. "You're worse than a coward," she hollered back to him.

Stephen dashed down behind her, sliding on his backside. Dirt covered them both as they walked toward camp. He didn't touch her again, much to her relief. After minutes of silent walking, he said, "Johanna, they would have killed me. And what good would that have done? More to the point, Dugan wanted to do God knows what... he would have hurt you. I couldn't let that happen. No matter how you feel about me, Johanna. Believe that of me, I wanted to prevent him from harming you."

She stopped and glared at him. "Thank you, Stephen. Thank you for saving me and your precious hide!"

"We have the mission, Johanna." He came closer, reaching for her, but she stepped far away. "And we have each other. You must stop mourning the past, damn it! And don't think for a moment that your Ryan Majors has honorable intentions, because he doesn't."

"No!" Her scream echoed in the canyon. "Get this through your head, Stephen. I'll never, ever marry you! And if Ryan Majors will have me then I'll marry him and no one can stop me."

~ * ~

The stallion allowed Johanna to brush and saddle him. She sat sidesaddle, echoing her aunt's sentiments that it would be easier to ride like the men. She felt grateful that she'd brought along her own saddle despite the extra weight it meant in her wagon. Years of lessons paid off as she rode with ease and control on the animal's back. She forded the river on a slant upstream. The slope proved gradual, easy to ride across. Wild ducks, startled by her horse, quacked madly and flew into the distance. Johanna envied their freedom to wander. She thought of the time in her childhood when she donned a costume with paper wings for a school pageant, the one and only performance attended by her father. She told him later that she longed to be as free as a bird. He laughed and told her to enjoy her childhood and that being a grownup tied one to matters of the world.

Johanna stopped the horse. She dried her eyes with her riding gloves. "Oh, I can't go on like this," she chided herself, "thinking of the past... it hurts too much." She yanked on the reins, spurring the horse onward. The stallion carried her across the rocky terrain and up and down the riverbeds. She rode at an even pace with the wagon train, ducking the low branches of cottonwoods and skirting around the willows that edged the banks.

The trail led to a spectacular view of the Rocky Mountains, snow-capped spires of green and brown landscape. She inhaled the sweet scent of the pine trees and the brisk air. "Oh, it's so beautiful," she told Mabel as she rode up to the wagon. Narrow streams gurgled along the dirt path as they descended from the higher elevations. Drinking in the beauty of the woodland decked with assorted white and yellow flowers, low shrubs, and scraggly brush, she put aside her own troubles for the moment.

Upon arriving at South Pass, Johanna led the stallion to a wide stream to drink. She listened to the chirping of the jays and the caw of blackbirds in nearby trees. Then she cupped her hands and dipped them in the cool water. The water felt good on her heated face. She led the horse back to the wagon, tied him to the backboard and walked over to Mabel.

Mabel's brow shot up in concern, and she put down her knitting. "What's wrong, Johanna? You look quite peaked!"

Arching her back and stretching her stiff legs, Johanna said, "It's been a long time since I rode a horse, Auntie. Years in fact. I've grown used to the luxury of the carriage and the wagon."

"You should have stayed with the wagon or walked."

"No, it feels good to ride. I see so much of the countryside," she added with a soft chuckle. "Ah, I know it sounds silly, but riding father's horse makes me feel a little closer to him."

"Hmm." Mabel cocked her head to one side. "I guess so. I felt that way when I kept the Captain's snuff box under my pillow. I couldn't stand it when he used snuff, but when he died, I missed those quaint little things he did."

Johanna sat beside her aunt. "Has meeting Seamus made you stop mourning for him?"

"Not at all, I still love the Captain, but I love Seamus, too."

Johanna opened her diary, pressed a primrose in its center then shut it. "I suppose that's how I feel about Robert now. I have the memories and what we had is important, but I love Ryan." She shrugged. "It's different somehow."

"I'm glad that you've made up your mind to marry." Mabel resumed her knitting. "It's high time, and to a man as good as Ryan."

"I didn't say that I'd marry him."

Mabel looked puzzled. "But you said you loved him."

Johanna shrugged. "I know... but marriage... it's a big step."

"It's high time, Johanna. High time. With your father gone, you'll need a man to look after you."

Johanna stood, took a deep breath then said, "I'll tend to the mules. No, when I'm ready to marry, I will. It's too soon. And I can manage on my own."

Mabel opened then shut her mouth, as the sounds of laughter and a baby's soft cry interrupted them. Johanna glanced across at the source. Tom Le Fleure sat beside Sally McPherson on a tree stump. Sally held Tom's baby in her arms, cooing down at the infant. "Why,"

Johanna said softly, "Sally looks so much like that child's mother." She shook her head. "No, she's much too young."

"Too young!" Mabel sniffed. "Indeed not out here, Johanna. In two more years Sally will be of a marrying age. She's not too young."

Johanna sensed the sharp rebuke meant for her. She knew her aunt's implication that she was far from a tender age. "Could they, no."

"Be in love?" Mabel finished Johanna's thought then shrugged her shoulders. "Possibly."

Johanna turned from the couple, and caught her aunt's nod of assent. "But it's so soon. How could they? Megan hasn't been dead that long."

Mabel tucked her knitting inside the wagon. "You're such a romantic, thinking that love runs eternal. You thought you'd never love again after your fiancé died, but look into your own heart. Haven't you fallen in love again?"

"Yes," Johanna admitted.

"And so it is the way of things," Mabel cupped her niece's face. "Listen to me, I know you've been distraught over your father's death. It's as if your heart is broken again. You're afraid, aren't you?"

"I guess so, it hurts to lose someone you love."

"I know." Mabel held Johanna, allowing her to lean against her shoulder. Mabel stroked Johanna's hair, comforting her. "Alas, I know how well the heart pines for those we love. And yet, life goes on. We're more resilient than we know." She pointed to Sally and Tom. "They're both so young. Tom needs a wife and his child needs a mother. And Sally is no longer a child. They're too young to give up on love." Mabel turned Johanna's face toward her own. "And I hope you won't be as stubborn as your father, my dear girl. Don't be afraid to listen to your heart and all will be right. A man will only wait so long!"

She followed her aunt's stare to the shadows of a figure; Ryan sat alone by his campfire. She listened to the strains of the harmonica as they floated to her... calling her over.

~ * ~

The next day the wagons reached a fork in the trail. Ryan and

Stephen locked horns over which trail to take. Johanna came to Ryan's defense. A meeting was called to order to decide between the Slate Creek cut-off, which Ryan claimed would shorten the trip, and Stephen's insistence on staying the course to Fort Bridger. The minister stood atop a small boulder gazing down at his audience. As usual the Emerson sisters stood at the front of the crowd of comely farmers.

"I have a map." Stephen unfolded a map and pointed out some markings on it. "The officers at Fort Laramie advised that we follow this route which leads to Fort Bridger. Now if the government officials advised the route, we should follow their advice. There we can dispose of Grizzly Dugan."

"That'll take you a hell of a lot longer," Ryan cut in. "By taking the cut-off, we'll go on over Emigrant Springs, up to Fort Hall and deliver Dugan, restock on supplies and go on along the Snake River."

"I'll go for saving time," Seamus said, standing beside Ryan. "I'd advise the rest of ya to follow suit. Food is a mite scarce, so is water. We been followin' rivers but half ain't fit to drink."

"The water has made everyone sick," Tom Le Fleure said, joining Seamus and Ryan. He turned to the crowd. "Let's listen to Monsieur Majors and take the Slate Creek cut-off." He turned to the men and women around them, asking, "We have come this far with this man, shall we not go all the way?"

Several heads nodded in assent. "You, see, Reverend," Tom went on, "the majority rules."

Stephen shook his fist in anger. "You'll be following the devil himself."

"I'd as soon follow Ryan," Seamus said, "then the likes of you. At least, he didn't bring that to us." He pointed to Dugan. Everyone turned to look at the man who sat shackled and grim-faced in the cart. Dugan spat at Seamus.

"Why you low-down, dirty..." Seamus balled his fist and rushed toward Dugan.

Ryan intercepted the ruddy-faced farmer. "No! Let him be, Seamus." He turned to Dugan. "You best mind your manners or you'll be hangin' from that cottonwood."

"We should have hung them both," Seamus said in disgust.

Johanna stepped in front of Stephen. "Reverend Green may have acted foolishly, but he didn't know what else to do."

"Horse manure!" Seamus said, "Some minister, he is, leading the sheep for the slaughter. And now he wants to lead us astray."

"Let's hang them both!" John O'Dowd shouted.

"I got a rope in my wagon," Amos Fletcher said.

Ryan waved his hand for silence. "Wait a moment, folks! If you kill the minister, you'll be as much a murderer as Dugan. And there's no need for it."

"Yes, no need," Johanna added, "and what would Reverend Wade have said? He wouldn't want any more killing. Right?"

"She's right," Mary O'Dowd said, pushing her husband's arm and grabbing the rope from between his hands. "There won't be anymore killing here."

"No, no more bloodshed," Tom agreed. "We've got to get along." He glanced at his sleeping baby. "For our sake and that of our children."

"Let's pray." Johanna bowed her head. "Oh Lord, we beseech Thee for guidance in our hour of need." She led the gathering in a brief prayer service, ignoring Stephen's narrow gaze.

"I did what any good Christian would do, Stephen," Johanna said when Stephen thanked her in mock sincerity. "I forgave my enemy. But I will never forget what happened." She stormed off, leaving Stephen to stare at her back and listen to the infernal cackling laughter of the madman Dugan.

~ * ~

"The prisoner escaped!"

John O'Dowd lay on the ground. His head twisted to one side; blood saturated the ground around it. Johanna had to fight back the urge to vomit as she glanced at the contorted and marred features of the gentle man. Seamus had shouted the call, and now stood holding Johanna as she grabbed her stomach. They glanced at the overturned prisoner's cart.

Ryan pulled Johanna's shaking form. "How could Dugan have gotten loose?" he asked then smacked his hand against his furrowed brow. "Green! Green let him go."

"No, Stephen may be desperate but he'd never stoop so low as to release the prisoner."

"I haven't seen Stephen since yesterday, have you?" Ryan asked Johanna as he examined O'Dowd. "Ain't it convenient, he's gone, so is Dugan."

"Did you think that I'd just walk out on you?"

They both turned around to face a pale, drawn-faced Stephen. Upon seeing the gruesome sight of the dead man, Stephen spun around and vomited. Ryan stepped over and clamped him on the shoulder.

"Where the hell were you?" he demanded. "Dugan escaped!"

Stephen wiped his mouth on a once white handkerchief. "Are you blaming me?"

"Oh, my poor John!" Mary O'Dowd pushed past them and ran to the dead man. "Oh, my God. He's dead. And... his ear's gone. That savage bit off John's ear!"

"I wasn't responsible for this!" Stephen said, peering at the crowd that had gathered about the dead man. "Furthermore, I have no idea what happened."

"Where were you then?" Johanna asked.

"Off hunting," Stephen said. "I got lost in the woods, believe me, I haven't slept a wink all night. I kept walking in circles until sunrise when I found my own tracks and the way back here."

Ryan examined the bits of rope which lay on the ground. "Damn, they've been chewed through like an animal. He chewed the ropes off his wrists." Then he walked around, carefully examining the ground. "He couldn't have gotten far... we'll catch up to him soon enough."

"Come on, Mary." Johanna gathered her close. "I'll help you and the children."

"I won't leave my John," Mary wailed, pulling away, "There'll be no wolves feasting upon him."

"Shh." Johanna held Mary, allowing her to cry on her shoulder.

~ * ~

After John O'Dowd's burial, Ryan led a few of the farmers on a desperate search through the backwoods and hillside for Dugan. They rode for half a day then returned to camp. Ryan jumped down from his horse, a bitter grin on his face. "He won't get too far. I'll catch him soon enough then there's no mercy this time."

Johanna listened to his rage, feeling as bitter and angry. Instead of lashing out as Ryan did, all her mixed emotions erupted in a flood of uncontrollable tears. She wept shamelessly on the wagon cover until Ryan held her. "Shh... I'm sorry, Johanna. You've as much pain as I, and I've been blind in my rage."

"You're to leave us?" She asked, wiping the last of her tears.

"No," he whispered. "Not yet, not until I fulfill my duty to this wagon train. No, your father hired me and I intend to see that you and the rest get to the Valley safely."

"Oh, Ryan!" Johanna melted against him, letting him soothe her with his soft, incoherent mumbling and the tender touch of his fingers along her hair.

Stephen rode up to them. "You can run after Dugan in your own good time, Majors. Now you're in our employ and you'd better deliver us to the Valley or else."

"Or what?" Ryan challenged. "Give it up, Green. You're not in charge, I am. As I told Miss Wade, I'm not about to quit."

"Good," Stephen said. "I've got more families now who'll follow me. Johanna, if you know what's best you'll do the same."

She stood facing him. "No. I wish you well, Stephen. I have faith in Ryan."

"God help you then." With that Stephen turned his horse and rode off.

~ * ~

"What happened to Dugan?" Johanna asked Ryan as they sat peering into a glowing campfire. "Why is he after you?"

Ryan cupped her hand in his then told his tale. "About fifteen years or so ago, me and my brother Chet was hunting. A grizzly bear, taller than two men and more ornery than four, come into our camp one night. Dugan and his squaw, a Bannock woman, had been celebrating their wedding. There had been too much drinking. Dugan saw the bear but couldn't stop him from grabbing his wife. Me and Chet heard the screams from our tent. We rushed out, fired our rifles.

Chet's missed the bear and hit the woman. The grizzly took advantage and dragged her into the woods. We ran, so did Dugan, to the woods. I fired, killing the bear, but it was too late. My God." Ryan shook involuntarily and choked on a sob. "You should have seen her... half eaten by that monster. Her belly slit, her head bashed to the side, and blood every which way."

"Oh, Ryan!" Johanna held him. She felt him tremble and stroked his hair as he leaned into her.

"Well after that, Dugan swore at us. We didn't believe him, he was so filled with whiskey. I never thought he'd come back and kill Chet."

"So," Johanna said, noting the deep sigh as Ryan sat back, "you think Grizzly Dugan blames you and your brother for what happened?"

"Course he does."

She stood, hands folded across her front. "And we're paying the price."

"Unless he's plumb foolish," Ryan said, hugging her, "he won't be back here. I meant what I said, Johanna. If he comes near you again, I'll kill him."

Twenty-one

Fort Hall to Fort Boise

Twenty families gathered around the campfire after supper. Stephen stood before them, hands clasped. He led them in a brief prayer then called for silence.

"Tonight you must decide whom to follow to the Willamette Valley. Reverend Wade gave me charge of the missionary work before he died."

"Liar!" Johanna shouted.

He ignored her look of defiance, focusing on those who stepped forward and looked interested enough in what he had to say. "Reverend Wade set in motion what brought us here today. It's the backing of the mission board and a few generous and supportive ladies." He nodded toward the Emerson sisters who smiled at him. "That's what brought us this far and will see us to the Valley and our new lives there. We can do this together." His glance rested on Johanna and she turned away. "Or apart... but either way, you must decide whom to follow, me or Ryan Majors."

"I've taken care of these people," Ryan cut in, walking up to him.

"And you snuck off to be with the Pawnees while we were left on our own."

Ryan held up his hands. "No, I did what I believed to be right and I came back."

"Eh," Seamus snickered. "What about you, Green? You led that murderer, Grizzly Dugan, to us. And you untied him, too!"

"What?" Johanna's jaw dropped open. She quickly recalled how Stephen had disappeared the night that Dugan escaped. "Is it true?"

"No." Stephen stepped back as Ryan's hands clenched at his sides.

"I told you that I had been lost in the woods," Stephen said, raking his fingers through his hair as beads of perspiration broke out along his forehead.

"Yeah, I'll bet," someone accused. "How convenient."

Stephen mopped the sweat off his brow with a handkerchief and looked everywhere but at the crowd coming closer. "I'm telling the truth with God as my witness."

"No, he's not," Jamie Jones said. "I seen him cut the ropes and flee into the woods."

"He's lying." Stephen cowered against a tree trunk. "You can't believe the word of a ten-year-old over a preacher."

"Yes, we can," Johanna said as she stood by Ryan's side. "I thought as much, Stephen, but I didn't want to believe that you'd stoop so low as to free the very man who caused my father's death."

"You've no proof, Johanna," Stephen said, "none at all. Why on earth would I free such an evil man as Dugan? I am a God-fearing man." His gaze swept the crowd and he choked back a sob. "Who, who could believe such a horrendous thing of me? I who have laid these healing hands on the afflicted." He extended his hands. "I who baptized and saved you from damnation... Who could believe that I'd do something to harm you?"

"Not I," Abigail Emerson said, swishing the skirt of her black dress as she rushed to Stephen's side. "I believe Reverend Green is telling the truth."

"So do I," Charlotte said, clasping Stephen's arm, "and the rest of you should be ashamed to think ill of him. He's a God-fearing man."

"Fearing all right," Seamus said. "Fearing his own hide that is."

"All of you, settle down," Ryan shouted as arguments arose in the crowd.

"A vote," Johanna shouted. "Let's take a vote. Men and women should be included in the decision. Raise your right hands if you want to go with Stephen."

Ten hands waved high in the air.

Ryan shot Stephen a look of utter contempt. "I guess I'm still in charge, Green."

Stephen stared at Ryan who led the crowd back to the wagons. He hollered after them, "Ryan Majors wants to lead you to your death. Do you dare trust your lives and the lives of your children with him?"

Johanna stopped in her tracks, turned then strode up to Stephen. With a stiffened back and hands on hips, she huffed, "That's not true!"

Viola stood beside Johanna, and turned on Stephen. "Ryan saved my Charlene from a buffalo stampede. I trust my very soul with him."

"So do I," said Ellie McCrory. "If it hadn't been for Ryan, my family would have been killed because of my blunder."

"You tell 'em," Tom Le Fleur said, joining the small bevy of women circling the young minister. "Monsieur Majors did all for us."

"Ya hear that, Reverend?" Seamus asked as he linked arms with Mabel. "We listened to you once and you led us astray. You brought in Dugan and look what happened. That map ain't worth the paper it's scrawled on."

Stephen scowled. "Are you going to listen to a drunk? Mabel, you of all people should know better! You're a woman of proper breeding, a Bostonian, for God's sake!"

"I'm not a fool, Stephen," Mabel replied with a huff, "and neither are these farmers."

"It seems as if you've lost your sheep," Johanna added, glaring at the Emerson sisters, "except for a few foolish enough to do your bidding."

"Who do you think got the extra food and cattle we needed?" Stephen asked his audience. "Who? Not Ryan. I bought it with the money left to me by Reverend Wade."

"What money?" Johanna asked. "Father never mentioned giving any money to you."

"I got three hundred dollars for the missionary work, it came from the mission board," Stephen went on. "And Miss Wade, there, showed little interest in our mission. Ryan Majors has corrupted her. Like Eve in the garden, she's a fallen woman."

"Balderdash!" Mabel shouted. "How dare you insult my niece!"

Stains of scarlet tinged Johanna's cheeks as she fumed inwardly. By now, a few families had returned and began to bicker about who could lead them. "Be quiet!" Johanna shouted then turned on Stephen. "Of all the nerve." She shot him a look of indignation. "I've had the interest of the mission from the start... how dare you insinuate that my morals have been compromised." Grateful that Ryan hadn't returned with this crowd, Johanna swallowed the lump in her throat and addressed them.

"Like many of you, I've given up a great deal to be part of this missionary... my life in Boston, my work as a governess, and the comforts of home. I've risked my own life." Her voice wavered but she continued, "and I've lost my father... because of him." She pointed at Stephen with her upturned chin. "Furthermore my father had no money from the board. I should know, he wrote to me monthly about the trip."

"What?" Abigail Emerson gaped at Stephen. "But... but you said the board financed your trip here."

"It only financed part of the trip," Mabel said, putting her arm around Johanna's shoulders. "We, Johanna and I, raised money back in Boston... through the ladies' auxiliaries and donations given at the church. We requested help with the missionary work."

"You lied to us, Stephen." Charlotte Emerson waved an angry fist at him. "And we gave you so much... a good sum from our inheritance."

"Shh!" Abigail whispered to her sister. "Don't tell everyone about it, silly."

"Please, listen to me." Stephen raised his hands for silence. When the crowd quieted, he said, "I didn't lie, here's the money Reverend Wade gave me." He held up a velvet pouch that looked oddly familiar to Johanna.

She leaned next to Mabel. "Isn't that the purse that Evening Star brought to our camp?" Mabel nodded. "Stephen, that pouch looks like the one Evening Star brought here... the one belonging to Ryan Majors."

Stephen ignored her. "As I said, Reverend Wade gave me the sum in here, and I spent part of it on food and supplies. There'll be enough left to purchase what we need in the months ahead.

Mollie Fletcher rushed to Stephen's side, dragging her husband Ned and her son Zachariah with her. Jacob Fletcher followed them, his face crimson with embarrassment.

The boy trembled when Johanna looked at him. She knew that Molly ran the household and nothing she could say would change that. "It's all right, Jacob," she mouthed to him. "I understand."

The Emerson sisters stepped forward, arms locked in a gesture of unity. With head held high, Abigail said, "I believe Stephen has our best intentions at heart." She elbowed her sister, "Isn't that correct, Charlotte?"

"Oh, yes," Charlotte said with an edge of doubt to her voice.

"Pshaw!" Mabel blurted. "As Seamus said, Stephen brought the Sioux upon us."

"Very well, Stephen," Johanna said, "You may have won a few 'converts' but not the majority of us. We shall sever all ties to you and your followers. God help you all."

Stephen ignored her scowl, bowed his head in a reverential pose, and prayed. "May God bless us all." With a pointed look at Johanna, he added, "May we meet again in the valley."

"Amen," Molly's voice rang out.

Stephen's words sent a shiver up Johanna's spine, reminding her of the lines from the Twenty-third psalm about the valley of death. She waited until everyone returned to their wagons then confronted Stephen.

"You're not only a liar and a scoundrel, you're a thief."

"You're wrong, my dear. It is you who is at fault... you're so blinded by your own love for that man." When he pointed toward Ryan who sat at Tom Le Fleure's campsite, Johanna growled in frustration. "Don't deny it—I know you've fallen in love with that back woodsman. And to think of what we could have had."

"This isn't about my life or who I love, Stephen," she snapped. "You know you stole that money. Give it back at once." She held out her hand.

Stephen swung the pouch in her face then pulled it from her grasping fingers.

"You won't get away with this, Stephen."

~ * ~

"I have to stop him, Auntie," Johanna said over supper. "Ryan hasn't come back from the Indian village. He was only going for a few hours. I'm going to find him." She helped Mabel wipe and stow away the dishes then saddled her horse.

"It's too late to be out alone." Mabel grabbed Johanna's elbow. "Those people will follow Stephen no matter what. They're drawn to him like moths to the flame and..."

"They'll be scorched all the same," Johanna finished. "I must find Ryan. After all, it's his money that Stephen stole."

The sound of a horse racing toward their camp made them look up. Johanna knew by the rider's face and form who it was. She never failed to thrill at the sight of him and she mustered a weak smile as he neared but sighed at the thought of what she had to tell him.

He dismounted, tied up his horse, and stepped over to her.

She knew he read her distress when his warm smile evaporated and his brows knitted in concern.

"Why, Johanna, you look as if all hell broke loose."

"It did," She said, leading him to the tree behind the wagon. He kissed her quickly then held her at arm's length.

"It's Stephen," she said, peering down at his dirt-crusted moccasins. "He's convinced half a dozen families to follow him."

Ryan rubbed the back of his neck. "Is that all? Well, they can go to hell with him."

"No, that's not all." She paused a moment, wondering how he'd take the news.

"Stephen stole your money."

"What?" He frowned, and a veil of fury darkened his eyes. "Ya mean, he stole the money Dugan took from the warehouse?"

"Yes."

"The money Chet got killed for?" When she nodded affirmatively, Ryan balled his hands into fists. "I'm going to kill the bastard with my bare hands. Why didn't you tell me sooner?"

"I... I just found out. After the meeting, you left for the village and Stephen told me." Frightened by the hatred in his eyes, she grabbed his clenched hands and stroked them. "Please... no more killing. Go and get your money back, but let him go on his way. Let those people go if they want to. He's convinced them that you weren't fit to lead the wagons and that you'd leave us as soon as you got what you wanted."

Ryan cupped her chin. "Do you really think I'd leave you?"

"No."

He sighed his relief and a slow smile lit his eyes. "I'm glad on that account... 'cause the last person I want to hurt is you."

"Oh, Ryan." She pressed her face against his chest, then he held her close a moment before loosening his grip and peering into her eyes. He traced the outline of her lips with his thumb before covering them with his own. The kiss heated her to the core, making her feel light. She didn't care what anyone thought. As long as Ryan stood beside her, what more could she want? As he moved away, placing her at arm's distance, she read the depth of love in his eyes. Then he stared into the distance, and his face became a hard mask of anger.

"I'm going to get that money back."

Johanna remained silent as Ryan escorted her back to the wagon. Upon hearing Seamus calling after them, they both stopped.

"He's gone," Seamus said, panting and trying to catch his breath as he met them.

"Who?" Johanna asked.

"Why Reverend Green, that's who," Seamus said, "I tried to talk to the Fletchers and the Emersons... but I might as well argue with my mule. At least my mule had a lick of sense. They packed it in and headed off after supper. Damn bunch of fools should know better than to travel by dark. That minister convinced them they'd reach the valley a lot sooner that way."

"Of all the..." Ryan cursed aloud. "I'll tear him to bits if I catch up with him."

"Somehow we'll get the money raised and help your kin in Missouri," Johanna said, rubbing his tense shoulder blades and trying to control her own wrath toward Stephen. "No good can come from that blood money."

~ * ~

Frustration and anger boiled in Ryan like the waters of a turbid sea. He took out a flask of whiskey given to him by his friend Courtney. He took a swig then in mild disgust threw the flask into the woods where it shattered on a tree trunk. He remembered Jed Thompkins' words when his brother Chet died... drinking wouldn't help matters. *No*, Ryan thought, *it only makes it worse.*

He stamped out the campfire and crawled into his sleeping bag. He stretched out, tucking an arm behind his head. He tried not to think too much about the consequences of losing the money. *That money would have meant a lot to Sara and the children. How are they now?* he wondered, peering up at the twinkle of light in the night sky. It had been three months since he stood with Sara at the edge of a wheat field by Chet's farmhouse. Sara reminded him then of the girl she'd been—the one he once loved. Standing there and wishing on a star for luck and happiness, she rekindled a yearning he thought had burned out. And all he offered her was financial support. *Perhaps,* he thought bitterly*, that's all she needed from me anyway.*

Leading the missionary parties brought on his envy for all his brother once had—a home, a good woman, and children. Whenever he watched the emigrant children at play, he imagined Chet's children on the farm. Sitting with the families who offered him a quick meal reminded him of those fleeting times when Chet and Sara greeted him with open arms, welcoming him back like the prodigal son.

Now Ryan wanted more than sharing a meal with someone else's family. He'd had his fill of trying to find solace in the arms of painted ladies or squaws eager to share their mats. Johanna Wade changed all of that. He vowed never to let her down. But before he could settle down, he had to take care of the promises he made to his family.

He came so close to having Dugan. So close. And now, the money was gone.

"Damn it!" He recalled his promise to his nephew Samuel. The words still resounded in his head. *You're gonna get that man, ain't ya, Uncle Ryan? You're gonna get that man that killed my Pa?*

"I tried," he said aloud.

"What ya gonna do now, Uncle Ryan?"

He startled then realized the sound of the wind playing through the trees and his own exhaustion had filled his mind with fancy. Or maybe it was what Johanna once called his conscience that bothered him. He had to set things right... for Chet's sake and for Sara. He lay down again and shut his eyes, willing himself to sleep.

Ryan dreamed of Chet's bloodied body. As he bent down to shut the eyelids, a harsh cackle taunted him. He turned to face Grizzly Dugan.

"Come on," Dugan said, brandishing a knife as he held aloft the velvet pouch containing money. "Come on and get it."

Ryan rushed like a vexed bull to butt Dugan. They struggled on the ground.

Suddenly Ryan lost his footing and began to fall. His hands grasped for a hold along the rocky ledge of a cliff. He lost his grip and slipped, spiraling downward...

"No!" Ryan sprang up, fully awake and bathed in sweat. He caught sight of an enormous bird perched upon the limb of a tree above him. As the bird's head bobbed up and down, Ryan recognized it as an eagle. He stood, and the bird screeched before taking flight.

Ryan felt beneath his buckskin shirt for his stone pendant shaped like an eagle. The eagle symbolized power and connection to the Great Spirit. His mother's sister once told him to be filled with the courage of the eagle. Ryan needed courage now; so many depended on him. He did what he hadn't done in a very long time. He bent on one knee and prayed in the language of his mother's people to find the eagle within him.

~ * ~

At Fort Hall, both Ryan and Johanna made inquiries about Grizzly Dugan. The kindly factor claimed that he didn't see the "no-account skunk" and hoped to never see him after he took off with some money that one time in a card game back in Missouri. "We're not getting any closer," Ryan said in disgust as he walked down the dirt trail from the fort. He walked along the Snake River, staring into its muddy water.

Johanna knew it was no use to dissuade him from his mission; she had her own. It warred with the growing need to make up her mind once and for all about the man she loved. Turning around, she touched Ryan's shoulder, "Let's go back to the camp, everyone traded or bought the supplies they needed."

Halfway to camp, a white-haired squaw rushed out to them screaming.

"What the devil?" Ryan asked as the wild woman rushed up and crushed him to her chest. When she let go of her vise-like grip, he could breathe again. A broad chuckle bubbled up as he recognized the lined copper face and crescent-shaped brown eyes as belonging to none other than his beloved aunt, his mother's sister. "Whoopee!" he yelped and spun her around.

Johanna stared in bewilderment at the display of affection between Ryan and the old woman. "This is my Auntie," he explained, "my mother's sister. She brung me and Chet up when my Ma died. Ah, ya haven't changed a hair!"

The twinkle lit her eyes and her smile widened. "And where's brother?" she asked him as they walked for awhile.

"Chet is dead," Ryan said. "Shot by a no-good trapper."

His aunt leaned into him and wept bitter tears. Ryan cradled her like a child until she stopped.

She peered up through her teary eyes. "You stay alive, my son. Spirit of the mountains in you."

He recalled the talk of spirits and totems which guarded a life. All nonsense, he figured, and as useless like the white man's religions. Yet, it comforted his kin. He pulled away from her and fingered the stone fetish of the eagle. Even though he scorned all beliefs, he couldn't part with this token of faith and gratitude. It somehow comforted him. "I will," he told his aunt who quickly pulled him along.

"Come, we make feast for our son who returned." His aunt paused a moment to glance at Johanna. "You come too."

"No, thank you, I've plenty to do at camp." She caught Ryan's look of disappointment before leaving them. For some reason, she wanted to be alone and she felt Ryan needed time with his family. She had wondered about Ryan's past; now she had proof of his heritage.

~ * ~

Dugan followed the meandering course of a stream as it led through thick undergrowth. He came out into a clearing and spied two men in brown uniforms. A small fire smoked in front of them. Soldiers! Mexican soldiers! *What the hell could they be doing way up here?* He cautiously crept closer, hunger getting the better of him as he smelled the cooked bacon and the coffee.

One man lifted his head, and the wide-brimmed hat revealed the face of an old friend. "Eduardo Juarez!" Dugan shouted. The man pulled a pistol from the top of his boot then aimed it at Dugan. As he neared him, he lowered the pistol and a grin broke across his broad face, revealing several gold-capped teeth.

"Juan? Juan Dugan?" He stood staring a moment.

"Yep, same one." Dugan stepped forward and breathed a sigh of relief as Juarez tucked the pistol back into his boot. "Ain't you fighting the war?"

"War is over," Juarez said. "The gringos took me prisoner... I escape and came here. I work for Atkins."

Dugan looked at the two revolvers Juarez packed, the one in his boot top and the other in his belt. "How'd you like to help me, Juarez, get back at them gringos and make a ton of money?"

Juarez stared with interest.

"And there's a wagon filled with women... enough *mujeres* to make a man's blood boil."

"*Mujeres*?" Juarez grinned.

"Yes, *mujeres*... women." Dugan outlined a woman's curves with his hands.

"*Si*. I come. This is Sanchez, my cousin."

Dugan looked at the younger man beside Juarez. "Any good with a gun?"

"*Muy bueno*," Juarez said. He spoke in Spanish to Sanchez, and the latter stood and pulled his revolver from his belt. He aimed it at a squirrel racing up the tree and fired. The squirrel exploded.

Dugan smiled broadly. "Hot damn! He's keener than I was at his age." Without being invited, Dugan sat and ate bits of bacon from the pan. He washed them down with the tequila Juarez offered. "At least someone round here knows the meanin' of hospitality."

Later that evening, he listened to a rendition of a Mexican love ballad then sang a bawdy song his mother taught him years ago in the brothel. He wiped his lips on his sleeve and said to the waning moon, "We'll soon see who's the better man, Majors." After polishing off the rest of the tequila, he saluted the moon then fell headlong onto the ground.

~ * ~

September 1848

Three weeks later the wagon party stopped at the Hudson Bay trading post of Fort Boise situated on the northern side of the Snake River. The adobe buildings reminded Johanna of Fort Hall. Here the families stocked up on supplies. Mabel complained of the costs, but she delighted in the variety of materials available to them. "It will be awhile now, Auntie," Johanna said, "before we reach the mountains. So, we'll need to rest up and get what we can while we can."

After spending a brief time camped alongside the riverbank, the travelers moved westward again with Ryan inspecting every wagon in turn.

~ * ~

About two weeks later they reached the base of the Blue Mountains. Johanna rode her father's stallion out from camp, needing to be alone. She needed time to think things through. She threw Mabel's words of caution to the wind. Still, she carried her pistol in her apron in case of trouble.

But standing there now, peering at the majestic blue mountains with their white caps of snow, she felt above all concern. The pine-clad surroundings and the crisp air invigorated her. She tied the horse to a tree and stretched her arms to release the tension of riding. She pulled her backpack from the saddle and sat. She wrote a few pages in her diary, confessing her love for Ryan and her apprehension for what lay ahead. *Could happiness be possible?* Johanna shut the book and leaned against a tree trunk. The horse whinnied and hoofed the ground. "Easy boy," she soothed, standing and rubbing his mane. For some reasons she felt as agitated as the stallion. "Oh, why can't I be satisfied?" she muttered.

"Ah, ah... maybe you can."

The hairs on the back of her neck lifted. She knew that voice—it haunted her dreams nightly. *Run*, her mind screamed—but she couldn't move, it was as if her feet were rooted to the earth. *Oh, God, let this be a dream*, she prayed, forcing herself to turn toward the voice.

Her heart hammered in her chest when she looked into the soulless black eyes of Dugan. "You! What... what are you doing here?" Looking wildly about, Johanna inched closer to her horse.

Swift as a snake, Dugan's hand shot out and grabbed the horse's reins. "Not leaving so soon, are you?"

"Let go of my horse!" Johanna slapped at his hand.

"She's a feisty, *muy bonita*, eh, Dugan?"

Johanna's head snapped around. The gold-toothed smile of the Mexican soldier widened as he stepped from behind a tree. Dugan tossed the reins to him. "Here, Juarez, take the stallion. I have a mare to catch."

Dugan grabbed Johanna's wrist and yanked her sharply to him.

"Let go of me!" Johanna pulled with all her might. Dugan laughed. Choking on his fetid breath, Johanna stamped hard on his foot.

"Ouch! You bitch!" Dugan slapped her face.

With a startled cry, Johanna staggered back, pulling Dugan with her. They crashed to the ground. Dugan fell on top of her, knocking the breath from her lungs. He cursed when her knee caught him in the groin. Then he rolled over, doubled in pain. Johanna scrambled away, clawing at the ground. Jaws stinging and gasping for breath, she hauled herself up and started to run.

Juarez' laughter and Dugan's curses rang in her ears as her feet pounded across the hillside. But her legs couldn't move fast enough. Juarez took one route and a man dressed similarly to Juarez took another. Dugan headed them off and his arms grabbed her by the waist. She struggled wildly to loosen from his grip.

"We meet again, Miss Wade," he said, pinning her arms behind her back. "And this time there's no one to help you."

Dugan motioned to the two soldiers. "Go on boys, help yourself to the wagons down there... there must be something of value." The two men mounted their horses. One of the men held the reins of Johanna's horse. They laughed then rode off toward the defenseless wagons...

Thank God Mabel is down by the stream with the others, Johanna thought. The handle of Dugan's knife rubbing against the small of her back stopped her thoughts.

"Don't worry about 'em," Dugan said. "You and me got business first. When we're done, I'll go after your man."

"No!" Johanna screamed, hoping someone would hear her then quickly realizing that the rest of camp were at least a mile away. She screamed again then something struck her head and darkness claimed her.

Twenty-two

Mountain Crossings to Fort Vancouver

Ice-cold water slapped Johanna awake. She shivered, sat up and moaned from the sudden pain in her arms and legs. She hugged her bruised knees to her chest. The only sound came from the running water of a brook as it cascaded over a bed of rocks. *I'm alone,* she thought. *Thank God.* The pounding in her head increased as she stood. She held her forehead and willed the pain to stop. One glance at her torn dress brought her to the quick realization of what her tormentor had tried to do. Piercing sunlight invaded the forest floor allowing her to see the narrow dirt trails, which led in different directions. *How do I get back to camp? How do I warn the others? What happened with the soldiers?* The questions only made her head ache more.

"Well, well, missie," Dugan's voice floated down to her.

She screamed, backing away from him as he stepped from a cluster of trees. "No!" She willed her feet to move despite her aches. *Any path,* she thought, *take any path and get away from him.* She didn't see the bramble as its thorny vines tripped her. Dugan pulled her up and trapped her against his chest. She felt faint as she inhaled his hot, fetid breath. "Got ya now, Miss Wade. Thought I'd have to do it with a dead woman... but ah, you're alive..." He rubbed his grubby hands along her hip. "So, tell me, where's your damn fool Ryan?"

"I don't know," she mumbled. She felt in her apron pocket.

"Were you looking for this?" Dugan held up the pistol. "It fell out and I picked it up. So, you've got no choice but to give in to me or tell me about your damn lover... Ryan."

Her eyes widened. "You... you saw us?" Now she knew who had been walking in the woods that day at Fort Laramie.

"Oh, yep, I seen you all right... naked as a jay under that tree. I seen what you two did... and you, a minister's daughter. Bah! And I so love to watch you bathe... there's a stream back there... maybe we can bathe together. I'll rub you in all the right places."

The mere thought of his hands on her naked skin made her want to retch. She struggled and he tightened his grip. She'd die before he'd have his way with her, she vowed.

"I could use me a fine wife," he cooed against her neck, "a lady like you. I lost my woman cause she got shot up."

"Ryan tried to protect her from a grizzly bear," Johanna muttered with contempt. She tried to pry Dugan's fingers from her waist, but he proved far too strong for her.

Dugan snorted in amusement. "Is that what he told you?"

A glint of madness in his eyes made her spine tingle. "Yes."

"He was after her... like all the others. He couldn't have her so he shot her."

"You're mad! Ryan didn't want your woman." Johanna felt his hold loosen. "He tried to save your lives. And you're not about to end his nor have mine." With all her might, Johanna hefted her knee up and kicked him in the groin. As he reeled back in agony, she fled.

The bramble's thorny branches cut and scraped her legs and arms. Tears blinded her vision, and she stumbled over rocks and fallen branches. "No!" she cried upon hearing the crunch of leaves and the snap of branches as Dugan ran after her.

"Help!" Her scream sent a flock of crows from their perches. They cawed down as she ran on. She knew he was gaining on her and that at any moment he might reach her. Her chest heaved as she panted for air. Fear catapulted her onward. Soon she arrived at a place where the stream widened. Large rocks formed a natural bridge to the other shore. Camp lay on the other side. She had to cross over. Her boots hurt her feet. She leaned on a tree, pulled them off, and discarded them on the ground then began to traverse the rock bridge.

"Miss Wade," Dugan called from one side. He held her boot in one hand. "Now that them boots are off, how about that little bath?"

"No!" she screamed as she toed the water. She lost her balance on the moss and slipped into the stream.

Feeling a sudden need to go off into the woods to hunt, Ryan primed his rifle. The woods gave a man a place to think or not think about things. The families had spent the day fishing and resting up by a lake. They didn't need him now. All remained quiet at camp, except for the movement and braying of several mules. *Odd*, he thought. He rode, rifle against his pommel, to the McPherson wagon. The children had gone on with their father. So who was throwing around the furnishings in the wagon? That's when he saw the wide-brimmed hat and the brown uniform. "Hey!" he called out. "What ya doin?"

"Gringo!" a man shouted, his dark gaze meeting Ryan's.

Mexicans! Ryan realized who these men were and what they came for. He aimed his rifle at the man and shouted, "Stop!" To his surprise, the bandits took flight. One turned and fired at him but missed. As he watched them dash off, he noticed one leading a stallion. *It's Johanna's!* Her aunt told him that she'd gone riding alone that morning. She's a fool, he told Mabel. The woods... *Johanna's in trouble. Those bastards have her hidden somewhere, and I've got to get to her before it's too late.* "Damn it!" he kicked his horse into a full gallop and followed the tracks of her horse into the thickening woods.

As he rode through the pine-cloaked forest, his pulse quickened with the thought that Johanna was in the hands of desperadoes, possibly even dead. Bile rose in his throat, and he spat out on the dusty trail and rode like hell. The low branches of trees brushed the sides of his horse, but on he rode in a race with time. *It's my fault,* he thought, *for not keeping an eye on her.* "Damn it, woman!"

As he came upon a torn sleeve of a dress caught on a bramble, he picked the white cloth up and noticed the blood. With horror he realized the sleeve belonged to Johanna's dress; Ryan braced himself against the side of his horse. A piercing cry broke the stillness and drew Ryan's attention to the gray sky. A lone eagle circled overhead. Listening to some inner voice, Ryan followed the eagle's course. It led to a wide stream. Ryan crossed using a natural bridge and came to a sandy bank. Thick bushes blocked his view as he scanned the shoreline. He rode several yards when a woman's scream stopped him short. "Johanna?" he called. A man's deep-throated laughter resounded along with the sudden slap and a muffled cry of pain.

Like a man possessed, Ryan leapt from his horse and charged forward, pushing aside the brambles in his wake. With his hand on his rifle, he hid behind the large trunk of a spruce. He looked out at the clearing. A few yards away, a man wrestled with a woman on the grass. Ryan crept on his belly with his rifle in one hand. He came close enough to decipher the couple. Grizzly Dugan, bare-chested and brandishing a knife, hunched beside a bruised-faced Johanna.

Ryan stood and cocked the trigger of his gun. "Leave her be, Grizzly."

Dugan turned around, a look of wicked satisfaction lit his dark eyes. "Heck, if it ain't Ryan Majors himself. We was talkin' about you, Majors. This woman offered her service if I didn't go after you. Ain't that right, honey?"

"No!" Johanna shouted. "Ryan, he'll kill us both."

Dugan pulled Johanna to her feet, and held the knife against her throat. "Drop your gun, Majors and I'll let her go. Then you and me can fight man to man."

"Put the knife down." Ryan stepped closer.

"Naw, not till I get what I come for," Dugan sneered. "You took my woman, now I got yours 'less you'll fight me for her."

Ryan slowly laid the gun on the ground, watching Dugan's every move. Johanna gathered the remnants of her torn and mud-stained dress. She sat back in a daze as the two men rushed headlong at one another in mortal combat.

Dugan head-butted Ryan, sending him backward. When Ryan got his breath back, he struck Dugan's chin. Dugan stumbled then charged again, delivering a quick jab to Ryan's chest. Ryan managed to move in and shove him back. Grizzly's fists bloodied Ryan's lips and bruised his cheek. Ryan fought back with an upper cut. Dugan fell with the impact. As Ryan came toward him, Dugan tackled him. The two rolled over and over on the ground. Ryan dodged Dugan's gouging fingers as they aimed for his face. He rolled from under Dugan and knocked him down. Straddling Dugan's back, Ryan pinned his arms. "Give up Dugan!"

"Never!" Dugan bucked forward, bouncing Ryan off. Ryan rolled sideways then stood. He ducked Dugan's swing. Blood trickled down his face.

"Ryan!" Johanna rushed to him. Dugan grabbed her and held the knife to her neck.

"It's you or her, Majors." Dugan dragged Johanna backwards.

"No!" Ryan held up his hands in surrender. "Let her go."

"Go on, missie," Dugan said, pushing Johanna onto the ground.

Dugan lunged at Ryan, slashing his forearm. Blood spouted out as Ryan stumbled back. He clutched his arm and fell backward over the cliffside.

"Ryan!" Johanna's scream echoed through the wood when Dugan stepped toward her, she dove for her pistol on the ground where he had left it and pointed it at him.

"Go to hell!" Johanna fired the pistol, hitting Dugan in the heart. Blood gushed from his chest as he slumped to the ground. His gaped mouth gurgled with blood as he breathed his last. The black eyes, which terrified her for so long, were now blank and lifeless.

Paralyzed with shock, she stood, smoking pistol in hand, and stared at Dugan's wretched face. An eagle's screech brought her back to the clearing. "Ryan! Oh God, where are you, Ryan?"

She raced to the top of the hill, and saw him lying still at the bottom. Blood pooled around his shoulder. She climbed down to him and felt for a pulse. "Oh, thank you, God," she cried up to the heavens. "He's alive." She sat and cradled his head a moment. His eyes fluttered open.

"Dang, it hurts, woman." He glanced about. "Where's Dugan?"

"Dead, I killed him."

A shadow fell over them, Johanna peered up to spy the eagle again. Ryan's head fell back against her arm; his eyes were shut tight and his breath came shallow. "Damn it, Ryan, you're not going to die on me."

Gently she eased him onto the ground then ripped his sleeve to assess the wound. Using the torn material, she fastened it around his upper arm. After knotting it, she used a stick to hold the makeshift tourniquet there then knotted the cloth again. She twisted the stick once then bandaged his forearm with a piece of her torn dress.

"I've got to get help," Johanna whispered to Ryan. "Otherwise, you'll die here." She kissed his forehead. The shuffle of hooves and a loud snort alarmed her; she turned to find Ryan's horse standing there and watching her. Johanna stood and stroked the horse's mane. "We've got to get help, Daisy." She mounted the horse and raced toward camp, praying all the way that she'd get back to Ryan before nightfall.

~ * ~

"He's still breathin'," Seamus said as he listened to the rise and fall of Ryan's chest. With Tom's help, they lifted Ryan up and placed him on a travois tied to Seamus' mule. "Get a move on, Bessy," Seamus said, slapping the mule's rump. They walked up the hill, pausing once to glance at Dugan. Johanna turned away from the grotesque feature with its twisted mouth and vacant eyes.

"Damn bastard don't deserve no buryin'," Seamus said, kicking the body, "except to be fed to the wolves. Let's move on it."

A shotgun blast startled Seamus' mule. The Mexican soldiers rode toward them, whooping and hollering as they fired more shots.

"We best hide over yonder," Seamus pointed to a thick grove of trees. Johanna quickly followed him and Tom to the spot.

"Indian?" Tom asked, as he peeked out between the branches.

"No," Johanna said, "They're Dugan's men, ex-soldiers. It looks like they're after Dugan's hide. They've put him on top of my horse."

"Mexican soldiers... murdering trappers..." Seamus muttered as they reached the edge of the camp site. "I dunno what's next. I'll be pleased as punch to reach Oregon."

Seamus looked at Tom then at Johanna. "Go on, Johanna. We'll be stayin' here in case them Mexicans show up again."

"Don't be long," Johanna begged. She refused to linger a moment more; Ryan needed care. She took the reins and led the mule-drawn travois into camp.

~ * ~

For what seemed to her like endless hours, Ryan lay unconscious on the cot. Johanna patted his fevered brow with a damp rag and prayed for his recovery. "God, don't let him die," she whispered.

Mabel hugged her. "Ryan lost a lot of blood from that knife wound and the fall. Only time and faith can heal him. Have faith, Johanna, all will be well." She poured tea into two porcelain cups and handed one to Johanna, then sat on a stool beside her.

"Thanks, Auntie," Johanna said, grateful for the warm, mint tea which took some of the chill away. She stared into the dwindling flames, thinking over the events of the day. When she looked up at Mabel, she put down her cup. "Oh, I'm so selfish," she said, touching Mabel's arm. "You're worried about Seamus, aren't you?"

"A bit," Mabel said, between sips. "He's off in the woods with crazed killers. And it's so late."

"If only I had stayed in camp, none of this would have happened."

The blast of a bagpipe made Mabel drop her teacup, shattering it on the hard ground.

"Good Lord!" Johanna glanced down at the shard pieces then at her aunt's radiant smile.

"It's Seamus!" Mabel shouted, clapping her hands together. "It's Seamus, at last." Two men stepped from the shadows, one clasping a bagpipe and the other tugging the reins on Johanna's horse.

Mabel ran to Seamus as he put the bagpipe on the ground. She kissed him hard on the lips.

"The two love birds," Tom said. "Ah, *magnifique*. And here is your horse, Johanna. The Mexicans had fallen asleep, we crept into their camp and grabbed the rifles and the horse."

Johanna took the horse's reins and smiled up at Tom. "Thank you."

"Those devils carted away half me wagon," Seamus said with a scowl, "but they didn't take the bagpipe. I'd have clobbered them good with it if I'd had the chance."

"You got one shot in," Tom interrupted, "and that one won't get far before the vultures pick his bones."

"Mercy me." Mabel sighed. "But praise the Lord, you're both all right."

"And what of Monsieur Ryan?" Tom asked Johanna.

Sally rushed over then and hugged her father. "Oh, Pa, you're alive." She glanced at Tom. "And Tom, too." She gave him a shy smile.

"Yes, Sally," Tom said with a broad grin. He gave her a quick hug then sniffed the air. "Hmm, you've been cooking, *mon cheri*?"

Sally chuckled. "Yes, Tom. I roasted that pheasant you gave us."

Mabel turned to Johanna, and whispered, "This is getting serious—he's giving her wild pheasants. A step above rabbits."

Johanna nudged her with her elbow. "Now, Auntie. Let's be grateful for their safe return."

"And where's Monsieur Majors?" Tom asked.

Johanna shook her head. "His fever subsided, but he hasn't revived yet."

Seamus picked up the bagpipes. "If he can rest through this, he's not alive at all."

"Oh, no, not again Papa!" Sally covered her ears as Seamus blew on the pipes.

"Damn it," Ryan moaned, "Stop that infernal racket, it's killing me. Johanna, where the hell are you?"

A smile lit her face and Johanna laughed with joy. "From the sound of him, I'd say Ryan is far from dead." She rushed into the tent to find Ryan wincing in pain as he gripped the blood-caked bandage on his shoulder. "You're undoing my handiwork," she scolded, kneeling beside him and tending to the bandage.

"It's about time woman, I've been waiting for you. What the—?" His eyes widened with measured trepidation as he looked at the knife in her hand. "What do you plan to do with that?"

"I've got to take that off." She pointed to the bandage. "Put on a fresh one." With that she set to work, cutting layer upon layer of cloth.

"Damn it, Johanna." Ryan grimaced. "It's my arm you're poking not a sack of flour. And get me something for my thirst."

"If you aren't the bossiest man on earth, I don't know who is." She shrank back at the sight of the festering wound, which made her gag. Pus crusted part of it. She prayed gangrene wouldn't set in. "I'll be right back," she told Ryan as she backed from the tent.

"I ain't goin' nowhere." He leaned his head on a pillow and watched her exit.

Johanna retrieved her medicinal supplies from the back of her wagon and returned.

"I learned a thing or two," she said as she ground dried linseed into powder, "from the squaws in the last village." She mixed powder with cornmeal and added water to form a paste. Satisfied with its consistency, she applied the poultice to the festering wound on Ryan's arm. He yelped as she touched the sore. "Lie down," she ordered when he bolted up, writhing in pain. "Lie down or I'll have Seamus blast his bagpipes."

"No... no not that," Ryan pleaded, "anything but those damn bagpipes."

"I'll give you some cold water." She filled a gourd and helped him drink. His appreciative smile warmed her. Then she tucked a light blanket about him. "Rest."

"Only if you join me," he tried to grab one of her hands but winced from the pain. "You've wrapped my arms as tight as the corsets you wear."

"Shh!" When he finally rested, she left him. She needed to rest too. The events of the day drained her so that she fell asleep the minute her head touched the blankets she'd placed outside the tent.

~ * ~

It took five days before Ryan's face regained its color and his fever subsided. When he coughed and opened his eyes, Johanna exclaimed with relief, "Thank God, you're better!"

Ryan smiled as she brought a cup of broth to his parched lips.

His hand pushed it away as he touched her hair. Pain creased his features, but he managed a weak smile. "You're an angel... and I'm in heaven."

"Not quite," Johanna said with a soft chuckle. He tried to sit up, but she held him back. "Steady, Ryan. You're still weak." She sensed his frustration yet he let her coddle him. She lovingly brushed away a lock of stray hair that had fallen across his forehead. "Your fever is gone. So is the infection. You've lost weight, Ryan, and you must take the broth to stay well." He acquiesced and she spooned the broth into his mouth.

He coughed and spat it out. "It's bad enough I got cut up without your poisoning me."

"It's not poison." Johanna forced another spoonful between his lips. "It's venison broth. Tom and Seamus shot a deer. They shared it with the camp. Drink."

"Venison?" He eyed her with suspicion then sniffed the cup. "Yep, venison. And what of you, did you shoot deer too?"

"No." She looked away as he took the broth. "I killed a grizzly... Grizzly Dugan."

"Grizzly Dugan?" Ryan knocked some broth onto his lap, and yelped when the hot liquid scalded his skin. "You... you killed him?"

"Yes. And Seamus shot one of the Mexican soldiers. They took off with Dugan's body."

"There was a reward on him, for gosh darn's sake!"

"It's over, Ryan, he's dead. He can't hurt us now."

"You don't understand, I wanted that reward for my kin. And I should have killed Dugan."

"Why? So you can avenge your brother's death?" She stood, hands on hips. "That's it, isn't it, Ryan? Your sole purpose has been to revenge your brother's death."

"I wanted revenge, all right, and money for my kin." He gazed away. "I never thought I'd fall in love."

"And you're sorry now?" She swallowed a lump in her throat.

"No." He clenched her hands in his. "You're the best thing that ever happened to this flea-bitten, down-on-his-luck trapper." He smoothed back her hair and brushed her cheeks with his lips. "And you're worth more than any bounty. You done saved my hide, Johanna. I owe you my life." He tried to pull her closer, but a jolt of pain forced him to sit back.

She smiled through her tears. She went to a corner of the tent and pulled out a round tin. She unscrewed the lid then held up a velvet bag. "This is for you, Ryan. To make up for the money you've lost."

He opened the cloth bag. His eyes widened in surprise at the sight of the diamond ring, pearl necklace, and silver brooch. "Are these yours?"

She nodded. "I've no need now for Robert McEntee's gifts nor for an engagement ring I'll never wear. That part of my life is over. You keep them. You earned it for all you did for the wagon party. Perhaps you can help your kin with it."

"Johanna, I can't take them." He began to hand them back to her.

"I insist." She closed his fingers over the pouch. "You can trade them in if you like." Then she stood. "Get some more rest. We need you, Ryan." She paused a moment and smiled. "I need you. Seamus can lead this wagon party only so far. You have to see us across the Blues!"

"Ah, the Blues... we'll get across somehow, I swear it." He fell asleep with the jewelry pouch in his palm. Johanna took the pouch and stored it in his satchel.

~ * ~

Several days later an old trapper wandered into their camp. Ryan called him Manny James. Johanna listened to their conversation about the weather and the trapping season then her ears perked up when she heard the old man talk about a wagon train led by a minister. With her attention focused on Ryan's care and continued improvement, Johanna had not thought much about Stephen.

"They was headed by a preacher named Green."

"Green, huh?" Ryan spat out his chewing tobacco. "Guess they're miles ahead of us now."

"Oh, don't reckon so." The trapper's gaze lowered. "A number of 'em came down with cholera. I didn't stay long enough to catch the names of the rest of 'em."

"Cholera!" Johanna exclaimed. "What horrible luck."

"And to think he'd have us with him." Seamus snickered.

"You can't blame Stephen if they became ill." Johanna stood and paced before the camp. She turned to Ryan. "Is there anything we can do?"

He shook his head. "We wouldn't get to them in time, Johanna."

"Oh, how awful," Mabel said. "Perhaps we could say a brief prayer?"

"You're right." Johanna lowered her head and prayed aloud. At

Ryan's loud "amen", she looked up and smiled a slow, sad smile. Despite all Stephen had done, Ryan had some compassion for him.

~ * ~

The next morning, they rode out with Ryan in the lead. Johanna marveled at his recovery. Only days before, he looked as if he lay on death's door and now he looked stronger and, she sighed, more virile than she'd ever imagined him. Tall in the saddle, back erect, and chin thrust outward, he cut a handsome figure against the backdrop of azure blue sky and pine-clad mountains.

Johanna inhaled the bracing air and listened to the sweet sound of songbirds flitting through the boughs of the tall conifer trees. Along with the other women in the party, she gathered a good supply of wild berries and edible wild plants to supplement their diet. The men worked under Ryan's supervision at disassembling the wagons for the decline down the steep mountainsides. After a lunch of roasted venison and stewed vegetables, everyone busied themselves with the tasks involved in getting down the mountain.

Ropes tied to wagon beds would serve as pulleys for lowering the wagon down the mountain. Ryan rode up and down the formation, ensuring that everyone followed his orders. The emigrants scaled the narrow, steep grade with ropes knotted to the thick trunks of trees on the mountaintop. Ryan helped a few of the children and the weaker elders down. Johanna marveled at Ryan's strength, knowing that his injuries bothered him. Yet he never complained. She helped with the children too, carrying them papoose-style. The rocks scratched her legs and arms as they slid downward, ever fearful that the rope would break or a child would slip from her back. A glance below sent a shiver of panic, which Johanna suppressed, praying silently to the Almighty for deliverance. She arrived on the bottom without incident.

Ryan sat beside her at camp that night, holding her hands while they watched the flames of the campfire lick the crisp night air. Despite the noise and chatter around them, Johanna felt as though they were the only couple there. Mabel sat with Seamus. Most members slept from their fatigue. Johanna found it hard to sleep.

"We're almost at the Columbia River, aren't we?" Johanna asked, breaking the silence that had descended on them after the meal.

"Yes," he said, pulling his hands away.

She sighed, leaned against his chest and shut her eyes, weariness overtaking her. "I pray the good Lord will see us through, like he did the other times."

He twisted her to face him and cupped her chin. Then he moaned as she leaned on his arm. "Miss Wade, you make the perfect picture for an injured man."

"Injured? A tad delirious, maybe, but I saw how you managed to take people across the mountain today. You stopped Sue Ellen from falling down the face of a mountain, blocking her as she began to slip. I doubt that you're that injured."

"Maybe not." His lips grazed hers. When she reached up to bring him closer still, he moaned with pain and pulled away from her grip. He frowned in frustration. "I guess I'm a mite sore."

"Yes, a mite." She massaged the muscles in his broad shoulders and back. "It takes time," she whispered as he leaned into her. "It takes time to heal. You taught me that."

"I hope it don't take too long," he groaned, lifting his good arm to grasp her hand. "I don't think I can stand much more of this..." His dark gaze met hers, and she felt a warm rush of need.

"Ryan," she said.

"Hmm?"

"You asked me awhile ago to marry you."

"Yes?" He sat up straight. "Will you?"

"I need a little more time... until we're settled in the Valley."

"That could be months from now."

"I know, but you told me you had to go back to your kin in Missouri."

He nodded. "I have to."

Her shoulders sagged. "I thought as much and I've no idea when you'll be back."

"You will if you come with me as my wife."

She stood, trembling with a mix of emotions. "I've got to continue my father's work. I'm needed by the settlers, you know that."

"I need you, too," he said, taking her hand and kissing the palm. "All right, if that's what you want to do. Then I'll return to you,

Johanna. I can't live without you."

He stood and held her close. "You've talked of faith, Johanna. Have faith in me."

"I want to," she said, shaking her head. "But you'll be hundreds of miles away. And..."

"And what?" Ryan touched her chin.

She twisted from his grip. "And you're going back to Sara. You told me that you once loved her, that Chet won her heart, and with Chet dead..." her voice trailed into an inaudible whisper.

Ryan shook her. "Are you crazy, woman?"

"Let's stop fooling ourselves." She spun on her heel and rushed off before Ryan could witness her tears.

"Johanna! Come back here!"

~ * ~

October 1848

Two weeks later, Ryan sold the jewelry Johanna gave him at Fort Vancouver. John McLoughlin, the fort's factor, provided lively entertainment for the emigrants in the form of a square dance. Johanna avoided Ryan's attempts to get her to dance with him. She busied herself with preparing for the remainder of the trip, purchasing supplies and visiting the families in the wagon. *The busier I am*, she told herself, *the less time I'll have to think about Ryan.* Avoiding the problem, didn't make it go away. In her avoidance of one man, she'd captured the attention of several others—young soldiers at the fort.

"Johanna, what the devil is wrong?" Mabel asked as they sipped punch. "First you spurn Ryan then you have every young, eligible man here running for cover. You had your pick of some of the handsomest men west of the Missouri."

Johanna shrugged. "You know me, Auntie. I place duty above all else."

"Hmmm... I see. Well, I'm not about to melt into the wall... Seamus is calling me over for a reel. I mean to have a good time while I can. Take my advice, and do the same."

Feeling utterly miserable, Johanna decided to go out and walk along the stockade. The moon shone in brilliant white ribbons, skimming off the stream that ran past the fort. Here and there, Johanna caught sight of a couple walking together and she felt a pain of jealousy and loss.

"I thought I'd find you here," the familiar, deep voice called from behind her.

"Ryan!" She grasped her shawl about her shoulders. "I needed some air."

"And to get away from me." He walked beside her, following the stone path toward the stream. "I've thought over what ya said a few days ago, Johanna. It's plumb crazy, that's all. Way back when, I loved Sara. I was young and foolhardy, but not the right one for her. And she wasn't right for me." He held out his hand to her. "Don't give up on me, Johanna. You didn't when you thought I was dyin', why now?"

A bubble burst inside her as the floodgates opened and tears streamed down her cheeks. "Oh, Ryan, I want to trust you. I want to believe you'll return to me. But..."

"You've had a lot of heartache, I understand." He reached into his leather satchel and pulled something out. "Here, I've held it awhile now... it's a small bauble my mother's kin gave me, but I want you to have it to remember me and my promise to return to your side."

Johanna glanced at the turquoise stone with its intricate bear-claw carving on a silver bangle. Ryan placed it on her wrist and held her by the hand. He led her to a brook and they sat a moment staring at their reflection in the silver stream. "Come, let's make our vows here."

"Here, by a stream?"

"Why not? We don't need a fancy ritual, Johanna. Oh, I guess we do." He lifted her chin and wiped away the tears that cascaded down her cheeks. "Marry me."

She knew there could be no one else for her. And she gave into the need to be held by him. He caressed her arms, her shoulder then removed the shawl. His lips traced kisses up and down the exposed skin of her neck, and found her lips. She parted her lips, allowing him access to the warmth and wetness. He tasted of salt and sweet wine from the punch. She grew heady from the kiss and leaned against him, pulling his head closer to her own. When they parted, she looked deep into the dark pool of his eyes.

"My love," he said in a husky tone.

She nestled against him, listening to the thumping of his heart. There would be little time for this, she knew, for they were close to their destination. "Ryan, it will be months before we see each other," she said, breaking the silence. "But I will wait for you, and we will marry in a proper wedding."

He pulled her tighter. "You won't regret it." They stayed huddled until the dance ended and Mabel called her over.

"Not a word to my aunt," Johanna begged him. "She'll worry every day that you're gone." She stood then added, "And so will I."

That night outside her tent, Johanna stared up at the stars. A bright one flew overhead, its tail flickering in an orange glow. She recalled her uncle's telling her of shooting stars and comets. Whatever it was, she made a wish. "Please God, may he come back to me."

Twenty-three

Willamette Valley, Oregon
September 1850

Johanna stared around the large log room with its modest furnishings. Seamus did his best to make the log cabin livable, but it took Mabel's finesse to make it a home. Lace curtains hung over the lattice windows. Pine table and chairs formed the dining area. Wildflowers in a vase over the stone hearth added splashes of purple and yellow. Wax candles glowed from the brass sconces on the wall and the oak cabinet leaned against one wall. She stared at the scrimshaw and the nautical instruments, and was reminded of another time and place. Seamus' bagpipe stood near a rough-hewn shelf of books. She read the titles to herself and smiled; most of them had been in her father's collection, but some came from her childhood days. She felt glad to give them to her extended family.

Johanna circled the wooden toy that lay on the floor. "I see Seamus is making a train set." She picked up the caboose and smiled.

"Yes." Mabel sighed. "He's a proud new grandpa. Even though Sally's baby is only a month old, Seamus will have a whole railroad set up before little Emile is two. It's not enough that he tills the fields from morn to night, but he whittles away all evening, too."

"Oh, does he?" Johanna said with a sly grin.

"Johanna!" Mabel dropped the blue blanket she had been knitting. "That's not what I meant."

Johanna stooped and handed her the blanket. "And you are the indulgent grandma."

"I'll do the same for you, Johanna." Mabel started knitting again. "That is when you finally settle down."

"With a nice cottage by the schoolhouse and a garden, I have settled down. There'll be plenty of work with all the children being born around here. I do miss Sally at the school. She was a good helper, but Melissa will do."

"Johanna, you have to get out of that schoolhouse. Come to the church supper on Sunday. The new minister has a friend visiting us from the East."

"Are you matchmaking again?"

"Never." Mabel laughed good-naturedly. She tucked the blanket into a basket then escorted Johanna to the front door.

Johanna kissed Mabel's cheek. "I'll think about the supper. I like Reverend Amos and his wife Mary. The board made a good selection. I think Father would have been glad for such dedicated clergy."

With a wave, Johanna stepped out into the sunlight. Its warmth bathed her face and lifted the veil of self-pity which threatened to color her mood. "Not today," she whispered to herself as she plucked a red rose from her aunt's trellis, one of the amenities Seamus agreed to when he built the log cabin home for Mabel and his family. The trellis and the small garden of herbs and wildflowers added a bit of cheer against the brown wooden structure. The wildflowers along the path—daisies, buttercups, and blue violets—reminded Johanna of the fields of wildflowers she'd passed on her journey to Oregon. She forced away the image of herself in Ryan's arms. A woman's voice broke into her reverie. "Johanna!"

She turned to face the ruddy-cheeked and mirthful grin of Mary O'Dowd. "Hello, Mary."

"Johanna, it's so good to see you. How's little Emile and Hanna Mary?"

"Both are growing bigger. Hanna Mary is a precocious but beautiful child and Emile is simply adorable. Seamus and Mabel fuss over them so."

"They're good to the young uns, all right." Mary reached into her basket and handed Johanna a jar of preserves. "Now, I can't pay you for your lessons. My Nelly is doing so well with her 'rithmetic and spelling since she came to you. But here's something for your table."

"Thank you." Johanna smiled, having grown used to payment in food or services around her schoolhouse and cottage. She had a small stipend from the mission board to help with other expenses, but bartering came with the territory. She had enough food from that and her garden to last the winter. "I appreciate it." Mary left her, heading down another path to the settlement, which stood out with its row upon row of log cabins and clapboard houses.

In two years, the wide-open spaces had become cluttered by housing and the beginnings of the small town. Not only farmers but merchants had come to settle there. A large warehouse had been built, and the owner, whoever he was supposed to be, was to arrive soon. She threw a furtive glance at the establishment then ambled up the hillside and the clover-lined footpath that led to the schoolhouse. Many a time since arriving, Johanna had longed to have her father beside her. He would have been proud to see the fruits of his labor— the small community he helped to organize which had taken root in the Willamette. She had longed for another man—Ryan—to share this beautiful land with, to take away her loneliness, and to fulfill his promise. *How could he not return to me?*

The afternoon sunlight played through the trees and for a moment she imagined herself in a meadow and Ryan holding her tight. Then the image faded and again she saw the valley with its settlers and farmland. She threw the rose on the ground and reprimanded herself for her foolish fancies. After all it had been two years—two long and lonely years—since she'd seen him. So much for promises made at the end of the trail. It irked her to think that she'd so readily fallen for the mountain man. No one, not even dear Aunt Mabel, knew why she'd worn the silver bangle with the turquoise stone and bear claw carving on her right wrist. If anyone inquired, she told them it had been a gift from a grateful pupil whose tribe she'd visited during her ministry work. Despite her better judgment, it remained a link to Ryan. She couldn't part with it even though it now reminded her of his broken promise. For all she knew he probably moved in with that sister-in-law. "Stop it!" she shouted aloud startling a chipmunk that scampered across her path. *I've more than enough to do with my life without that man.*

With a soft sigh, she entered the schoolhouse and inhaled the scents of chalk and musty books. She put on her bifocals, hating the way they looked on her and sat like a weight upon her nose.

The settlement had an eye doctor who prescribed them despite her protests about looking old and ugly. The middle-aged doctor had smiled and teased her. "Nothing can make your face ugly, Miss Wade." Then he asked her to the barn dance that weekend. She refused, the first of many such refusals from men trying to find a wife in the settlement. Despite all her aunt's attempts at matchmaking in the last year, Johanna stuck to her decision. No one could come close to what she'd known in Ryan's arms.

Sally told her that some papers had been misplaced. The children needed the papers in order to prepare for their next test. Johanna sat at her pine desk and pulled open the drawer. As she fumbled through the layers of papers within it, her fingers touched the edge of an envelope. She pulled it out and glanced at the faded letters. Temptation made her open it, again. The letter had yellowed from time and was wrinkled from her perusal. Once again she read the hastily scrawled print of Ryan's letter, thanking her for the jewelry which paid for so much and helped his kin. Her finger traced the final words... words about love and waiting for him to return. "Bah!" She said, crushing the letter as tears blurred her vision. What good did it do her? Two years wasted with waiting and fighting off the advances of other suitors who came her way. Men, old or young, came pouring in seeking wives. She rejected each one in turn, closeting herself up in the cocoon of her work and her little garden. She peered out the open window at the wildflowers waving in the gentle breeze. Why on earth did she grow wildflowers? Her aunt suggested roses or trees.

A knock interrupted her thoughts. "Who is it?" She put the crumpled letter down and waited. When she didn't receive a reply, she opened the drawer where she kept her pistol.

Rumors of marauders raiding houses made her cautious these days. She placed the pistol in her pocket and stood behind the door as she opened it. The floorboards creaked as the visitor stepped into the room. Swinging round, pistol poised, Johanna said, "Not a step further, mister!"

"Johanna!"

Her heart leaped to her throat and she fell back against the chalkboard. "Ryan! It's you. It can't believe it!" The handsome face she'd dreamed about grinned at her; those dark brown eyes that sent a spasm of warmth into the pit of her stomach matched the smile.

"It's me, all right. And what kind of way is that to greet a man?" Ryan took the pistol from her hand and placed it on the desk.

As he moved toward her with the sure-footed grace of a predator after its prey, she stepped away. "Oh, no you don't!" She flailed her arms in the air. "How dare you suddenly show up in my life after having been away? It's been two years."

"I know." He looked down at her desk, picked up the crumpled letter, and gave it a cursory glance. "I'm sorry, Johanna. It took awhile for me to get enough money to be able to support a family and to be worthy of you."

"And what of the family in Missouri?"

He grabbed her by the shoulders. "Johanna! *Look* at me."

Tiny lines creased the corners of his eyelids, and a few gray hairs streaked his shoulder-length hair. Nevertheless, he cut a handsome and sophisticated looking figure in his tailored nut brown suit jacket with matching trousers, white shirt and striped cravat. A stranger would not have recognized him as a man reared in the mountains who trapped for a living, rode dusty trails for months on end, and who fought with savage fury to defend the settlers he led. Yet not everything had changed. Despite her wanting to resist, Johanna felt the same strong, magnetic pull tugging her toward him. She took a deep breath and inhaled the scent of bay rum and laughed a shrill, nervous laugh. "You've really come back to me!'

"I told you I would. With the help of the outfitting company in Missouri, I was able to buy the trading post in the Valley. By the way, these are for you." He picked up something from the doorway. She smiled at the bouquet of wild daisies and blue violets. "Collected them on the way here. Better than an apple for the teacher, eh?"

"You stole them from my garden!" She sniffed the flowers then put them beside the pistol on her desk.

"Your garden? That's some spread of land you have, Johanna."

"Don't tell me you're like the others."

"Others? Have other men courted you?" His eyes narrowed dangerously.

"And what if they had?"

"Why I'd..." His fist curled at his side then he looked away. "I couldn't blame you, I guess. But I thought you'd wait. Maybe I was wrong." He looked at her beseechingly.

"No, Ryan. I haven't been courted by anyone else." He released a relieved breath and she leaned into the warmth of his chest then pulled away. "Why did you come back?"

A muscle in his jaw twitched as he slammed the door shut behind them. She turned from his angry gaze to the gray slate board. His words thundered around them. "You know why, damn it!"

She gripped a piece of chalk so tight it snapped in two. "No, I don't."

"You're still wearing it!"

"What?" Johanna pulled her sleeve down over her wrist.

Ryan hovered behind her and touched her shoulders. She felt the soothing caress as it massaged the growing knot of tension. "You're wearing the bracelet I gave you... for a promise I intended to keep as soon as I could." He turned her to face him. She read the longing in his gaze and bit her trembling lip. She wanted him to kiss her again, the way he did that last time. He didn't make a move, but went on with his explanation. "That money I made from the jewels helped my kinfolk. Thank you."

She choked on the sob that threatened to escape her lips then glanced at the dust-covered floor beneath her feet. "You didn't have to come half a continent to tell me that." She fidgeted with an eraser then scowled at him. "How is Sara, your sister-in-law? Or is she your wife now?"

"Good God, woman." Ryan pulled her to his chest. "How can you think I'd wed Sara? She's got her own family. They're getting on. Samuel... takes after Chet all right. He's helping her run the farm. And Jed is a right sort."

Johanna pulled away from him in surprise. "Jed?"

"Yeah, Jed Thompkins. He's the one who set me up in the trading post after I spent a few months trying to make a living from trapping again. He and Sara wed last month. I couldn't stay for the wedding and told 'em I was needed back here." He cupped her face in his hands. "Tell me, Johanna, tell me... am I needed back here?"

"You are the owner of the warehouse? You're the visitor at the church supper?"

"Yeah, ain't that something? I've been invited to the new minister's church supper. When I heard about a young minister and his wife heading the settlement, I thought you had gotten married. Mabel told me otherwise."

"Mabel? You've talked to Mabel and she never said a word to me..."

"I told her not to." Ryan put his hands around Johanna's waist. "I wanted to surprise you."

"Shock the living daylights out of me, you mean." Johanna pulled away. "I saw Mabel this morning and she didn't even tell me about seeing you."

"I talked to Tom and Sally, too. They're a fine pair. I knew they'd get along well."

"Yes," Johanna interrupted. "And now they have a baby. It looks like children are being born every month. There's so much work around here. Mabel and Seamus are a happy match too. Yes," she said, idly playing with the crumpled letter on her desk. "Everyone is very happy."

Ryan grabbed hold of her hands, looked down at the crumpled letter a moment then at her face. "Everyone is happy?"

His calloused fingers brushed away the tears which streamed down her cheeks. Then he placed a velvet pouch in her hand. It was the pouch she'd given him. "This is for you. It's one jewel I'd like you to keep."

Her hand shook as she held the pouch. She opened it then stared in surprised wonder at the sparkling gold band. A sapphire gem gleamed in its center.

"I got it back in Missouri. Traded with a California prospector for a month's worth of fur hides." He held the ring to the light of a candle. Shimmers of gold bounced across the room. "I hope it fits. The jewel matches your eyes... I often dreamt of them on those lonely nights away from you."

Struck speechless, Johanna gaped at the ring.

Ryan picked up a piece of chalk and wrote on the slate board.

I love you. Will you marry me?

Without a moment's delay, she scrawled back. *Yes*

He placed the ring on her finger. "I hear there's a good preacher in town. I know those things mean a lot to a woman... you can have a fancy party and all that."

She reached out to him and kissed his lips before he could say more. The kiss that had been a long time coming filled her with warmth from head to toe. His embrace left her breathless and restored all the faith she'd lost in the power of love. When their lips parted, she sighed and said, "I don't need a party or anything else. All I need is you. I love you."

He stroked her hair and held her so close she felt they'd melt together. His voice came husky as he looked at her again. "I've loved you since the day I first set eyes on you, Johanna Wade. And I'll keep right on loving you forever."

She smiled with the radiance in her soul. "That's a very long time, Ryan."

"Yes, I know." He scooped her up into his arms and nuzzled her neck, growling "Ah, but there's so much more we can teach each other, my love, it'll take forever."

As their lips touched in a fevered kiss, Johanna realized the truth of Mabel's sage words—*follow your heart, and all will be right.*

Meet Catherine Greenfeder

The American West and the pioneer days has been a fascination for Catherine Greenfeder since fifth grade when her teacher, Mrs. Seguine, created a "pioneer day" complete with square dancing and venison stew. Her trips to Oklahoma to visit her parents, who relocated to Tulsa from New York City, sparked an interest in the plight of the Native Americans and those earlier settlers in the frontier states. A fan of romance fiction since high school, Catherine Greenfeder decided to write her first romance novel after careers in publishing and advertising. *Wildflowers* is the product of several years of research and writing.

Catherine attributes her love of writing to growing up in a household of storytellers, especially her mother who loves to entertain with stories about the past.

Membership in the New York City chapter and the New Jersey Chapter of Romance Writers of America encouraged Catherine to pursue her writing career and provided a network of support and encouragement she cherishes immensely.

Wildflowers, a historical romance, is her first novel, but it is the second book which is being released in electronic format and Print on Demand (POD). *Angels Among Us,* a paranormal romance, is her first book released by Wings ePress, Inc. in

2006. Catherine is thrilled to be able to share Johanna and Ryan's adventures and romance on the Oregon Trail during 1848.

"In some ways I identify with the storytellers or the shamans who told their tales around the campfires long ago. It's both a craft and an art to bring characters to life, pass along the culture, and entertain. I hope that I have done this and to continue to tell tales which will fill the pages of my books."

Catherine Greenfeder lives in Nutley, New Jersey with her husband Wayne, her son Jonathan, and beloved Labrador retriever, Maxi.

VISIT OUR WEBSITE
FOR THE FULL INVENTORY
OF QUALITY BOOKS:

http://www.wings-press.com

Quality trade paperbacks and downloads
in multiple formats,
in genres ranging from light romantic
comedy to general fiction and horror.
Wings has something
for every reader's taste.
Visit the website, then bookmark it.
We add new titles each month!